Also by Eugene Vesey

Ghosters (Novel)
Opposite Worlds (Novel)
Italian Girls (Novel)
Venice and Other Poems
Thirty-nine Poems

GHOSTERS

Eugene Vesey

www.newgeneration-publishing.com

New Generation **Publishing**

for

Xiaoqian

CHAPTER ONE

'Ahem. Remember, Fran, it's not a holiday camp you're going to.'

Fran knew his dad was going to say something, because he had given one of his little coughs first. Annoyed, he carried on looking through the train window at the passing scenery, pretending not to have heard above the rat-a-tat-tat of the wheels on the rails. He knew he wasn't going to a holiday camp! He was going away to the seminary to become a priest.

'This part of Lancashire is called the 'Fylde',' his dad told him, looking at his map – he loved maps. 'That's an old word for 'field'.'

Fran nodded, but carried on looking through the train window at the fields flashing past. They were as flat and green as billiard tables, with sheep grazing in them. There were hedges around them and a few bushes, but no trees. After a while they started to look marshy and he wondered if the sheep were safe. They must be, he supposed, or they wouldn't be there.

Suddenly the sea came into view. That meant they must be getting near, he thought excitedly, because the seminary was by the seaside. He gazed at the sea with awe. Actually, it wasn't really the sea, but sand, stretching away almost as far as he could see. It looked as smooth as glass, but muddy and not very nice for playing on, not like the sand at Blackpool. The sea itself was like a thin strip of silver foil a long, long way away on the horizon beneath a pearly sky.

'Is that the Irish Sea?' he asked his dad, keeping his eyes on it as it came nearer and nearer.

'Yes, that's the Irish Sea,' his dad said, proudly.

'Does that mean Ireland is over there?'

'Right over there,' his dad said, even more proudly. Ireland was right over there! The thought sent a thrill through him.

Ireland was where his mum came from and where they went for their summer holidays. They had just come back a few days ago. They always stayed on his uncle's farm in County Cavan, where his mum had been born and brought up, before she came to England to be a nurse. His dad didn't come from Ireland – he was born and brought up in Manchester like himself – but his dad's parents had and he considered himself Irish.

'This must be Morecambe Bay,' his dad said, studying his map.

'Do we go through Morecambe?' Fran asked, glancing at him.

'No, there's a viaduct over the bay so we miss it.'

'Oh,' Fran said, disappointed.

His dad had taken them to the seaside at Morecambe for a day out last year and he had really enjoyed it. He wasn't really disappointed though. He didn't really want to go to Morecambe. He was going to the seminary to become a priest. That was much better than going to Morecambe. He could hardly wait for the train to arrive. He watched impatiently as the sea came closer and closer …

'Ahem. Did you hear what I said, Fran?'

Fran nodded, but kept looking through the window, annoyed again. Why did his dad have to say that? Probably because last year he had gone to Butlin's holiday camp in Wales with the school for two weeks. He hadn't even enjoyed the second week, he had been so homesick. He knew he wasn't going to a holiday camp now! He hoped he wouldn't be homesick at the seminary. No, it'd be different, he told himself.

He had wanted to be a priest for as long as he could remember, had never wanted to be anything else, had dreamed of this day for years. Now that it was here and he was actually going, he could hardly believe it. He was half-afraid it was still only a dream and at any moment he would wake up. That was why he could hardly wait for the train to arrive and why his dad's remark annoyed him so much.

The trouble was, his dad didn't understand. He didn't really want him to be a priest. His mum understood. She wanted him to be one. That was partly why he wanted to be one himself, because he knew it would make her happy. His dad wasn't as religious as his mum. And he thought he was too young to leave home.

'The lad *is* only twelve years old, after all,' he had overheard his dad saying to his mum in the kitchen the other day, to his alarm. 'Do you really think he knows what he's doing?'

'Sure, he can always change his mind if he doesn't like it, can't he?' his mum had replied gruffly, and to his relief his dad hadn't said anything else.

He was afraid his dad might try to say something to make him change his mind even now. That was why he didn't want to talk to him and kept his eyes fixed on the view – the sea was getting closer and closer. He wished his dad hadn't come with him now. He hadn't wanted him to. He'd wanted to go with the student from the seminary like the other new boys. He'd look mard in front of them, having his dad with him.

To his relief, his dad didn't say anything else. He took his pipe out of the pocket of his tweed jacket and started filling it. As he did so, he sang one of his favourite songs softly to himself, 'I'll Take You Home Again, Kathleen', which was an Irish song, like most of the songs he sang. He was a good singer, his dad – during the war, when he was a soldier, he used to sing in concerts for the troops. He had even sung on the wireless!

His dad struck a match, lit up his pipe and began puffing clouds of smoke all over the compartment. He loved the smell of his dad's tobacco and suddenly realised he wouldn't smell it again for three months, when he went home for Christmas. He wouldn't hear his dad sing again for three months either. He wouldn't *see* his dad again for three months!

Suddenly, he felt guilty for wishing his dad wasn't with him. He had been glad his dad was going with him when he said goodbye to his mum on the station. He had felt sad then, especially when she gave him a last hug. He had felt even more sad watching her wave goodbye as the train pulled out. She would be at work in the hospital now, in her blue nurse's uniform. He wouldn't see her again till Christmas. The thought sent another pang of sadness through him, so he stopped thinking about her.

He hoped his dad didn't think he was being cheeky by not answering him. Even worse, he hoped he wasn't committing a sin. Well, if he was, it was only a venial sin, he told himself, not a mortal sin. A venial sin was like one little black spot on your soul, whereas a mortal sin made your whole soul black and meant you would go straight to Hell if you died, for ever and ever. God would say to you: 'Depart from Me, ye cursed, into the everlasting fire that was prepared for the Devil and his angels, where there shall be weeping and gnashing of teeth.' The very thought of hearing God say those words to him sent a tremor of terror through him.

A venial sin wasn't nearly as bad as a mortal sin, but it was still bad. It meant you couldn't go straight to Heaven if you died, but had to go to Purgatory first. Purgatory was a place of punishment like Hell, except that it didn't last for ever. In Purgatory there was fire, as in Hell, but it was purifying fire, to purify your soul so that you could be admitted to Heaven. How long you had to spend in Purgatory depended on the state of your soul when you died. You could reduce the time you spent there by saying special prayers that had 'indulgences' attached. For example, some indulgences were worth three hundred days in Purgatory. Best of all were 'plenary' indulgences – they excused you from Purgatory completely, until you committed another sin.

You could offer up indulgences for yourself or for the souls already in Purgatory. Fran preferred to do that, because they couldn't help themselves and he felt sorry for them. He imagined them imprisoned in cages surrounded by flames. Although they were suffering terribly, they weren't making any sound, just standing there silently with their hands clasped and tears streaming down their faces, gazing towards Earth, towards *him*, for help.

Thinking about them, he felt so sorry for them that he decided to say a prayer for them now: 'Eternal rest grant unto them, O Lord, and let perpetual light shine upon them. May they rest in peace. Amen.' He repeated it three times as usual, hoping the indulgences it was worth might just be enough to release one of the poor souls. He imagined the Archangel Gabriel, clad in a golden suit of armour, entering Purgatory, unlocking one of the cages and letting one of the souls out. Then he led the soul up a steep flight of marble steps to the golden gates of Heaven, where they were let in by St. Peter, and along a marble hall, like the hall of a palace, only bigger and better than any palace on Earth, with marble columns going up to the clouds and choirs of angels and saints singing hymns of joy all along the way, to the throne of Almighty God Himself.

Sometimes, when he thought about the souls in Purgatory, he wondered how God could let them suffer like that even for one minute. But God had to, he supposed, because they had to be cleansed of their sins before they could be allowed to enter Heaven. It was their own fault if they were in Purgatory, because God gave everyone free will not to commit sin if they didn't want to. Besides, God didn't have to let anyone into Heaven. No one had a right to it. It was only out of His mercy that He let anyone in and He couldn't even do that if He hadn't sacrificed His only Son, Jesus, for men two thousand years ago, by sending Him down to Earth to die on the cross. That was because, since Adam and Eve, everyone was born with original sin on their soul.

Our Lord didn't have to die on the cross for us. God the Father only asked Him to, and He only agreed, because They both loved us so much. Purgatory was nothing compared with what Our Lord had suffered! If it did seem terrible, it just showed how bad even a venial sin was, how much it hurt God. The thought that he might have committed a sin, even only a venial one, by ignoring his dad, filled him with shame. He would have to tell it in Confession, just in case. He needed something to tell, anyway.

Suddenly he had an even more worrying thought – what if, by continuing to ignore his dad, the sin was getting worse every moment? What if by now it had become a mortal sin? If the train crashed and he was killed, he would go straight to Hell! He had better say an Act of Contrition quick, just in case, he decided.

He was just about to start when there was a deafening clatter and his heart leapt into his mouth – the train was running over a long bridge made of iron girders with the sea right underneath! He made a quick Act of Contrition: 'Oh, my God, I am sorry and beg pardon for all my sins. I detest them above all things, because they have deserved Thy dreadful punishments, because

5

they have crucified my loving Saviour, Jesus Christ, and most of all because they have offended Thine infinite goodness. But I firmly resolve, by the help of Thy grace, never to offend Thee again and carefully to avoid the occasion of sin in future.' That made him feel better, but he continued to stare down at the sea with his heart in his mouth until the train left the bridge.

'What was that?' he asked his dad, looking back.

'That was the viaduct,' his dad told him. 'It carries the railway across the bay. Otherwise, it'd have to go all the way round. There's a Latin word for you – 'via' is the Latin word for road or way.'

Fran nodded, keeping his eyes fixed on the sea, which was now right beside the railway line. On the other side there were flat, green fields and, in the distance, mountains. He didn't want a Latin lesson from his dad any more than a lecture about not going to a holiday camp. He knew he would have to learn Latin at the seminary and his dad was only trying to help him, but he preferred to wait until he arrived. His dad didn't really know Latin, anyway. He was a teacher, but only in a primary school.

The train suddenly gave a long, shrill whistle and started to slow down. This must be it, Fran thought, moving to the edge of his seat.

'Wait till it stops,' his dad told him, emptying his pipe into the ashtray and putting it back in his pocket. 'Pull your socks up and straighten your tie.'

Fran did as he was told. The train ground to a halt in a tiny station and the engine gave a gasp, as if it was exhausted, letting out a huge cloud of steam. His dad stood up, put his trilby and mac on and told Fran to put his mac on. Then he took Fran's suitcase down from the luggage rack. He opened the window by letting it down with the leather strap, leaned out of the carriage to open the door, stepped down onto the platform and lifted the suitcase down.

'Careful,' he said to Fran, offering him a hand, because the carriage was a lot higher than the platform, but Fran jumped down on his own.

The first thing Fran noticed was the salty tang of the sea on the fresh breeze. He could see it, too, through a small window in the side of the station wall. It looked cold and grey, like lead.

The station had only two tracks and two platforms. It was built of grey stone, with glass roofs over the platforms supported by brown iron posts. To Fran's surprise, there were flowers – nasturtiums and geraniums – in pots on the platforms, just like his mum had outside the front door at home. It made him miss her and home again.

'Follow me,' his dad ordered him.

He followed his dad to the end of the platform, where a porter took their tickets and they were met by a student from the college. The student had frizzy red hair and a freckly face with wire specs. He was wearing a royal-blue blazer and long grey flannels. That was the school uniform, which he had been told in a letter he would have to buy himself, only short trousers like the ones he was wearing now. His mum had also had to buy him a lot of other new things, such as sheets, a dressing-gown, leather slippers, football boots and wellingtons, all of which were in the suitcase his dad was carrying for him.

'A late vocation, eh?' the student joked, in a Scottish accent, shaking his dad's hand, which made his dad chuckle.

Then the student shook his hand, saying, 'Hello, laddie,' and led them through a tunnel under the railway to the front of the station. There a priest in a black cassock, with a bushy black beard, was waiting beside a minibus full of other new boys and their luggage. The priest said hello in a deep voice and shook hands with them both, while the student put his suitcase in the minibus. The priest was big and fat and there was something funny about one of his eyes.

'There seems to be no room for you, I'm afraid,' the priest said to his dad, in his deep voice.

'Ahem. Yes, I see,' his dad said. 'Well, never mind, Father. I'm sure he's in good hands. I'll just go for a walk round the town till it's time for my train back.'

The priest gave his dad directions. Fran knew his dad would have liked to go to the college, but he was glad there was no room for him – he already felt mard in front of the other new boys.

'Ahem. Well, cheerio, Fran,' his dad said, shaking hands with him. 'Remember, work hard and be good.'

'Yes. Goodbye, Dad,' Fran said self-consciously and climbed

into the back of the minibus.

The priest shut the doors, heaved himself into the driver's seat, making the minibus wobble, and started the engine.

'Procedamus in pace,' he intoned in his deep voice and drove off.

His dad waved goodbye as they drove away and Fran waved back shyly through the window. Then they drove around a bend in the road and his dad disappeared.

CHAPTER TWO

The minibus drove along a winding country road. On one side there was a steep hill covered with trees and on the other a low, grey, dry-stone wall, covered with ivy. Behind the wall there were a few bushes and trees, through which Fran could see fields with cows, sheep and horses grazing in them. The fields were flat, just like the ones he had seen from the train, except that, right in the middle of them, there was a round, wooded hill.

'That's where the college is,' the ginger-haired student informed them, in his thick Scottish accent, 'but ye cannae see it frae here because o' the trees. Dinnae worry, though, yous'll be seeing it soon enough.'

After a while, the wall at the side of the road became higher, with gaps in the top like the wall of a castle. They turned right and pulled up in front of a pair of big, black, iron gates. The Scottish student jumped out to open them. On each side of the gates there was a square, grey, stone pillar, with 'CASTLE' written on one and 'HEAD' on the other. On the left, outside the gates, there was a small, quaint-looking house, with pointed roofs and tall chimneys, also built of grey stone, on which was written, 'GRANGE LODGE'. Behind the wall, to the right of the gates, there was a sign with a badge on it that said:

ST. MARY'S COLLEGE
MISSIONARIES OF THE HOLY GHOST
JUNIOR SEMINARY
'Euntes Ergo Docete Omnes Gentes'

'Do any of you little blighters know what that means?' the priest asked, in his deep voice, looking at them with his funny eye in the driving mirror.

9

They were all silent. The only Latin that Fran knew was the Latin for serving Mass, which he had learnt when he was seven, but he didn't even understand that properly. The priest drove through the gates and pulled up again to wait for the student to close them. Then he turned and stared at the boys, one eye moving from boy to boy, the other not moving at all, and Fran suddenly realised it must be a glass eye, just like the one his aunty in Ireland had.

'It means,' the priest said, staring at them with his one good eye and speaking in a sepulchral voice, 'Abandon hope all ye who enter here.'

The gates clanged shut behind them and the priest slowly turned to the front again. With his bushy beard and eyebrows, glass eye and deep voice, he looked and sounded like an ogre in a pantomime. A few of the boys let out a titter. The priest swung round.

'You'll find that I like little boys!' he intoned, staring at them with his one good eye, and paused for dramatic effect. There were a few more titters. 'Fried!' he boomed, making them jump. 'In oil!' he boomed after another pause for dramatic effect. 'Preferably with onions,' he added, after another pause, licking his thick lips and rubbing his hairy hands together.

The boys were silent, not sure whether he was joking or not. The student got back in the minibus and the priest turned back to the wheel. Some of the boys started to snigger, but he ignored them and drove off. They drove slowly down a long, narrow drive as straight as a ruler. They had to drive slowly, because it was so narrow and also full of potholes, so that the minibus bounced up and down like a boat on a rough sea.

'This is the Grange drive,' the Scottish student said, turning to them. 'Yous are allowed tae walk doon it during recreation, but only as far as the last telegraph pole there.' The boys all turned to gaze at it in awe as they lurched past. 'The area between that and the gates is called, 'No-Man's Land',' he rasped on, 'and it's strictly oot o' boonds. If you're caught breaking boonds by straying intae it, you're for the high jump.'

'What does that mean?' one of the boys piped up.

'That means six o' the best,' the student said, with a glint in his bespectacled eyes. 'You know what that means, don't you, laddie?'

The boy nodded sheepishly and the others sniggered.

'Yous'll not be laughing if you get it,' the student said, with an even more manic glint in his eyes.

'What 'appens if you go out of the gates?' another boy asked.

'Then you're for the nine forty-three, laddie,' the student said, enigmatically.

'What's that?' the boy asked.

'That's the train hame, laddie. Every morning at nine forty-three, change at Carnforth. There's a train the noo.' He pointed across the fields and they saw a train chugging into view from behind a cliff.

'The cliff there is called the 'Bluff',' the student told them. 'Yous'll be goin tae it for walks. The trains run along that embankment across the bay tae the bottom o' that other hill. That's called 'Grange Fell' – hills aroond here are called 'fells' – and the toon of Grange is at the bottom. The embankment, as well as carrying the railway, acts as a dam tae hold back the sea. All this land aroond here used tae be under the sea till it was reclaimed in the last century – that's why it's sae flat and fertile. The sea used tae come right up tae the college. O' course, it wasnae a college then, just a big hoos. This is the farm.'

They turned a sharp bend in the drive and stopped beside a high redbrick wall while a herd of cows crossed the drive in front of them. The cows were being herded through a gateway in the wall by a sheepdog and a fat, red-faced farmer wearing a beret, dungarees and wellingtons. When the cows were all in, he came and talked to the priest who was driving the minibus. The priest called him 'Brother' and he had an Irish accent. Some of the boys wrinkled their noses and sniggered at the smell of manure, but Fran didn't mind it, as it reminded him of his uncle's farm in Ireland.

'This is the rose garden,' the Scottish student told them, as they lurched on past the farm. 'Yous'll be doing the odd bit o' weedin' in it, nae doot. The big sta'ue in the middle is a sta'ue o' Saint Theresa, Saint Theresa o' Lisieux, that is, no' Avila, otherwise known as 'The Little Floor'. She's the patroness o' the missions.'

They turned right through some trees, drove half-way around

a large, semi-circular lawn with a statue of Saint Joseph in the middle, and stopped at the foot of a broad flight of stone steps, with stone lions crouching at each side.

'Oot yous get,' the Scottish student ordered them, jumping out to open the rear doors of the minibus.

When they had all got out and unloaded their luggage, he told them to wait there with him, while the priest went up the steps into the house, holding his cassock up as he did so, as if he was ascending the altar steps. Fran looked up at the house. It too was built of grey stone and looked like a castle, with 'battlements' around the roof and a verandah around the bottom.

Suddenly, at the left-hand corner of the verandah, a ghostly figure drifted into view. It was wearing a long black cloak and its skull-like head was bent over a book. Fran's heart missed a beat – it looked like Count Dracula, he thought, but it was only a priest reading his breviary. When he reached the verandah railing, the priest stopped, turned, and glided back out of view around the corner of the house without looking up.

'Yous see the letter 'M' up there,' the Scottish student said, pointing to the top of the verandah. They all looked up and saw an 'M' carved in the wood. 'We say that stands for 'Mary', the Mother o' God, because the order is named after her, or the Immaculate Conception, to be precise, as well as the Holy Ghost. Originally, though, it stood for 'Mucklow'. That was the name o' the last owner o' the hoos, the chap the order bought it frae.'

'When was that?' one of them asked.

'That was in nineteen o' seven, laddie.'

'Is this Mucklow dead then?' another one asked.

'Och, aye, o' course he's deid, laddie,' the student replied scornfully. 'Or no' exactly – his ghost is still aroond. They say he cannae rest in peace because he's supposed tae have murdered his wife.' He paused for dramatic effect. 'O' course, he was a Protestant, no' a Catholic,' he added, with a contemptuous curl of his lip.

' 'ow did he murder 'er?' another boy asked. They were all agog.

'Ye can ask him that yourself when you meet him next week at your initiation ceremony, laddie,' the student replied. 'He likes tae shake hands wi' all the new boys tae welcome them.'

They all looked at him, wondering whether he was joking or not, when the priest in the cloak floated into view at the corner of the verandah again.

'Is that him?' Fran asked. They all burst out laughing.

'Sssh!' the student hissed, glancing nervously at the corner of the verandah. 'I see we have a joker in the pack,' he sneered, when the priest had drifted away again. 'What's your name, laddie?'

'Francis,' Fran answered sheepishly.

'Your surname, laddie – we dinnae use first names here.'

'Walsh,' Fran said.

'Ah'll be keeping ma beady eye on you, Mister Walsh, so you'd better watch your step.'

Fran blushed and bowed his head.

'As ah was aboot to say, before ah was sae rudely interrupted,' the student carried on, 'Mucklow wasnae the builder o' the hoos – he only added the verandah. The hoos itself was built by a rich bod called John Wilkinson in seventeen sixty-five. He was an iron founder frae hereaboots. He helped James Watt tae build the first steam engine. He also built the first iron ship. That was launched on the river that flows through the groonds. It's called the Winster, by the way. Anyhow, your man Wilkinson, being an iron founder and having made all his money oot o' iron, asked tae be buried in an iron coffin. After he died, that is, no' before.'

They all burst out laughing again.

'Ssh,' the student said, glancing at the corner of the verandah. The priest in the cloak had hovered into view again. 'So,' he continued, when the priest had disappeared, 'he got his wish and was buried in an iron coffin in the rose garden, where the sta'ue o' Saint Theresa is noo, wi' an iron monument he'd designed himself on top o' his grave.'

'Is 'e still buried there?' one of the boys asked.

'Och, no. The coffin and the monument were removed when Mucklow bought the hoos. The monument was re-erected in Lindale – that's the local village. It's still there – yous'll see it when yous go there for a walk.'

'What 'appened to the coffin?' another boy asked.

'That's a wee bit o' a mystery – naebody kens.' He paused for dramatic effect again. 'It was supposed tae have been re-buried in the village churchyard,' he carried on, 'but there's nae gravestone. They say that, being made o' iron, it was so heavy it broke the cart they were using tae carry it oot, as if your man didnae want tae leave, and they couldnae find another one strong enough, so they put it back.'

'You mean, in the rose garden?' one of the boys asked.

'That's another mystery – naebody kens exactly where. Yous could be standing on top o' him right noo.'

The boys looked down and shifted their feet uneasily.

'He wanders aboot, too, just like Mucklow, despite his iron coffin – especially on the verandah,' he added.

At that moment the priest in the cloak wafted back into view, bent over his breviary, turned and disappeared again.

'No, that's no' him,' the student said, putting a finger to his lips to stop them laughing. 'That's Father Egan, the Dean o' Studies. Dinnae worry, yous'll be seeing plenty more o' him. And Mucklow. And Wilkinson.'

'Was Wilkinson a Catholic?' one of them asked.

'Och, no, he was worse than Mucklow,' the student said, pausing as if unable to bring himself to say it.

What could be worse than being a Protestant, Fran wondered?

'He was an *atheist*,' the student spat the word out. 'Do any o' yous know what that is?'

They all shook their heads. 'An atheist is somebody who doesnae believe in God,' the student said, with a sneer.

Somebody who didn't believe in God? Fran was shocked. How could anybody not believe in God? It meant you would go straight to Hell when you died! That must by why Wilkinson couldn't rest in peace – he must have gone to Hell. A shudder of horror went through him and he wondered whether he should say a prayer for the repose of his soul, just in case.

Just then several boys in blue blazers came charging through the front door of the house. Seeing the student at the bottom of the steps, they skidded to a halt, piled into each other and fell in a heap on the verandah floor, giggling.

At that moment, the priest in the cloak reappeared at the corner of the verandah. He stopped in his tracks, slowly raised his bony head, rotated it like a robot and glared at them so fiercely that they instantly stopped giggling, picked themselves up and dusted themselves off. Even the new boys, standing at the bottom of the steps, felt afraid. The priest continued to glare at the boys on the verandah for a while, then slowly, in the same robotic way, rotated his head back, lowered it to his breviary, turned around and glided away again without saying a word.

'Yous are lucky,' the Scottish student said. 'I've a good mind tae send the lot o' yous up tae Father Director anyway. Running through the Fathers' hoos! It'd be bad enough at the best o' times, but in front o' new boys, who yous are supposed tae set an example tae.'

'Please don't send us up, Gyp,' one of them pleaded. 'It's only the second day.'

'Ah'll think aboot it,' the Scottish student said. 'Noo come and help these new boys with their luggage.'

'Thanks, Gyp!' they exclaimed and ran down the steps to do so.

There weren't enough of them to carry all the suitcases, so Fran had to lug his own with two hands up the steps and through the front door. As he did so, he bumped into a big brass dish on a tiny table just inside the door. It crashed to the tiled floor of the hall and rolled round and round several times with a deafening clatter, until it finally came to a standstill.

A deathly silence descended. Fran stood staring at the now stationary dish for a few moments, his face burning with embarrassment. The others had all stopped and turned to stare as well, some of them sniggering. Blushing, Fran put his case down and bent to pick the dish up.

'You clumsy eejit!'

Fran jumped back like a startled rabbit and looked up to see the priest in the cloak standing in the doorway, glaring at him fiercely, just as he had done at the boys on the verandah. Nervously, he bent down again to pick the dish up.

'Leave it!' the priest hissed and pointed with an outstretched arm. 'Go! Go! Get out of my sight!'

Terrified, Fran grabbed his suitcase with both hands and scurried down the tiled hall after the others. Half way along there was another statue of Saint Joseph in an alcove in the wall, where they turned right and filed down a narrow, stone-flagged corridor. On the right, they passed a door with black iron hinges and an arched top, just like a door in a castle. That was the chapel, one of the old boys told them, and this was all part of the Fathers' house, which was normally out of bounds. It smelt of a mixture of polish and incense, Fran noticed.

At the end of the corridor there was another door like that of the chapel. They passed through it into a large room with two rows of bare wooden tables and benches, on which a fat, bespectacled boy in a blue blazer was laying cutlery. There was a smell of polish here, too.

'This is the ref,' one of the old boys told them. 'We eat at these tables and Father Director eats at that one.' He pointed to a small table standing on its own at one end of the room, with a white linen tablecloth on it and a dining chair behind it.

'Who's that?' a new boy asked, looking at a bust in an alcove in the wall.

'That,' the old boy explained, 'is the Venerable Father Francis Libermann, who founded the order in eighteen forty-eight. He's still only a Venerable, not a Saint yet, but they're trying to have him canonised in Rome. They have to make him a Blessed first, though.'

The Venerable Father *Francis* Libermann! Fran was pleased he had the same name. However, he had a big nose and looked rather ugly, Fran thought, feeling disappointed, though he knew that was silly. He wondered if not being a saint meant you couldn't pray to him.

'Where did 'e come from?' another new boy asked.

'He was a French Jew who was converted to the faith,' the old boy answered. 'You'll be learning all about him soon, because his life story is read out at dinner every day this term, from the rostrum there. We always have reading at meals, except on Sundays and free days. What's for supper, Biffo?'

The boy who was laying the tables suddenly clutched his stomach and bent over making retching noises, pretending to be sick.

'Oh, no, not Spam!' the old boys groaned.

'Only jossing,' Biffo said, returning to normal. 'It's dead dogs' eyes, actually – special treat for the new boys.'

16

'Flog off, Biffo! What is it?'

'Go and see,' Biffo said, carrying on with his work.

They filed through a pair of swing doors into a stone-flagged passage. In the wall on the left there was a serving hatch, on which were piled several metal trays covered with slices of a sweaty, slimy, pink material.

'Oh, no!' the old boys groaned in unison. 'He wasn't jossing! Yuk!'

Just then a short, podgy, red-faced man in a chef's hat and apron appeared at the hatch, carrying another tray of the same slimy-looking material, which he placed on top of the others.

'Good evening, Mister JohnSTONE!' the old boys chorused, abruptly changing their expressions to one of beatific delight.

'Good evening, ssonnies,' the man lisped haughtily in reply and waddled back into the kitchen.

'That's Cyril, the cook,' one of the old boys explained, as they filed through another pair of swing doors onto a landing, where evening sunshine beamed in through the frosted glass of metal-framed windows. The landing had a stone floor and the bottom half of the walls was bare brick, while the top half was painted a pale blue. In the corner there was a large statue of Our Lady on a wooden pedestal.

'We call him 'Cyril' among ourselves,' the boy continued, 'but you have to say 'Mister Johnstone' when you speak to him.'

'Mister JohnSTONE', ssonny,' another one corrected, imitating the cook's lisp and stressing the second syllable as they went up some stone stairs. The others all guffawed.

The boy at the top of the stairs put down the case he was carrying, turned and halted them with a raised hand. At the same moment, a priest appeared in the open doorway behind him and stood watching, with his hands on his hips and a wry grin on his face. He wasn't at all like the priest on the verandah, Fran noticed with relief, but young, tall, dark and handsome. He wasn't wearing a cloak either, but a black cassock with a girdle around the waist and a short shoulder cape. His teeth were very white and regular, except for one gleaming gold one in the middle.

'Not 'Mister JohnSTONE', ssonnies,' the boy with the

17

raised hand proclaimed pompously, imitating the cook. 'Your Holiness!'

He held the back of one hand towards them, as if for them to kiss an episcopal ring, while with the other he pretended to be holding a crozier, and waited for them to laugh. When they didn't, he looked puzzled for a moment, and then winced as the truth dawned on him. Cringing, he turned around.

'Never mind the clowning, Sheehan, get these boys into the dorm and unpacked,' the priest ordered, cuffing him on the back of the head. Then he hurried off downstairs. The other old boys chortled gleefully at Sheehan's misfortune as they carried on up the stairs.

'That's Father Director,' one of them said. 'He's in charge of us. We call him 'Greg', because he looks like Gregory Peck. He was born in India, that's why he's so dark.'

Fran knew who Gregory Peck was, because his dad used to take them to see cowboy films, but actually he thought the priest looked more like Gary Cooper, who was his favourite cowboy actor.

They went through a pair of swing doors into the biggest room Fran had ever been in in his life. It was long and wide, with four rows of iron beds, each with a blue blanket on top and a wooden chair beside it, over which a towel was draped. The floorboards were completely bare, the bottom half of the walls was bare brick and the top half was painted blue, like the landing. All along each side there were metal-framed windows, but there were no curtains on them. On the wall at the far end hung a huge, almost life-size crucifix.

'This is the dormitory, or 'dorm' as we call it,' one of the old boys informed them.

'We also call it 'the barn',' another one added, 'because it's so big and draughty.'

The old boys led them to the far end, found each of them a bed with his name on it, told them to wait by it and rushed off. Fran put his case down with relief and looked at the bare mattress, noticing that it was both stained and torn, with horsehair sticking out. He sat down on it and there was a loud 'ping!' as one of the bedsprings broke. He jumped up, blushing, then sat down on it again more carefully and waited.

He suddenly felt lonely. Most of the other new boys were talking and laughing together – they already knew each other, because they had come together on the train. He wondered where his dad was now, if he was on the train home or had already arrived, but that made him feel more lonely. He looked at his case, which his mum had packed for him the day before, but that made him feel even more lonely!

To distract himself, he decided to try and count the number of beds in the dormitory. The rows were all more or less the same length, so he reckoned that by counting one and multiplying by four he would get roughly the right number. It wasn't easy, because the rows were so long and he kept losing count. Eventually, though, he managed to count about twenty beds in a row, which meant that there were about eighty altogether!

'Francis Walsh?'

'Yes,' Fran said, standing up, to a tall, gangly boy in a royal-blue blazer and long grey flannels, who was reading the label on the foot of his bed.

'Tony Fisher,' the tall boy said, shaking hands. 'I'm your 'Guardian Angel'. That means I'll be looking after you and showing you the ropes.' He had a funny accent that Fran had never heard before. 'Are you from Manchester?'

'Yes,' Fran nodded.

'Another Mancunian, eh?' his Guardian Angel joked.

'Are you from Manchester, too?' Fran asked, shyly.

'Why, no, man – I'm a Geordie.'

'What's that?' Fran asked.

'That means I come from Newcastle way. Do you know where that is?'

'It's in the North-East, I think,' Fran said, remembering an old geography lesson.

'A bit of a clever one, eh? Right, well, the first thing to do is unpack your case.' He picked up the case, plonked it on the bed and opened it. 'This is very neat – who packed it for you?' he asked.

'Me mum,' Fran said, proudly.

''Me mum',' his Guardian Angel mimicked him, making him blush – nobody had ever made fun of his accent before.

His Guardian Angel helped him to unpack and showed him

where to put everything. At the end of the dormitory there was a curtained rack, where he had to hang up his new navy-blue mac. Above this there were some lockers, one with his name on, which he had to stand on a chair to reach, in which he had to put all his other clothes. On the chair next to his bed he had to put his toilet bag with his towel draped over it, like all the others.

Next, his Guardian Angel showed him how to make his bed, which he told him he had to do every morning after Mass. First, the bed had to be stripped completely and the mattress turned over. Then the sheets, pillow and blankets had to be put on, with the blue blanket on top over the pillow and tucked in all around. Pyjamas had to be left folded neatly under the pillow and dressing-gown laid tidily across the foot of the bed. Finally, the bed itself had to be left in line with the others, both down and across. If it wasn't all done properly and everything left 'shipshape and Bristol fashion' when the dorm was inspected, his Guardian Angel warned, he would be 'in the soup'.

He also warned him that it was strict silence in the dorm at all times and most of the time the dorm was out of bounds. That was one of the strictest rules of the college, he warned, which you could be expelled for breaking. The very word 'expelled' frightened Fran so much he resolved there and then never to break the rule, though he didn't understand why it was so important. The thought of being expelled was almost as terrifying as the thought of going to Hell!

Suddenly, a bell started clanging somewhere downstairs. 'That's the bell for Benediction,' his Guardian Angel told him. 'It means you've got five minutes to get to chapel and you mustn't be late or you'll be in trouble. Follow me.'

Fran did as he was told. He wanted to go to the toilet, but was too shy to ask. When they reached the chapel, his Guardian Angel showed him to the front bench with the other new boys and left him.

He was surprised by how small the chapel was, compared with the church he went to at home. It was already full, with boys in royal-blue blazers in order of seniority and size from front to back, youngest and smallest in the front pews, while the back pews were occupied by priests in their black habits. In the background an organ played softly. After a minute or two a bell rang, the congregation stood up and the thurifer, acolytes and servers, in black cassocks and starched white cottas, followed by the priest in his gold cope, processed slowly in. Then they entered the sanctuary, where the ruby-red lamp signifying the Divine Presence glowed warmly, and the familiar ceremony began.

The smells of incense, altar flowers and melting candle wax all mixed into a pungent, heady perfume. In the centre of the altar stood the gold monstrance, shining like a golden sunrise over the snow-white altar cloth. The sounds of tinkling bells and chiming gong mingled with the music of the organ into the sweetest of symphonies. And as their voices swelled in the familiar melodies of the Latin and English hymns, such as 'O Salutaris Hostia', 'Tantum Ergo' and 'Faith of Our Fathers', Fran's heart swelled with joy, that he was one of them, a seminarian at last.

CHAPTER THREE

The study hall was as silent as a sepulchre, except for the scratching of nibs on paper and the occasional rustle of pages being turned. Now and then one of the fluorescent lights hummed, accentuating the studious silence. The Dean of Studies, in his black cloak, padded silently up and down between the rows of desks, reading his breviary, like some spectral sentry. Nobody dared to make the slightest unnecessary noise or movement – already tonight he had given the strap to one boy for cracking his knuckles.

'I'll crack your knuckles for you!' he had declared gleefully, his own knuckles white on the clenched fist in which he gripped his 'pandybat' – a leather cosh, reinforced with whalebone and weighted with lead, Fran found out later, which he had brought with him from the order's school in Ireland and which he then whacked down as hard as he could on each of the luckless boy's hands, making him yelp with pain.

Fran opened the lid of his desk as carefully as he could to put away his maths books. On the underside of the lid he had sellotaped some holy pictures of Our Lady and his favourite saints, Saint Francis of Assisi and Saint Patrick; a photograph of his mum in her nurse's uniform; his class timetable and the daily timetable, which was as follows:

6.30 Rising.
6.45 Morning Prayer.
7.00 Mass and Thanksgiving.
7.40 Bed-making.
7.45 Morning Study.
8.15 Breakfast. Recreation.
8.45 Functions.
9.15 Class.

10.45 Elevenses.
11.00 Class.
12.30 Recreation.
12.45 Visit to Chapel.
 1.00 Dinner. Recreation.
 2.15 Class.
 4.30 Tea. Recreation.
 5.00 Rosary.
 5.15 Study.
 7.00 Supper. Recreation.
 8.00 Library.
 8.30 Spiritual Reading.
 8.45 Conference.
 9.00 Night Prayer. Bed.
 9.30 Lights Out.

This was the timetable every day except for Wednesday and Saturday afternoons and Sundays. On Wednesday afternoons, instead of class, there was football or cricket and on Saturday afternoons there was manual labour. Sunday was the best day of the week, because they got up at seven o'clock instead of half-past six. In the morning they had to go to two Masses, a Low Mass as usual and then, after breakfast and recreation, a High Mass, after which they had to do English Composition for an hour and a half, followed by Spiritual Reading.

In the afternoon though, they went out for a walk, in groups of three in a 'crocodile' – the only time they were allowed out. In the evening, instead of study, they had letter writing, to the accompaniment of classical music on the gramophone, followed by Benediction and supper. After supper they had the longest recreation of the week – one and a half hours, from half-past seven until night prayer at nine o'clock. Usually during this recreation there was some form of entertainment, such as a sing-song, debate, quiz, film or slide show by a priest home from the missions.

Fran looked at his class timetable to see what he should do next. At the same time he glanced at the photo of his mum. He missed her so much it hurt. He was tempted to look longer at it, but resisted, because it only made him miss her more. Looking back at his class timetable, he decided he had better do his Greek homework, so started to take out his 'Dr Smith' textbook and exercise book. But suddenly a shadow fell across his desk and he realised the Dean of Studies was looking over his shoulder. A shiver went down his spine.

'And which of God's holy saints is this, Mister Walsh?' the Dean of Studies enquired sarcastically, pointing a bony finger at the photo of his mum.

'It's me mum, Father,' Fran answered, blushing – he knew the others had stopped to look and listen, glad of a diversion.

'"It's me mum, Father',' the Dean of Studies mimicked him, and there were titters from those around.

'Silence!' the Dean of Studies snapped and the titters stopped abruptly. 'I've had my beady eye on you, Mister Walsh,' he said to him, 'and you haven't exactly accomplished much in the last few minutes. You've been gawping at this instead, haven't you?'

'No, Father,' Fran denied, burning with both embarrassment and indignation. 'I was – '

'Don't contradict me, Mister Walsh!' the Dean of Studies cut him off. 'Remove it!'

'What, Father?'

'"What, Father?',' the Dean of Studies mimicked him and there were more titters, which he silenced abruptly again. 'The photograph, you eejit!' he snarled.

'But, Father, it's me mum,' Fran said timorously.

'"Me mum'!' the Dean of Studies mimicked. 'Remove it!'

Oh, no, Fran thought – the Dean of Studies was going to confiscate it! With trembling hands he did as he was told, taking care not to tear it, and tried to put it in his desk. However, the Dean of Studies snatched it from him and strode over to the nearest wastepaper bin, where to Fran's horror he ceremoniously tore it into pieces and dropped them in.

'Let this be a lesson to all of you,' he announced to the study hall, brushing his bony hands together as if soiled. 'Anyone else who has such a frivolity stuck on his desk lid or anywhere else in his possession had better dispose of it by tomorrow. Such frivolities are distractions, as Mister Walsh here has demonstrated tonight. They are distractions from the twin purpose for which you are here, which is to pray and to study. You must forget the outside world, leave it behind, erase it even from your memories. You must cut all ties with it, even ties of blood. That is what Our Divine Lord meant when he said, 'Leave all and follow Me'. That is the supreme sacrifice He asks us to make if we wish to be priests. If there are any among you who are not prepared to make that sacrifice, you should go and pack your bags now.' He paused dramatically, pointing with a bony finger towards the doors. No one moved. 'Good. Now carry on with your work. I want no more distractions tonight. Especially from you, Mister Walsh.'

With a lump in his throat and tears in his eyes, Fran took out his Greek books, carefully closed his desk lid, laid the books on the desk and opened them. The Greek characters looked even more indecipherable than ever through the blur of his tears. He blinked them back and looked at the exercise. Then he remembered that he needed his Greek dictionary, so opened his desk again. However, in doing so, he let go of his textbook, which slid off the desk and hit the polished parquet floor with a resounding smack, making his heart jump. He bent down to pick the book up, but it was kicked away by the shiny black shoe of the Dean of Studies.

'Go and pick it up, you clumsy eejit!' the Dean of Studies hissed, pointing at the book with outstretched arm.

Trembling, Fran did so, put it back on his desk and started to sit down again.

'Kneel!' the Dean of Studies commanded.

This was the Dean of Studies' usual punishment for anyone who dropped anything. Burning with shame, Fran did as he was told. There was a snigger from the boy behind him. The Dean of Studies, who had started to walk away, swivelled round.

'Was that you, Mister Walsh?'

'No, Father,' Fran said, his voice quavering.

'Well, who was it, then?'

'It was – ' Fran was about to say the boy's name, when he realised it would be 'spragging', and stopped himself. 'I don't know, Father,' he said instead, his voice quavering even more.

'You don't know, eh? Well, now, let's see if we can jog your memory, Mister Walsh.' He drew his pandybat from the pocket of his cassock like a sword from a scabbard. 'Stand up!'

'But it wasn't me, Father,' Fran pleaded, standing up, his legs wobbling like jelly and his stomach churning at the sight of the pandybat.

'Out with your paw!' the Dean of Studies ordered, ignoring him and raising the pandybat in the air.

Fran held out a trembling hand and the pandybat smashed down on it, making it drop. A shock of red-hot pain shot up his limp arm like an electric current. Tears sprang to his eyes again, but he blinked them back.

'And the other one, laddie!' the Dean of Studies ordered, wagging a bony finger at him.

Fran held out his other trembling hand and the pandybat smashed down on it, making it drop. Another current of red-hot pain shot up his limp arm. More tears sprang to his eyes, but this time, to his horror, something even worse happened – he dirtied his trousers.

'Now kneel down and get on with your work,' the Dean of Studies ordered, stuffing his pandybat back in his cassock pocket.

'I – I need to go to the toilet, Father,' Fran whimpered.

'Well, go, go!' the Dean of Studies said testily. 'And don't take all night.'

Fran scurried to the nearest door and tried to open it, but his hands were so numb with pain he couldn't turn the knob, so the boy sitting next to it had to do it for him. Then, keeping his knees together and his throbbing hands under his armpits, and trying to keep the tears from his eyes, he scuttled along the stone-floored corridor, which it was his job to clean every morning during 'functions', through the swing doors at the end and past Father Director's office, through some more swing doors and down some stone steps into the washroom.

There, with difficulty, he turned on one of the taps and held each throbbing hand under cold water for a while. Then he went into one of the toilets to clean himself. His underpants were so dirty that he had to take them off and return to the washroom to rinse them under cold water, feeling sick with shame and disgust. He wrung them out and wondered what to do with them.

He thought of flushing them down the toilet, but was afraid they might block it up – it had happened to another boy a few days ago and Father Director had really blown his top about it in 'Conference'. The boy had been found out because his name was on them, as their names had to be on all their clothes. He thought of burning them in the furnace, which was in the boiler room opposite the toilets, but didn't dare – the boiler room was strictly out of bounds and anyway he was afraid he wouldn't be able to open the furnace door. In the end, he decided to hide them in his locker in the boot room.

He scurried along the short, stone-flagged corridor that led from the washroom to the boot room, feeling cold without his underpants, stuffed them, damp and stained, into the back of his wooden locker, behind his football boots and wellingtons, and closed the door. Then, still fighting back tears, he hurried back to the study hall, where the Dean of Studies made him kneel at his desk until the end of study.

It was dark in the dorm, except for the occasional glow of the moon through the bare windows and the blue night light above the door at the end, which led to the toilet and Father Director's bedroom. Father Director himself was walking around in his carpet slippers as usual, saying his rosary, with his hands crossed behind his back, rosary beads in one hand and a torch in the other. Every now and then he shone the torch on somebody's bed and sometimes he stopped to talk to them quietly.

Outside, the wind whistled through the trees on the hill and whined down the drainpipes, while from time to time an owl hooted eerily. Inside, the only sounds were the breathing or snoring of sleeping boys, the occasional creak of bedsprings as somebody turned over, the jingle of Father Director's rosary beads and the rustle of his habit as he passed or the murmur of voices when he stopped to talk to somebody.

Fran lay awake in bed, thinking about what had happened. He had felt cold all evening, because he had no underpants on, and was still a bit smelly, because he hadn't been able to clean himself properly. He had been afraid the other boys would notice and make fun of him, as they did of 'Smelly Kelly', another new boy who was always dirtying and wetting himself. To his relief they hadn't, but he still felt dirty and ashamed. He felt worried, too, because he wouldn't be able to clean himself properly for three days until Friday evening, when it was his turn for a bath – you weren't allowed to use the bath at any other time – and he didn't want to put clean underpants on till he had done so.

More than anything though, he felt homesick. He had felt more and more homesick all evening – by now it was as if there was a huge weight on his chest, crushing him, so that he could hardly breathe. He was sorry he had come to the seminary now. He wanted to go home. He missed home, especially his mum, so much that it hurt. He struggled, as he had struggled all evening, to keep the tears from his eyes, but now it was more difficult than ever.

He felt so lonely! He had no friends here, because it was against the rule to have friends. The Dean of Studies seemed to have it in for him and none of the other priests were very friendly, not even Father Director. He kept hoping that Father Director would stop and talk to him, but he never did – he always passed him by and, whenever he stopped to talk to someone else, he felt even more lonely. At least in bed at night at home he could talk to his brothers, because they all slept in the same room.

Suddenly, from outside, there was a long, forlorn whistle, followed by the muffled sound of a train in the distance as it crossed the bay. He could hold back the tears no longer. They gushed out and he started sobbing, the tears streaming down his cheeks. He knew the others could hear him if they were awake, but he didn't even care any longer – all he wanted to do was go home!

'What's the matter, son?'

It was Father Director. He was crouching down beside his bed and had put a hand on his shoulder. His face was so close to his that he could see his gold tooth and smell his aftershave. He hoped Father Director couldn't smell him.

'I - I want to go home, Father,' Fran sobbed.

'Why do you want to go home, son?'

'I – I miss me mum, Father,' Fran sobbed.

'I'm sure you do, son,' Father Director squeezed his shoulder. 'That's only natural. I'm sure she misses you, too, doesn't she?' Fran was surprised by the question. 'I – I don't know, Father,' he sobbed. 'I – I suppose so.'

'Oh, I'm sure she does, son,' Father Director said, squeezing his shoulder again. 'She loves you, doesn't she?'

'Y – Yes, Father.'

'But she hasn't come to take you back, has she?'

Fran shook his head, puzzled, trying to stop sobbing.

'Why hasn't she, do you think, son?'

'I – I don't know, Father.'

'Because she's given you to Our Lord, son, just as you've given yourself. You don't take back a gift, once you've given it, do you, son?'

'N – No, Father,' Fran said, gulping back a sob.

'And you have given yourself to Our Lord, haven't you, son? You do want to be a priest, don't you?'

'Y – Yes, Father,' Fran said, stifling another sob.

'That's a good boy. I'm sure Our Lord wants you to be a priest, too. But it's not easy, son. 'Leave all and follow Me' – that's what He said to His disciples and that's what He says to us. He asks us to leave home, family, friends, everything. And that's not easy, is it, son?'

'No, Father,' Fran sniffled, starting to feel better – Father Director understood how he felt.

'No, it's not easy for any of us, son. Being a priest is a great privilege, the greatest privilege that God can give to any man. But it's a long, hard road. Most people fall by the wayside. 'Many are called, but few are chosen,' as Our Lord said Himself. He has called you – that's why you're here. You're feeling homesick tonight, but that's only natural, nothing to be ashamed of, son. Everyone feels that way sometimes. Ask Our Lord to help you get over it. Remember, He knows how you feel – He had to leave His own mother and father. Will you do that for me? Will you ask Him?'

'Yes, Father,' Fran sniffled.

'I'll pray for you, too, son,' Father Director said, giving his shoulder another squeeze and taking his hand away.

'Thank you, Father,' Fran sniffed, feeling better, but sorry that Father Director was going.

'Now, son, dry your eyes and blow your nose. Where's your hanky?'

'In my trousers, Father,' Fran said, without thinking.

Father Director turned to the chair beside his bed and shone his torch on it to look for his trousers. Fran was afraid he would notice his underpants weren't there, but to his relief he found his hanky and handed it to him without noticing. Fran wiped his nose and dried his eyes with it. Father Director took it and put it back in his trousers.

'Where are your underpants, son?' he asked, shining his torch around the floor.

'I – I haven't got any, Father,' Fran stammered, trying in vain to think of a fib.

'Why not, son?'

'I – I had to wash them, Father.'

'Why, son?'

'I – I had an accident, Father.'

'What do you mean, son?'

'I – I dirtied them accidentally, Father,' Fran admitted, almost bursting into tears again.

'I see, son. What have you done with them?'

'I put them in my locker in the boot room, Father. I – I'm sorry, F – Father,' he started to sob again.

'It's all right, son,' Father Director patted his shoulder. 'It's nothing to worry about. It could happen to anyone. Did you clean yourself?'

'Y -Yes, Father,' Fran sniffled. 'B – But not properly.'

'Do you want to have a bath, son?' Father Director asked.

'What, now, Father?'

'Yes, son. You'll sleep better.'

'Yes, please, Father,' Fran said, already feeling better.

'Right, son, out of bed you get,' Father Director told him, pulling back his bedclothes. 'Put your slippers and dressing gown on, bring your toilet bag and follow me.'

Fran did as he was told. Father Director led him by torchlight to the end of the dorm, where he popped into his bedroom. Then he led him down the stone stairs all the way to the washroom. It was spooky and Fran was half-afraid of seeing the ghost of Mucklow or Wilkinson, but he supposed they would be afraid of Father Director, since he was a priest.

When they reached the washroom, to his relief Father Director put the light on. The washroom was a large square room with a tiled floor, a big wooden table in the middle and washbasins all around the walls, with flyblown mirrors above them. In each of the two far corners there was a cubicle, one of which was the senior bathroom, one the junior.

To Fran's surprise, Father Director led him into the senior bathroom, which was slightly bigger than the junior one. It contained only a rusty cast-iron bath, a wooden chair and on the tiled floor a cork mat for standing on. Fran supposed Father Director would leave him then, though he hoped he would wait outside, because he felt nervous about being left on his own down here. However, to his surprise, Father Director closed the door, locked it, took off his camail or shoulder-cape, which he hung on the hook on the back of the door, and rolled up the sleeves of his habit. 'Right, son, take off your things and I'll run the bath for you,' Father Director told him, bending over the bath to do so.

Embarrassed but obedient, Fran took off his dressing gown and pyjama jacket, which Father Director hung on the back of the door for him. Then Father Director bent down to test the water. Fran was too embarrassed to take off his pyjama trousers while Father Director was there, so waited for him to go.

'All right, son, in you get,' Father Director said, turning off the taps and standing up.

Fran hesitated, embarrassed, wanting Father Director to go out.

'Go on, son, don't be shy. Take the trousers off, too,' Father Director told him and joked: 'You can't have a bath with them on!'

Blushing, Fran did as he was told and stepped into the bath. Father Director held his arm to help him and told him to stand up in the water, so he did so, though he didn't understand why. He hoped Father Director wasn't going to stay and watch him having a bath!

But not only did Father Director stay, he started to wash him with his soap and flannel. He washed him all over, even between his legs. Fran blushed furiously and wished he had never told Father Director he wanted a bath. He didn't need Father Director to bath him – he wasn't a baby, he was twelve years old!

After a while though, he stopped feeling embarrassed and even started to enjoy being bathed. It was very kind of Father Director to look after him like this, he thought. When he had finished washing him, Father Director rinsed him off, helped him out of the bath, dried him and rubbed Johnson's Baby Powder all over him – even between his legs. That made him blush again, though he tried not to. Then Father Director helped him to put on his pyjamas and dressing gown and led him back up to the dorm by torchlight, where he tucked him up in bed.

'All right, son?' Father Director asked, crouching down by his bed and putting a hand on his shoulder. 'Feel better?'

'Yes, thank you, Father,' Fran whispered.

'You can put some clean underpants on tomorrow morning. Now go to sleep.'

'Yes, Father.'

'Say an Act of Contrition before you go to sleep, won't you, son?'

'What for, Father?' Fran asked, puzzled.

'You should always say one before you sleep, son – just in case.'

'Yes, Father.'

'Goodnight and God bless, son.'

'Goodnight, Father.'

Father Director gave his shoulder a squeeze, stood up and carried on walking around the dorm, saying his rosary, beads jingling. Outside, the wind whined, an owl hooted and another train passed with a forlorn whistle, but these sounds didn't make Fran feel homesick or lonely any more.

He snuggled down in bed, shut his eyes and said an Act of Contrition, as Father Director had told him. Then he said a prayer to Our Lord to help him stay and become a priest, as he had promised Father Director earlier. Finally, as always before going to sleep, he asked God to bless his mum, dad, brothers and sisters and all his relations, in England and Ireland, naming each of them one by one. But, before he got though all the names of uncles, aunties and cousins, he had drifted off ...

CHAPTER FOUR

Father Director, standing behind his small table at one end of the ref, said the 'Benedicite', or grace before meals, and they sat down on their benches – in silence – to wait for breakfast. The reader began reading from 'The Imitation of Christ' on the rostrum. While they waited, stomachs rumbled – it was now quarter-past eight and they had been up since half-past six. At last the servers in their white aprons brought in the tins of porridge – or 'pigswill' as they called it – and gave one to each table. The head of each table then divided it into six with a knife and started to dole it out into their plastic bowls.

Suddenly Brother Michael, bacon-faced and burly, burst through the door from the Fathers' house into the ref, slinging a girdle around his generous girth, and hurried over to Father Director. A current of excitement went around the room. There was a whispered 'confab' between Brother Michael and Father Director, who was munching his corn flakes, during which Father Director glanced out of the window and nodded several times. With each nod, the boys' excitement increased.

Brother Michael bustled out, but Father Director carried on eating his cornflakes, keeping them in suspense. Not until he had finished, and daintily dabbed his mouth with his white linen napkin, did he at last tinkle the little bell on his table to stop the reader and announce what they wanted to hear: 'As the weather seems to have dried up, Brother Michael says that potato picking can start today, so – '

Before he could go any further, a cheer went up from the boys – this was what they had been waiting to hear for a week, but had been prevented by constant rain. Today, though, the skies had cleared to a cold, bright blue. Potato picking meant no class or study for three days, followed by a 'dies non' or free day – almost a whole week off!

'Silence!' Father Director shouted, ringing his bell loudly, and the cheering stopped abruptly. 'So,' he continued, 'no more reading. Finish your breakfasts as quickly as possible in silence and when you have finished – quiet, Aspinall! – go and get changed and congregate in the quad, where the Master of Manual Labour will give you your instructions. Aspinall, do you want six of the best to warm you up before you go out?'

'NO, FATHER!' Aspinall, a new boy from Manchester like himself, answered in his loud, raucous voice.

'There's no need to shout, Aspinall,' Father Director reprimanded him.

'I'm sorry, Father,' Aspinall said, just as loudly. 'It's me nature, Father.' The whole ref burst into laughter.

'Silence!' Father Director bawled, ringing his bell as loudly as he could, and the laughter stopped. 'Aspinall, go and wait outside my office and we'll see if we can change your nature.'

'But I 'aven't finished me breakfast, Father,' Aspinall protested, to splutters of laughter.

'Aspinall, if you're not outside my office in one minute, this will be your last breakfast,' Father Director threatened him, glowering.

Aspinall stood up and left the ref with his tail between his legs.

'Now carry on with your breakfasts, in silence,' Father Director ordered the rest of them sternly.

They did so. For them, breakfast meant cold, watery, lumpy porridge, a slice or two of stale bread with a tiny ration of margarine, or 'axle grease' as they called it, and a cup of 'dishwater' tea from an aluminium jug, with milk and sugar already added by Cyril the cook. Unfortunately, he always watered the milk down and, they joked, counted in the sugar as meanly as possible grain by grain.

For Father Director though, and the other Fathers in their elegant dining room, breakfast was somewhat more sumptuous. *They* had a choice of fresh fruit or fruit juice, porridge or corn flakes, tea or coffee, bread or toast with butter, marmalade or jam, a boiled or poached egg or fried egg, bacon and tomato. The head server now brought the rest of Father Director's breakfast in on a silver tray and placed it obsequiously in front of him. The aromas of coffee and bacon wafted around the ref, making their mouths water, but they could only look forward to their turn to serve, when the head server might, if they grovelled, toss them a titbit or two from the Fathers' leftovers.

Chattering and laughing, they trooped down the drive to the potato field, togged out in a motley collection of work and football clothes several layers thick against the biting October wind and carrying an assortment of buckets and basins. At the field, which was as big as several football fields, they were instructed to string themselves out in groups of six according to their tables in the ref. Each group marked out its territory by kicking a line across the first few furrows – not without some territorial dispute – which they then had to clear of weeds and stones ready for the tractor.

After much tinkering, the tractor, driven by Brother Michael, growled into life and came rumbling along the first furrow, the digger behind spraying out a shower of spuds, soil and stones. As soon as it had passed, they had to charge forward, collect the spuds in their buckets and basins as fast as they could and empty them into sacks, then retreat before the tractor came along again.

At first it was fun, but after a while it became tiring and it was a relief when the tractor broke down, as it frequently did. Then they either rested or, to keep warm, played games, such as seeing who could run the fastest or jump the farthest over the furrows, though they weren't supposed to. They also held spud-throwing contests, though they weren't supposed to, and these were completely stopped when a particularly big spud landed on the frizzy, red-haired head of Gyp, the First Auxiliary, who sent the culprit up to see 'Father Director'.

At eleven o'clock there was a tea break, which they had all been eagerly looking forward to, not only for refreshment and a rest, but also because the mail was given out. Fran had been looking forward to it ever since he had woken up at half-six, because it was Tuesday, when he always received a letter from his mum. The tea was dispensed by the Head Refectorian from an urn brought down to the field in a wheelbarrow, while the mail was distributed by the First Auxiliary in his overalls.

Fran joined the throng of boys around the First Auxiliary rather than the queue for tea, a letter from home being far more important than food or drink. The First Auxiliary read out the name on each letter, which had already been opened and 'censored' by Father Director, then slung it towards its lucky recipient to a chorus of cheers or, if it fell to the ground, jeers. Fran waited expectantly for his name to be called, until the First Auxiliary reached the last letter. This must be his, he thought, but the Auxiliary called out the name of someone else and sent the letter flying towards him. 'That's your lot, laddies,' he declared, striding away.

Fran stood there for a few moments, hardly able to believe it. Oh, well, it must have been delayed in the post and would come tomorrow, he told himself, choking back his disappointment, and traipsed over to join the tea queue.

'What's it like?' one of them asked.

'Dishwater, as usual,' another said.

'Dishwater?' said a third. 'I reckon Cyril's washed his socks in it.' They all laughed, except for Fran.

By dinner time though, he had cheered up. After the 'Benedicite' and reading from the New Testament in Latin, Father Director gave a 'Tu autem', at which they all cheered, because it meant there was no more reading and they could talk. By then, after nearly four hours in the field, they were so ravenous they devoured even the rotten spuds, mushy swede and gristly bangers with gusto. For afters, it was tinned peaches and custard, which they called 'carrots and paint' and gobbled up with chunks of bread as a filler.

After dinner there was a short recreation and then they had to go back down to the potato field. In mid-afternoon there was another tea break, this time with jam 'butties' – though they were made with margarine or 'axle grease' rather than butter. When it got dark, the tractor made its last run, they combed the field for missed spuds, then trudged, tired but cheerful, back up the drive to wash and change for supper at seven.

At supper Father Director gave another 'Tu autem' and again a loud cheer went up. While they waited, chattering excitedly, for the 'doss' to arrive, the heads of table divided the small blocks of 'axle grease' up into six with a knife and the second heads of table sawed off six slices of bread and distributed them. They continued to wait hungrily, but the 'doss' still didn't arrive. After a while, some of them succumbed to the temptation to eat their bread and marge. Eventually, a chorus of 'Why are we waiting?' started up, accompanied by the banging of cutlery on the table tops, but Father Director stopped it by ringing his bell angrily and telling them not to be 'Balubas', which was the name of a tribe in Africa.

At last the servers came in carrying trays and another loud cheer went up, not only because the 'doss' had arrived at last, but also because it was one of their favourites – fried eggs. There was only one each, but at least it was warm and the grease could be mopped up with bread. Fran felt happy – after supper there was a long rec to look forward to before Conference, followed by bed. After lights out, Father Director would probably come and chat to him as usual, if he was still awake. And tomorrow there was the best thing of all to look forward to – his mum's letter!

But his letter didn't come the next morning or the following one. The First Auxiliary slung the last letter to its recipient with his usual, 'That's your lot, laddies,' and strode off. Fran stood there, shocked. He couldn't believe it. His mum hadn't written to him! She had forgotten about him! She didn't care about him any more! She didn't love him any more! Tears sprang to his eyes.

'Oh, Walsh?' the Auxiliary called, suddenly stopping and turning towards him.

'Yes?' he asked, startled, blinking back his tears and hoping the Auxiliary hadn't noticed them.

'Parcel. Father Director's office. Collect it before dinner.'

The Auxiliary strode off again. It took Fran a moment or two to realise what he had said – there was a parcel for him! It must be from his mum. That was why he hadn't received her letter – it must be in the parcel! She hadn't forgotten him after all! She still loved him as much as ever!

'Come in!' Father Director called out, when Fran knocked on the door of his office a couple of hours later.

'Laus tibi, Christi,' Fran panted, going in. He had run all the way downstairs from the dorm, though it was against the rule.

'Nunc et in aeternam. Amen,' Father Director responded, turning round from his desk, where he was reading his breviary, and looking at him.

'The First Auxiliary said I had a parcel, Father,' Fran panted.

'That's right, son. Close the door and bless yourself first,' Father Director told him.

Fran closed the door, dipped his fingers in the holy water font next to it and blessed himself, ashamed of having forgotten.

'You look as if you've just been dragged though a hedge, son,' Father Director said.

Fran blushed – he had been in such a hurry to get his parcel that he hadn't dressed himself properly. He hoped it didn't mean Father Director would give him a bad mark for deportment on his weekly report.

'Come over here, son,' Father Director said.

Nervously, Fran did as he was told, afraid Father Director might be going to give him the strap. But all Father Director did was straighten his collar and tie for him. Fran was relieved, but embarrassed. Then Father Director asked him for his comb and combed his hair for him. While he did so, Fran glanced eagerly around the office for his parcel. At first, to his dismay, he couldn't see anything, but then he caught sight of a brown-paper parcel tied up with string on the window sill.

'There we are, son, you look a bit more presentable now,' Father Director said, giving him his comb back and gazing at him.

'Can I open my parcel now, Father?' Fran asked, embarrassed again.

'Can't wait, eh?' Father Director grinned, so that Fran could see his gold tooth at the front.

'No, Father,' Fran said, wishing Father Director would let him go and get it.

'Patience is a virtue, you know, son,' Father Director said.

'Yes, Father,' Fran nodded, feeling as if he had been told off.

'All right, son, go and open it. It's over there on the window sill. Here are some scissors.'

'Thank you, Father,' Fran said gratefully, taking the scissors and going over to the window sill.

Eagerly, he cut open the parcel and to his delight saw that his mum had put in his favourite sweets – Mars bars and Rowntree's fruit gums – as well as biscuits, cakes, a pot of jam, a tin of syrup and some apples and oranges. There was also a letter in the usual blue Basildon Bond envelope, with 'Master Francis Walsh' written on it in his mum's familiar handwriting. His heart swelled with gratitude. She hadn't forgotten him! She still loved him! He was so sorry for thinking she didn't. A lump came to his throat and he almost wanted to cry.

'Bring it over here, son,' Father Director said from behind him.

Fran slipped the letter into the inside pocket of his blazer. Then, blinking back tears, he gathered up the parcel and took it over to Father Director, who told him to put it on his desk.

'Who is it from, son?' Father Director asked.

'Me mum. Father,' Fran said, proudly.

'My, my, she has done you proud, hasn't she?' Father Director declared, examining the contents of the parcel, which made Fran feel even more proud of her.

'Wasn't there a letter?' Father Director asked, glancing at him.

'No, Father,' Fran fibbed, trying not to blush – for once he wanted to open it himself and be the first to read it.

'Are you sure, son?' Father Director asked, looking him straight in the eyes.

'Yes, Father,' Fran said, reddening despite himself. It was a fib, but he'd tell it in Confession, he thought – he needed a few sins to tell, anyway.

'That's a bit strange, isn't it, son?'

'I don't know, Father,' Fran shrugged, guiltily avoiding Father Director's eyes.

'She's probably written separately,' Father Director said.

'Yes, Father,' Fran nodded in agreement. 'I hope so.'

'Don't worry, son, I'm sure she has – it'll probably come tomorrow,' Father Director reassured him, making him feel even more guilty.

'I hope so, Father.'

'She really loves you, doesn't she?'

'Yes, Father!'

'And you love her, do you?'

'Yes, Father,' Fran said, surprised at the question.

'That's good, son,' Father Director said, still looking straight at him. 'But you know that if you want to be a priest, you have to detach yourself from all human love, don't you, son?'

'You mean, I shouldn't love my mum any more, Father?' Fran asked, perplexed.

'Not exactly, son,' Father Director said. 'You should still love her, of course, because she's your mother, but in a more spiritual, detached way. Detachment is one of the virtues we have to acquire if we want to be priests. That's one of the reasons why you are here, to learn detachment from all earthly ties. Do you understand, son?'

'Yes, Father,' Fran nodded, though he didn't really,

'It's natural, too, that as we grow older we become more detached from our parents, isn't it? People grow up and get married, for example. Do you understand?'

'Yes, Father,' he said, though he didn't really.

'That's a good boy. Now, you can choose one item from the parcel to keep.'

'You mean, I can't keep it all, Father?' Fran asked, dismayed.

'Just one item, son – the rest has to go in the communal kitty.'

Fran was so disappointed he almost burst into tears. He picked up a Mars bar in one hand and a packet of fruit gums in the other, unable to make his mind up between them. Then, suddenly, the bell rang for chapel.

'Hurry up, son,' Father Director said.

'I'll take the fruit gums, please, Father,' Fran decided, reckoning he could make the fruit gums last longer.

'All right, son, put them in your pocket.'

Fran slipped the packet of fruit gums into his blazer pocket, but couldn't bear to relinquish the Mars bar.

'Go on, son, take that as well,' Father Director said.

'Thank you, Father!' Fran exclaimed, slipping it into his pocket with the fruit gums. He felt like flinging his arms around

Father Director's neck and kissing him, but of course couldn't.

'All right, son – off you go and don't be late for chapel,' Father Director said, standing up and opening the door for him.

'Thank you, Father,' Fran said again, and as he went out Father Director patted him on the head.

Fran hurried up the stone stairs to the chapel. He felt happy – happy because Father Director had been so kind to him and happy because he had his sweets to look forward to eating. Most of all, though, he felt happy because he had his mum's letter to look forward to reading. And for once he'd be able to open it himself!

CHAPTER FIVE

'Atchoo!'

Fran couldn't stop sneezing during supper, each time interrupting 'In the Steps of the Master' by H. V. Morton. He didn't feel like eating his chunk of stale cheese – he didn't like cheese anyway – and asked the Head of Table if could leave it.

'Geddit down yer, yer little flogger!' was the Head of Table's sympathetic response.

Last week the Head of Table had caught him trying to slip it into his blazer pocket and forced him to eat every last bit, including the rind. He made him do the same tonight and again it almost made him sick.

After supper Father Director took his temperature in his bedroom and sent him to bed. It felt strange, being in bed so early all on his own in the darkness of the dorm. From below he could hear the muffled sounds of the other boys talking and laughing during recreation, the bell for the end of recreation, doors opening and closing, chairs scraping the study-hall floor, their voices saying the 'Ave Maria', Father Director's voice giving Conference, and then their footsteps shuffling upstairs to go to bed.

When the lights went on, Fran closed his eyes and tried to sleep. He heard them saying Night Prayer as they knelt by their beds and getting ready for bed. Then he started to fall asleep. The last thing he heard was the ghostly voice of the First Auxiliary in the darkness after lights out, intoning the final prayer of the day in his Scottish brogue: 'Remember that at any moment you may die and enter into eternity. If you die in a state of grace, you will live forever in eternal happiness; if you die in a state of mortal sin, you will burn forever in the Hell of the damned that was prepared for the Devil and his angels.'

'Benedicamus Domino!' shouted Father Director, switching on the lights and clapping loudly.

'Deo Gratias,' those who were awake mumbled sleepily, sitting on the sides of their beds with the covers over them for modesty and starting to get dressed. It was half-past six in the morning, pitch-black outside and freezing cold.

Father Director swept around the dorm, shouting 'Benedicamus Domino!' and clapping his hands loudly to wake everyone up. If any boy didn't get up, he pulled the bedclothes off him and maybe gave him a prod in the ribs.

Fran forgot that he was supposed to stay in bed and out of habit started to get up, but Father Director put a hand on his shoulder, gave it a squeeze and told him, 'You stay where you are, son.'

He was glad, because he felt hot and shivery, and it was nice to be able to lie in while everyone else had to get up. When they had all gone downstairs to the study hall for Morning Prayer, he dozed off. He was woken up again by the banging and clanging when they came back to make their beds after Mass and Thanksgiving an hour later. After they had gone downstairs to the study hall for morning study, he dozed off again …

'Wakey, wakey!'

Someone was shaking his shoulder. He opened his eyes. It was the Infirmarian, a boy from the Fourth Form called Zak. He gave Fran a basin of water to wash his face and brush his teeth in, then sent him to the toilet. When he came back, Zak had made his bed for him. He told him to get back in and stuck a thermometer in his mouth. After a minute or so, he took it out and looked at it, frowning. 'Oh, dear,' he said, shaking his head.

'What's wrong?' Fran asked, alarmed.

'Nothing – don't worry,' Zak said solemnly. 'Sit up and Father Haynes'll be along in a few minutes.' He puffed up his pillows for him and picked up the basin of dirty water to go.

'Father Haynes?' Fran asked, puzzled. 'What for?'

'To bring you Extreme Unction,' Zak whispered in his ear and bustled off with the basin.

Extreme Unction – that was the sacrament for the dying, wasn't it, Fran thought? Oh, God, he must be going to die! He must have caught pneumonia or something on the potato field! He was going to die all alone here in the dorm! He would never see his mum and dad or brothers and sisters again! And he was only twelve years old! Oh, God, he prayed in panic, please don't let me die! I don't want to die! I'll do anything for You, if You don't let me die!

Suddenly, through the swing doors at the end of the dorm, he heard the tinkle of a bell and his heart missed a beat. He turned his head to look and listen, holding his breath. There was another tinkle, a little louder and nearer, and another. Then the dorm doors opened and his heart leapt into his mouth: a server in cassock and cotta appeared, holding an altar bell in one hand, followed by another carrying a candle, followed finally by Father Haynes in an alb, with a humeral veil around his shoulders, under which he was carrying something.

Slowly and solemnly they processed up the long, narrow aisle between the rows of beds on his side of the dorm, the server in front tinkling his bell every few steps. Aghast, Fran slid down in the bed and covered his head with the bedclothes, pretending to be asleep, hoping they wouldn't even see him. But the tinkles of the bell came nearer and nearer and with each one his heart thumped harder and harder. In panic he prayed that they wouldn't see him, that they would pass by and go away, that it was all a mistake, a bad dream, he wasn't really going to die ...

Someone shook his shoulder. Fran pulled the bedclothes off his head and stared. The server with the bell was leaning over him. Father Haynes and the acolyte were standing at the foot of the bed.

'Sit up – Father Haynes has come to give you Holy Communion,' the server with the bell said.

With relief, Fran realised that the Infirmarian had been 'jossing'. He sat up and the server put a communion plate under his chin. He closed his eyes, joined his hands and put out his tongue. He heard Father Haynes say the words of Communion: 'Corpus Domini nostri Jesu Christi custodiat animam tuam in vitam aeternam. Amen.' Then he felt the Sacred Host on his tongue. Keeping his eyes closed, he let it melt a little and swallowed it without touching it with his teeth, as you were supposed to.

When he opened his eyes, Father Haynes and the two servers had gone. He suddenly felt lonely in the empty dorm. Then he remembered that Our Lord was now present inside him. He said a prayer of thanks to Him for not letting him die and asked Him to make him better. He told Our Lord that he loved Him more than ever and promised Him fervently that he would become a priest one day, just like Father Director.

Then he lay back on his pillow and dozed off again ...

'Not dead yet?' Zak, the Infirmarian, enquired, bringing him breakfast on a tray. 'Well, this'll finish you off.'

Fran smiled wanly and sat up. 'Breakfast' was the usual 'pigswill' porridge and bread and marge with a cup of 'dishwater' tea. He could only drink the tea. After breakfast, Zak came back and told him to get out of bed and put on his dressing-gown and slippers.

'It's Emergency Ward Ten for you,' Zak said.

'What's that?' Fran asked, doing as he was told.

'The infirmary.'

'Why, what's wrong with me?' Fran asked, alarmed.

Zak pursed his lips, took a deep intake of breath and declared: 'You've got flu.'

'What's that?'

'That's short for influenza. It's a viral disease of the upper respiratory tract,' Zac informed him gravely, as if he were a doctor.

'Can you die from it?' Fran asked.

'Twenty million people died from it just after the First World War.'

'You're jossing.'

'I'm not jossing. It's in the history books. Father Director told me. He said we have to isolate you, because it's contagious, and there's only one cure.'

'What's that?' Fran asked.

'You have to sweat it out.' He yanked the blankets off the bed. 'Come on. Follow me.'

Frightened, Fran did as he was told. The infirmary was a small room next to the ref, with a sloping ceiling. There was nothing in it except two beds, two chairs, a small table and a crucifix on the wall. However, Fran enjoyed being there, though he was too hot under all the blankets the Infirmarian had put on his bed. It had curtains on the window and lino on the floor, so it was almost like being in a proper bedroom again. It reminded him of the attic he used to sleep in at home when he was seven.

He remembered how he had been ill in the attic once, with measles. When he got better, his mum bought him two goldfish in a bowl, but they died after only a few weeks. He came home from school one day and his mum showed them to him, lying immobile on a piece of newspaper on the kitchen table. He couldn't believe it – that morning they had been swimming around happily. His mum helped him to bury them in the front garden and make a cross out of twigs to mark the grave. That was the first time he had really understood what 'dead' meant.

He hoped Zak was only jossing and he wasn't going to die. He brought him dinner and tea on a tray, though all he could eat was some of the Fathers' soup at dinner, which was a special treat because he was ill. Whenever Zak came in, he said, 'Not dead yet?', and whenever he took his temperature, he shook his head, pursed his lips, took a deep intake of breath and said something like, 'Not much hope left', but he was only jossing, Fran soon realised.

After tea and recreation, when the bell went for Rosary, Fran took his rosary beads out of his pyjama pocket. They were in a small, black, leather pouch, with the name of the Cistercian abbey in Ireland where his mum had bought them for him stamped on it in gold letters. They were really good ones, made of cowhorn, with a little glass tube of Lourdes water in the crucifix, which was made of black turf. Fran had also attached to them various medals, including a St. Christopher medal and the 'miraculous' medal his granny had given him the last time he had seen her, last year, before she died. He started to say his rosary under the bedclothes, but before he finished he fell asleep ...

'Aaaargh! Aaaaaargh!'

He tried to scream but hardly any sound came out. There was something at the window – a skeleton with a black cloak, bloody fangs and huge glass eyes, staring straight at him. In one bony hand it held a big black stick and with the other it was clawing at the window, as if trying to get in. It looked like a cross between Dracula and the Dean of Studies. He tried to jump out of bed, but was paralysed.

Suddenly the light went on and someone was shaking his shoulder. 'Wake up, son – it's all right.'

Fran opened his eyes to see Father Director sitting on the edge of his bed and a wave of relief swept over him.

'Were you having a nightmare?' Father Director asked, keeping his hand on his shoulder.

'Yes, Father,' Fran said, feeling silly now.

'What was it about?'

'I – I can't remember, Father,' Fran fibbed. He couldn't very well say he had been having a nightmare about the Dean of Studies!

'Just as well,' Father Director smiled. 'And how do you feel?'

'Very hot, Father.'

'My, my, you're like a furnace!' Father Director said, putting his hand on his forehead. 'Are you sweating?'

'I think so, Father.'

'Let's have a look.' Father Director pulled back the bedclothes and put his hand under his pyjama jacket. 'Good grief, you're sweating cobs!' he exclaimed.

'I'm not going to die, am I, Father?' Fran asked, scared.

'Of course not, son. Who told you that?'

'The Infirmarian, Father.'

'That infirmarian! I'll have his guts for garters!'

'He said I had flu and twenty million people died from it after the First World War.'

'That's right, son. You have got flu and twenty million people did die from it after the First World War. But that was forty years ago. You're not going to die. What else did he say?'

'He said I had to sweat it out.'

'Yes, you do, son, but – how many blankets have you got here?' Father Director took his hand away from under his pyjama jacket and counted them. 'Ten! Suffering catfish! No wonder you've been having nightmares! That infirmarian's a right Baluba!' He stood up and pulled all the blankets off the bed, handed Fran his dressing-gown and said, 'Come with me, son.'

Fran got out of bed, put on his dressing-gown and slippers, and followed Father Director to his bedroom. Father Director was just going to give him some medicine, he supposed. However, when they got there, Father Director locked the door, took off his camail, hung it on the back of the door and rolled up the sleeves of his habit. 'Take your things off and put them on the bed, son,' he told him, going over to the washbasin.

Puzzled, Fran took off his dressing-gown and pyjama jacket and put them on Father Director's bed. Father Director was running water in the washbasin with his back to him.

'Shall I take off my scapular, Father?' Fran asked. That was the scapular of the Sacred Heart that Fran wore round his neck.

'Yes, everything, son,' Father Director said, his back to him.

Everything – did that mean his pyjama trousers, too, he wondered, taking off his scapular and putting it on the bed? He hoped not!

'And the trousers, son,' Father Director said, glancing over his shoulder at him.

Embarrassed, but obedient, Fran did as he was told and stood naked in the middle of the floor, wondering what Father Director was going to do.

'Almost ready,' Father Director said, taking a towel off the rail and turning round.

He spread the towel on the floor, told Fran to stand on it with his legs apart and gave him some rosary beads to hold. Blushing, Fran did as he was told, wondering nervously what Father Director was going to do. Father Director turned back to the washbasin and ran some more water.

While he waited, Fran glanced around the room, trying to stop himself blushing. It reminded him of his bedroom at home, because it had curtains on the window, wallpaper on the walls and brown lino on the floor. It also had a wardrobe, a chest of drawers and a wooden bed instead of the iron ones they had in the dorm. On the wall above the bed hung a crucifix. On the locker beside the bed there was an alarm clock and some books, including a breviary. The top of the chest of drawers was covered with bottles of medicines and tablets and toiletries. It looked like a chemist's shop, Fran thought.

'Now, son,' Father Director said, turning to him with a flannel in his hand. 'There's nothing to be afraid of. I'm just going to give you a wash, to freshen you up. It'll make you feel better. It's what they would do if you were in hospital. Just lift your arms up, close your eyes and say your rosary. That's a good boy.'

Fran did as he was told. Father Director crouched down and began to wash him all over with the soapy flannel, even between his legs, which made him blush again. After Father Director had soaped him down, he rinsed him off with the wet flannel. Fran blushed even more fiercely when it went between his legs, but he kept his eyes shut tight and tried to pray, as Father Director had told him.

Finally, Father Director dried him off and rubbed Johnson's Baby Powder all over him, including between his legs. That made his face feel as if it was on fire!

'There you are, son, you'll feel a lot better now,' Father Director said at last.

'Thank you, Father,' Fran said, opening his eyes and moving towards the bed to pick up his things.

'Just a minute, son,' Father Director said, putting a hand on his thigh. 'I want to look at something.'

Fran flinched and felt his face flare up again – Father Director was holding his thing!

'Relax, son,' Father Director said, stroking his thigh with one hand and still holding his thing with the other. 'There's nothing to be afraid of. I won't hurt you. I just want to look at something.'

Fran shut his eyes tight and tried to do as he was told, but it was impossible – now Father Director was holding his thing with one hand and feeling underneath it with the other. His face burned.

'I think you've got something here, son,' Father Director said. He sounded serious. Fran suddenly felt scared again – there was something wrong with him after all! The Infirmarian was right!

'I think you've got a varicocele, son,' Father Director said, still holding his thing. 'Do you know what that is?'

Fran shook his head, keeping his eyes shut tight.

'It's nothing to worry about, son,' Father Director said. 'It's just like a varicose vein. Do you know what a varicose vein is?'

Fran nodded, eyes still shut tight – he knew, because his mum had varicose veins in her legs and had had an operation on them, but he couldn't understand how he could have one there. Did that mean he would have to have an operation! The idea terrified him. Oh, God, no, he prayed!

'Don't move, son,' Father Director said, standing up.

Fran peeped through his eyelashes. To his alarm, Father Director went over to the chest of drawers, picked something up, came back and crouched down in front of him again with something in his hand. It wasn't a pair of scissors, was it, Fran wondered fearfully, peeping down, but couldn't see.

Suddenly, he felt something cold touch his thing and flinched.

'Keep still, son,' Father Director told him. 'I'm not going to hurt you. I'm just going to rub some ointment on. That's all. Look.'

Nervously, Fran opened his eyes and looked down to see what Father Director had in his hand. To his relief, it was only a tin of Germolene!

'Now close your eyes again and say your prayers, that's a good boy,' Father Director told him, starting to rub the ointment on his thing. 'There's nothing to be afraid of. I'll speak to the doctor about it tomorrow.'

Fran tried to do as he was told, but it was difficult – he felt embarrassed as well as afraid. What exactly was wrong with him? Why did Father Director have to speak to the doctor about it? What if it was serious? What if he had to go to hospital? What if he had to have an operation? Oh, God, no, please, he prayed again! Please, God, I'll do anything!

'All right, son, that'll do for now,' Father Director said.

Fran opened his eyes to see Father Director putting the lid back on the tin of ointment. He hoped he would let him go now.

'By the way, son,' he said, still crouching in front of him and putting a hand on his thigh again, 'what kind of underpants do you wear?'

51

'I'm not sure what you mean, Father,' Fran said, blushing again.

'I mean, are they the loose types – you know, like football shorts?' Father Director asked, his hand still on his thigh.

'Yes, I suppose so, Father,' Fran said, puzzled, wishing he would let him go.

'Well, we'll have to change them for the other type – you know, Y-fronts, like swimming trunks. You need support there.' Father Director put his hand under his thing, making him flinch again. 'Do you understand?'

'Yes, Father,' Fran said, though he didn't really.

'All right, son, you can put your things back on now,' Father Director said, patting his thigh, standing up and helping him on with his pyjamas and dressing-gown.

'A few more days of this treatment and we'll soon have you back in circulation,' he said, ushering him to the door with an arm round his shoulders. 'You'll still have to come to Infirmary with the other thing, though. Do you understand?'

'Yes, Father,' Fran said.

'Infirmary' meant when boys went to Father Director's bedroom at bedtime for any medicine they needed. The boys jokingly called it the 'pyjama parade'.

'Good boy,' Father Director said. He unlocked the door and opened it, but then closed it again. 'One other thing, son – you must never say anything about this or any other medical matter to anyone, not even your parents. It's private and confidential, between you and me, just like Confession. Do you understand?'

'Yes, Father,' Fran said. As if he'd tell anyone – he'd be too embarrassed!

'Good boy. Off you go, then, back to bed and sweat it out,' Father Director said, giving his shoulder a hug and opening the door again.

'Thank you, Father,' Fran said, with relief hurrying out.

He went back to the infirmary, got back into bed and snuggled down under the bedclothes. Father Director was right – it felt better, because there weren't so many blankets on now. He felt nice and clean and fresh after his wash, too, just as Father Director had said he would. Father Director was very kind. He was sorry he had been so embarrassed when he was washing him now. It was only what they would do if he was in hospital, he supposed, as Father Director had said – not that he had ever been in hospital, except sometimes when he went with his dad to meet his mum.

He hoped he wouldn't have to go to hospital or even worse have an operation. He was scared stiff of that. He didn't really need to be, though, he thought – Father Director would look after him. He seemed to like him, unlike the Dean of Studies. He liked Father Director, too – it was almost like having a dad again.

He started to feel sleepy. He decided to say another decade of the rosary before he fell asleep, so took his rosary beads out of his pyjama jacket pocket. But before he started, he offered it up to Our Lady to help him become a priest, just like Father Director ...

CHAPTER SIX

December 1st – only twenty-two days till they went home for Christmas!

As usual, the first thing Fran did when he came down to the study hall for morning study was open his desk and cross off the number of days to going home on the calendar he had sellotaped under the lid, along with an array of holy pictures. December 23rd was the big day and round it he had drawn a circle in red, with rays of sunshine radiating outwards.

However, there was a big black cloud on the horizon before going home – the Christmas exams. He was nervous about them, though he had got good marks all term and been on the Honours List every week – more than any other boy in the class except one, a Polish boy called Zapolski, or 'Zappo' as he was nicknamed. He was hoping to come top of the class, to please both his parents and Father Director, but to do so he had to beat Zappo, as well as all the others. That was going to be hard, so from today, December 1st, he had resolved to study – and pray – harder than ever.

Before the exams, though, there was something to look forward to – December 8th was the feast of the Immaculate Conception of the Blessed Virgin Mary and a 'dies non' or free day. He wasn't sure what 'Immaculate Conception' meant until he looked it up in his missal, where it said: 'Mary was preserved from all stain of original sin from the first moment of her conception and so was prepared for the surpassing dignity of Mother of God'. He still wasn't sure what 'conception' meant, but guessed it was another word for 'birth'.

According to his missal, the dogma of the Immaculate Conception was solemnly defined as a truth of the Catholic faith by Pope Pius the Ninth on December 8th, 1854, which meant that if you were a Catholic you had to believe it. His missal also had two beautiful pictures of Our Lady, one called, 'The Immaculate Conception', by the seventeenth-century Spanish painter, Murillo, and the other called, 'The Mother of God, Preserved from Sin as a Pure Tabernacle for the Messias', by the Florentine artist, Botticelli (1444 -1510).

For several days before, visiting members of the order came from all over. The most important was Father Provincial, an eccentric old man of about seventy, who was in charge of the English province. The boys called him 'Pop' and made merciless fun of him, especially his stammer, which was supposed to be a result of his having been gassed during the First World War when he was a chaplain to the troops.

On the evening before the feast day, Pop gave them a 'Conference', which according to the old boys was exactly the same every year and a lot of which they had already heard in impersonations, especially the introduction: 'My g-g-good boys, you are like t-t-tomatoes in a, in a, in a 'ot'ouse ...' As soon as Pop started to stammer out these words himself, several boys burst into giggles and before long most of the boys were giggling giddily. However, Pop didn't seem to notice or mind and stammered wheezily on regardless about the Immaculate 'C-C-Conception' and 'p-p-priestly p-p-purity'.

A priest, Pop told them, had to be as 'p-p-pure' and ''oly' as the 'B-B-Blessed V-V-Virgin 'erself,' who not only never committed a sin in her life, but was conceived without the stain of original sin on her soul, the only human being since Adam and Eve to have had that privilege, except of course for Our Lord. Fran still wasn't sure what exactly 'conceived' meant, but would look it up later in his Concise Oxford Dictionary, he decided.

The realisation that Our Lady had not only been born without original sin, but had never committed even a venial sin in her life, inspired him with a new reverence for her. He imagined her as she looked in holy pictures and church statues, clad in snow-white and sky-blue robes, with the earth at her feet, beams of light radiating from her outstretched hands and a halo of stars around her head, looking both holy and beautiful. She had to be both, because she was the mother of God. Yet she was their heavenly mother too, Pop told them, and loved them especially, because they were going to be priests. She more than anyone would help them, if they prayed to her.

There and then Fran resolved that he would pray to her more than ever – he already had a special devotion to her, ever since he had been to Lourdes the year before and seen the grotto, the very place where she had appeared a hundred years ago to Saint Bernadette. He would begin a novena to her tonight, he resolved, not only to help him to become a priest, but also to do well in the exams and come top of the class.

The feast-day itself, the next day, was celebrated with Solemn High Mass. That meant the celebrant was assisted by a deacon and sub-deacon, all wearing the best blue and white silk vestments, blue and white being the liturgical colours for Our Lady. There were also more servers than usual, including acolytes and a thurifer, all wearing newly-washed and starched white cottas. The altar was adorned with flowers, all the candles were lit and the brass candlesticks, specially polished in manual labour the day before for the occasion, gleamed like gold. The Mass itself was sung in plainchant, which they had been practising for weeks before in singing class.

The Mass wasn't quite as solemn as it should have been, because Pop was the celebrant and besides his stammer he had a voice like a foghorn when he sang. As a result, by the First Gospel, most of the congregation were convulsed with laughter and a few boys even had to stagger out of the chapel in stitches. However, as in 'Conference' the night before, Pop didn't seem to notice, stammering and honking on regardless.

The most solemn part of the Mass, the Consecration, was the funniest, even funnier than the most exaggerated impersonations. Not only did Pop stammer out the sacred words like a misfiring old banger – ''oc, 'oc, 'oc est enim C-C-Corpus Meum', ''ic, 'ic, ''ic est enim C-C-Calix Sanguinis Mei ...' – when he genuflected and elevated the sacred host and chalice, he did so with comically clockwork, jerky movements. And like most of the others, Fran couldn't help laughing.

By the end of the hour-and-a-half-long ceremony, though, he didn't feel like laughing. His knees and back were aching and his tummy was rumbling with hunger, hunger accentuated by thoughts of the special feast-day dinner they were going to have. But that wouldn't be for another hour and a half, until after recreation and visit to chapel.

When dinner did come, it was good – they had a bottle of pop each instead of just water, roast potatoes instead of boiled, pork chops instead of 'bangers' and apple pie and custard instead of 'carrots and paint', as they called the usual tinned peaches with cream. Also, Father Director gave a 'tu autem', which meant there was no reading and they were allowed to talk. The Head of Table made them laugh by imitating Pop as he shared out the 'doss': ''oc, 'oc, 'oc est p-p-porkus chopus tuus ...'

Fran even tried imitating Pop himself by pretending to be drunk on his bottle of lemonade: ''ic, 'ic, 'ic,' he hiccupped, flapping his arms up and down the way Pop did and swaying from side to side. The others guffawed, but the Head of Table didn't like his thunder to be stolen.

'Hey! Who do you think you're imitating?' he demanded, pointing his knife at him.

'Pop,' Fran said, sheepishly.

'Pop?' the Head of Table sneered. ''Father Provincial' to you, you cheeky little flogger!'

Abashed, Fran bowed his head and started to eat his 'doss'.

After dinner they went on a long walk, in the usual 'crocodile' of groups of three, led by Father Director, to Hampsfell Hospice. This was a square stone shelter on top of one of the 'fells' or hills, built in the last century by a local benefactor for the use of travellers. To reach it they had to wind their way up the hillside through a wood, the ground iron-hard with frost and most of the trees bare, and then file across a rocky windswept moor. The only vegetation here was grass, heather and a few gorse bushes and the only other visible living creatures birds, sheep and rabbits.

Just before the hospice there was an expanse of flat white rock, which the head of their group told them was limestone and which they had to step across carefully, because it was full of deep crevices. To Fran it looked like the surface of the moon or some other planet. In some of the crevices the bones of animals were stuck – they must have got trapped and died, he supposed, with a ripple of horror.

As soon as they came within sight of the hospice itself, they were allowed to disperse and with a cheer they raced off across the rock to it. There were some steps on one side going up to the roof, which Fran climbed up with some of the others. From the top there was a panoramic view of the mountains of the Lake District and a revolving indicator with the names of mountains and other places on.

After looking at the view from the top for a while, Fran went down the steps and inside with a few of the others – it was so small that there was only room for a few at a time. It was also bare, except for a wooden bench around the walls, on which were carved names and dates from as long ago as the last century. Around the top of the walls there was a wooden board with a poem written on it. There were two small windows with no glass in them, so that the wind blew right through.

'It's not much of a shelter,' one of them said, shivering.

'Just like the dorm,' another one joked, and they went out.

Fran stayed behind. He had noticed some words in Greek carved in the stone above the doorway – RODO DAKTYLOS HOS – and was trying to translate them, but couldn't. Suddenly, he felt a hand on his shoulder and turned with surprise to see Gordon Lewis, a fifth-former, beside him again. He had been beside him on the roof, too, where he had pointed out some of the sights with the revolving indicator for him. In fact, Fran suddenly realised, Gordon Lewis always seemed to be beside him these days.

'It's from Homer,' Lewis said, keeping his hand on his shoulder, which made him uneasy, because it was against the rule. 'Have you done any Homer yet?'

'No,' Fran shook his head, wishing Lewis would take his hand away.

'No, I don't suppose you would have,' Lewis said. 'Can you translate it?'

'No,' Fran said, somewhat ashamed – Lewis was supposed to be the best Greek scholar in the school and was doing it for A-level, whereas he had only studied it for three months.

'Do you want me to translate it for you?' Lewis asked, keeping his hand on Fran's shoulder.

'All right,' Fran said, uncomfortably.

'It means, 'Rosy-fingered dawn',' Lewis explained. 'Beautiful phrase, isn't it?'

'Yes,' Fran agreed, with a shiver, as a gust of wind blew through.

'Are you cold?' Lewis asked, putting his arm around Fran's shoulders.

Fran flinched and at that moment a figure appeared in the doorway. It was Father Director, in his black trilby and raincoat. Lewis removed his arm from Fran's shoulders like lightning.

'What's going on in here?' Father Director demanded sternly, stepping in.

'Nothing, Father,' Lewis said, blushing. 'I was just translating – '

'Were you touching this boy?' Father Director demanded angrily, cutting him off.

'No, Father,' Lewis lied, blushing furiously.

'Was he touching you?' Father Director demanded of Fran.

'He just put his hand on my shoulder, Father,' Fran fibbed, hoping Father Director hadn't seen Lewis's arm around his shoulders.

'I want to see you in my office as soon as we get back, Lewis – now get out of here!' Father Director shouted at him.

Lewis slunk out. Fran's legs were shaking like jelly, though he hadn't done anything wrong as far as he knew.

'What was he doing, son?' Father Director demanded.

'He was just translating the Greek for me, Father,' Fran said, pointing up at it with a trembling hand.

'And he put his hand on your shoulder – are you sure that's all?'

'That's all, Father.'

'Did he touch you anywhere else?'

'No, Father,' Fran blushed.

'Tell me the truth, son.'

'That – that is the truth, Father.'

'You swear it?'

'Yes, Father.' It wasn't really the truth – it was a lie. He'd have to tell it in Confession. But Father Director seemed to have calmed down now.

'All right, son,' he said. 'Go and join the others. I'll see you in infirmary tonight as usual.'

Relieved, Fran scampered out and joined his group in the re-forming 'crocodile' to go. They wound their way down the other side of the fell to the road that ran through the floor of the valley, in order to circle back to the college. By the time they reached the road, dusk was falling and they were cold, tired and hungry.

To keep them going as they trooped along they had the thought of tea to look forward to when they arrived back, followed by recreation. He'd spend some of it revising for the exams, Fran thought, and some of it reading his library book – 'A Tale of Two Cities' by Charles Dickens – next to one of the radiators in the study hall. After recreation there was Benediction, followed by supper, and after supper there was going to be a 'singsong', which he was really looking forward to.

After that, it would be bedtime. In infirmary Father Director would take care of him as usual – he had been embarrassed about it at first, but now he didn't mind it, even enjoyed it. Then, after lights out, Father Director would probably come and chat to him as usual – if he was still awake.

But the best thing of all to look forward to was in two weeks' time – GOING HOME!

The next morning, Gordon Lewis left. Word went round that he had been expelled, though no one seemed to know exactly why. Fran suspected it had something to do with what had happened in the hospice, but he didn't tell anyone. For one thing, it was against the rule to speak about someone who had left, especially if they had been expelled, and for another he would have been too embarrassed.

They knew when someone was leaving, because instead of making their beds immediately after morning Mass and Thanksgiving, they were told to go straight down to study. That meant that someone was in the dorm packing. They could guess who it was from the empty desk in the study hall and the empty place in the ref at breakfast, as he was given breakfast on his own in the parlour of the Fathers' house. Then he was whisked off by car to the station to catch the 'nine forty-three'. No one was allowed to speak to him or even see him, especially if he was being expelled – it was as if he had suddenly contracted leprosy.

After he had left, no contact of any kind was allowed. They weren't even allowed to talk about him, though they usually did, out of earshot of prefects. Officially, he became a non-person. All traces of him were erased, so that it was as if he had never existed. Boys left regularly, especially from the First Form, or were expelled, usually for 'impurity' – Father Director was fanatical about that. Of the twenty-two who had started in the First Form with Fran in September, five had already left. They left because they were homesick, because they couldn't stand the discipline or because they decided they didn't want to be priests after all.

Fran was sure he would never leave or, as Father Director put it in 'Conference', 'fall by the wayside'. He would keep his hand to the plough and one day, with God's help, be a priest, religious and missionary, as he had always wanted to be – just like Father Director.

The Dean of Studies strode grimly into the study hall in his black cloak, clutching a ledger to his meagre chest. The assembled school rose to its feet, boys at their desks and Fathers at the front on either side of the rostrum, facing them. The Dean of Studies dropped to his knees on the rostrum step, made a brisk sign of the cross and recited the first half of the 'Ave Maria', in response to which they recited the second half all together.

The Dean of Studies made another brisk sign of the cross, mounted the rostrum, positioned the ledger on it, opened it and pressed down the pages with a clenched fist. Then he threw back his cloak, pulled forward the padded chair and sat down, all but his skeletal head disappearing from view. Only then did the rest of the assembly sit, the boys at their desks, the Fathers on chairs facing them, hands resting on their knees or tucked into the sleeves of their habits, heads slightly bowed.

A solemn silence ensued, as if the study hall were a court room, the Fathers the jury and the Dean of Studies the judge. After a few seconds' suspense, during which the only sounds were the humming of one of the fluorescent lights and a nervous cough or two, the Dean of Studies announced in a steely voice: 'Here are the Christmas examination results.'

He read them out form by form, from the Sixth Form down, boy by boy in alphabetical order of surname, subject by subject, with a mark and class position for each subject, followed by an average and class position, finishing with an average for the form as a whole. As each boy's results were read out, he had to write them down on a results sheet in front of him, to take home. At the end of each boy's results, if he had done exceptionally well he was ordered to stand and coolly commended, but if he had done badly he was given a public dressing-down and ordered to report to the Dean of Studies' room afterwards for the strap.

'Stand up, Duggan,' the Dean of Studies ordered a third-form boy from Yorkshire, who had come bottom of the class even though he was repeating the year. 'Stand up, so that everyone can see what a dunce and a dunderhead looks like.'

Duggan, a big, ungainly boy with lop-sided shoulders, rose slowly to his feet, blinking nervously and blushing.

'What have you got to say for yourself?' the Dean of Studies demanded.

'Nothing, Father,' Duggan mumbled.

'Take the straw out of your mouth and speak up!' the Dean of Studies snapped.

'Nothing, Father,' Duggan repeated, blinking and blushing like a Belisha beacon.

'Nothing, eh?' the Dean of Studies said sarcastically. 'To use a plain bit of Anglo-Saxon, you don't give a tuppeny damn, do you, Duggan?'

'Well, I'm not worried, Father,' Duggan mumbled, with a shrug of his lop-sided shoulders.

The Fathers sitting at the front lowered their eyes, a smile flickering over some of their faces. Among the boys a few sniggers broke out, but these were instantly quelled by a dagger-like glance from the Dean of Studies.

'So you're not worried, aren't you?' he said to Duggan, with a sarcastic sneer.

'No, Father,' Duggan shrugged again.

'Well, you damn well ought to be!' the Dean of Studies yelled at him. 'You will come and see me afterwards and we'll see whether you're worried or not. Now kneel in the aisle for the rest of the results.'

'No, Father.'

A shockwave went round the study hall.

'What did you say, Duggan?' the Dean of Studies demanded, daggers in his eyes.

'I said, 'No, Father', Father,' Duggan mumbled, blinking and blushing furiously. There was a deathly hush – even the fluorescent light suddenly stopped humming.

'Kneel!' the Dean of Studies snarled, springing up in the rostrum like a demented jack-in-the-box. Father Director stood up too, hands on his hips, and glared at Duggan.

'No, Father,' Duggan said yet again.

'Father, deal with this boy, will you?' the Dean of Studies said to Father Director, doing a little dance of rage on the rostrum.

Without further ado, Father Director pulled his 'cosh' from his cassock pocket and rushed up to Duggan. 'Kneel!' he bellowed at him, brandishing the cosh, but Duggan just stood there, blinking and blushing more furiously than ever.

'I'll break your stubborn pride for you!' Father Director barked and started belting him about the body with the cosh. 'Kneel! Kneel!'

Duggan raised his arms to protect himself and backed away, knocking his chair over, but Father Director followed him, belting him about the body as hard as he could and bellowing, 'I'll break you, boy! I'll break you!'

At first, waiting tensely for his results, Fran had felt annoyed with Duggan for making the Dean of Studies 'shirty', but now he felt sorry for him and wished Father Director would stop hitting him.

By now Duggan had crumpled into a heap on the floor with

his arms over his head to protect himself, pleading, 'No more, please, Father, no more!', but Father Director kept on raining blows down on him, bellowing, 'I'll break you! I'll break you!', as if he had gone raving mad. Fran was shocked. He wished one of the other Fathers or senior boys would stop him, but no one moved – the other Fathers either stared impassively or bowed their heads still lower.

'Now get out!' Father Director roared at Duggan, when he was too tired to hit him any more.

Duggan crawled to the door, which was opened by the boy sitting nearest, and crawled into the corridor, whimpering.

'Thank you, Father,' the Dean of Studies said to Father Director as he resumed his seat and continued reading the results in an even steelier voice than before to the shocked study hall.

Fran waited more tensely than ever for the Dean of Studies to reach the First Form and at last he did so. With a trembling hand he picked up his best Parker fountain pen, which his mum had bought him for going away to the seminary, and said another quick prayer. His name was the last but one, the last being Zappo, his arch-rival. By the time the Dean of Studies reached it, there were only two positions in the class left – first and second.

Hand trembling, he wrote down his marks for each of the nine subjects that they studied: English language, English literature, Latin, Greek, French, mathematics, history, geography and religious instruction. They were all good. He waited for his average – that was good, too. Then he waited, with bated breath, for the most important thing of all, his position in the class: 'Second'.

A stab of disappointment went through him, followed by a stab of envy as he heard Zappo beat him by one mark to come first, for which he was commended by the Dean of Studies. However, both feelings were quickly swept away by a wave of relief that the suspense was over and gratitude that he had done well, for which he said a quick prayer of thanks. Now he could look forward without worrying to tomorrow when, unbelievable as it seemed, they were going home!

After summing up, the Dean of Studies wished them all a

happy and holy Christmas and a good vacation, from which he hoped that they would return with 'batteries recharged' to work harder than ever. Then he picked up his ledger, knelt on the rostrum step, led them in the 'Ave Maria' again and strode out, clutching the ledger to his chest, as grimly as he had stridden in, followed by the rest of the Fathers except Father Director.

The study hall immediately burst into cheers, but Father Director silenced them and mounted the rostrum to give them their 'Holiday Notes', which they had to write down. These were a list of rules, both 'dos' and 'don'ts', which they had to observe during the vacation.

The 'dos' were mainly spiritual. They had to attend, or better serve, Mass and receive Holy Communion every day, two Masses on Sundays. They had to say their morning and night prayers and one decade of the rosary every day. They had to go to Confession once a week and Benediction on Sunday evenings. And whenever they passed a church, they had to pay a visit to the Blessed Sacrament.

The 'don'ts' were mainly about girls. Father Director sounded very strict as he spoke about them. The strictest rule of all, he stressed, was that they were not allowed to go out with girls – as if he would want to, anyway, Fran thought. Not only that, though, they were not allowed to go anywhere there were likely to be girls, such as parties, coffee bars or mixed swimming pools. They were not allowed to have anything to do with girls at all, not to talk to or even look at them. Girls, Father Director warned, were the agents of the Devil, which he would use to try to lure them from their vocations, just as he had used Eve to tempt Adam in the Garden of Eden.

Apart from avoiding girls like the plague, Father Director went on to dictate, they were not allowed to read newspapers, magazines or novels. They were not allowed to look at suggestive pictures. They were not allowed to go to 'A' or 'X' films. They were not allowed to listen to pop music, especially 'Billy Presley', as Father Director called him. They were not allowed to wear teddy-boy clothes or mix with teddy-boys. They were not allowed to go to pubs (it was lucky they didn't live in a pub any more, Fran thought), nightclubs or betting

Eugene Vesey

shops. They were not allowed to drink alcohol, smoke or chew chewing-gum. Finally, they were not allowed to go to non-Catholic services or mix with non-Catholics.

After the 'Holiday Notes', Father Director gave out their train tickets for the next day, a ritual they had all been eagerly looking forward to. Even when he held his ticket in his hand, Fran could still hardly believe he was going home tomorrow. He wanted to shout and jump for joy. When Father Director left, telling them that they could have recreation until visit to chapel before dinner, he joined the others in a rapturous cheer and jubilant chorus of:

'One more day to go,
One more day of sorrow;
No more Latin, no more French,
No more sitting on the old school bench,
We'll be home tomorrow!'

'Never mind, son,' Father Director said, as he treated him in infirmary that night. 'Maybe you'll beat him at Easter.'

'I'll try, Father,' Fran said.

He was standing naked on a towel in the middle of Father Director's bedroom floor as usual, with the electric fire on to keep him warm. His eyes were closed, his arms outstretched with his rosary beads in one hand and his legs apart. If only he had beaten Zappo, he thought, how pleased Father Director would've been! He'd try really hard at Easter.

'All packed for tomorrow?' Father Director asked, rubbing Germolene on his thing as usual.

'I think so, Father.'

'Are you looking forward to going home?'

'Oh, yes, Father!'

'What are you looking forward to most?'

'Seeing my mum again, Father.'

'Will she be meeting you?'

'No, Father. I think my dad's meeting me.'

'What about your mum?'

'She'll be at home, making tea, I hope, Father.'

66

'And rolling out the red carpet?'

'I don't know, Father,' Fran laughed.

'I'm sure she will, son, I'm sure she will.'

Father Director continued rubbing the Germolene on him. He wasn't embarrassed by it any more. He even enjoyed it, though he tried not to, because he knew he wasn't supposed to. He suddenly realised, with a twinge of regret, that this was the last time Father Director would be treating him for three weeks. He wondered if he would be all right, not having ointment on for three weeks, or if he would have to do it himself, but he was too shy to ask.

'I want to ask you something, son,' Father Director said, and stopped rubbing the ointment on.

'Yes, Father?'

'You are coming back, aren't you?'

'Of course, Father,' Fran said, offended.

'Open your eyes, son, and look at me.'

Fran opened his eyes. Father Director was kneeling in front of him, his face level with his chest, gazing up at him. He looked worried. 'Promise me you will come back, son,' he said.

'I promise, Father – I want to come back,' Fran said. 'I want to be a priest.'

'That's a good boy!' Father Director exclaimed, suddenly throwing his arms around him and hugging him tightly.

Fran felt embarrassed now, because Father Director had never done that before. He wished he would let him go, but he kept holding him tight, his head pressed against his chest. He was going a bit bald on top, Fran noticed with surprise.

'That's what I wanted to hear you say, son,' Father Director said, taking his arms from around him at last, but keeping his hands on his thighs. 'I'm sure Our Lord wants you to come back, too. I'm sure he wants you to be a priest. Pray to him for help, won't you?'

'I already do, Father.'

'Good boy,' Father Director said, letting go of him and standing up. 'That'll do for tonight. Let's put your things back on.'

Father Director helped him back on with his pyjamas, dressing gown and slippers, then unlocked the door for him, but didn't open it. 'Just one last thing before you go, son,' he said, turning back to him. 'Remember, this is a medical matter between you and me, so you won't say anything to anyone about it, will you, not even your parents?'

'No, Father,' Fran said, offended again – Father Director didn't need to tell him that again. Anyway, he'd be too embarrassed to tell anyone!

'Promise me.'

'I promise, Father.'

'Good boy,' Father Director said, opening the door for him and patting him on the head. 'Now off to bed with you. Goodnight and God bless.'

'Thank you, Father. Goodnight, Father,' Fran said, going out, along the short passage and back into the dorm.

The dorm was dark, except for the blue night light above the doors. He made his way down the aisle back to his bed as quietly as he could, so as not to disturb any of the other sleeping boys, bumping into suitcases once or twice. When he reached his bed, he took his dressing-gown off, spread it on top for extra warmth and jumped in quickly, because the dorm was freezing cold.

At first, the sheets felt as cold as ice, but they soon warmed up and after a few minutes he was as snug as a bug in a rug. He still couldn't believe he was going home tomorrow. He was almost afraid to fall asleep in case the lights went on and it was only a dream, as so often before. He knew it wasn't though, because he had his train ticket in his blazer pocket to prove it.

Suddenly, from outside, came the muffled sound of a train crossing the bay. Instead of the usual pang of homesickness, it sent through him a thrill of anticipation. He could hardly wait for morning! He was going to see his mum and dad and brothers and sisters again! It was funny – he tried to remember what they looked like, but couldn't properly. Their faces were all fuzzy!

Oh, well, never mind, he thought – he would see them again tomorrow. He must say a prayer for them and all his relations before he fell asleep, as he usually did. In his excitement he had almost forgotten! He started to do so, but as usual before he got to the end of the list, including all his relations in Manchester and Ireland, he had drifted off ...

CHAPTER SEVEN

'Are you sure you want to go back, Fran?'

That was what his mum had asked him the day before, as she helped him to pack his suitcase at the end of the Christmas vac.

'Yes, of course,' he had answered, impatiently. Then she had tried to give him a hug, but he had pulled away, embarrassed. He was even more embarrassed when he noticed there were tears in her eyes. Why was she crying, he wondered? She wanted him to be a priest, didn't she?

Now, sitting on the train, chatting and laughing with the other boys, all in their royal blue blazers, he felt glad to be going back. Every now and then though, he turned to gaze through the train window at the snow-caked fields speeding past in the murky dusk and felt guilty. He felt guilty for having spoken to his mum like that and for feeling glad to be going back.

He had been looking forward to going back for the last few days. After the first few days he hadn't felt happy at home, though he had tried not to show it. The trouble was, he didn't really fit in any more: he felt different from his brothers and sisters, who had started making fun of him, calling him names like 'Holy Joe'. When he had first arrived home, he was shocked by how small the house seemed. He was shocked by the way his brothers and sisters argued with each other all the time. He was even more shocked by how cheeky and disobedient they were to their mum and dad.

He had felt offended by his mum's question because she knew better than anyone how much he wanted to be a priest. It was she who had given him the idea. It was mainly to please her that he wanted to be one. Even if he hadn't wanted to go back himself, he would have gone back just to please her. It puzzled him – he loved his mum and dad and his brothers and sisters, yet within a few days of going home he had started wanting to go back.

He tried not to think about it, and the nearer the train got, the easier it was, because the more excited he felt. But he started to feel anxious, too. Would he be able to do as well in his studies as he had done last term? Would he be able to keep all the rules and stay out of trouble? What would his new function be? Whose table in the ref would he be on? Where would his new desk in the study hall and bed in the dorm be? Father Director had told them in Conference that all these things were changed every term to prevent 'attachment' and 'possessiveness'. And would he be able to keep his place on the school football team?

'Hey! Guess what?' one of them said, coming back from another compartment, where there were some other boys. 'Dracula's going to be taking us for R. I. as well as French!'

'Oh, no!' they groaned in chorus. 'You're jossing, Kipper?'

'I'm not. Beanpole said so.' 'Beanpole' was the nickname of a senior boy, so that seemed to confirm it.

'What's happening to Father Duffy?' someone asked.

'He's being sent back to the missions,' the bearer of the bad news told them.

'You'd better get off at the next station, Frankie boy!' they started jossing him, knowing that Dracula, or the Dean of Studies, had a particular dislike for him.

'It's all right, I've got my crucifix,' Fran said, making a joke of it, and they all laughed.

He was secretly worried by the news, but they started talking about horror films and he quickly forgot. Soon the sands of Morecambe Bay came into view, which meant they were almost there, and a thrill went through him. The sands swept past, a muddy expanse stretching to the horizon. Then the train ran with a deafening clatter over the viaduct and past the Bluff onto the embankment.

The round, wooded hill hiding the seminary buildings came into view in the middle of the flat, snow-bound fields and the boys erupted into a chorus of boos and groans, which Fran joined in. However, when the train gave a whistle and pulled into the tiny grey-stone station by the sea, he was the first to spring up, grab his suitcase from the luggage rack overhead and jump off.

Waiting to meet them with the minibus at the front of the station as usual was Father Bursar, otherwise known as 'Yogi Bear', the burly, bearded priest who taught them maths and liked little boys, as he frequently reminded them in his lugubrious voice, 'fried ... in oil ... preferably with onions'.

'And you, Walsh, how would you find your way if you were lost in the middle of the desert?'

Father Haynes was preparing their composition topics for Sunday with them. He had already asked several boys the same question and their answers had provoked increasing merriment, so that he had finally raised his hand and declared in his pompous way: 'That's enough levity.'

'I'd ask a policeman, Father.'

The class burst into guffaws and Fran immediately knew he had put his foot in it.

'Silence!' Father Haynes shouted, his eyes bulging even more than usual and already ruddy face turning tomato-red with rage.

A deathly hush fell on the class. Fran wished the classroom floor would open up and swallow him.

'Leave the room, Walsh.'

Fran didn't move. He couldn't believe it! Father Haynes was sending him out, just for saying that? He had never been sent out of class before. English was his best subject, too!

'Did you hear me, Walsh?' Father Haynes pointed at the door and shouted: 'Out!'

Blushing, Fran stood up and walked slowly towards the classroom door, hoping his classmates would plead for mercy for him, but all he heard were sniggers. When he reached the door, he paused, still hoping, but no one spoke up. He opened the door and stepped backwards into the corridor, still hoping for a last-minute reprieve, but Father Haynes shut the door in his face.

The corridor was eerily empty and silent. Feeling like an outcast, Fran looked through the frosted-glass windows of the door, hoping Father Haynes would call him back in quickly. Through the glass he could see the blurred shape of Father Haynes in his black habit and the blurred, blob-like faces of his classmates. He could hear Father Haynes' plummy Oxford voice, which they all made fun of, as well as the voices of his classmates. Then, to his relief he saw Father Haynes coming towards the door. He was going to let him back in! The door opened.

'Go and stand on the other side of the corridor, Walsh,' Father Haynes told him, eyes still bulging and face still glowing tomato-red.

Crushed, he did as he was told. It seemed as if Father Haynes was going to leave him out until the end of class. He looked up and down the corridor, which he knew so well from having swept and dusted it every morning as his function last term: the red stone floor, the bare redbrick lower walls, the fire extinguisher, the metal-framed windows, the six classroom doors with their brass doorknobs, the three bookcases – junior, O-level and A-level – and the life-size statue of the Sacred Heart on its wooden pedestal at the far end.

After a while, feeling bored, he started to sidle along the corridor, looking at the framed school photographs and paintings on the walls. Most of the paintings were religious, by artists with foreign names that he wasn't sure how to pronounce, but which fascinated him, because they were the names of men who had lived long ago and far away, yet here they were. They must have been very holy as well as clever, he thought. It would be good to be an artist like them, but not as good as being a priest – nothing was as good as that.

He came to the notice board and stopped to look at the 'Honours List' and 'Black List'. If your name was on the 'Honours List', which was typed in red, it meant that all your marks on your weekly report were over seven. His name was on it as usual, which cheered him up a little. If your name was on the 'Black List', which was typed in black and considerably longer, it meant that you had two marks or more under five. He was glad he wasn't on it and never had been, but felt sorry for those who were, especially as they always got the strap off the Dean of Studies.

He moved on to look at the picture of Our Lord's crucifixion, by an artist called 'El Greco', in which the figures were all strangely elongated, including that of Our

Lord Himself. It made Him look as if He was really suffering and as always Fran felt sorry for Him. He moved away quickly to look at another picture and was just starting to think this was better than being stuck in class, when suddenly, from the classroom behind him, he heard a sound that made his heart leap into his mouth – the Dean of Studies' steely voice telling the class to put down their pens and the Head of the Class to collect the work.

He looked at his watch – 'Dozo' Dobson, the 'regulator', had forgotten to ring the bell for the end of class! The classroom door behind him opened. Panic-stricken, he scooted along the corridor and hid beside the junior bookcase, just in time to see the Dean of Studies sweep out of the classroom in his black cloak and come goose-stepping grimly along the corridor towards him. He held his breath and waited like a statue, his heart thumping.

To his relief the Dean of Studies strode straight past him, but then suddenly stopped, turned on his heel with a swish of his cloak and fixed him with a hawk-like stare. Fran felt his insides turn to jelly.

'What are you doing in the corridor, Mister Walsh?' the Dean of Studies demanded.

'I – I was sent out, Father,' Fran stammered, unable to think of a fib and too terrified to tell one, anyway.

'Why are you skulking in that corner? Come here and stand in front of me,' he beckoned with a bony finger.

Fran did as he was told, his legs shaking. At the same time, the third-form classroom door burst open, 'Dozo' Dobson dashed into the corridor, grabbed the bell from a windowsill and rang it as if the school were burning down, grinning inanely at him as he did so.

'So you were sent out,' the Dean of Studies gloated, when the din had stopped. 'And who sent you out?'

'F – Father Haynes, F – Father,' Fran stammered, stomach churning.

'And what did Father Haynes send you out for?'

'F – For talking,' Fran fibbed – Father Haynes would probably have called it 'impertinence', but he didn't dare tell the Dean of Studies that.

'For talking, eh?'

'Y – Yes, F – Father.'

Fran knees were knocking so hard he felt as if he might fall down. Classroom doors began opening and teachers coming out to change classes or return to the Fathers' house, books under their arms, boys to rush to the toilets. Fran hoped that Father Haynes wouldn't come out and tell the Dean of Studies the truth – then he would really be in the soup!

Suddenly, Father Director came striding through the swing doors at the end of the corridor, a pile of exercise books under his arm, on his way to class.

'This boy has been sent out of class, Father,' the Dean of Studies said, stopping him.

Father Director glanced at Fran. He shrivelled with shame, but hoped Father Director would save him.

'Would you like to deal with him, Father?' Father Director said to the Dean of Studies, to Fran's dismay.

'With pleasure, Father,' the Dean of Studies smiled coldly at Fran, as Father Director swept off to his class.

The Dean of Studies placed his books on the window-sill, pulled his pandybat out of the pocket of his habit and raised it. 'Out with your paw,' he ordered Fran.

Fran held out a trembling hand. The Dean of Studies raised himself to his full height – which was little more than Fran's – and swiped the pandybat down on it as hard as he could. Fran let out a gasp of pain and his arm fell limply to his side, as if he had had an electric shock.

'And the other one,' the Dean of Studies ordered, wagging a bony finger.

Fran raised his other trembling hand and the Dean of Studies swiped the pandybat down again as hard as he could, knocking his arm down to his side, where it hung limp and burning like the other one. His face was burning, too, with embarrassment at being seen by both Fathers and boys passing. Tears sprang to his eyes, but he blinked them back.

'Now get back to your class and remember – I've got my beady eye on you, Mister Walsh,' the Dean of Studies said, stuffing his pandybat back into his habit, picking up his books and striding off through the swing doors, black cloak billowing.

At that moment, the door of his classroom opened, Father Haynes came out, glanced haughtily at him and also strode off through the swing doors.

A sudden flame of resentment flared up inside him – resentment against Father Haynes for sending him out in the first place, against his classmates for not speaking up for him, against the Dean of Studies for having a down on him and giving him the strap, and most of all against Father Director for not saving him. He wouldn't go back into class! He'd run away and leave! That'd teach Father Director! That'd teach all of them!

Holding his throbbing hands under his armpits, he scurried off to the washroom and ran some cold water on them. Then he darted out across the quad between the study hall and the games huts, across the grass-covered 'oval', where they played football during recreation, through the rose garden and down the drive. When he was safely out of sight of the buildings, he stopped running and walked as fast as he could, swinging his arms to cool his still burning hands in the cold air for a while, and swerving round the ice-covered potholes.

He hurried past the entrance to the farm, hoping that Brother Michael, the farmer, wouldn't see him. There wasn't a soul in sight – on one side of the drive the flat, frosted fields stretched away to the snow-capped fells, on the other to the railway embankment, beyond which lay the sea. It was freezing cold, but he didn't care – he was nearly free! No more rules! No more getting up early! No more functions and manual labour! No more bells! No more silence! No more Dean of Studies! No more strap!

He came to the 'elbow', from where he could see Cyril the cook's house – 'Castel Gandolfo' as they jokingly called it – at the foot of the hill. Cyril himself would be in the school kitchen now, cooking the dinner. That was something else he would never have to do again, he thought triumphantly, eat Cyril's rotten 'doss': gristly bangers, black-eyed spuds, sweaty Spam, slimy corned-beef, stale cheese, watery porridge, dishwater tea ...

He passed the 'elbow' and started running again, eager to make good his escape. When he reached the last telegraph pole, he stopped, panting for breath and clutching his side, because he had a stitch. Between this and the big, black gates it was 'No Man's Land', strictly out of bounds. All he had to do was cross it, push open the gates and he would be free!

But he couldn't. It was as if there was an invisible wall in front of him. He suddenly realised that home was over a hundred miles away and he had no money for a train ticket. He could try getting on a train and giving his name and address, but he might be arrested. He could try hitching a lift, but it was a long way and he had never done it before. The driver might even take him back to the college or to the police – after all, he was only twelve years old. Anyway, not a single car or lorry passed the gates. And suddenly he started to feel both cold and hungry, without even money for a bar of chocolate.

But there was an even stronger reason holding him back. If he ran away, he could never be a priest. He would be letting his family down, especially his mum. He would be a failure. He would have to live at home again, where at Christmas he had felt so out of place, and he would have to go back to his old school. He would be letting down his relations in Ireland, too – they all expected him to be a priest. The very thought of facing them, having left, made him squirm with shame. And what would he be, if he didn't become a priest? He had no idea. There was nothing else he wanted or had ever wanted to be.

There was someone else, even more important, he would be letting down if he ran away – Our Lord. How could he ever have thought of doing it, just because he had been sent out by Father Haynes and given the strap by the Dean of Studies? He remembered with a pang of pity and guilt the picture of Our Lord's crucifixion by El Greco in the school corridor – Our Lord had suffered and died on the cross for him! He had been scourged and had nails hammered through His hands and feet, whereas he had only one of the strap on each hand! His hands hardly even hurt any more!

There was another thing – by running away he would probably be committing a mortal sin. If he died or was killed on the road, he would go straight to Hell! His whole body would burn, not just his hands. He remembered with a shudder the frog one of the boys had tossed on the bonfire on bonfire night, how it had hissed and crackled like a sausage on a frying pan, before shrivelling to a cinder. But at least the frog had died quickly, whereas in Hell you burned for ever and ever and ever ...

Suddenly, the seminary didn't seem so bad, not even the Dean of Studies or Cyril's rotten 'doss'. In fact, he felt so hungry now that he could even eat one of Cyril's gristly bangers. He was freezing cold, too. He pulled up his socks, buttoned up his blazer, turned and ran back up the drive as fast as he could. He was just in time to join the others going upstairs to the ref for dinner.

'Where the flog have you been?' Cooper, one of his classmates, whispered, breaking silence.

'I got nabbed by Dracula,' he whispered back, nervously.

'How many did you get?'

'Two, *fangs* to you lot for letting Tom Haynes send me out.'

Cooper tittered. A prefect turned and gave them a warning glance.

'Anyway, you missed a Greek test, you jammy flogger,' Cooper whispered, as they shuffled past the hatch. 'Oh, no, not flogging bangers again! It's enough to make you do a bunk!'

'Cooper, see Father Director afterwards,' the prefect said, turning again.

'Oh, flog!' Cooper swore under his breath, and it was Fran's turn to titter as they filed into the ref.

A week later it was Ash Wednesday, the first day of Lent. After Mass they had the ceremony of the putting on of the ashes – the black smudge was still on all their foreheads in morning study. In Conference the night before, Father Director had told them that it was a symbol of penance and a remembrance of death, a leftover from the days of sackcloth and ashes.

Earlier they had had to write down what penances they were going to do for Lent on a piece of paper, which Father Director collected. This, he explained, was to make sure that nobody tried to do anything excessive or dangerous, in misguided imitation of the saints, who had lived in different times and circumstances. Examples of penances that were not allowed were putting stones in their shoes, wearing home-made hairshirts, throwing themselves naked in beds of nettles, tying anything tight around any part of their bodies, self-flagellation (although Fathers didn't have to give up flogging boys, they joked later) or any form of self-mutilation. Crucifixion, Father Director warned, was definitely out.

That was because last year, during Holy Week, two boys had performed their own passion play, like the one at Oberammergau, except that one of them had tried to crucify the other for real on top of the hill. They had been discovered in the nick of time by a search party of priests and prefects and expelled. The hill may have been their Calvary, but Grange railway station was the last in their Stations of the Cross, Father Director joked blackly.

But the penances that Father Director recommended, such as saying an extra rosary or making an extra visit to the Blessed Sacrament, didn't seem like real penances to Fran. At home he used to give up sweets and sugar in his tea for Lent, but he couldn't do that here – no sweet parcels were allowed in Lent and their 'dishwater' tea already came with next to no sugar in it.

Anyway, he wanted to do even more than give up sweets or sugar in his tea. He wanted to suffer physically for Our Lord, despite what Father Director said, just like the Cure d'Ars, the Little Flower and Mat Talbot, all of whom he had read about in Spiritual Reading, or like the pilgrims who went to Croagh Patrick and Lough Derg in Ireland and walked barefoot over stones, fasted and stayed awake all night praying. He knew about it because his mum used to do it and had told him all about it.

Sometimes he even wished he could die for Our Lord, like the early Christian martyrs or the English martyrs of the Reformation, whom he had also been reading about. However, he wasn't sure if he would have been brave enough to endure the rack or being hanged, drawn and quartered, and he certainly wouldn't have fancied being thrown to the lions, so he was secretly glad he hadn't lived in those times. Anyway, there wasn't much chance of becoming a martyr nowadays, even as a missionary in Africa – though some priests from the Belgian province of the order had been killed in the Congo only a few weeks ago, he recalled uneasily.

He might never be a martyr, but at least he could suffer a little for Our Lord, Who had suffered so much for him, he resolved. As Lent went on, he found ways of doing so, without directly disobeying Father Director's orders. He didn't scratch himself when he had an itch, he knelt for as long as possible on only one knee in chapel, if a stone accidentally got in his shoe, he left it in, and, after having a haircut, he deliberately left the hairs down the inside of his vest, which made him feel itchy all over for several days.

He was inspired to these 'excesses' by the lives of the saints, but especially by the story of Our Lord's Passion and Death, as told in the Gospels and portrayed in the Stations of the Cross. During Lent they did the Stations of the Cross in chapel every Friday evening before Confessions. According to his missal, by decree of the Sacred Penitentiary of October 20th, 1931, every time you did all the Stations, you gained a plenary indulgence, plus an additional plenary indulgence if you received Holy Communion on the same day or any day of a month in which you made the Way of the Cross ten times.

That meant that every time they did the Stations of the Cross, they gained at least two plenary indulgences, he reckoned, since they had to receive Holy Communion every day. Next month, he decided, he would try to gain at least one more by doing the Stations a few extra times, though it would be hard to find time. However, according to his missal, it didn't matter if you started and didn't finish, because you gained a partial indulgence of ten years for each Station if you started the Way of the Cross, but 'for some reasonable cause could not complete it'.

At the beginning of the Stations, the priest said a prayer before the High Altar that set the mood: 'O Jesus Christ, my Lord, with what great love didst Thou pass over the painful road which led Thee to Thy death; and I, how often have I abandoned Thee! But now I love Thee with my whole soul, and because I love Thee, I am sincerely sorry for having offended Thee. My Jesus, pardon me, and permit me to accompany Thee on this journey. Thou art going to die for love of me, and it is my wish also, O my dearest Redeemer, to die for love of Thee. O yes, my Jesus, in Thy love I wish to live, in Thy love I wish to die.'

Then the priest, accompanied by two acolytes, began the Stations by going to stand in front of the first picture, entitled, 'Jesus is Condemned to Death'. The congregation had to turn to each picture as he came to it and genuflect with him as he said each time, 'We adore Thee, O Christ, and bless Thee', to which they had to respond, 'Because by Thy holy cross Thou hast redeemed the world'. The priest read a short explanation of what was happening in each picture and everyone had to meditate silently on it for a few moments. Finally, the priest said a special prayer for each one, which always ended, 'I love Thee, Jesus, my love, above all things. I love Thee more than myself. I repent with my whole heart of having offended Thee. Never permit me to separate myself from Thee again. Grant that I may love Thee always and then do with me what Thou wilt.' This was followed by an Our Father and then they passed on to the next Station.

Fran liked doing the Stations, but they made him feel sad. At the tenth Station, Jesus, having been scourged and crowned with thorns, having fallen three times under the weight of His cross, having met His mother and had His face wiped with a towel by the holy woman, Veronica, was stripped of His garments to be crucified. The priest read: 'Consider the violence with which the executioners stripped Jesus. His inner garments adhered to His torn flesh, and they dragged them off so roughly that the skin came with them. Compassionate your Saviour, thus cruelly treated.'

By this point, Fran would have a lump in his throat and tears in his eyes. He felt like crying, just like the women of Jerusalem, who had wept at the sight of Jesus in the eighth Station. But he always swallowed hard and blinked back his tears – it would have been too embarrassing to cry in front of his fellow seminarians.

The last week of Lent was Holy Week, during which Our Lord's Passion and Death were commemorated. From Maundy Thursday, when they had finished their exams, until Easter Sunday, they were on retreat, which meant three days of even more spiritual exercises, manual labour and silence than usual. The ceremonies were very solemn and sad, especially the ceremony on Good Friday afternoon, with the chanting of Our Lord's Passion and Death in Latin. At the point where Jesus, having been mockingly offered a drink of vinegar by the Roman soldiers, said, 'Consummatum est', bowed His head and died, there was a pause, during which everyone had to kneel and meditate on His death.

Strangely enough, at that very moment, the sky outside the chapel darkened, there was a flash of lightning followed by a deafening clap of thunder and a storm started, just as was supposed to have happened when Jesus actually died on the cross. Fran felt a shudder of dread go through him. What if there was an earthquake, as in the Gospels, he thought, and it was the end of the world? He imagined the mountains of the Lake District all around erupting like volcanoes, the earth splitting open, corpses arising from graves, buildings falling and people tumbling into chasms of fire and smoke, including the chapel and themselves. So, just to be on the safe side, he said a quick Act of Contrition.

To his relief, it wasn't the end of the world yet. The thunder rolled away, the chapel remained intact and the celebrants continued their chanting, about how the Jews wouldn't let the bodies remain crucified on the sabbath the next day, so asked Pilate that they might have their legs broken, in order that they would die more quickly, and be taken away. When they came to Jesus, they found Him already dead, so they didn't break His legs, but one of the soldiers pierced His side with a spear and immediately blood and water flowed out. That was to fulfil the prophecies in the Scriptures: 'You shall not break a single bone of His' and 'They will look upon the man whom they have pierced'.

The next day was Holy Saturday. In the morning the exam results were read out by the Dean of Studies in front of the assembled school, as at Christmas. Fran was beaten into second place again by Zappo. He was disappointed, but glad the exams were over and he could look forward to the next day, Easter Sunday, when his family were coming to visit him, because they weren't allowed to go home at Easter. In the afternoon they had manual labour, which they had to do in complete silence, since they were still on retreat. The whole school, inside and out, had to be given a spring-clean in preparation for Easter. Fran was assigned to weed the rose garden with a gang of others.

While they were working with their hoes, they were supposed to be meditating on the Passion and Death of Our Lord. Our Lord was now lying dead in the tomb, with a rock against the entrance and Roman soldiers guarding it, at the request of the chief priests and Pharisees, in case any of His disciples tried to steal His body and claim that He had risen from the dead. However, that hadn't stopped Our Lord rising from the dead. There was another earthquake and an angel, his countenance like lightning and his raiment white as snow, descended from Heaven, striking terror into the guards, and rolled back the stone ...

Fran had read the story over and over in his missal, thrilled by it, and thought about it while he hoed the weeds. However, he couldn't help thinking about the next day as well, about seeing his family again for the first time in three months, especially his mum, and showing them around the school. He felt guilty about it, but the thought thrilled him even more than that of the Resurrection.

He couldn't help thinking about it even more during the ceremonies of the Easter vigil that night. The ceremonies themselves were beautiful: the Blessing of the New Fire, the Blessing of the Paschal Candle, the Paschal Proclamation, the Lessons from Sacred Scripture, the Litany of the Saints, the Renewal of Baptismal Vows and finally Solemn High Mass. While the ministers vested for Mass in the sacristy, the second part of the Litany of the Saints was chanted and the altar was prepared – new, snow-white altar cloths were put on, the candles were lit and the altar was decked with vases of daffodils, lilies and ferns, so that it was gradually transformed before their eyes into a resplendent display of flowers, linen and brass.

At the end of the litany, the 'Kyrie eleison' was chanted and the ministers returned to begin Mass. They genuflected and ascended the altar. The celebrant kissed it and incensed it with the thurible. Then he intoned the 'Gloria in excelsis'. All through the 'Gloria' bells were rung – the Mass bell by one of the servers on the altar and the Fathers' house bell by the regulator in the corridor outside the chapel. At the same time the violet cloths were taken off all the sacred pictures and statues in the chapel.

The sounds of the singing and bells sent through him a surge of joy – Lent was over, Our Lord had risen from the dead and in just a few hours he would be seeing his family again! He felt as if he were floating on a cloud, like Our Lord when He ascended into Paradise. He followed the rest of the ceremony on this cloud of rapture, rapture heightened by the mingled scents of incense, flowers and melting wax, by the flicker of candle flames, by the gleam of gold and silver altar vessels, by the blood-red glow of the sanctuary lamp and rubies encrusting the Paschal candle, by the chimes of the gong and jingle of bells, by the murmur of the familiar Latin prayers, by the swelling chords of the organ and by the chorus of their voices singing the plainchant, resounding exultantly around the walls of the chapel, radiating out into the night, out in expanding, circular waves of joyous sound through the sky to the farthest planets and stars, to the boundary of the universe and beyond, to harmonise with the choirs of angels and saints in Heaven itself ...

After Mass there was a 'collation' of cocoa – or 'mud' as they called it – and biscuits in the ref, amidst a cacophony of excited chatter. Their excitement was the excitement of both release and anticipation – release from six dreary weeks of Lent and anticipation of seeing their families again in a few hours, after three long months. There was something else to look forward to as well – the blissful luxury of a lie-in till eight o'clock in the morning!

CHAPTER EIGHT

The summer term was the best – it was warm, so they could go swimming in the river, there were several free days and there was a whole week's holiday at Whit, when they were allowed visits from their families again. It was also the shortest term, only twelve weeks, with the long summer vac to look forward to at the end.

One evening after supper they went swimming at the bend in the river as usual. They were playing 'pirates', using two rafts they had made by tying some empty oil drums to old doors as their ships. They had already floated out of bounds beyond the bend several times and had to be whistled back by Father Director, who was on lifeguard duty as usual. He was sitting on the bank in his swimming trunks, with the lifebelt beside him.

Fran was one of 'Captain Morgan's' crew, who had just tipped the crew of the 'treasure ship' into the water and boarded it amidst whoops and yells of triumph, when it suddenly see-sawed and he himself was catapulted into the water. He went under, came up and made a grab for the raft, but was pushed away by a foot in the chest. He went under and came up again, winded, only to see the raft well away from him, with the 'battle' still in full swing. Finding nothing to hold onto, his feet felt for the bottom, but instead he just went under again. He came back up, spluttering and thrashing in panic, but went under yet again, down, down, down into the bottomless blackness …

Then suddenly he was being held up in the air and could breathe again. He had been saved! It was Father Director who had saved him, he supposed, but he could see Father Director standing on the bank, with his hands on his hips, gazing anxiously at him. It wasn't until his rescuer had waded to the bank and dumped him unceremoniously on it, joking, 'This river isn't half full of rubbish!', that he realised who it was – Gerry Hanlon, a fourth-former who came from Northern Ireland.

'Shouldn't you be studying, Gerry?' Father Director demanded, putting a towel round his shoulders as he sat shivering on the bank.

He said that to Gerry because Gerry's class would soon be starting their O-levels and were supposed to do extra study after supper, instead of swimming, and Gerry wasn't very clever. But it seemed a funny thing to say to him after he had just saved him from drowning. He wanted to thank Gerry, but Gerry swam off, without even answering Father Director.

'Are you all right, son?' Father Director asked him, drying him off with the towel.

'Y – Y – Yes, Father,' Fran said, his teeth chattering with cold.

'You'd better get dressed,' Father Director said, and to his embarrassment helped him to do so. His teeth were still chattering.

'They sound like castanets,' Father Director joked, putting the towel around him and helping him off with his trunks.

Fran laughed shyly and tried not to blush as Father Director dried him off, then helped him on with his underpants and trousers ...

'Hey, Walsh! Greg wants you!'

It was Wednesday afternoon and they were on their way down the path by the river to the playing fields to play cricket. The usually muddy path had been baked as hard as concrete by the heat-wave and the grass on either side was up to Fran's waist. On the other side of the river the newly-mown cricket pitches looked like two strips of pale green in the middle of two dark-green, oval carpets, cut out of the even deeper, darker pile of the field.

Fran was looking forward to cricket, not because he liked the game itself much, but because it meant no class and being outside in the sunshine for the afternoon. When not batting, bowling or fielding, they lounged in the long grass, chatting or reading or fooling around. Like the others, he was wearing 'whites': a white shirt, a cream pullover with a coloured pattern around the edges, which his mum had knitted for him, long white flannels – the only long trousers first-formers like himself could wear – and white pumps, newly whitened for him by Gerry Hanlon, who was by his side as usual.

Since the day he had saved him from drowning, Gerry had become his 'best' friend, though it was against the rule to have 'best' friends. He went with him whenever he could, gave him little presents, such as sweets or fruit, and did him favours secretly, such as whitening his cricket pumps, polishing his shoes, pressing his trousers and even cleaning his comb for him. The others had already noticed this and started making fun of them in the usual way, calling him 'Gerry' and Gerry 'Frank'.

Upset by this 'jossing' and afraid of getting into trouble for 'grouping', Fran had tried to avoid Gerry for a while, but given up, because Gerry had only stuck to him even more closely and been even more friendly. Anyway, it was nice having a friend like Gerry and besides, so far he hadn't got into trouble for it. However, when he heard that Father Director wanted him now, a current of alarm went through him. They all turned to see Jimbo, a second-former, running towards them.

'Greg wants you,' Jimbo gasped, reaching them.

'Who, me?' Fran asked.

'Yeah, you,' Jimbo panted.

'You're jossing,' Fran accused, because Jimbo was known as a practical joker.

'He's jossing,' the others all agreed, turning to go.

'It's no joss,' Jimbo insisted, still panting. 'He wants you. Honest.'

'Now?'

'Pronto.' That was one of Father Director's favourite expressions and seemed to confirm it.

'What for?' he gulped.

'Haven't the foggiest, but you'd better hurry up – he sounded shirty.'

'Six of the best!' Mahony, a fellow first-former, taunted gleefully.

'Shut up, Fishface!' Gerry said, brandishing a cricket bat at him. Then he turned to Jimbo and grabbed him by the throat. 'If you're jossing, I'll beat your brains out!' he threatened.

'He hasn't got any brains!' one of them gibed and they all laughed.

'I'm not jossing, honest!' Jimbo whined, cringing in Gerry's clutch.

'You'd better go,' Gerry said to Fran, letting go of Jimbo. 'Here, I'll take those.' He took the pads Fran had been carrying from him.

'Thanks, Gerry,' he said, and started walking nervously back to the house.

'Wrong way!'

'Declared already?'

Boys he passed on their way down made funny remarks, but he was too nervous to take any notice. Why on earth did Father Director want to see him now, right at the beginning of cricket? Maybe a prefect had reported him for 'grouping' and Father Director really was going to give him six of the best. Or maybe he was in trouble for something else, though he couldn't think what. Anyway, it was a funny time for Father Director to want to see him. Maybe Jimbo was jossing after all.

He was climbing the steps up to the back lawn when he was struck by an even more worrying thought – what if something had happened at home? What if his mum or dad had died? Only last week a boy had been called out of class because his dad had died. A wave of panic swept over him. *'Oh, God, no, please, I beg You!'* he prayed silently, hurrying past the boot room.

'Hey, Gerry! Where's Frankie?' some boys coming out of the boot room called and started singing:

> 'Frankie and Gerry were lovers,
> Oh, Lordy, how they could love!
> They swore to be true to each other,
> True as the stars above.'

Fran was too worried to take any notice. He hurried into the building and knocked on the door of Father Director's office with a trembling fist, but there was no answer. That was strange, he thought. The only other place Father Director might be was his bedroom. He ran upstairs and knocked nervously on the door.

'Come in,' Father Director called out.

He opened the door, but didn't go in – to his surprise, Father Director was standing with his back to him at the washbasin in his trousers and vest, with his braces hanging down, brushing his teeth. Also, the curtains were closed, though it was the middle of the day, so the room was in semi-darkness.

'Jimbo said you wanted to see me, Father,' he said, terrified that something had happened at home.

'Grrrrrrrrgh!' Father Director threw his head back, gargled and spat into the washbasin. Then he examined his teeth in the mirror. As usual they gleamed brightly in his handsome brown face, especially the gold one in the middle. 'Yes. Come in and close the door, son,' he said, turning towards him.

Fran's stomach lurched – it sounded serious. He stepped in and closed the door, his stomach churning. *'Oh, God,'* he prayed, *'please don't let anything have happened at home, especially not to my mum. Please, God! I beg you!'*

'Go and lie down on the bed, son,' Father Director told him.

Oh, God, Fran thought, not moving. Something had happened at home and Father Director wanted him to lie down before he told him, in case he fainted. In a daze, he did as he was told and lay down on Father Director's bed. *Oh, God, not my mum, please! Not my mum!*

Father Director went over to the door and turned the key in the lock. Then he came and sat on the edge of the bed. He looked really serious. Fran stared at him, his heart fluttering like a trapped bird's. Something had happened at home, he knew it.

'Have you got your rosary beads on you, son?' Father Director asked.

Fran shook his head – he wouldn't have his rosary beads on him playing cricket!

'Here, hold these,' Father Director said, handing him some from the bedside locker,

Fran took them. His mum had died! Father Director was preparing him for the shock. Father Director's face blurred. The room started to spin. Fran felt as if he was going to faint, even though he was lying down.

'I've got something to tell you, son,' Father Director said, putting a hand on his shoulder.

Fran shut his eyes, held his breath and waited, his heart beating wildly. His mum was dead! He'd never see her again!

'It's about your varicocele.'

'Oh,' Fran gasped, with relief. His mum wasn't dead! *Oh, thank You, God! Thank You! I'll be a priest for You, I promise!*

'I spoke to the doctor this morning,' Father Director continued.

Fran opened his eyes in alarm. 'The doctor, Father?' Was something wrong with him?

'That's right, son,' Father Director said. 'He said we have to take extra-special care of you in this hot weather. Do you understand?'

Fran nodded, though he didn't.

'Good,' Father Director said. 'Close your eyes and say your rosary. That's a good boy.'

Puzzled, Fran closed his eyes. To his surprise, Father Director unbuttoned his white cricket trousers.

'Lift up, son,' Father Director told him.

He did so and Father Director pulled down his trousers and underpants, making him blush. Then Father Director told him to lift up again and spread a towel under him. Fran tried to pray, but was too embarrassed. Father Director had never made him lie on the bed like this before. What was he going to do?

'That's a snazzy pullover,' Father Director said, rolling it up. 'Did your mum knit it for you?'

'Yes, Father,' Fran said proudly.

'A labour of love, eh?' Father Director said, standing up and moving away from the bed.

Fran heard some water running. He opened his eyes to see Father Director coming towards him with a basin of water in one hand and a flannel over his arm, just like the server at the Lavabo in Mass. What was he going to do, he wondered nervously? Was he going to do an operation on him?

'Close your eyes and say your rosary, that's a good boy,' Father Director told him, sitting on the edge of the bed again and putting the basin of water on the floor. 'I'm just going to bathe you with cold water, as the doctor ordered, that's all, son. Don't worry, I won't hurt you.'

Relieved, Fran closed his eyes and started to say some 'Hail Marys', but when he felt the cold flannel touch his thing, he flinched.

'It's all right, son, don't worry, I won't hurt you,' Father Director said. 'Just keep your eyes closed and say your rosary. That's a good boy.'

Fran did as he was told. After a while the flannel didn't feel cold any more and he didn't feel embarrassed. He even started to enjoy it. It was nice, lying here on the bed in Father Director's bedroom, with Father Director looking after him like this, while all the others were playing cricket – he could hear their shouts in the distance through the open window and even the occasional click of leather on willow.

'By the way, son,' Father Director said, as he 'bathed' him with the cold flannel.

'Yes, Father?'

'There's something I want to ask you.'

'Yes, Father?'

'Open your eyes and look at me.'

Fran did as he was told. Father Director was looking at him, with the flannel in one hand and the other on one of his thighs. 'I want you to look me in the eye and tell me the truth, son. Will you?'

'Yes, of course, Father,' Fran said, trying not to blush.

'It's about Gerry.'

Fran started to redden, despite himself.

'Has he become friendly with you?'

Fran hesitated, blushing furiously – the truth could get them both into trouble.

'Tell me the truth, son – you don't need to be afraid.'

'A little bit, Father,' Fran said.

'That's not what I've heard, son,' Father Director said, suddenly stopping 'bathing' him. 'I've heard that he's become *very* friendly with you. Is that true?'

'I suppose so, Father,' Fran admitted, feeling guilty for betraying Gerry.

'Now, son, I want to ask you something else and it's even more important that you tell me the truth. Not only both your vocations, but both your immortal souls are at stake. Do you understand, son?'

Fran nodded, his face burning.

'Will you promise to tell me the truth, son?'

'Yes, Father.'

'Has Gerry ever touched you?'

'What do you mean. Father?'

'Has he ever touched you impurely?'

'No, Father,' Fran shook his head, his face on fire.

'Are you sure, son?'

'Yes, Father!'

'Thank you, son – that's all I need to know. Now, let's dry you off.'

Father Director dried him off with the towel he was lying on, then rubbed Johnson's Baby Powder on him. When Father Director's hand touched his thing, he flinched, but then relaxed and let Father Director do it. Finally, Father Director pulled his underpants and trousers up, took the rosary beads from him and told him to get up.

Fran stood up and moved towards the door, hoping Father Director would let him go now – he was ashamed for telling him about Gerry and afraid he might even give him the strap for 'grouping'. He waited for Father Director to open the door for him, eager to go back down to the cricket field.

'Before you go, son, I want you to do something for me,' Father Director said. 'I think I sprained my shoulder bowling last week. Rub some of this on for me.' He handed Fran a bottle of liniment from the top of his chest of drawers, sat 'backwards' on the wooden chair and put his hand over his shoulder. 'Go on, son, don't be shy. Just there. I can't reach it.'

Blushing even more than before, Fran took the bottle, poured some of the liniment out and started to rub it timidly on the back of Father Director's shoulder.

'Go on, son, don't be shy. Rub it in hard.'

Fran did as he was told, glad Father Director couldn't see his burning face.

'Harder, son,' Father Director ordered. 'Put some elbow grease into it!'

Fran rubbed the liniment in even harder, blushing furiously.

'All right, son, that will do. Good boy,' Father Director said at last, standing up, taking the bottle of liniment from Fran, putting the top back on and replacing it on the chest of drawers.

With relief, Fran turned to the door again, more eager than ever to escape back down to the cricket field. Father Director came over to the door, turned the key and started to open it for him, but then closed it again. 'Oh, just before you go, son,' Father Director said. 'Remember – you mustn't say anything about these medical matters to anyone. They're confidential, just like Confession. Do you understand?'

'Yes, Father,' Fran nodded, impatient to escape. The room felt like a furnace!

'Good boy,' Father Director said, opening the door at last. 'Off you go. I'll see you in infirmary tonight.'

'Thank you, Father,' Fran said with relief, stepping out of the room quickly, in case Father Director called him back.

He ran downstairs two or three at a time, though it was against the rule, and out through the back doors into the bright, hot sunshine. He stopped for a moment, dazzled by the brightness of the sun, then, with a whoop of delight, ran as fast as he could all the way down to the cricket field with his arms outstretched, pretending to be a World War One fighter pilot like Biggles, the hero of the book he had been reading in library.

After Mass and Thanksgiving the next morning, Gyp, the First Auxiliary, told them to go straight down to study instead of making their beds. That meant only one thing – someone was leaving. Fran had a horrible feeling it might be Gerry, because he hadn't seen him in the dorm the night before, nor had Gerry left a sweet under his pillow as usual. He hadn't seen Gerry this morning either.

When Gerry didn't appear in morning study or at breakfast, he knew it must be true, but still couldn't believe it. He could hardly eat his porridge, which seemed even colder, runnier and lumpier than usual. It almost made him sick, but he had to eat it, because he knew the Head of Table wouldn't let him leave it. To make matters worse, other boys kept glancing at him. Maybe

Gerry was just ill in the infirmary, he hoped, but knew deep down that he wasn't.

When they went to the dorm after breakfast to make their beds, there could no longer be any doubt – Gerry's bed had been stripped and left covered with the blue top blanket, with the pillow and other blankets folded underneath, so that it looked as if there was a dead body in it. The chair beside the bed had been cleared of its towel and toiletries. Choked, Fran went to make his own bed. Under the pillow he found a sweet and an envelope, both of which he slipped into his blazer pocket.

While he was making his bed, he saw some of the others raiding Gerry's bed for its mattress, pillow and blankets, like vultures. Tears sprang to his eyes. He wanted to stop them, but didn't dare. He wanted to see Gerry before he left, but knew it was impossible. He would never see him again. Blinking back his tears, he finished making his bed as quickly as possible and hurried downstairs to do his function, cleaning one of the classrooms.

Later, a rumour went round that Gerry had been expelled, even though he was supposed to start his O-levels in a few days. Fran felt sad, sorry and guilty. He felt sad because he would never see Gerry again – in the letter he had written to him, Gerry had asked him to write to him and even visit him during the vac, but he knew he couldn't, because it was strictly against the rule and he would be expelled himself if he did and was found out. To be safe, he tore the letter up into tiny pieces and dropped them into several different wastepaper bins. He felt sorry because Gerry had been expelled, especially just before his exams. And he felt guilty because he knew Gerry's expulsion was because of him, though it wasn't his fault.

'You're not upset about Gerry leaving, are you?' Father Director asked him, as he rubbed Germolene on his thing in infirmary that night.

'No, Father,' Fran fibbed, closing his eyes even more tightly to stop tears coming.

'That's a good boy,' Father Director said, giving him a pat on the thigh. 'You paddle your own canoe.'

'Girls,' Father Director said in his sternest voice, and paused dramatically.

He was sitting on the rostrum at the front of the study hall, camail slung back over his shoulders so that the black silk lining shone in the fluorescent light. It was the evening before Whit Monday, when the annual garden fete was to be held, and he was giving them a 'pep talk' about how they must behave in front of the visitors.

'There will be girls around tomorrow,' he continued sternly, 'but remember – girls are the AGENTS OF THE DEVIL. The Devil will use them to try and lure you from your vocation, just as Eve lured Adam in the Garden of Eden. So, as regards girls tomorrow, the same rules as for vacations apply. As far as possible, you will avoid any contact with them. You will not speak to them except to exchange courtesies as briefly as possible. You will not – I repeat NOT – engage in conversation with them. You will observe, even more strictly than usual, 'custody of the eyes': you will not look at them, even if you have to speak to them. You will keep your eyes down. I repeat: DOWN. They will be invisible to you. And I warn you now – if I catch anyone or hear of anyone either speaking to or looking at a girl for a moment longer than necessary, he will be on the nine forty-three the next morning. I hope I make myself clear. There will be NO MERCY. You have been warned.'

Fran couldn't understand why Father Director made such a fuss about girls. They all knew they couldn't have anything to do with them, if they wanted to be priests. He couldn't understand why anyone would want to, anyway – girls were sissies and they couldn't be priests. He certainly didn't want to speak to them or look at them, except maybe to say hello to his sisters. He was looking forward to the fete though – especially to seeing his mum and dad again.

The fete was held on the back lawn, which sloped down from the bottom of the hill to the study hall and the back of the Fathers' house. The night before, the statue of Saint Joseph that normally stood in an alcove in the hall of the Fathers' house was left out on the verandah to intercede for fine weather. The boys joked that Father Bursar – alias 'Yogi Bear' – spent the night on his knees there himself, hands clasped and eyes cast heavenwards in pecuniary supplication. Father Director finished his 'pep talk' by urging them to pray for the same intention.

God must have listened to their prayers, because though it had been wet for the last few days, Whit Monday dawned miraculously sunny. They spent the morning filling the stalls that they had erected the day before and making hundreds of sandwiches. Bunting was strung up and the papal flag run up the flagpole on top of the Fathers' house. At two o'clock the fete was declared officially open by Father Superior and was soon thronged with visitors, mostly boys' relations. Father Bursar strolled around beaming beatifically and licking his lips at the sight of so much cash dropping into glass jars and old biscuit tins.

It was strange to see so many people, especially women and children, dressed in ordinary clothes and making so much noise, swarming about in places that for them were normally out of bounds or places of silence. It was even stranger to see and hear them doing things that they were never allowed to do, such as holding hands, kissing, hugging, whistling, smoking, chewing chewing-gum, swearing, handling money ... Being able to break some of the rules added to the fun of the fete for them, but remembering Father Director's 'pep talk' the night before, they had to be careful not to go too far.

Fran enjoyed seeing his mum, dad, brothers and sisters again and they all enjoyed the fete. Yet he felt shy with them and when it was all over, the visitors had gone and everything was back to normal, he couldn't help feeling a sense of relief.

The feast of Corpus Christi, less than two weeks later, was a free day. In the morning there was Solemn High Mass and in the afternoon there was a procession down the drive, which they had to decorate at intervals with designs made of flower petals. Fran worked on a design of the Holy Ghost in the form of a dove. There was keen competition between groups to see who could produce the best design. It was good fun, especially as it meant they could go out of bounds to collect flowers.

The procession was led by Father Superior in gold Benediction cope. He carried the Blessed Sacrament under a canopy held over him by four servers in cassocks and cottas, preceded by acolytes with lighted candles and thurifers walking backwards swinging thuribles of incense. Behind followed priests in cassocks and cottas, followed by boys in best blazers and order of seniority, with the rear taken up by Brother Michael and Cyril the cook in best bib and tucker.

The procession began from the chapel with Father Superior uttering the words, 'Procedamus in pace', to which the response was, 'In nomine Christi. Amen'. As they processed down the drive, their feet scattering the floral designs that they had laboured over so earnestly earlier, they sang hymns to the Blessed Sacrament. The procession finished in the rose garden with Benediction at a specially erected altar in front of the statue of Saint Theresa – 'of Lisieux that is, no' Avila', as Gyp, the First Auxiliary, was fond of pointing out.

During the ceremony, the spicy smell of incense mingled with the sweet scent of roses into a heady perfume, while the hot midsummer sun beamed down like a divine benediction upon their heads bowed before the Blessed Sacrament. Fran felt truly blessed. He wanted to be a priest more than ever, so that he too could one day wear a cope of gold and bless the congregation with the gleaming monstrance that contained the Body of Christ, here in the rose garden or better still on the missions in Africa, for that was what he really wanted to be, not just a priest, but a missionary priest, saving souls for Christ.

On the following Sunday they went by coach to a local convent to take part in another Corpus Christi procession. However, the main attraction for them was not so much the procession as the High Tea that the nuns laid on afterwards. This, as they quickly came to appreciate, was the culinary high spot of the year! There were white linen tablecloths on the tables – which itself was a novelty – and they were laid with the best bone china tea-sets and silver cutlery, rather than the plastic crockery and battered old cutlery they were used to. On the tables too there were jugs of unwatered-down milk, bowls of sugar, dishes of butter and pots and pots of homemade jam. There were also real teapots full of piping hot tea and, best of all, there was plate upon plate of scrumptious homemade scones, cakes, tarts and pies of every kind, with cream, all followed by trifle. It was like being back at home! Billy Bunter – he was reading the Billy Bunter books in library – would have been in Heaven! *They* were in Heaven!

The trouble was, there was too much to eat, a problem they solved by stuffing as much as they could into their mouths and then into their pockets. Another problem was that for days afterwards Cyril's 'doss' seemed even more disgusting than usual. However, the only solution to that, short of leaving, was to wait for the summer vac. That wasn't too far away now, since they were just over half way through the summer term. According to the calendar underneath his desk lid, there were only five more weeks to go – that was thirty-five days, which according to his calculations, was eight hundred and forty hours, which was fifty thousand, four-hundred minutes, which was three million and twenty-four thousand seconds ...

'You are coming back, aren't you, son?' Father Director asked, as he rubbed Germolene on him in infirmary the night before going home for the summer vac.

'Yes, of course, Father!' Fran said, offended as always by the question.

He was standing in the middle of the floor of Father Director's bedroom, his pyjama trousers around his ankles and his legs wide apart as usual, while Father Director crouched in front of him. He wasn't embarrassed any more when Father Director treated him – in fact he enjoyed it, though he tried not to, because he knew he wasn't supposed to.

He was still embarrassed sometimes when Father Director treated him on Wednesday afternoons before cricket, as he usually did, or when Father Director made him rub something on him, such as liniment or Germolene, as he sometimes did. But it was silly to be embarrassed, he told himself, because as Father Director had told him, it was only 'doctor's orders'.

'You do still want to be a priest, don't you, son?'

'Yes, of course, Father!' he said again, trying not to sound annoyed.

'That's a good boy. I'm sure Our Lord still wants you to be one, too.'

'I hope so, Father.'

'Oh, I'm sure he does, son. All you have to do is pray to Him. You will, won't you?'

'I always do, Father.'

'Good boy. I'll pray for you, too, and I'll offer up Mass every morning for you.'

'Thank you, Father.'

'I think Our Lord wants me to take special care of you, because He's chosen you specially. That's why you're here now. Do you understand, son?'

'Yes, Father.' Fran felt pleased.

'Are you sleepy?'

'Not really, Father.'

'You're too excited about going home, I suppose.'

'I think so, Father.'

'I'll tell you what, I'll make you a mug of warm milk – that will help you to sleep – and you can sleep here tonight. All right?'

'Yes, Father,' Fran shrugged, surprised.

Father Director pulled his pyjama trousers up and tied them for him. Then he went over to the bed and pulled back the covers.

'In you get,' he said and hesitantly Fran did so.

Father Director went out, locking the door behind him. Fran lay in the bed and waited, wondering. Was Father Director going to sleep in the bed with him? He felt embarrassed by the idea, but shouldn't, he told himself. After all, Father Director was only being kind and looking after him. He was lucky – he was Father Director's favourite among all the boys!

After a few minutes, Father Director came back with a mug of warm milk for him and sat on the bed, watching him while he drank it. When he had finished, he told him to lie down and tucked him it.

'Goodnight and God bless, son,' Father Director said, kissing him on the forehead. 'I'm going to check the dorm.

You try to sleep.'

'Goodnight, Father,' Fran said. 'Thank you, Father.'

Father Director switched on the bedside lamp, switched off the main light and picked up his torch from the chest of drawers before he went out, locking the door behind him again. Fran lay in bed with his eyes shut and tried to sleep, as Father Director had told him, but it was difficult, because he couldn't stop thinking about going home tomorrow and wondering where exactly Father Director was going to sleep.

After a few minutes though, the warm milk began to take effect and he started to drift off. He was half-asleep when Father Director came back, locked the door and switched the bedside lamp off. He heard him taking off his habit, brushing his teeth at the washbasin, taking off the rest of his clothes and putting on his pyjamas.

Then he got into bed beside him and put his arm around him. By now, Fran was too sleepy to be bothered. In fact, he felt happy that Father Director liked him so much, more than any of the other boys. He felt even more happy at the thought that tomorrow he was going home and would see his mum and dad and brothers and sisters again ...

CHAPTER NINE

By the time Fran reached the Sixth Form, there were only ten boys left in his class. At the end of the year they would take their A-level exams, receive the habit of the order and take their first religious vows of poverty, chastity and obedience. Then they would go to the novitiate for a year, at the end of which they would take their final vows. After that, they would go to the senior seminary to study philosophy and theology for six years, towards the end of which they would be ordained priests at last.

He was seventeen now and more committed than ever to becoming a priest, religious and missionary. He wanted to devote his whole life to the service of God in the practice of poverty, chastity and obedience and the pursuit of the salvation of souls in Africa. That was what he had always wanted, for as long as he could remember, even as a little boy. He had never wanted to be anything else, and even less so now, after five years of hard prayer and study at the junior seminary.

He prayed harder than ever for God to give him the necessary grace and strength. What kept him going was the thought of the day of his ordination and giving his first blessing to his family, especially his mum – how proud and happy she would be! Then there was the thought of saying his first Mass to look forward to – for the first time changing the bread and wine into the Body and Blood of Our Lord and giving Holy Communion to his family! And finally, there was the thought of going to Africa – Africa, about which he had read and dreamt so much ever since boyhood!

Most of those who left did so because of women – or rather the absence of women. Fran couldn't understand it. How could anyone give up the idea of being a priest just because of women? When one of his classmates had told him last year that he was leaving because he couldn't stand the thought of living without a wife, Fran felt scornful as well as sorry, and thanked God he didn't feel the same way.

Sex wasn't really a problem at all for him, as it seemed to be for most of them – he couldn't quite understand why. Before Mass every morning there was a special Confession for those who wanted to confess to having masturbated, or 'tugged their toggles' as they jokingly called it, the night before, so that they could receive Holy Communion in a state of grace. They had to queue up outside the sacristy, where everyone could see them.

Fran had never joined the queue and never needed to. He couldn't understand how anyone could do whatever it was they were supposed to do – he wasn't even quite sure what it was. And he certainly couldn't understand how anyone could bear the embarrassment of being seen in the queue – that alone, apart from the threat of Hell, since it was a mortal sin, would have been enough to deter him from doing it.

He didn't have a very clear understanding of sex at all, which was hardly surprising, considering his education in the subject ...

At the beginning of his third year, when he had just turned fourteen, Father Director had called him to his office for 'direction'. As usual, he blessed himself from the font just inside the door and said, 'Laus tibi, Christi,' to which Father Director responded, 'Nunc et in aeternam. Amen,' then told him to sit down.

He sat down in the brown leather armchair and Father Director turned the chair of his desk round to sit facing him, legs crossed beneath the skirt of his habit, camail turned back to show the shiny black silk lining. Fran felt uncomfortable, partly because he wasn't used to armchairs any more (though now at least he wasn't swallowed up by it) and partly because he was apprehensive about what Father Director was going to say.

As usual the first question Father Director asked was, 'How's your vocation, son?', to which as usual he replied, 'It's fine, thank you, Father.' It sounded silly, but he could never think of what else to reply. Again, when Father Director asked him how both his 'spiritual life' and his studies were, he couldn't think of what else to reply except, 'Fine, thank you, Father,' silly as it sounded too.

Father Director asked him a few questions about both and then if he had any problems he wanted to talk about. As always, Fran found this question embarrassing, because he could never think of any problem worth mentioning – it was a bit like trying to think of sins for Confession. As usual he said no and with relief leaned forward to get up, but Father Director stopped him. 'Before you go, son, there's something else I want to talk to you about,' he said, even more serious than before.

Fran sat awkwardly on the edge of the seat, elbows on the arms, and waited.

'Now that you're fourteen and have started to grow,' Father Director said, 'you will find that certain other changes happen to your body. They're nothing to worry about, just part of the natural process of growing up that we all have to go through. For example, your voice will start to sound deeper. You'll start to grow hair in places it never grew before. And sometimes, during the night, while you're asleep, you'll find that there's a hardness in your pyjama trousers and you emit a white fluid, which leaves a slight stain on your pyjamas and maybe on your sheet. You'll find that this happens when you have certain dreams. Now, as I said, son, this is nothing to worry about – it's natural and normal and starts to happen to all of us at around your age. It's the way God has made us and there's nothing we can do about it. All you have to do is ignore it and carry on with your prayers and studies as usual. Pray especially for priestly purity, because that's what a priest needs above all, purity of both mind and body. Do you want to ask me anything?'

'No, Father,' Fran shook his head, too embarrassed to ask a question even if he wanted to.

'Here's something for you to read,' Father Director said, seeming embarrassed himself, because he turned away quickly, picked up something from a pile on his desk and handed it to Fran without looking at him. It was a Catholic Truth Society pamphlet entitled, 'Where Do Babies Come From?'

'If you have any questions about it, you can come and see

me,' Father Director said, turning back to his desk. 'That's all, son. Now back to study.'

Fran had gone back to study feeling confused. He had no idea what the 'hardness' and 'white fluid' that Father Director had spoken about were, because they hadn't happened to him yet. He couldn't understand what or where exactly the 'hardness' was supposed to be. Nor could he understand what the 'white fluid' was or where it was supposed to come from. At first he thought it must come from his belly button, but couldn't quite believe it. The only other place he could think of was his thing, but he could hardly believe that either.

It wasn't until a year later, when he was fifteen, that he had started to have 'wet dreams' and understood. Meanwhile, he was worried that something was wrong with him. He wondered if it might have something to do with his 'varicocele' – but Father Director had stopped treating him for that at the end of his second year, when he was still thirteen, so he supposed he was better. Father Director never made him go to his bedroom on Wednesday afternoons any more either. In fact, after his second year, Father Director had suddenly stopped giving him any special attention at all, so that for a long time he had felt rejected, as well as mystified.

Where did babies come from? According to the Catholic Truth Society pamphlet, strangely enough they came from their mothers' stomachs. Even more strangely, when they were born they came out of the hole that women had instead of a thing – he knew about that because he had seen his sisters without clothes on. But no matter how many times he read it, he couldn't work out how a baby got into its mother's stomach in the first place. Somehow it came from its father, but exactly how was not explained. It was yet another mystery, like a mystery of faith, he supposed.

He had started trying to find out about it, somewhat guiltily, from the only sources available – reference books, even those in the senior library, which they weren't supposed to read until they were in the Fifth Form. It was fascinating, like trying to solve a murder mystery, except that in this case the mystery wasn't about how someone had died, but how they were born. The investigation was made doubly difficult by the fact that Father Director fanatically censored all books for references to sex or women – other than women saints. He either inked them out, stuck brown paper over them or simply cut them out with scissors.

No matter how fanatical Father Director was though, he couldn't read every word of every book. Besides, there were references to the subject in the most innocent of sources, such as history books, Shakespeare plays, even the lives of the saints, his missal and the Bible itself. So gradually Fran had put the pieces of the puzzle together and realised that babies were produced or 'conceived' by a husband and wife doing something together with their private parts in bed, which was why they slept together, like his own mum and dad.

What it was exactly that they did, he still couldn't quite work out. Nor could he work out when exactly they did it. He supposed it must be at night, when they were in bed. But how long did it take? Did it take all night? Did that mean they had to stay awake all night? Or did they do it in their sleep? For all he knew, they did. After all, you could talk and even walk in your sleep, as boys often did in the dorm at night – including himself, according to the others. One night he had walked all around the dorm and then tried to get in the bed of the boy next to his by mistake!

He couldn't find out any more and didn't really try to – it all seemed rather disgusting. It was even more disgusting to think that his mum and dad must have done it to produce him and his brothers and sisters. He couldn't understand how a man could want to do that with a woman. He was more glad than ever that he was going to be a priest and would never have to get married, even though it meant he would never have children.

At the beginning of his sixth and final year, Fran was appointed 'guardian angel' to Mark Brown, a new boy of thirteen, from the south of England. Mark went straight into the Second Form, because he had already done a year at grammar school. However, he hadn't done any Latin or Greek, so Father Director also assigned Fran to tutor him privately in those subjects, which he was doing, as well as English, for A-level.

He taught Mark two afternoons a week in a free classroom, while the others were having singing or elocution class. Mark was blond-haired, blue-eyed and smooth-skinned, with an angelic face. He sang like an angel, too, so went straight into the choir. While Fran was tutoring him, he had to sit close beside him at one of the desks and found himself wanting to sit closer and closer. Gradually he did so, till sometimes their thighs touched, filling Fran with an excitement he had never felt before.

He sensed it was wrong, but couldn't resist, especially since Mark didn't seem to mind. Anyway, he told himself, it wasn't really wrong, as he wasn't actually doing anything. He started to look forward to his twice-weekly lessons with a new eagerness. Mark was a good pupil and looked up to him. He started thinking about Mark all the time and glancing at him secretly, even during Mass. He also started going with him more and more often during recreation, though he knew he risked getting into trouble for 'grouping' – but he had a good excuse, he told himself, in that Mark was his 'protégé'.

After a while though, he started wanting to do more than just sit close to Mark. He wanted to touch him, to stroke his blond hair, smooth cheeks and slim body. Then he wanted to put his arm around him. Finally, he wanted to kiss him. That would definitely be wrong, a mortal sin, he told himself, resisting the temptation with all his willpower. Besides, Mark would probably be shocked if he did anything like that. He would probably tell Father Director and Father Director would probably expel him. That thought, as much as the thought of Hell, was enough to deter him, despite the sometimes almost irresistible temptation.

Ashamed of his feelings, Fran thought of going to see Father Director to tell him about them and ask him for 'direction', but was too afraid. He thought of telling his confessor in Confession, but couldn't bring himself to do that either. He knew they would both tell him he had to stop teaching Mark, and he couldn't bear the thought of that. He prayed that the feelings would go away, but they didn't – if anything, they became stronger. So he prayed at least for the strength to resist them.

One morning at Mass, he read in his missal the story from the gospel of the Last Supper – how, during the meal, Our Lord kept His 'favourite' disciple, Saint John, next to Him, how Saint John was the one He 'loved most' and how, during the meal, Saint John didn't just sit next to Our Lord, but 'reclined on His breast'. A current of excitement went through Fran – that was exactly how he felt about Mark! If it was all right for Our Lord, it must be all right for him! He read the story over and over again, more and more excitedly, all the time glancing at Mark a few benches in front of him on the other side of the chapel. He could hardly wait to sit beside him again.

'Are you sure it's all right?' Mark asked, in the soft southern accent Fran liked so much.

'Our Lord did it with Saint John,' Fran said. 'You read it, didn't you?'

'Yes, but ...'

'So there can't be anything wrong with it, can there?'

'I suppose not.'

'Of course not.'

'It doesn't actually say Our Lord kissed Saint John, though, does it?'

'No, but that's what it means obviously. If you love someone, you kiss them, don't you?'

'I suppose so.'

'There you are, then. I love you just as Our Lord loved Saint John.'

'Do you?'

Mark looked up at Fran with his big blue eyes full of admiration, so that Fran's heart fluttered. They were sitting next to each other in the classroom on their own, Fran with his arm around Mark's shoulders, Mark with his head on Fran's chest, just like Our Lord with Saint John at the Last Supper, according to the gospel.

To his delight, Mark had let him put his arm round him without any resistance after he had shown him the story in his missal, which was still open on the desk in front of them. Tremulously, he had tried to kiss Mark on the cheek, too, but

Mark had recoiled.

'Yes, I do,' Fran said, in answer to Mark's question, his voice sticking in his throat, and gave Mark a quick peck on the cheek. 'There you are – that didn't hurt, did it?'

'No,' Mark smiled, making Fran's heart flutter even faster.

'Do you love me?' Fran asked.

'Yes,' Mark whispered.

'So we love each other then?'

'Yes, I suppose so.'

'Let's promise to be best friends and love each other for ever, shall we?' Fran suggested, to which Mark nodded eagerly. 'I promise,' Fran declared, putting his hand on the missal.

'I promise,' Mark said, putting his hand on top of Fran's on the missal.

They looked into each other's eyes. Fran's heart was pounding now, with both fear and excitement. He put his other arm around Mark, pulled him close and did what he had been longing to do for so long – kissed him on the lips. Then he hugged him tight against his wildly beating heart.

Unable to stop himself, despite the danger, Fran went around with Mark more and more. When he wasn't with him, he couldn't stop thinking about him – during class, during study, even during Mass. He couldn't bear to see Mark with anyone else without feeling jealous. He did him little favours and gave him presents. He even started writing him poems!

At night he dreamt about him. Sometimes he dreamt that he was in bed with Mark, hugging him tight, and woke up wet. These dreams worried him and he thought he should tell his confessor about them, but couldn't bring himself to, because they also gave him a feeling of indescribable ecstasy. Besides, he knew that his confessor would tell him not to see Mark and he couldn't bear the thought of that.

Sometimes he was afraid that he was committing a mortal sin through his friendship with Mark and worse, by going to Holy Communion every morning, committing sacrilege on top. But he wasn't, he convinced himself, because he was only doing what Our Lord did with Saint John and he never did more than kiss Mark. He wanted to touch him 'impurely', but never dared to. He dreamt of doing it sometimes, but a dream couldn't be a sin, he told himself.

Somehow – probably because he was both Mark's 'guardian angel' and 'private tutor' – they got away with it through the Christmas and Easter term, without being caught and 'sent up' for 'grouping'. Towards the end of the Easter term, during one of their private lessons, Mark asked him how he thought he would do in the Easter exams, which were also their mock A-levels.

'Oh, I'll probably come second again, as usual,' he said, though it pained him to say it.

'Not first?' Mark seemed disappointed.

'Zappo always comes first.' Oh, how it pained him to say it!

'Haven't you ever beaten him?' Mark asked, surprised.

'No,' he admitted, squirming.

'I bet you could if you wanted to,' Mark said.

'Do you think so?' He was touched by Mark's faith in him.

'I think you're just as clever as he is.'

'Oh, I don't know,' he said modestly, but decided there and then he would try to beat Zappo, for the first time ever, just to impress Mark.

He swotted harder than he had ever swotted before, getting up an hour early at 5.30 a.m. to do so. During the day he carried a Latin or Greek vocabulary notebook around with him and studied it during every free moment. At night, after lights out, he even studied under the bedclothes by the light of a torch, though it was against the rule. It was his very last chance to beat Zappo, apart from in the A-level exams themselves, and he became more and more determined to do it, mainly to please Mark, but also for his own satisfaction – after five years, he was fed up with coming second!

During the results ceremony, when the Dean of Studies came to his name, 'Walsh', there were only two positions in the class left as usual – first and second. Nervously, he wrote down his marks for each subject. In English he came first. In Latin he came second. In Greek he came third. His heart sank. He hadn't done it. Mark would be disappointed in him! Then the Dean of Studies read out his position in class: 'First'.

He felt an explosion of triumphant joy, though he was careful not to show it. The Dean of Studies, for the first time in six years, told him to stand up and publicly commended him. Afterwards, Mark was the first to come and congratulate him, saying, 'So, how does it feel to be top of the Sixth Form?' He smiled, feeling on top of the world. Some of his fellow Sixth-Formers came to congratulate him, too, but he noticed that Zappo, who had come second, was not among them.

In fact, Zappo mysteriously went missing and a search party had to be sent out. He was eventually found huddled in one of the outside toilets, sobbing uncontrollably. He was sent home the next day, never to return. He had had a 'nervous breakdown', they said. Frank felt sorry for him, but not sorry for having beaten him, because now Mark idolised him more than ever.

'Father Director wants to see you,' the First Auxiliary said, giving him a tap on the shoulder during study one evening early in the summer term.

His stomach lurched – he knew straightaway it must be about Mark. He had been dreading it for ages and knew it had to come sooner or later. Slowly, he stood up, placed his chair under his desk and left the study hall. Then he walked as slowly as possible along the corridor towards Father Director's office, trying to think of what he would say and summon up the courage to say it.

Nervously, he knocked on the door and Father Director called him in. He could tell by the sound of his voice that he was shirty. He went in, with a trembling hand blessed himself from the font by the door and said, 'Laus tibi, Christi' as usual.

'Sit down,' Father Director said curtly, without responding or even looking up from his desk, where he was marking exercise books with a red pen.

He went over to the brown leather armchair, sat down on the edge with his elbows on the arms and waited, bracing himself for the confrontation ahead. After a while, Father Director threw down his red pen, swung round and glowered at him.

This was one of Father Director's ploys to intimidate people, Fran knew, but he held his gaze, refusing to be intimidated. Doing so, he noticed for the first time that Father Director had started to look old: his hair was going grey at the sides and thin on top, there were shadows under his eyes and there were lines on his still handsome, tanned face.

'Have you become friendly with Mark Brown?' Father Director demanded at last, without beating about the bush.

'What do you mean, Father?' Fran asked disingenuously, struggling not to blush.

'You know what I mean!' Father Director shouted. 'Don't prevaricate! Have you become friendly with him?'

'No, Father,' Fran gulped, blushing despite himself.

'That's not what I've heard,' Father Director accused. 'Have you or have you not become friendly with him?'

'No, I haven't, Father,' Fran said, his voice wavering.

'Don't lie to me!' Father Director shouted, banging his desk with his fist and making Fran jump.

'I'm not lying, Father,' Fran said, but his red face gave him away.

Who had reported him, he wondered? He could think of one or two in his own class who might have done it, because they were jealous of him having come first.

'You *are* lying!' Father Director shouted, banging the desk with his fist again. 'Tell me the truth!'

'That *is* the truth, Father,' Fran insisted quietly, trying to stop blushing.

'If it's the truth, swear it on the Bible!' Father Director ordered, grabbing a Bible from his desk and thrusting it into Fran's trembling hand.

Fran held the Bible in one hand and gripped the arm of the chair with the other. His heart pounded painfully.

'Go on!' Father Director shouted. 'Swear it on the Bible! Have you become friendly with him?'

The lie rose in his throat, but stuck there, choking him. He didn't dare lie on the Bible – he could go to Hell for it! Father Director had trapped him.

'Just a little, Father,' he admitted, in a tremulous voice.

'Tell me the whole truth and nothing but the truth!' Father

110

Director shouted, banging his desk with his fist again. 'I've heard! I know all about it! Swear on the Bible – have you become friendly with him or not?'

'Yes, Father,' Fran confessed, his face burning.

'Ahah!' Father Director exclaimed triumphantly. 'The truth at last!'

'I'm his Guardian Angel and I tutor him in Latin and Greek, that's why, Father,' Fran protested weakly.

'That's no excuse!' Father Director shouted, banging the desk yet again. 'You are no longer his Guardian Angel and you will not tutor him! I'll find someone else to do it! You will no longer have anything to do with him! You will not speak to him or go near him again! Do you understand?'

Never to speak to or go near Mark again? The thought went through him like a spear! And the thought of someone else tutoring Mark made him writhe with jealousy. A rebellious anger suddenly rose inside him. 'Why not, Father?' he asked, the Bible still in his trembling hand.

'Why not?' Father Director roared. 'Because your association with him is unhealthy and furthermore it's against the holy rule!'

'But Our Lord had a special friendship with Saint John, Father,' Fran objected, quaking at his own audacity.

'Our Lord? How dare you compare yourself with Our Lord? It's blasphemous!' Father Director bellowed at him.

Fran flinched – Father Director was in such a rage that he thought he was going to spring out of his chair and hit him with his clenched fist. He was now taller than Father Director, but Father Director was bigger and stronger. Anyway, he wouldn't dare hit him back – he was a priest, after all.

'I'm not comparing myself with Our Lord, Father, I'm just questioning – '

'It's not your place to question!' Father Director cut him off angrily. 'It's your place to obey, obey blindly! Blind obedience, boy, blind obedience! You will obey or you will leave this seminary! You will not receive the habit! Do you understand?'

This was the ultimate threat. Fran felt a shudder of terror at the thought and his rebellion evaporated. 'Yes, Father,' he said, meekly.

'Good!' Father Director declared. 'You will have nothing

further to do with Mark Brown. If I hear of you even looking at him, you will be on the nine forty-three. Do you understand?'

'Yes, Father,' Fran said, completely deflated.

'Now, I want to ask you something else and I want you to tell me the truth, to swear it on the Bible.' Father Director suddenly turned to his desk and shut his eyes, as if they were in Confession. 'Have you ever touched this boy?'

'What do you mean, Father?' Fran asked, though he knew very well.

'I mean, have you ever touched him impurely?'

'No, Father!' Fran denied indignantly.

'Do you swear it on the Bible?'

Fran hesitated. The Bible was still in his trembling hand. If he told a lie, he could go to Hell. But it wasn't a lie, he told himself – he had touched Mark, but not 'impurely'. There was nothing wrong with putting your arm around someone or even kissing them, if you loved them as he loved Mark, as Our Lord had loved Saint John. Was there?

'Swear it on the Bible,' Father Director insisted, head averted, eyes still shut.

'I swear,' Fran said, his voice quivering.

'Thank God,' Father Director gasped, suddenly dropping his head into his hands. 'You've let me down. You've betrayed the trust I put in you.' He spoke now more in sorrow than anger.

'I'm sorry, Father,' Fran said, abjectly.

'Go back to study,' Father Director ordered him, his head still in his hands, elbows on the desk.

Fran stood up, placed the Bible on the corner of the desk and left the room quickly. However, he didn't go back to study. Instead, he went to the boot room and sat on one of the benches, still shaking, to recover his composure and think.

One thing was certain, he thought – nothing must stop him receiving the habit in four weeks' time. It was what he had worked towards for the last six years. But what about Mark? He couldn't give up his friendship with Mark! He'd continue it secretly. He'd somehow have to tell Mark what had happened and warn him. But how? He'd write him a letter – that was it!

He stood up, took a deep breath and went back to the study hall to do so.

CHAPTER TEN

'Caught you! Father Director exclaimed triumphantly, bursting through the door of the games hut like a commando, camail flying.

They sprang apart and jumped to their feet. Fran had been sitting with his arm around Mark's shoulders on one of the benches, chatting in between games of table tennis. It was Wednesday afternoon and the others were playing cricket. Being about to begin his A-levels, Fran was allowed to miss cricket in order to study, but Mark, who was in cricket whites, should have been down on the cricket field.

'What are you doing?' Father Director demanded, hands on hips, eyes blazing.

'We were just talking, Father,' Fran answered, blushing, but knowing they had been caught red-handed.

'Don't lie to me, Walsh – I saw you with your arm around this boy!' Father Director shouted at Frank.

'That's all, Father – we weren't doing anything wrong,' Frank protested feebly.

'Is that all?' Father Director demanded of Mark.

'Yes, Father,' Mark said, to Fran's relief.

'Go to my office,' Father Director ordered him, pointing at the door. Mark slunk out.

'We weren't doing anything, Father,' Fran protested, in a last desperate attempt to save himself.

'Silence!' Father Director bellowed, banging his fist on the table tennis table. 'I saw what you were doing! You had your arm around that boy! You have broken the holy rule! You have disobeyed me! You have persisted in this unhealthy and unnatural relationship! You have committed mortal sin! You have defiled yourself and him! You will not receive the habit of this order! You will take your A-level exams and then you will

113

go from this seminary!' Father Director turned on his heel and stormed out, slamming the door behind him, before Fran could say anything.

Fran remained standing there, stunned. Slowly the full horror sank in – he had been expelled! He couldn't believe it. After six years he had been *expelled*! It was his worst nightmare. But it wasn't a nightmare. It was *real*!

In a daze, he walked out of the games hut and down to the river, where he sat on the bank, staring at the water, trying to think. Instead of receiving the habit in two weeks' time and going to the novitiate, he would have to go home, in disgrace. His family would be shocked. His mother would be devastated. And he would never be able to be a priest!

Two things were certain – he could never face life without being a priest and he could never go home. He couldn't stand the shame, especially if Father Director told them he had been expelled and even worse, why. He'd rather die! He'd rather throw himself in the river right now!

He stared at the glassy black water with horror. In it he could see his reflection, surreally mixed with those of the riverbanks, clouds and sky. A sudden breeze rippled the surface. His reflection writhed and wriggled grotesquely. It was like a reflection of his soul, he thought, in sudden self-disgust. Yes, he had sinned, sinned mortally, not just once, but hundreds of times, one sin leading to another – impurity, disobedience, pride, sacrilege ... He *deserved* to die!

But to die on a lovely summer's day, at the age of seventeen! To die by drowning, like a dog! *Oh, God, help me, please!* It was no use calling on God though. God had abandoned him. No, *he* had abandoned God, rejected Him, by his sin. *He* had cut himself off. As if to symbolise it, a cloud suddenly slipped across the sun, blotting out his reflection in the water. This was Hell in the true sense, as they had learnt in Christian Doctrine class, this sense of being cut off and cast into the 'outer darkness'.

As if to emphasise it, from the cricket field on the other side of the river, he could hear the click of balls on bats and the muffled yells of his companions playing cricket. They sounded so innocent, so carefree, so happy! He was no longer one of them though. He had cut himself off from them too. This place was his whole world and he had been cast out, like Adam out of the Garden of Eden. He was an outcast! Tears sprang to his eyes and ran down his cheeks. He tried to stop them but couldn't. He curled up into a ball and sank down onto the soft grassy riverbank, sobbing and shaking uncontrollably ...

'Hello,' Mark whispered.

'Hello,' Fran whispered back, glancing around nervously.

It was manual labour and they were weeding the rose garden, with several others. He didn't want to speak to Mark. He was ashamed of how he had felt about him. He had done nearly all his A-level exams under the sentence of expulsion and next week, after the last one, was going to ask Father Director for a reprieve. If they were caught together again, he knew there would be no mercy. Besides, it was supposed to be silence.

'What did he say?' Mark asked, hoeing busily beside him.

'He told me I couldn't receive the habit,' Fran said, hoeing busily too.

'You mean, he expelled you?'

Fran nodded.

'I'm sorry,' Mark said, pausing to glance at him.

'Keep working,' Fran said, terrified of being seen talking, especially to Mark.

'When do you have to leave?' Mark asked.

'When I finish my exams.'

'It's not fair. We didn't do anything wrong.' Fran didn't say anything. 'Are you going to see him?'

'Yes, but I don't think he'll change his mind. What did he say to you?'

'He just gave me the strap and told me I mustn't talk to you again.'

'How many did he give you?'

'Six of the best.'

Fran winced. 'Three on each hand?'

'No – all on the backside.'

Fran was shocked. 'Did it hurt?'

'Yes.'

'Did you cry?'

Mark nodded.

'I'm sorry.' He wanted to put his arm round Mark, despite himself. 'Does it still hurt?'

'Not too much – he put some cream on afterwards.'

'Oh.'

That was strange, Fran thought, moving away slightly. He didn't want to talk about it any more – he was afraid of getting into trouble for 'breaking silence', especially with Mark. However, Mark moved close to him again. They both hoed more busily than ever.

'He asked me if we had ever committed a sin of impurity together,' Mark whispered.

'What did you say?' Fran whispered back, embarrassed but intrigued.

'No, of course.'

'Good,' Fran nodded.

'We didn't, did we?'

'No, but we did break the rule.'

'Don't you like me any more, then?'

'Yes, but – ' Fran blushed, not quite knowing how to put it.

'But what?'

'We can't be friends any more. It's wrong. It's against the rule.'

'Father Director still likes me, anyway,' Mark said, sounding hurt, and moved away.

'What do you mean?' Fran whispered, moving beside him again.

'He likes me,' Mark repeated petulantly.

'What do you mean?' Fran insisted, a horrible thought starting to form inside his head. 'How do you know he likes you?'

'He looks after me.'

'What do you mean exactly?'

'It's private, like Confession. He said I mustn't tell anyone.'

'You can tell me, can't you?'

Mark sulked silently.

'Please, Mark,' Fran urged him. 'Tell me. I need to know. What exactly does he do?'

'He washes me.'
'All over?'
'Yes.'
'In his bedroom?'
'Yes.'
'Does he put powder on?'
'Yes.'
'And ointment? Germolene?'
'Yes.'
'I mean, on – you know – ?'
'Yes. He says I've got something wrong.'
'What?'
'I forget. I think it begins with 'v'.'
'A 'varicocele'?'
'Yes. That's it.'

The thought burst like a monster from an egg inside Fran's head: it was horrible but, he realised excitedly, he could use it to save himself.

'How long has he been doing it?' he asked.
'Since I came. Why?'
'It's all right. Thanks.'

He moved away, too shocked but excited to speak further. Anyway, the prefect in charge was looking at them. He started to hoe with renewed vigour, his mind whirling.

'Can I speak to you, please, Father?'

'What do you want?' Father Director demanded curtly, without even looking up from his desk, where he was reading his breviary.

Fran was glad he didn't tell him to sit down in the brown leather armchair – his knees were knocking, but he felt stronger standing.

'Can I receive the habit, Father?' His voice was as shaky as his legs. They had done their last A-level exam that day and were to start the long, ten-day retreat in preparation for the reception of the habit the next.

'You cannot!' Father Director shouted, swinging round and banging the desk with his fist, making Fran jump. 'You have disobeyed me! You have broken one of the strictest rules of this seminary! You have sinned against holy purity! You will pack your bags tonight and leave this place tomorrow!'

'I want to receive the habit, Father,' Fran insisted, tremulously. 'I've spoken to my confessor and he's told me I can.'

'It's not for your confessor to decide!' Father Director shouted, thumping the desk again. 'I am your director – it's for me to decide and I have decided! You cannot and you will not receive the habit! You will go! Go!'

Fran took a deep breath. This was it. 'If you don't let me, I'll go to the Superior and tell him everything,' he said, quaking at his own audacity.

'What do you mean, boy?' Father Director demanded menacingly.

Fran took another deep breath. 'I'll tell him what you do with Mark Brown and other boys. I'll tell him what you used to do with me.'

'What are you accusing me of?' Father Director demanded, even more menacingly.

'You do things with boys that you shouldn't do, Father. You do them with Mark Brown. You did them with me.'

'What things? What things? Be specific, boy!' Father Director shouted.

'Improper things, Father.'

Father Director jumped up, apoplectic with rage. Fran stepped back, afraid he was going to hit him. 'How dare you!' Father Director roared. 'I have never done anything improper with any boys!'

'Yes, you have, Father!' Fran shouted back, suddenly angry himself now, his vocation, his very life, at stake. 'You have! I know! And if you don't let me receive the habit, I'll tell the Superior!'

'Liar!' Father Director bellowed, shaking his fist at him, and lunged forward.

Fran moved back quickly behind the armchair to escape, holding onto the back of it to steady himself, his legs wobbling like jelly. 'I'm not lying, Father!' he replied, shaking.

'Why are you doing this?' Father Director asked, his rage

suddenly abating and a note of pleading entering his voice.

Fran noticed that Father Director looked old. His hair was grey around the edges and thin on top, his face haggard, with an almost ashen pallor, while his habit hung loosely on his once athletic frame.

'I really want to receive the habit, Father,' he said, calmly confident now. 'I think I deserve to. I've worked hard for six years for it. I want to be a priest. I want to be a missionary. My parents have made a lot of sacrifices for me. You can't stop me now. You can't destroy their expectations. If I broke the rule with Mark Brown, it was because of you. I'm sorry now. I've confessed it. If you stop me, I'll tell the Superior everything. I've already told my confessor.'

'What have you told your confessor?' he asked, his voice a whisper now.

'What you used to do with me. In infirmary. You know what I mean, Father.'

'Oh, my God!' Father Director gasped in horror and suddenly staggered towards him with his hands raised.

Frightened he was going to attack him, Fran dashed to the door and grabbed the knob, ready to make a break for it. However, Father Director simply sank to his knees on the floor, keeled forward and clutched his head in his hands, groaning, 'Oh, God, forgive me!'

'Can I receive the habit, Father?' Fran asked, alarmed.

But Father Director just knelt there, bent double, his head in his hands, groaning, 'Oh, God, forgive me!' over and over again.

'I'm going to receive it, Father,' Fran said, panicking, opened the door and fled from the office.

He ran upstairs to the chapel, which was deserted and dim, except for the ruby-red glow of the sanctuary lamp. Trembling, he knelt down in one of the pews, bowed his head before the Divine Presence and prayed as he had never prayed before.

'I have called you together at this unaccustomed time because I have some sad news to impart to you,' Father Superior, sitting on the rostrum in the study hall, said solemnly to the assembled school. He paused dramatically, hands clasped, bald head bowed, as if unable to speak further. The suspense in the study hall, already intense, immediately heightened. One of the fluorescent lights started to hum, as if to emphasise it. Sitting at his desk near the back, Fran felt a sickening sense of foreboding about what the Superior was going to say.

'This morning,' the Superior, raising his head, continued gravely, 'Father Director was found dead in bed.'

He paused and bowed his head again. A shockwave went around the study hall. Fran sat there stunned.

The Superior raised his head and continued even more gravely: 'Apparently, Father Director passed away during the night. Doctor Macready has been and diagnosed the cause of death as a sudden, massive heart attack. You did not know, because he did not want you to be disturbed, but Father Director had been having treatment for pains in his chest for the past few months. Evidently, the condition was much more serious than anyone suspected. The doctor thinks that he probably died in his sleep, so did not suffer. That, at least, is something that we must be grateful to Almighty God for.' He paused again.

'The obsequies will be held in the chapel on Saturday, with Solemn High Requiem Mass. The body will lie in the chapel until then and a watch will be kept, for which a rota will be put on the notice board later. Today and tomorrow, classes and examinations for those doing them will continue as normal. Those receiving the habit will begin their long retreat tonight as timetabled. This, I feel sure, is the way Father Director himself would have wished it.'

He paused and bowed his again, then resumed: 'Meanwhile, we will offer up all our prayers and devotions, including the holy sacrifice of the Mass, for the repose of Father Director's soul, although I do not think he will have much need of them. It was because of his holiness and regularity that he was entrusted with the most sacred charge of being your director. For the time being, Father Haynes will assume that responsibility. Now, let us all kneel and pray together for the repose of Father Director's soul.'

Father Superior rose and knelt on the rostrum steps. They all stood up, with a scraping of chairs, and knelt on the polished parquet floor. Then Father Superior led them in reciting the 'De Profundis': 'De profundis clamavi ad Te Domine, Domine, exaudi vocem meam ...' This was followed by three 'Requiem Aeternams'.

Fran said the words mechanically, still in a state of shocked disbelief, remembering what had happened the evening before in Father Director's office, what had happened in the games hut, what had happened a few years ago in Father Director's bedroom. He felt sick with shame and guilt and sorrow.

Afterwards, the rumour went around that Father Director had not died of a heart attack at all, but had committed suicide by swallowing a bottle of pills, of which he had plenty.

When he heard this, Fran said nothing, not even to Mark. He went to the toilets and vomited. Then he went for a long walk by the river, to think and to pray. He had to decide whether to receive the habit or leave the seminary. But he knew he could never leave. His only other choice would be to throw himself in the river. And the river looked as black as Hell ...

'Sure, it was a beautiful ceremony, wasn't it?' his mother sniffed, taking a hanky from the sleeve of her dress and dabbing her eyes.

'Ahem. The singing was very good,' his father remarked, embarrassed by his mother's display of emotion.

'Did you think so?' Fran said, absently,

They were standing on the back lawn with the other new novices and their relations, after the ceremony of the reception of the habit. The novices were all wearing their new habits – black cassocks, girdles and camails with white clerical collars – while their relations were dressed in their Sunday best. They all felt somewhat self-conscious and not quite sure what to say to each other.

Fran had kissed his mother, who looked old despite her make-up, jewellery and best summer dress, and made them all laugh by saying she looked like a duchess. He had kissed his sisters too, noticing how pretty they looked in their best summer frocks, with the minimum of make-up his mother had allowed. He had shaken hands with his father, making a joke about his 'middle-age spread', which they all laughed at, even his father himself, and with his two younger brothers, both growing tall like himself and looking smart in their best, Beatle-style suits.

'Yes, I thought the singing was very good,' his father said again.

'Sure, it was a beautiful ceremony altogether,' his mother said gruffly, dabbing her eyes and stuffing her hanky back up the sleeve of her dress. 'Don't you think so, Fran?'

Fran didn't answer, his mind elsewhere.

'Fran?' his mother repeated.

'Oh – yes,' he replied, coming to.

He couldn't help a wry smile – his mother, having little ear or taste for music, obviously resented this aspect of the ceremony being emphasised by his father, who had an excellent, trained tenor voice. She was right about the ceremony though. The chapel had been packed with priests, students and the relations of those receiving the habit, who were in the two front pews. The sun had beamed in through the stained-class windows, creating a kaleidoscope of colours, and the choir had sung sublimely, as his father had said.

Father Provincial, or 'Pop', had given an introductory homily, but Fran had hardly listened to it. Then he and the other nine postulants had gone out one by one to kneel on the altar steps and receive from Father Provincial the folded habit, the book of 'Rules and Constitutions', and the crucifix and rosary beads of the order. Then they went to the sacristy, where they put on their new habits, and returned to kneel on the altar steps again. There, on their knees before the True Presence in the open tabernacle, they had sworn to obey the rules and constitutions of the order and pronounced their first, 'simple' vows of poverty, chastity and obedience. Finally, Father Provincial had given a concluding homily and the ceremony was rounded off with the hymn they all knew so well, 'Veni Creator Spiritus'.

Yes, it had been a beautiful ceremony, he supposed, but he had hardly been aware of what was going on. He couldn't stop thinking about all that had happened. He couldn't stop thinking about Mark and Father Director. He was filled with confusion, guilt and self-disgust. He still wanted to be a priest, but he wasn't sure if he was fit to be one any more.

He had asked his confessor what he should do and he had advised him to pray. He had prayed long and hard, sometimes with tears in his eyes, for God to let him know His will, but God seemed to have turned a deaf ear. Or maybe that was God's way of telling him to leave, that He didn't want him to be a priest any more? But he couldn't bring himself to believe that. Deep down he knew he ought to leave, but he didn't have the courage. He didn't have the courage to tell his parents, especially his mother, because he knew it would break her heart. He didn't have the courage to face his family or the world outside. What would he do, if he left? The very thought filled him with despair. He would prefer to die, like Father Director, but he didn't have the courage to do that either. He was truly hopeless.

'Ahem. How do you think you've done in your A-levels, Fran?' his father asked.

'Er – all right, I think,' he answered, evasively.

'Do you think you've got university grades?' his father pursued the subject, to his discomfort – he was afraid that, under the strain of the last few weeks, he hadn't done as well as he should have. To his father at least, going to university was more important than becoming a priest, because he hadn't had the opportunity himself – he had had to spend six years fighting Adolf Hitler. He was probably going to disappoint on that score, too!

'Of course he has – he's brilliant, isn't he?' Terry, his sixteen-year-old brother, chipped in.

'I wouldn't say that!' he laughed, not quite sure whether Terry was being sarcastic or not. 'Actually, some of the papers were stiffer than we expected.'

'Fran doesn't want to be thinking about that today,' his mother butted in brusquely, to his relief. 'He has other things on his mind. He's had a hard time. Let him relax, can't yous?'

He smiled gratefully. Little did she or any of them know how hard a time he had had, how close he had come to being expelled and for what. A shudder went through him at the thought of them ever finding out.

'Who's he?' Molly, his elder sister asked, nodding towards one of the other novices.

Fran told her his name and where he came from, glad to divert the conversation from himself.

'He's good-looking, isn't he?' Molly commented.

'Mmm, yes!' Pat, his younger sister agreed. 'He looks like George Harrison, without the hair.'

'What a waste!' Molly quipped.

His sisters started giggling and he grinned, conscious of his own convict-style crew-cut executed only the day before, in contrast with the fashionably long hair of his brothers.

'That's enough of that!' his mother scolded them. 'They're not interested in that sort of nonsense here.'

'Who's George Harrison, anyway?' he asked.

'Ah, he's one o' them oul' Beatles,' his mother said scornfully, scowling and lapsing into her Irish brogue, as she did when she became agitated, and they all laughed.

'Are you sure he's not one o' them oul' Sthrollin' Bones?' Kevin, his younger, fourteen-year-old brother, asked, mimicking her and making them laugh even more. Fran didn't laugh, because he didn't get the joke and didn't want to offend his mother. He didn't feel like laughing, anyway.

'Ah, yous think yous are awful smart,' his mother scowled at them. 'If only yous were half as smart at your books!'

They stopped laughing and there was an awkward silence.

'Ahem. That was tragic about Father Director, wasn't it?' his father observed.

Fran nodded, trying not to redden – he knew it had to be mentioned sooner or later, but had been dreading it.

'Ah, terrible,' his mother said. 'He was such a fine man, too, wasn't he? God rest his soul.'

Fran couldn't bring himself to say 'yes'. If only she knew the truth, he thought! His clerical collar felt as if it was choking him, so he tried to loosen it.

'Are you all right, Fran?' his mother asked, anxiously.

'Just a bit hot,' he said – it was a sunny July afternoon.

At that moment, to his relief, he was called for a photo with the other new novices. He joined them on the steps of the Fathers' house.

'Say cheese!' the photographer ordered them.

Fran smiled, though he didn't feel like it. This should have been the happiest day of his life, he reflected bitterly, but the memory of what had happened hung over him like a big black cloud. He couldn't stop thinking about Father Director. He even had bad dreams about him. And it was only with the greatest difficulty that he had been able to resist speaking to or looking at Mark. Even now he had to struggle not to seek him out with his eyes.

The sooner today was over, the better, he thought. Tomorrow they would go to the novitiate for twelve months. It was supposed to be tough and the others were apprehensive about it, but he could hardly wait. It was going to be painful not seeing Mark again, but it was a pain he knew he had to endure if he wanted to be a priest. And, in spite of everything, he still wanted to be a priest more than anything else in the world!

CHAPTER ELEVEN

'Put your arms round each other!' Molly, his elder sister ordered, in her bossy nurse's manner.

She was taking a photo of his mother, himself and the statue of St. Joseph in front of the novitiate. The novitiate was situated in the middle of the flat midlands countryside and had once been a brewer's mansion, with columns all along one side like a Greek temple. He and his four fellow-novices had just made their profession of vows as religious before going to the senior seminary to study philosophy and theology for six years.

'Aw, hurry up, for God's sake!' his mother scowled at her. 'Me sciatica's killin' me, shtannin' here like this.'

Self-consciously he put an arm around his mother's shoulders, shocked at how old and frail she seemed since he had last seen her. He was ashamed of feeling embarrassed – after all, she was his mother, he reminded himself. She might as well almost have been a stranger though, he thought sadly, which was hardly surprising – he was now eighteen, had left home at the age of twelve and hadn't seen her for a year, since the reception of the habit. It was the same for the rest of his family – father, brothers and sisters – they all seemed like strangers.

The ceremony of profession had just finished in the chapel. Of the fifteen novices who had started the novitiate a year before, only five were left. The ceremony, which had been preceded by a 'long', ten-day retreat, had been short and simple. First, Father Provincial gave a homily on the significance of what they were about to do. Then, they came forward one by one, knelt on the altar steps in front of the True Presence in the open tabernacle and pronounced their vows of poverty, chastity and obedience. Next, they stood up one by one and signed their 'Last Wills and Testaments' on the altar itself, bequeathing to the order all their worldly goods and possessions. Finally,

Father Provincial pronounced them fully-fledged religious and members of the order and the ceremony was rounded off with the hymn they all knew so well, 'Veni Creator Spiritus'.

After the ceremony, high tea had been laid on for their families and themselves in the parlour. Then they had been allowed to spend some time with them in the grounds. As usual, Fran couldn't help feeling uncomfortable with his family, but this time even more so, for it had been a year since he had seen them. And, while at the reception of the habit last year the occasion had been clouded by what had happened before, this time there was something even more seriously wrong.

'Smile!' Molly ordered him, and he tried to do so.

'What's this, the Holy Family?' Kevin, his youngest brother cracked, and they all laughed except his mother, who simply said, 'Humph!'

'Hurry up, Molly, Saint Joseph's getting tired, too,' he joked, to show he wasn't offended.

'Yes, hurry up, Molly,' his father said. 'Then you can take one of me and Fran at the car.' His father had just bought a new car, an Austin Westminster, which was his pride and joy.

'Ah, go away with you and the car!' his mother retorted gruffly. 'Who wants a photo of the oul' car?'

'Who wants a photo of the oul' feller, you mean?' Molly, who still hadn't taken the photo, quipped.

'Come on, Molly,' Fran laughed uneasily with the others, not used to this family banter. 'Then we'll have one of Dad, me and the car.'

'Sure, it's not you he's interested in,' his mother said. 'It's the car. The car's more important than the lot of us.'

'Get on with it,' his father said testily, 'or I'll drive off and leave the lot of you.'

'Is that a promise?' Terry, his other brother, asked sarkily.

'A right family of smart-alecks I've got,' his father said.

At last Molly pressed the button and Fran removed his arm from his mother's shoulders with relief.

'I'll have to sit down, me back's killin' me,' she groaned.

'Dad might let you sit in the car, if you ask him nicely,' Terry joked.

'Do you want to?' his father asked her.

'Sure, it'd be like an oven,' his mother objected – it was a hot July afternoon, with the sun blazing down.

'There's a bench round the side in the shade,' Fran suggested, taking her arm and escorting her to it.

'All right?' he asked, when she had sat down.

'Yes, that's better, thanks,' she said, but to his shock he noticed that there were tears in her eyes.

'What's the matter?' he asked, embarrassed.

'Nuthin', nuthin',' she said, taking her hankie from her sleeve and dabbing her eyes.

'Would you like a cup of tea?' he asked, not knowing what else to say or do.

'I'd love one,' she said.

'I'll see if I can get it,' he said, turning to go, but she stopped him with a tug on the sleeve of his habit.

'Are you all right, Fran?' she asked.

'Yes, of course,' he laughed. 'What do you mean?'

'Are you happy?'

Did she suspect something, he wondered? Had she detected something about him, with her mother's intuition, even though she had hardly seen him for seven years?

'Of course,' he lied, blushing. 'I'll go and get the tea.'

He hurried off and as he turned the corner to enter the house, bumped into Molly.

'Is she all right?' Molly asked.

'She was crying,' he said. 'I'm going to get her a cup of tea.'

'Can I come with you?'

'Why?' he asked.

'I want to talk to you, Fran.'

He hesitated – to get to the kitchen, he would have to go through the 'cloisters', the part of the house closed to lay people. Also, he was afraid that Molly, in her solicitous, big-sisterly way, might have noticed something wrong with him and start asking him embarrassing questions, like his mother.

'OK, come on,' he said, deciding to dispense with the rule for once, and led Molly to the kitchen, where she helped him make the tea.

'Do you know why she was crying, Fran?' Molly asked him.

'I don't know – the emotion of the occasion, I suppose,'

he said.

'Not just that, Fran,' Molly said.

'What then?' he asked, uneasily.

'She's in pain, Fran.'

'What do you mean?' he asked, alarmed.

'She didn't want us to tell you, but I think you ought to know.'

'Tell me what?'

'She's got cancer.'

The very word was like a knife in his guts. 'Oh!' he declared, putting the kettle of boiling water down.

'Here, let me do it,' Molly picked the kettle up and poured the water into the pot.

'How long has she had it?' he asked, trying to appear calm.

'It was diagnosed a few weeks ago, but she's probably had it for months, if not years. She's going to have a mastectomy. Do you know what that is?'

'Does it mean – ?' he said, guessing it from his knowledge of Greek, but too embarrassed to say it.

'It means she's going to have a breast removed,' Molly explained in her no-nonsense nurse's way.

'When?' he asked, both embarrassed and horrified now, but trying not to show it.

'In a few days.'

'Will that – cure it?'

'We don't know – if it hasn't spread too far. Will you pray for her, Fran?'

He couldn't bring himself to say yes. For ironically, he had a cancer of his own, a cancer of the soul. He had just made his profession as a religious, before the True Presence in the open tabernacle, but he did not believe in it. He could no longer believe that God was present in a piece of bread, just because a priest had said a few words of mumbo-jumbo over it. Yet it was a basic doctrine of faith and if he couldn't believe that, he might as well not believe anything, and the ceremony of profession for him was a charade.

'Are you all right?' Molly asked.

'Yes, sure, just a bit shocked,' he mumbled.

'Don't worry, it might be all right,' Molly said, pouring out the tea and stirring it. 'Just pray for her, won't you?'

'Yes, of course I will,' he said, trying to sound as sincere as possible. 'Thanks for telling me. Will you take that to her and I'll just tidy up here?'

To his relief Molly took the cup of tea and left. Fran stood there, needing to be on his own for a while to absorb the shock. It was a double shock – his mother had cancer and he had started to lose his faith. He couldn't remember when exactly it had started, but it had been after Easter, when ironically he had been given the job of sacristan and so came into even closer contact than usual with the sacred vessels, a job he had secretly coveted and at first took pious pleasure in.

Until then the novitiate had not been too difficult, monastic though the regime was. The day began at six-thirty and consisted of prayer, study and manual labour, with just two or three short periods of recreation after meals to break it up. Meals were held in silence, accompanied by reading from religious books. They were allowed out only once a week, for a walk, on Sunday afternoons. Any transgression of the rule was punished with a penance – or expulsion.

It proved too rigorous for most, who left, but Fran was determined to survive and become a priest, despite what had happened at the junior seminary. He had a crisis just after Christmas, when they received a letter from the junior seminary with the news that Mark had left. The news shocked and pained him, for he realised it meant he would never see Mark again. He sank into a state of depression, a sort of dark night of the soul, not helped by the fact that it was the middle of winter, cold. dark and dead, with six long, grim weeks of Lent ahead ...

However, he had revived. His revival had coincided with spring and the revival of nature. He would get up early, sneak out of the house and stroll around the grounds, drinking in the sights, sounds and smells of nature with an almost mystical joy. Sometimes he felt as if he had been transported back to the Garden of Eden. He would stand and gaze in rapture at a bird, a blade of grass, a flower or one of the beautiful trees that adorned the grounds – the copper beech, with its slate-smooth bark and burnished leaves, the cedar of Lebanon, with its biblically evocative name and swaying fanlike boughs hung with cones, the horse chestnut with its great tongue-like leaves and candles of creamy blossom, a lone pine, whose scraggy outline and spicy scent reminded him nostalgically of both the Lake District and Ireland, or the line of Lombardy poplars standing like sentinels at the back of the house, with their exquisite elegance and delicate, silvery, heart-shaped leaves that fluttered gaily in the faintest breeze.

Not just nature, but the whole universe – sun, moon, stars and planets – filled him with a wondrous sense of God's presence and power. His presence and power pervaded all. He was within all, because He had created all, and it was His power that held all together from moment to moment and morning to morning in all its amazing, incomprehensible complexity and variety. Most amazing of all, he thought, God had made it all for man!

And although man had rejected God through original sin and continued to do so through sin, God had still not rejected man. He had sent down His only beloved Son, Our Lord Jesus Christ, to redeem him by dying on the cross for him, and continued to do so daily through the holy sacrifice of the Mass. Why had God done all this for man – created this beautiful world for him and then sacrificed His Son for him? There was only one possible explanation – LOVE! Love greater and more incomprehensible than the world itself, *infinite* love!

Why did God love man so much? Because He had made man in His own image and likeness and so was his Father. God was his Father! God loved him! The God Who was able to make a tree was also able to let His Divine Son die on a tree out of love for man, for *him*! The thought pierced Fran's heart with love, as Our Lord's heart had been pierced by the soldier's lance.

If necessary, he had resolved, he would die for God in return, give his very lifeblood. But if he couldn't die, at least he would live for God, as a priest, religious and missionary. At the end of the novitiate he would take the next big step towards that goal, by making his first profession of vows. Then he would be a religious, with only five years to ordination as a priest, the consummation of his life's dream and, he hoped and prayed ardently, his divinely ordained destiny.

But now, he reflected desolately, standing shocked in the

kitchen, his life's dream was in ruins. He could not believe in one of the most basic doctrines of the faith, that of transubstantiation. He had prayed in vain for the problem to disappear until finally, only a week ago, in desperation he had confided in his confessor, Father Mitchell.

Father Mitchell, whom they had nicknamed 'Torty' because he both looked and moved like a tortoise, was an elderly, semi-invalid, retired missionary. Fran didn't have much confidence in him, but had decided to accept his advice and make his profession. Gasping and wheezing pitifully because of his asthma as he lay on his bed, the feet of which were propped up with old altar missals, Torty had told him only what he had expected: that the True Presence was a mystery of faith, that God had probably sent him this trial as a test or that it was a last-ditch attempt by the Devil to divert him from entering the religious life and that he must pray, pray, pray. He had also reminded him that very soon he would be going to the senior seminary to study philosophy and told him that the study of scholasticism, the great philosophical system of St. Thomas Aquinas that provided a rational basis for the Church's doctrines, would help him to overcome any difficulties he might have as regards faith.

Clutching at this straw, Fran had gone ahead and made his profession. He was still determined to become a priest, as much for his mother's sake as his own. The news that she had cancer and could perhaps die any time made it all the more impossible to leave – if he did, it would probably kill her. He could only hope and pray that God would both restore his faith and cure her, so that in five years she would be able to enjoy the long dreamed-of day of his ordination and receive his first blessing.

'Mister Walsh?'

'Yes, Father?' It was the Novice Master, an ascetic, humourless, pedantic priest. He sounded shirty.

'Was that one of your visitors I've just seen breaking cloister?'

'Er – yes, Father,' he admitted, blushing. 'It was my sister. We were just making a cup of tea for my mother. She's – '

'I'm not interested in the whys or wherefores, Mister Walsh,' he said brusquely. 'You have broken one of the most

important rules of this house, allowing a lay person –
especially a female – to break cloister. I'm surprised at you,
Mister Walsh, today of all days.'

'But, Father, my mother – '

'Don't interrupt me, Mister Walsh!' the Novice Master said
irascibly. 'You will come and see me before vespers for a
penance. Now go back to your visitors.'

'Yes, Father,' he said meekly, and did as he was told –
after all, he reflected with bitter irony, he *had* just taken a
vow of obedience.

Eugene Vesey

CHAPTER TWELVE

One summer morning at the senior seminary, Fran got up early as usual, put on his black habit and went for a walk in the grounds. He walked with a limp, having injured his knee at football. He enjoyed his early morning walks, because he was all alone and the grounds were beautiful, with lawns, landscaped gardens, tennis courts and even a bowling green and pavilion. But he was far from happy.

He had been here two years now and just finished the philosophy course, but it hadn't helped him to regain his faith in the mystery of 'transubstantiation', as Father Mitchell had said it would. In fact, he had lost his faith in most of the other mysteries of faith as well, such as the incarnation, the virgin birth and the resurrection.

He had studied and prayed as hard as he could, often with tears in his eyes, but both prayers and tears had fallen on stony ground. In a couple of months he would be starting the four-year theology course. In four years, when he was twenty-four, he would be ordained – if he continued. That was what he had to decide. He knew he ought to leave, but after nine years, even though he had lost his faith, he still couldn't bring himself to do so. He may not have faith, he told himself wryly, but he still had hope.

Try as he might, he could not believe in 'transubstantiation' – the changing of the bread and wine into the Body and Blood of Christ by the priest pronouncing the words of consecration over them during Mass. The scholastic theory that was supposed to explain it was that of 'substance' and 'accidents'. According to this, all things possessed both 'substance' and 'accidents'. The 'accidents' of a thing were its physical properties, such as its shape, size, colour, texture and taste. These were perceptible to the senses and of secondary importance. The 'substance' of a thing, on the other hand, was what made it what it was, its essence or, in scholastic Latin terminology, its 'quidditas'. This was abstract, imperceptible to the senses and of primary importance – what mattered. Thus, when the priest changed the bread and wine into the Body and Blood of Christ, he did not change their 'accidents', which was why they continued to look and taste like bread and wine, but only their 'substance', which was invisible. He changed their 'substance' into the equally invisible 'substance' of Christ's Body and Blood, which was why it was called 'transubstantiation'.

Like the rest of scholastic philosophy it was ingenious, Fran thought, but only a clever, elegant theory. The scholastics could have devised a theory to explain anything, no matter how far-fetched. There was no way of proving it or, in the language of logical empiricism, 'verifying' it. Like all metaphysics, it seemed to him a meaningless misuse of language. He could see no reason to believe it, except wanting to believe it. He wanted to, wanted to desperately, but to him that wasn't reason enough.

Why had God imposed this trial on him, he wondered bitterly, this cross of iron and irony, of wanting to be a priest, but being unable to believe in the essential mysteries of faith? He had started to question other things, too. For example, how could a God of supposedly infinite love allow so much suffering? The Church's teaching that the human race had brought it on itself through Adam's 'original sin', and continued to do so through its misuse of free will, he found more and more unconvincing.

Passing the orchard and smelling with delight the fragrance of the ripening apples in the fresh morning air, he was reminded of the story of Adam and Eve and the apple. It was a charming story, he reflected, but utterly unsatisfactory as an explanation of the ills of the world – poverty, hunger, pain, disease, death ... According to Catholic philosophy, it all hinged on 'free will' – human beings, like Adam, were free to choose between good and evil. As far as he could see, though, this simply wasn't true, certainly not always. The whole concept of 'free will' was highly questionable, especially in the light of modern psychology.

Anyway, he thought, if all the ills of the world were the consequence of freedom, so-called, it would have been better to have had less freedom. The price was too high. Maybe it would have been better for humans not to have been created at all, but of course they had no 'freedom' of choice about that, as about so many other things. Why did God go ahead and create them and give them their 'freedom', if He was able to foresee what a mess they would make of it? Why did He go ahead, foreseeing that He would have to come down to Earth Himself and suffer and die to rescue them from the mess? If He hadn't gone ahead, neither He nor they would have suffered and He could have gone on being perfectly happy ad infinitum! It was all illogical, absurd, grotesque – more so than anything in Greek or Roman mythology.

He walked past the farm into the barley field and stood to watch the sunrise. It rose above the horizon, a dazzlingly bright ball of gold, bathing the earth in brilliant light, so that the young barley shoots shone like silver. His heart leapt with joy at the splendour of the sight and suddenly, like a sun bursting forth over the dark planet of his soul, he saw the answer to all his theological questions. It was so simple, so obvious, so logical, that he was amazed he hadn't seen it before. The answer was that *God did not exist*. There *was* no God!

'For me, the die is cast,' Jim said, cryptically.

'What do you mean?' Fran asked.

Jim Dwyer was in the same year as he. They were sitting chatting in Fran's room, clerical collars and girdles off and cassocks unbuttoned because of the afternoon heat. Fran was sitting on the chair at his desk, Jim on the edge of the bed, sandaled feet on the polished parquet floor. The tiny room contained nothing else except some bookshelves, filled with philosophy and theology books, and a curtained closet for clothes. On his desk lay his crucifix and some more books, including his breviary and, open, St. Thomas Aquinas' 'Summa Theologica', in Latin, which he had been reading.

'I've decided,' Jim said, still cryptic.

'Decided what?'

'I'm leaving.'

'You're leaving?' Fran was shocked, though not surprised.

They had known each other since their first year at the junior seminary, nine years ago.

'Yes,' Jim confirmed.

'Why? The lack of aggiornamento?' That seemed to be why a lot of people were leaving. The order was particularly slow at catching up with the reforms of the Vatican Council and in many ways was still stuck in the nineteenth century.

'No,' Jim answered. 'In a word, women.'

'Women?' As always Fran felt both embarrassed and puzzled – how could anyone give up the priesthood just for women?

'I've decided I can't live without them, Frank. I'd go crazy as a coot, like so many others around here. You know, sometimes I feel like rushing out and raping the first woman I see! No, celibacy's not for me. I can't do it. I've already applied to be released from my vows. What about you?'

'I'm leaving, too,' Fran admitted, though it pained him to do so.

'You are? Have you told the Superior?'

'No, not yet,' Fran acknowledged sheepishly – he hadn't had the courage to do that yet.

'Why are you leaving, then?' Jim asked. 'Women?'

'No, not really,' Fran said, blushing. 'I –I just don't believe in it any more.'

'What do you mean? Don't believe in what?' Jim pursued.

'In the faith, I suppose,' Fran shrugged, not sure he wanted to go into detail.

'What aspect of the faith?' Jim pinned him down.

'Any of it – the incarnation, the virgin birth, the resurrection, Heaven and Hell, the divinity of Christ, transubstantiation ...' Fran decided he might as well make a clean breast of it.

'Oh, I see.' It was Jim's turn to be shocked.

'Do you still believe in it all?' Fran asked him.

'Well, yes, I haven't really got a problem with that,' Jim said.

'I don't even believe in God any more,' Fran confessed daringly, deciding he might as well go the whole hog.

'Oh, come on, Frank, you can't be serious!' Jim expostulated.

'I am. I don't. I can't. Do you?' Fran put the ball back in Jim's court.

'Well, yes, of course. Why don't you?' Jim asked.

'I just can't see any evidence for God,' Fran shrugged.

'But the evidence is all around,' Jim declared. 'The whole universe is evidence! Someone must have made it.'

'Not necessarily,' Fran disagreed.

'Where did it all come from, then?' Jim wanted to know.

'I don't know – the big bang, evolution?' Fran suggested.

'They're only theories,' Jim said.

'God is only a theory,' Fran riposted.

'Come on – what about the human eye, for example? Do you think something as complex as that could come about by chance?' Jim demanded.

'No, but it could have evolved, over millions of years,' Fran argued.

'But how did it all start in the first place? Where does it all come from? Someone or something must have started it, created it. God, in some form or other.' Jim's argument was the classic 'first cause' one, for which Fran had no satisfactory answer.

'Maybe,' Fran conceded. 'Not a God of love, though, as far as I can see.'

'Why not?' Jim enquired.

'There's so much evil in the world, so much suffering,' Fran stated.

'There's both good and evil,' Jim asserted in reply.

'Yes,' Fran agreed, 'but, I can't believe that a God of infinite love and power would allow any evil at all, would allow even one child to suffer for one moment. I wouldn't, if I was God,' he added dryly.

'Ah, but you're not, thank God!' Jim laughed.

'I'm working on it,' Fran laughed also, glad to lighten the discussion a little, deadly serious as he was.

'What about the Five Proofs?' Jim was referring to the famous 'five proofs' of God's existence of St. Thomas Aquinas.

'I've just been reading them,' Fran said, waving his hand at the obese tome still open on his desk. 'They're very clever, but they're not *proofs*. They're arguments that can be refuted. They have been refuted, haven't they?'

'I don't know,' Jim shook his head. 'I do know you're in a hell of a position.'

'That's a good way to put it, actually,' Fran smiled wryly.

'What are you going to do?' Jim asked.

'I'll have to leave, I suppose,' Fran said sadly – the very thought sent a wave of despair over him. 'The trouble is, I daren't. I'm afraid of facing the world outside, having been locked away from it since the age of twelve.'

'I know what you mean,' Jim sympathised. 'I'm a wee bit nervous about it myself.'

'And I just don't know what to do, if I can't be a priest,' Fran disclosed.

'Most of us seem to end up as teachers or social workers,' Jim chuckled.

Fran smiled wryly again – neither prospect held any appeal for him. Nothing could compare with being a priest!

'When are you leaving, then?' he asked Jim.

'As soon as my dispensation comes through,' Jim told him. 'Within a week or two I hope. I don't want to spend any longer than necessary around here or I'll go cuckoo. What about you? When are you going to see the Superior?'

The thought made Fran wince. 'I don't know. The trouble is I've got to go to Lourdes with my mother next week. She's got cancer.'

Mentioning his mother sent a knife through his heart – she wanted to go to Lourdes in the hope of a cure for her cancer, which had recurred. The thought of going to Lourdes in his present frame of mind depressed him utterly. The idea that his mother might be miraculously cured of cancer, the idea of miracles in general, now struck him as absurd. Yet he hoped, deep down in the furthest recesses of his soul, that maybe, just maybe, not only might his mother be cured, but he, too.

'I see – I'm sorry,' Jim said. 'I'll pray for her.'

'Thanks,' Fran said, though he didn't believe in prayer any more, having prayed his guts out unsuccessfully for the restoration of his faith. 'And after coming back from Lourdes I've got to go into hospital myself for an operation on my knee.'

'Oh? What are they going to do?' Jim asked.

'Remove some torn cartilage, I think,' Fran told him – the prospect scared him, as well as delaying his decision.

Suddenly, there was a tap on the door, it opened and Mike Cummings, a student in his final year of theology and already ordained, stuck his bespectacled, owlish, balding head in. 'I'm going into town – anyone want anything?'

'Oh, yes, please, Mike,' Fran said. 'Could you get me a book from the library?'

'What is it?' Mike asked, putting his head in a bit further.

'It's called 'Ulysses', by James Joyce,' Fran informed him.

''Ulysses'' by James Joyce!' Mike expostulated, flinging the door wide open and stepping into the room, his bulldog jowls quivering with indignation. 'That – farrago of filth! That – bundle of – blasphemy!'

'Oh, you've read it, have you?' Fran enquired sarcastically, taken aback by this display of self-righteous indignation and resisting the temptation to congratulate him on his alliterative powers.

'I haven't read it and you're not reading it, either,' Mike decreed pompously.

'Oh, why not?' Fran asked, defiantly, though he was trembling inside.

'Because it's on the Index,' Mike declared triumphantly. 'Dangerous to Faith and Morals. It's not fit for any decent Catholic to read, never mind a seminarian and religious.'

'Oh, I see – well thanks for warning me, Mike,' Fran said, sarcastically again.

'I shall speak to the Superior about this,' Mike blustered, his jowls turning puce.

'Speak to the Pope about it if you like,' Fran retorted, trembling at his own audacity.

Mike spluttered with indignation and for a moment Fran was afraid he was going to rush in and hit him. He put his hand on his walking stick, with which to defend himself, just in case. However, Mike turned on his heel and stomped off, spluttering. Jim and Fran looked at each other and burst out laughing, though he felt more angry than amused, and more sad than angry – it was yet another sign that he didn't belong here any more.

Standing in front of the grotto at Lourdes, pretending to say the rosary with his mother and the other pilgrims, Fran felt revolted by both the morbid superstition and crass commercialism of the place. He found it incredible that anyone could believe what was supposed to have happened here – that the Blessed Virgin Mary, the 'mother' of God, had appeared to a fourteen-year-old French peasant girl a hundred years ago and as a result the water had miraculous properties, capable of curing disease. He looked at the statue of Our Lady in the niche above the grotto and at the crutches strung up across it with particular revulsion – the statue a typically sentimental idealisation and the crutches a pathetic, though poignant, testimony to people's credulity, gullibility and desperation.

His mother repeated the 'Hail Marys' fervently, fingering her beads, while he stood there mutely, holding his beads but unable to bring himself to say the words, which now struck him as so much mumbo-jumbo. For his mother, coming to Lourdes was the fulfilment of a lifelong dream – she believed in it all ardently, even that she might be cured of her cancer. Looking at her, he felt a pang of pity mixed with contempt, which was what he felt for all the other pilgrims, especially the invalids. For the priests swaggering about in their cassocks or black clerical suits like himself, he felt only contempt. The nuns he didn't mind too much – at least they were usually doing something useful, like looking after the sick.

The whole place was sick, he felt now, having been here seven days – thank goodness this was the last. Sickness seemed to permeate the very air, so that he felt sick himself, could hardly breathe, a feeling not helped by the swarming crowds, stifling heat and the fact that he was wearing a clerical collar. He wished he could escape up into the majestic, soaring, snow-clad mountains of the Pyrenees that rose above the town, the only thing about it that he liked. He could hardly wait to get on the plane tomorrow and fly away from it. He even hoped the plane might crash and then all his problems would be solved.

Ironically, at the junior seminary, he had been fascinated by Lourdes and read everything he could find about it. Then he had been in awe of Saint Bernadette. Now it was obvious to him that the poor girl had been suffering from hallucinations of some sort – maybe from eating too many mushrooms – just as it was now obvious to him that the whole place was the product of mass hysteria. Yet it still held a morbid fascination for him and at least until this afternoon he had even retained a shred of hope, if not belief, in it. Going to the baths for the last time this afternoon, to please his mother, he had challenged God with a last chance to prove Himself by miraculously curing his knee and thereby restoring his faith.

God, of course, had failed to take up the challenge. The idea was absurd, he knew, but no more absurd than the whole idea of apparitions and miracles. His knee was as painful as ever, especially standing like this. A couple of years ago, he reflected wryly, he would have offered up the pain for the souls in Purgatory. Now it just made him feel even more depressed. The idea of Purgatory and Hell now struck him as obscene, just like this place, full as it was of sickness, suffering and superstition.

For a while after that moment of 'revelation' in the barley field, when he realised that there was no God, he had felt euphoric, but the last few weeks had been ones of deepening depression as he came face to face with the implications. It meant that he could no longer believe in Catholicism and the whole structure of his faith had collapsed like a cathedral of cards, most of them jokers, from the preposterousness of papal infallibility to the stupidity of the Church's attitude to contraception, from the impossibility of a man rising from the dead to the quackery of a man having the power to forgive sin, from the pie in the sky of Heaven to the grotesquery of Hell, from the sorcery of transubstantiation to the medieval superstition of the Devil, from the pomposity of cardinals and bishops to the ostentation of the Vatican ...

It meant, of course, that he could not continue in the religious life or become a priest. He had to leave. But what was he going to do when he left? Every time he asked himself that question, he sank deeper into depression and despair. There was nothing else he had ever wanted to be except a priest. If there was no God, life was meaningless. It was all a meaningless, sick joke that started in slime, if Darwin was right, and finished in dust and ashes. Man – he, Francis Walsh – was no more significant than a monkey, reptile or insect. It was a devastating thought, but he could find no reason to think otherwise. So what reason was there to carry on living?

Suicide would be one way out. He felt like doing it and would have done, if he could have found an easy, clean, painless way, such as by swallowing a bottle of sleeping pills. But sleeping pills were not exactly standard issue in the seminary. He couldn't do it violently or bloodily. He had thought of slitting his wrists with a razor blade, but the very thought had made him feel faint. He had thought of hanging himself with the girdle of his habit – it was tailor-made for the job – but couldn't stand the thought of strangling to death. He wanted to die, but didn't have the guts to do it. He was a coward on top of everything else!

God, these were sick thoughts! But then, this was a sick place and he was sick in soul. He wished they would hurry up and finish the rosary – it grated more and more on his nerves. Besides, the pain in his knee was becoming unbearable with standing for so long. What on earth was he doing, he suddenly wondered, standing in front of a cave in the south of France with a crowd of gullible, superstitious people who believed a ghost had appeared here a hundred years ago? It was mad! Bernadette Soubirous had been mad! He was mad! They were all mad!

But then, he thought, Catholicism was mad. Christianity was mad. Christ himself – if he ever even existed – must have been mad, a megalomaniac whose ultimate madness was delusions of divinity. It all seemed so clear to him now. It was as if scales had fallen from his eyes. It was ironic that he should be in front of a cave, especially this one. He felt as if he had escaped from a cave, like the prisoner in Plato's allegory. Like the prisoner, though, he was blinded and terrified by the light, wanted to stagger back into the familiar, comfortable darkness, where he had been so happy for most of the first twenty years of his life …

'You're not losing your faith, are you, Fran?'

With a shock he realised that the rosary had finished and his mother was speaking to him. The words went like a dagger through his heart. She knew! But he couldn't bear to speak to her about it. He could hardly bear to speak to her about anything these days. His love affair with God, with the Church and with her was over. There was nothing she or anyone could do about it.

'I'm going for a walk – I'll see you back at the hotel,' he said, and walked away.

He walked back along the wall by the river Gave, wincing at the pain in his knee and wishing he had the guts to fling himself in – not that it looked deep enough to drown in, he observed wryly.

CHAPTER THIRTEEN

77 SLIPS BY BUSY SURGEONS
by
WILLIAM BRECKON: Medical Correspondent

British surgeons made major errors in 77 operations last year, according to a report by the Medical Defence Union.

In 44 cases they left swabs or instruments in the patient, and in 33 other cases they did the wrong operation.

It is the highest number of surgeons' slips ever reported in one year to the union, which represents doctors in legal cases and pays some of their damages.

Among the errors the surgeons made: Operating on a patient's left knee instead of the right and performing a hernia operation on a boy who needed only a cyst removed.

The figures are given in the annual report, which is to be published later this month.

One of the reasons for the errors is that the number of operations is going up every year and that many surgeons are grossly overworked.

Compensation claims are now running at above £3 million a year.

Dr. Philip Addison, union secretary, said yesterday: 'The errors are a very small proportion of the total number of operations.'

He said that some 1,500,000 operations had been carried out in British hospitals in the year.

He added: 'Nonetheless, we are concerned. A patient should never be subjected to a wrong operation.'

Fran read the newspaper article with grim fascination as he

sat in bed in hospital, waiting nervously for his operation and trying to kill time. He had a lot of time to kill – it was still only ten on the ward clock and he wasn't due to go to theatre till two. They had been woken up at six in the morning, had their pulses and temperatures taken and been brought basins of water to wash in. Then the other patients had been given a cup of tea, followed an hour later by breakfast – but those like him scheduled for surgery weren't allowed to eat or drink anything, not even water. NIL BY MOUTH, the sign above his bed said ominously.

He was used to being woken up early and to fasting in the seminary and felt too nervous to eat, anyway. However, he wasn't used to lying in bed till ten in the morning, but felt too nervous to enjoy that either. Nor was he used to being attended to by young girls in uniform, but found that embarrassing. He also found it depressing, because he could see that some of them were attractive, but felt no attraction to them, which only reinforced the shameful feeling that there was something wrong with him, that he might be – no, he didn't even want to think it.

The ward itself reminded him uncannily of the dorm at the junior seminary, with its rows of iron beds along each wall. When he had woken up this morning, for one ghastly moment he thought he was back there and was puzzled to see vases of flowers, bowls of fruit and greeting cards on the bedside lockers. These had definitely not been a feature of the dorm at the junior seminary! When he realised where he really was, he felt a wave of relief, but then remembered that this was the day of his operation and immediately sank into depression again.

The newspaper article didn't worry him too much – he didn't see how any mistake could be made in his case, since yesterday evening the leg to be operated on, the left one, had been shaven from hip to ankle, painted a radioactive orange with iodine and tied up in a white linen bag. 'Be careful, it's the leg of a holy man,' the hatchet-faced Irish Sister Docherty had said to the student nurse, as she showed her how to use the razor, making him cringe with both embarrassment and terror. If only she knew, he thought darkly – here he was, a seminarian and religious, and he didn't even believe in God!

In fact, he felt so depressed he hoped the doctors would make a mistake this afternoon and he wouldn't wake up from the anaesthetic. Judging from the article and stories his mother and sister, Molly – both nurses – told, it was far from impossible. His mother, when saying goodbye to him at the end of their Lourdes trip last week, had disconcerted him by making him promise to go to Confession before he went into hospital, in case anything did go wrong.

'We have to go to Confession every week,' he told her wearily.

'Promise me, anyway, Fran,' she insisted.

'Yes, of course,' he replied irritably, to his remorse. Of course, he hadn't gone. He hadn't been to Confession for months. He found the idea repugnant, especially as they went not in the privacy of a confession box to a priest who didn't know them, but to one on the seminary staff, kneeling on a prie-dieu beside him in his room.

Yesterday evening Molly, his sister, who worked on another ward, had popped in to see him. After telling him how good both surgeon and anaesthetist were, she asked him if he had been to Confession. 'We have to go every week,' he told her wearily, as he had told his mother, who he suspected had put her up to it.

'If you haven't,' Molly said sceptically, 'you should at least make an Act of Contrition before you go to theatre.'

'Why?' he asked, pretending not to understand.

'Because they're only human, you know, Fran, not gods.'

He couldn't help a wry smile. But what if they were right, he thought now – his mother, sister, fellow-seminarians and all the millions of others who did believe in God, Heaven and Hell? What if he didn't wake up from the anaesthetic? It was eleven on the ward clock now. By three o'clock he could be dead. At three o'clock he could be hearing those terrible words: 'Depart from Me, ye cursed, into the everlasting fire that was prepared for the Devil and his angels, where there shall be weeping and wailing and gnashing of teeth.'

The thought sent a tremor of terror through him. If they were right and there was a God, he would go straight to Hell! He would burn! He would burn just like that frog one of his classmates at the junior seminary had chucked on the bonfire one November the fifth. He had watched with horror as it squirmed, sizzled like a sausage in a frying pan, then shrivelled up into a cinder. But the frog had died almost instantly, whereas he would burn for ever! *For ever!* Maybe he ought to do what his sister suggested and make an Act of Contrition, just in case. What did he have to lose? Nothing, except his pride.

No, he resolved! He wouldn't! He wouldn't give in! This was the crunch, the first big test of his disbelief. He couldn't fail it. What would it be worth if he did? It would mean they had won, the Ghosters, the wizards, the sorcerers, the druids. This was his chance to prove to himself that he had beaten them, broken all those years of indoctrination and brainwashing. He was scared – scared of being put to sleep, scared of surgery and scared of dying, even though he wanted to die – but he wouldn't, he mustn't give in.

No, he didn't believe in God any more. He had vaguely hoped that God might have miraculously restored his faith at Lourdes, but ironically, if anything, Lourdes had confirmed him in his loss of faith. He shouldn't be scared of dying, since he didn't believe in God, Heaven or Hell any more. The more he thought about it, the more convinced he felt. How could the idea of Hell, of eternal punishment, be reconciled with a God of infinite love? It was sick! It was as sick as the idea of Heaven was silly!

He couldn't even believe that a God of infinite love could have created this world, with all its pain and suffering. Judging by the newspaper he was trying to read, the world was full of it: poverty, hunger, oppression, torture, bloodshed, riot, war, disaster, disease, death ... This ward was full of it! Fred, the man on his right, was going to have a kneecap amputated. On his left there was a little boy of six who was going to have his umpteenth operation to straighten his legs. How could a God of infinite love let that happen to an innocent child?

'Good morning, Dracula!'

It was Fred, speaking to a woman in a white coat who had come to take blood. She took some from Fred and then from him. But when she approached the little boy, he started to scream with terror and refused to let her do it.

'Come on, Peter,' one of the nurses coaxed him. 'There's

nothing to be scared of. It's only a little prick. It doesn't hurt. Look, Mister Walsh's had it. It didn't hurt, did it, Mister Walsh? There's nothing to be scared of, is there, Mister Walsh?'

'No, nothing,' he fibbed, though he was scared stiff, especially as there was worse to come. There was plenty to be scared of!

In the end, two nurses had to hold Peter down, screaming, while his blood was taken. Then one of them stayed with him while he whimpered for his mummy. It was heartbreaking. How could a loving God allow it?

'Shall I read him a story or something?' Fran suggested to the nurse.

'It's better not to excite him, thanks,' she said, to his relief, because he didn't really feel like it.

Some time later a medicine man in full regalia came into the ward and started flitting from bed to bed, talking to patients. However, this wasn't a doctor, it was a Catholic priest, as he could tell from his black clerical suit and white clerical collar. Aghast, he slipped down in the bed and pretended to be asleep, watching the priest through his eyelashes. The very last person he wanted to see was a priest!

On the other hand, he thought, maybe he should stop him and make his confession, just in case – it might be his very last chance to avoid eternal damnation before going under the anaesthetic. No, he told himself – he didn't believe in eternal damnation! As the priest approached his bed, he shut his eyes tight and waited for him to pass, his heart palpitating. When he opened them, he saw with relief that he had gone.

He shut his eyes again and tried to sleep, but it was difficult – he was too tense and the ward was like a railway station, with cleaners pushing beds around to mop the floor, nurses charging to and fro, doctors sweeping in and out and porters wheeling patients in and out on trolleys like parcels. Trussed up in the linen loincloth, operation gown and cap that he had been given to wear, with a plastic identity bracelet on his wrist, he felt like a parcel himself or worse, like a turkey waiting for the chop. He felt like jumping out of bed and running away, but couldn't – he had no clothes or money. He was trapped, a prisoner! It was like

149

the feeling he had in the seminary, of wanting to escape, but being unable to. If only he could fall asleep and never wake up! With a bit of luck maybe this afternoon he would.

He managed to doze off for a while, but was woken by screams. It was Peter, the little boy in the next bed. The nurses had come to give him his 'pre-med' injection. They had to hold him down again while they did so. Afterwards, he cried so much that one of them had to stay with him until the injection took effect. Then the porters came, lifted him onto a trolley and wheeled him away.

'Good luck,' Fran said, as he went, though by now he was probably too doped to hear.

'Your turn next,' the nurse said to him jauntily, as if it was a game.

He lay and waited with his eyes closed, too tense to sleep again, but trying not to think, wishing it was all over – not just the operation, but life, which had become so empty and meaningless. How wonderful it would be to go to sleep and never wake up! Blissful oblivion! And yet, he still couldn't help thinking, what if he was wrong and Hell did exist? As always, the thought sent a tremor of terror through him. It was one o'clock. Time was running out. If he was wrong, and he didn't wake up, he would go straight to Hell. For ever! For ever and ever! Was he really prepared to take that chance? Why not just say a quick Act of Contrition? No! He wouldn't! He didn't believe in it!

'Mister Walsh?'

He opened his eyes. There were two nurses by his bed. They had a small trolley with them. One of them pulled the curtain around his bed, while the other one picked up a syringe from the trolley. This was it.

'Time for your injection. Roll over on your side, please.'

He did so and they lifted his operation gown. He closed his eyes and braced himself.

'This will relax you,' the nurse said, jabbing the needle deep into his buttock, making him wince.

God, it felt like a blooming knitting needle! He grimaced and gripped his pillow while she squirted the solution in. It seemed to take ages. He was glad they couldn't see his face.

At last, to his relief, the needle was pulled out, though even that hurt. Then they opened the curtain and bustled off. He lay back limply and waited for the injection to take effect, trying to shut all thought out of his mind ...

By the time the porters came and bundled him onto a trolley, he wondered what he had been so worried about. As they wheeled him out of the ward, the other patients wished him good luck and he grinned back at them like a Cheshire cat – he was already lucky, because he was going for a ride, while they had to stay there.

It seemed to be a long ride, but he didn't mind – it was good fun, being wheeled along corridors and going in lifts. Where were they taking him, he wondered? It must be somewhere nice, because he felt so nice and there was a nice lady with him, in a blue dress, with a nice face, who looked just like his mum and kept leaning over him and smiling and asking him if he was all right, and he just smiled back dopily at her, because he was falling asleep, could hardly keep his eyes open, seemed to be floating on air ...

'It's the right leg, isn't it?'

He opened his eyes to find himself in a dazzlingly bright room, all white tiles and chrome, and crowded with Martians in green dresses jabbering away to each other. The nice lady had vanished. One of the Martians was leaning over him, staring at him with enormous glass eyes.

Slowly his brain cleared. He realised he must be in the anaesthetic room and the 'Martians' must be doctors. And it slowly filtered through to him what the doctor had said.

'No, no, it's the left leg,' he murmured drowsily, but the doctor had already walked away.

Oh, no, he thought, panic-stricken, remembering the newspaper article – they were going to operate on the wrong leg! He tried to raise himself up to call over to them, but was too sleepy and they were talking to each other with their backs to him. They were probably talking about what they were going to do to him. They were going to operate on the wrong leg! They might even cut it off by mistake! He might wake up with only one leg!

Maybe this was a sign from God, he thought, terrified.

151

Maybe God was giving him a last chance to repent. Otherwise, he might not only wake up with one leg, he might wake up in Hell! All he had to do was make a quick Act of Contrition. No, he told himself. I won't! I don't believe in God! I don't believe in Hell! No! No! No!

The doctors turned and came over to him. One of them lifted the white hospital blanket. He was wearing thick glasses.

'It's the left leg,' he murmured woozily.

'Yes, of course,' the doctor said, lifting the operation gown and removing the white linen bag from his left leg.

Another doctor pushed the sleeve of his operation gown up and took hold of his wrist with one hand. In the other hand, Fran noticed with a quiver of fear, he held a needle.

'I'm just going to give you an injection to put you to sleep,' he said. 'All you'll feel is a slight prick. Then you won't feel a thing. Try counting to ten if you like.'

Fran closed his eyes and winced as he felt the needle prick the back of his hand. This is it, he thought. You might be seconds away from eternity. You might be seconds away from eternal damnation. This is your very last chance. Say an Act of Contrition. Go on! Say it!

No, he murmured. No ... no .... no ... no ...

CHAPTER FOURTEEN

'Ah, awake at last!' the nurse smiled.

She was young and pretty, as slender as a daffodil, with blonde hair tied up beneath her nurse's cap and rose-petal skin. She was attractive, or at least she would be if he was normal, he supposed gloomily. He was grateful for the smile at least.

'How do you feel?' she asked, removing a tube from his mouth and lifting his wrist to take his pulse – her fingers, as light as butterflies, made his pulse beat faster. Maybe he was normal after all – not that as a seminarian he should be having such feelings …

'Thirsty,' he murmured groggily.

Her name, according to the badge on her bib, was Angela O'Grady and she was only a student nurse. From her name and her voice she was obviously Irish, as most of the nurses, including Sister Docherty, seemed to be. She poured a glass of water and held it to his lips.

'Thanks,' he gasped, taking a few sips from it. Never had water tasted so good! And never had a girl looked so pretty! Maybe he had died and gone to Heaven and she was an angel, as her name suggested, he reflected wistfully.

'We thought you were never going to wake up!' she laughed, a lovely Irish lilt in her voice.

He smiled weakly. Little did she know how he wished he hadn't, though he was glad he had woken up here and not in Hell.

Hell, though, came that night, when the pain of the wound in his knee made sleep impossible. He had been given a pain-killing injection of morphine, like all the others who had had surgery, but it brought relief for only an hour or so. For the rest of the night he lay sweating in agony. It felt as if a six-inch nail had been driven through his knee, making it throb unbearably. His whole leg, which had been encased in a metal splint and swathed with bandages, burned as if being barbecued over a bed of red-hot embers. The splint and bandages seemed to trap the heat in, making it even worse. On top of everything, it was a stiflingly hot August night, so that the ward felt like a furnace, even though all the windows were open, and because of his leg he couldn't move or even turn over.

It was no better for the others, judging by the chorus of moans and groans that went on most of the night, especially from Fred, who had had his kneecap amputated, and Bruno, a husky, athletic young Italian, who had had his toes operated on. Peter, the little boy who had had his legs straightened, cried so loud and long that eventually the nurses removed him to a room at the end of the ward, where he could still be heard bawling pitifully.

The pain was just about bearable during the day, because there were distractions, but the second night was even worse than the first. They wouldn't give any more morphine injections, on the absurd grounds that they might suddenly turn into junkies. Instead, they gave them two sleeping pills each, which were as useless as Smarties when you had had your kneecap amputated or a knife plunged into the middle of your knee. By midnight Bruno, who had been begging the nurses for an injection for hours, was crying like a bambino for his mama. After much palaver, the night nurse fetched Sister Docherty, who reluctantly gave him a jab and was then obliged to give one to anyone else who wanted.

'This had better not happen tomorrow night,' she decreed sternly as she left, lips pursed.

Excruciating as the pain was, he didn't take an injection. He was too proud to beg and knew that the relief didn't last long anyway, as was confirmed when the moaning and groaning resumed after an hour or so. By the third night, though, he couldn't stand the pain any longer. All day his knee had felt as if a blowlamp had been trained full blast on it by some fiendish torturer. His whole leg, encased as it was in splint and bandages, felt as if it was on fire, the bone from hip to ankle like a glowing, red-hot poker. It had also become maddeningly itchy, but the splint and bandaging, as well as trapping in the heat, made it impossible to scratch. On top of all that, it was another stiflingly hot night, so that the ward felt like a furnace again. There was no possibility of sleep and he couldn't stop thinking about both the past and the future, feeling crushed between them.

By two in the morning he could stand the pain no longer, neither the pain in his knee nor the pain in his heart. He covered his head with the sheet and broke down crying like a baby. He cried until there were no tears left, then lay there for the rest of the night, burning in his own private hell of pain, desolation and despair ...

'How do you feel?' Molly asked, giving him a peck on the cheek and sitting on the chair beside his bed.

'Still pretty sore,' Fran said, with effort summoning a smile, for his leg still felt like a red-hot poker.

'That's a good sign,' Molly commented.

He looked at her with a frown – she evidently had no idea how painful it was, just like the other nurses. They became insensitive, even callous, to pain, he supposed, being surrounded by it all the time. It was the same with death. Early that morning an old man who had been brought into the ward after a road accident had died and he had watched with horrified fascination as the nurses despatched the corpse swiftly and unceremoniously to the mortuary, while the new day dawned and the birds began their morning chorus, blithely oblivious of the old man's dismal end. A few minutes later the nurses were giggling together about something in a magazine, seemingly oblivious themselves, as maybe they needed to be. He wished he was like the old man, dead and out of it, the fever and the fit.

'It's the healing process,' Molly explained, 'the tissues knitting – '

'Please, spare me the details,' Fran cut her off.

'You look tired. Didn't you sleep again?' she asked.

'Not very well,' he fibbed – he hadn't slept at all.

'Did you take some pills?' she asked.

'Yes, but they're useless,' he said, testily. 'They should give you a proper painkiller of some sort.' He immediately regretted saying it, because it sounded as if he was both complaining and, indirectly, criticising her, too.

'They can't, Fran,' she said.

'I know, I know,' he agreed wearily, in no frame of mind to argue with her.

He closed his eyes, wincing as the blowlamp on his knee suddenly seemed to switch back to full blast. He was half-afraid he might break down crying, as he had done last night, to his shame, crying as much because of the wound in his heart as that in his knee, a wound he knew unlike that in his knee would never heal, the gaping wound of loss, loss of all that he had ever believed in.

'Is there anything else the matter, Fran?' Molly asked.

'Of course not,' he said, irritably. 'Sorry. It's a bit depressing in here, I'm afraid.'

Did she suspect something, he wondered? Had his mother been talking to her? Maybe he should tell her – this would be as good a moment as any.

'Never mind,' she said. 'You'll be out in ten days or so and you'll be able to go back.'

'I'm not sure I want to go back,' he said, seizing his cue.

'What do you mean?' It was her turn to frown.

'I've been thinking – I'm not sure I would make such a good priest.' What an understatement, he thought!

'Don't talk nonsense, Fran,' she replied, dismissively. 'I think you'll make a very good priest.'

The words burned with bitter irony in his brain. He was foiled. He didn't have the courage to tell her the full truth, that he had lost his faith, that he might be sexually abnormal. He didn't know how to tell her. If she couldn't understand the pain in his knee, how could she understand the pain in his soul, kind and caring as she was? She was trying, but she couldn't communicate with him. How could she? For the last nine years their lives had been totally separate. She was his sister, but they were like strangers!

'Well, I'd better go,' she said, standing up.

'OK. Thanks for coming.'

'I'll try to pop in again this evening when I come off,' she said. 'Don't worry, you're feeling low because you've had an operation, but you'll feel better in a few days.'

He nodded and gave her a strained smile. She bent and gave him a peck on the cheek.

'Hey! What's this? Preferential treatment?'

'Do we all get one of those?'

'Do we need a prescription?'

'Go on! Give us one!'

'I'll give you something else in a place you won't like, if you don't shut up and behave yourselves,' Molly retorted to the quips of the other patients, provoking guffaws of laughter as she left.

Amused, despite his pain, Fran slipped down in the bed, closed his eyes and tried to sleep. He felt lonely after his sister had gone, frustrating as her visit had been. Some of the patients, ironically, thought she was his girlfriend. The idea was doubly ironic, since he felt no attraction to any of the nurses – except perhaps Nurse O'Grady – or, indeed, girls in general. But that wasn't surprising, he reflected bitterly – after all, he had been brainwashed against them for nine years.

The thought that he might be homosexual lurked at the back of his mind like a monster, a monster he didn't dare to confront. It made the prospect of leaving the seminary even more daunting, because if he did, he knew he would have to confront it. As if it wasn't daunting enough already, he thought morosely: like parachuting out of a plane at night over alien territory, without maps or directions, not knowing the local language or customs, and now with a gammy leg, too.

If only he could sleep, he thought, though sleep brought bad dreams, dreams about Mark, about Father Director, about his mother. If only he could fall asleep and never wake up! If only he had never woken up from the anaesthetic! If only the pain in his knee would subside! If only they would give them something effective to help them sleep at night! The sleeping pills they gave out were useless, as he had told his sister.

Suddenly, though, an idea struck him – he'd continue to accept them, but not take them and save them up. It would be tricky, because the nurses usually waited and watched until you had put them in your mouth and swallowed them, but he'd get round that. He'd get round that if it killed him.

'Wakey, wakey!'

He opened his eyes and turned towards Fred in the bed next to his.

'Here comes Torquemada,' said Fred, with a grin. He turned to look the other way and saw the white-coated, female physiotherapist entering the ward. He smiled wryly at the nickname he had coined for her himself, but groaned inwardly and braced himself for the agonizing torture of trying to raise his leg a couple of inches off the bed.

Over the next few days the pain in his knee gradually subsided as the wound healed and he was able to sleep at night, though sleep brought back bad dreams, as he had feared. The wound in his heart did not heal – if anything it gaped wider and wider. He continued to collect the sleeping pills: he had decided he would take them the night before he was due to be discharged, which was also the night before his twenty-first birthday.

The thought of committing suicide, even with sleeping pills, terrified him and he wasn't sure if he would have the nerve to go through with it. But he had no choice – he couldn't stay in the seminary and become a priest, after all that had happened and having lost his faith. On the other hand, he didn't have the courage to leave, couldn't face the thought of life without faith, without being a priest. Nor could he face the thought that he might be sexually abnormal in any way.

There was only one faint glimmer of light in the darkness and that was Nurse O'Grady. To his surprise, she seemed to like chatting to him. At first he had felt embarrassed, as always with women, but gradually he found that he was able to relax and actually enjoyed chatting to her, even started to like her. He hardly dared think it, but maybe it meant that he wasn't abnormal after all.

'What is it you do?' she had asked him early on.

'I'm – er – a student,' he said evasively.

'And what do you study?' she asked.

He had been hoping she wouldn't ask that. He was trapped. If he answered truthfully, it would give the game away that he was a seminarian and she wouldn't be interested in him any more.

He thought of telling a fib and saying simply that he was a student of philosophy – which was half-true – but decided there was no point, as she was bound to find out the truth sooner or later and he was probably only fooling himself in thinking she liked him anyway.

'Theology,' he admitted, sheepishly.

'Theology?' she said, surprised. 'Are you a clerical student?'

'Yes,' he confessed, as if to a crime, amused by the quaint term.

'Oh,' she said.

'Oh, what?' he asked.

'So you're the holy man, then?'

He cringed inwardly – that was what Sister Docherty called him – though there was a note of irony in her voice.

'Not at all,' he objected and thought he might as well tell her the truth now. 'In fact – '

'I've a brother who was a priest, but he quit,' she interrupted.

'Oh, why?' he asked, fascinated despite himself.

'He met a girl. He's married now, with three kids,' she laughed.

'Was he a secular?' he asked.

'He was with the Passionate Fathers. Oh, God,' she laughed. 'That sounds funny. I'm sorry.'

'It's all right,' he smiled, amused himself.

'Which order are you with?' she asked.

'The Holy Ghost Fathers,' he said, blushing – the very name was embarrassing! 'We call them the 'Ghosters'.'

'I never heard of them,' she said.

I'm not surprised, he thought, but resisted saying it. 'What do they do?' she asked.

'They work on the missions in Africa mostly,' he said.

'So you're going to be a missionary?'

'Well, actually – '

But before he could finish, the ward sister, Sister Docherty, swept in and directed a dagger-like glance at Nurse O'Grady.

'Sure, that's grand,' she said and bustled off, to his dismay.

Oh, well, that's that, he thought, lying back on his pillow and closing his eyes. She wouldn't be interested in him any more now. It was probably just as well. He was only fooling himself.

She wasn't really interested in him at all. She was just being kind. She was a nurse. It was her job to be kind.

She was nice though. It would be nice to kiss her. Or be kissed by her. He had never thought that about a girl before. He would never know, he supposed. The thought sent a stab of pain through his heart, a pain from which there was no escape, except to sleep, preferably for ever ...

'So when will you be ordained?' Nurse O'Grady asked him later.

The question embarrassed him. He decided to tell her the truth, though it pained him to admit it. 'I don't think I ever will be,' he said.

'What do you mean?' she asked.

'I've decided I don't want to be a priest after all.'

'Why ever not?' she asked.

This was even more painful. He hesitated again.

'I don't believe in God,' he confessed.

'What do you mean, you don't believe in God?' she asked, shocked.

'I don't believe in God,' he shrugged. 'Do you?'

'Of course I do,' she said. 'Why don't you?'

'Well, for one thing, because there's so much suffering in the world. In this very ward, for example.' He didn't want to mention his own suffering, not even to her.

'Sure, that's not God's fault, is it?'

'Whose fault is it, then?'

'Suffering is the result of sin, isn't it?'

'Sometimes, maybe,' he conceded, 'but not always. Not in babies and children, surely? What did Peter there do to deserve that, for example?'

'I don't know. Nothing, I suppose, the poor little divil.'

'Anyway, the point is, I think that a God of love wouldn't allow so much suffering – or any suffering at all, for that matter.'

'Maybe He has His reasons, which we don't know.'

This was a cliché of Catholic theology that irritated him, though he was careful not to show it. 'Such as?' he asked.

'That's just it – we don't know.'

'I can't accept that. If I'm going to be punished, I want to know why at least. I want to know the reason. Besides, God is supposed to be like a father. I wouldn't allow my children to suffer for any reason, if I could prevent it. Would you?'

'No,' she agreed. 'But you have to allow your children their freedom eventually and then they will suffer, won't they? That's what God does with us, isn't it?'

It was a good point and he couldn't think of a good answer. 'Maybe,' he conceded.

'Anyhow,' she said, 'it's not all suffering, is it? There are lots of good things in the world, too, aren't there?'

'I suppose so,' he agreed, trying to sound positive, though he didn't feel it.

'You're just feeling low because you've had an operation,' she said cheerfully, just like his sister – it must be in the training manual, he thought. 'You'll feel better in a few days, when you're up and about again.'

He was trying to think of something positive to reply when Sister Docherty came into the ward and homed straight in on them.

'Nurse O'Grady,' she said, in her vinegary voice, 'there are other patients in this ward.'

He smiled wanly at Nurse O'Grady as she hurried away. If only it was as simple as she had said, he thought, lying back on the pillows and closing his eyes. She was lovely, but she didn't really understand – how could she? Her life had been so different, so normal, growing up on a farm in Ireland with her parents and six brothers and sisters, whereas his had been so abnormal. How he envied her her normality!

She seemed to like him though, and he found himself starting to like her. He enjoyed talking to her. Maybe he was normal after all! He watched her surreptitiously as she attended to other patients, feeling jealous. Was he falling in love with her? He had been reading 'A Farewell to Arms' by Ernest Hemingway. Maybe she would be his Catherine Barkley. He'd leave the seminary and run away with her!

No, it was stupid to even start thinking like that, he told himself. He was fooling himself. She didn't like him in that way

– she was just naturally friendly and kind. Why should she? Apart from being a 'clerical student', as she quaintly put it, he was an emotional and physical wreck. If he wasn't a seminarian and wasn't in hospital, she wouldn't be interested in talking to him at all.

Anyway, the thought suddenly struck him, even if he were to leave the seminary and run away with her, people would think he had left because of her. His mother, especially, would hold it against him – and against her. No, it was impossible, ridiculous ...

He shut his eyes and tried to shut her out of his mind, too. However, her image remained hovering there, lovely and luminous, like a new moon casting its light, no matter how pale, over the dark and desolate planet of his soul, bringing to his tormented spirit for the first time in months a tiny glow of solace and hope.

He wanted to tell her how he felt about her, but was far too shy and wasn't sure about his feelings, anyway. Then he had an idea – he'd write a poem about her. It would help him to clarify his feelings. He hadn't felt like writing anything for a long time. The last poem he had written had been for Mark. So this must mean something! He picked up pen and paper from the bedside locker, sat up and started.

'What are you writing?' she asked, catching him at it.

'A poem,' he said, hiding it.

'So you're a poet as well, are you?' she asked, impressed.

'I wouldn't call myself that,' he said, with a self-deprecating laugh, 'but I do like writing.'

'That's very good,' she said.

'Is it? Why?' he asked.

'We don't get many poets in here,' she said.

'No, I suppose not,' he smiled.

'Can I read it?' she asked.

'It's not finished yet,' he said.

'Go on,' she coaxed.

'I'll let you read it when it's finished,' he said. 'In fact,' he screwed up the courage to add, 'it's about you, anyway.'

'Go away with you!' she laughed, blushing, but he could see she was pleased.

'It is,' he said, blushing himself, surprised at his own boldness.

'Why would you be writing a poem about me?'

'To tell you what I feel about you.'

'What's that?'

'I'm not sure. It's all in the poem – that's why I'm writing it.'

'Sure, you shouldn't be writing poems to me.'

'Why not?'

'You're going to be a priest.'

'I told you, I'm not,' he said, sounding annoyed despite himself. 'I'm going to leave.'

'Not because of me, I hope.'

'Partly.' He could hardly believe he was saying this to a girl.

'You mustn't.'

'Mustn't what?'

'You mustn't leave'

'Why not?'

'You'll make a good priest one day, I'm sure.'

'But I told you – I don't believe in God any more. I can't be a priest if I don't believe in God, can I?' He couldn't help sounding slightly exasperated.

'You really don't believe in God?'

'No.' It still pained him to admit it.

'What do you believe in, then?'

'Nothing.'

'That's a terrible thing to say.'

'It's true.'

'It can't be – you must believe in something.'

'You're right, it's not really true. I do believe in something.'

'What's that?'

'Love.' Disturbingly, Mark's image flashed through his mind – it wasn't the one he wanted to see.

'What kind of love?'

'All kinds of love,' he said. 'The kind of love a man feels for a woman, for example.' Again he could hardly believe he was saying this to a girl, but somehow it was easy with her. Was it just because she was a nurse? Was it because he had been

163

reading 'A Farewell to Arms'?

'Love is what makes life worth living,' he added for good measure.

'That's a lovely thought,' she said.

'Do you agree, then?' he asked.

'I'd better go,' she said.

'Why?' he asked, disappointed. He wanted to continue the conversation, surreal as it seemed to him, almost as if it was somebody else saying the words. Maybe it was the anaesthetic and the drugs!

'Sister Docherty'll be here any minute. She's already ticked me off for talking to you.'

'Has she?' Damn her, he thought.

'Yes, the old dragon,' she said.

'Speak of the devil,' he said, glimpsing Sister Docherty's hatchet face entering the ward.

'Bye. I'm going off duty now,' she said.

'Oh,' he said, disappointed again. 'See you tomorrow.'

'It's my day off,' she said.

'Oh,' he said, even more disappointed.

'If you like, I'll pop in to see you though.'

'Will you?'

'On one condition.'

'What's that?'

'That you give me the poem.'

'Do you really want it?'

'I suppose I might as well have it, if it's about me,' she laughed.

'All right, it's a deal,' he agreed.

He watched her leave, then put pen to paper again. As he wrote, he suddenly realised that not only could he feel no pain in his knee, even the pain in his heart seemed to have eased and it was beating with a new, though faint, excitement at the thought of seeing her again ...

He waited expectantly all day, but she didn't come. He felt betrayed and angry, but more angry with himself than her. He told himself he had been a fool to even start thinking she liked him or there could be anything between them. He crumpled up the poem and dropped it in the rubbish bag hanging on his bedside locker.

By the end of visiting time he felt utterly depressed. No one had come to visit him – not that he wanted anyone except Nurse O'Grady, not even his sister, certainly not anyone from the seminary. He was truly alone. He felt like crying, but couldn't – it was as if he had no tears left. Anyway, it was too late for tears – there was only one way out.

Before lights out, he wrote a last letter to his parents, in which he told them he was doing what he was doing because he had lost his vocation and could not face life outside. He did not tell them he had lost his faith or thought he might be homosexual, because he knew that would devastate them totally, especially his mother, though he knew she suspected the former. He sealed the letter, put it in an envelope and placed it on the bedside locker, among the birthday and get-well cards.

When the nurses came round with the night-time medications, he took two sleeping pills as usual and put them in his mouth, but didn't swallow them, taking them out after they had passed by. He now had twenty altogether – that should be enough to put him to sleep for ever, he thought, ineffective as they were.

Half an hour before midnight, when the ward had settled down for the night, he took them out, slipped them into his mouth a few at a time and washed them down with water. Then he lay back, closed his eyes and waited, listening to the last beats of his heart.

This was it, he thought. He had done it. He was going to go to sleep and never wake up. All his problems were over! Tomorrow he would be twenty-one, but he would never see it. A lump came to his throat: it was sad to die so young, but he couldn't carry on. Life without faith was impossible. Anyway, he deserved to die. He was a failure. He was a sinner. He was a traitor. He was sick!

He started to feel drowsy.

How had it come to this, he wondered? He had been so happy as a child, until he went to the junior seminary. That was when the trouble had started, with Father Director. Father Director was to blame. If it hadn't been for Father Director, he would never have fallen in love with Mark. Or maybe he would – it was such an abnormal place. Mark's face appeared before him and his heart swelled with a mixture of pleasure and pain. Maybe he should have written Mark a letter? No. He still loved Mark, but he knew it was an impossible love. That was another reason why it was better to die – he was abnormal.

He felt sleepy now.

Why had God allowed this to happen to him? Because there was no God! There couldn't be a God. God could not have allowed this to happen to him. All he had ever wanted in his life was to love and serve God as a priest. That was all he had ever lived for. Without that, there was nothing to live for. Without God, life had no purpose or meaning. Human beings were no more important than insects. It was a devastating thought. It was a thought he couldn't live with. It was another reason why it was better to die.

He felt very sleepy now.

What if he was wrong though, he suddenly thought? What if there was a God, after all? In a few minutes he could be in Hell! This was his very last chance. Maybe he was wrong. Maybe he ought to say a quick Act of Contrition, before it was too late. No, he thought, no! If he did, it would make his death pointless. And they would have won, the men in black, the wizards, the druids, the sorcerers, the Ghosters. No, he thought, no! I won't. I won't. I won't. No. No. No. No. No. No ... No ...No ...

CHAPTER FIFTEEN

'Wakey, wakey, Mister Walsh!'

Someone was shaking his shoulder. He opened his eyes with difficulty, as if the eyelids had been glued together. It was Nurse O'Grady, looking lovelier than ever.

'About time, too!' she exclaimed, sticking a thermometer in his mouth and holding his wrist to take his pulse.

God, was he glad to see her! His pulse was racing. She was so lovely! Why hadn't she come to see him yesterday though?

'I'm sorry I didn't come to see you yesterday,' she whispered, as if reading his mind. 'I came to the ward, but Sister Docherty was on duty, so I didn't dare to come in. You know she doesn't like me talking to you, the old dragon.'

Damn Sister Docherty, he thought, nodding. It was like having his mother around! But at least Nurse O'Grady was here now and he was still alive! The pills hadn't worked, thank goodness, and no one seemed to have realised what he had done. In fact, he had had his first decent night's sleep since coming into hospital. He was glad to be alive. He felt much better, especially seeing Nurse O'Grady.

'So, twenty-one today,' she said, glancing at the cards on his locker.

Fran nodded again, the thermometer still in his mouth.

'Congratulations,' she said. 'I thought you'd never wake up to see it.'

He smiled weakly, glad he couldn't speak because of the thermometer – he wouldn't have known what to say. He was happy just to hear her voice with its soft Irish lilt, which filled his ears like the music of a flute. What would it be like to kiss her, he wondered, his pulse racing even faster ...

'And you're leaving us today, too, are you?' she asked, dropping his wrist and taking the thermometer out of his mouth.

'Mm,' he murmured, depressed by the thought.

'You don't sound very happy about it.'

'I'm not,' he shrugged.

'Sure, you'll feel better once you're back in your own environment.'

'I don't think so,' he said, with a wan smile.

'Sure you will. Why wouldn't you?'

'You know why.'

'Well, it's bound to be better than here.'

'I'm not so sure. Not with you around.'

'Ah, don't be coddin' me,' she blushed.

'I'm not. I'll miss you.' He blushed too. He wondered if he should ask her if she still wanted the poem, but hesitated, hoping she would ask him about it. He was sorry he had crumpled it up, but he could easily rewrite it – if she wanted it.

Unfortunately, before either of them could speak again, Sister Docherty swept in and darted a dagger-like glance at them.

'That's grand,' Nurse O'Grady said and bustled away to the next patient.

He watched her jealously doing the same for other patients, then shut his eyes again and lay back on the pillows. She hadn't said anything about the poem. She must have forgotten about it. She obviously wasn't interested. His euphoria evaporated.

Then he remembered why he had taken the pills – he had lost his faith and didn't believe in God any more, yet had to return to the seminary, only to leave. The thought plunged him even deeper into depression. On top of that, he was making a fool of himself by looking at Nurse O'Grady through romantic eyes – she wasn't interested in him, especially knowing he was a 'clerical student' as she called it. He wouldn't know what to say to her or any girl, anyway. He was sorry the pills hadn't worked after all.

The only escape was to try to sleep again, though sleep brought bad dreams. He pulled the white sheet up over his face and dozed off ...

'Ole!'

He was at a bullfight, but instead of a bull, it was Mark and himself in the arena, naked, and instead of picadors on the horses, it was priests in their black habits, Ghosters. They were chasing them round and round, jabbing at them with their lances, in front of hundreds of jeering, cheering spectators: the Pope, cardinals, bishops, priests, his fellow-seminarians, his relations, even his mother and father. One of the picador-priests stuck his lance in Mark and paraded gloatingly round with his dead, naked body on the point. Then one of them came charging towards him ...

'No!' he screamed.

'Wake up, sleepyhead!'

Someone was shaking his shoulder. He opened his eyes, terrified. To his relief, it was Nurse O'Grady. 'Were you dreaming?' she asked.

He nodded sheepishly.

'It must've been frightening,' she said. 'You were screaming the ward down!'

'I'm sorry,' he said, glancing round embarrassed at his fellow-patients, but none of them seemed to have noticed.

'I hope it wasn't about me,' she joked.

If only it had been, he thought, smiling, and joked back: 'No, it was about Sister Docherty.'

'Oh, God, don't!' she said, stifling a laugh.

Why had he dreamt about a bullfight, he wondered? It must have been because he had gone to one with his mother in San Sebastian, where they had spent a week before going to Lourdes. He had gone out of curiosity, curiosity aroused by reading Hemingway. The spectacle had sickened him, though he still liked Hemingway, especially 'A Farewell to Arms'.

'Do you want to sit up?' his own Catherine Barkeley asked.

He tried to pull himself up into a sitting position, but couldn't – he felt weak and his left leg was like a lead weight tied to his body. Nurse O'Grady put her arms under his shoulders and hauled him up. 'There you are,' she said, fixing his pillows.

'Thanks,' he gasped, hoping she couldn't see that he was blushing and his heart was beating faster, while his mind whirled with delight at the thought of what it would be like to feel her arms around him in an embrace.

'So, are you going to give me the poem or what?' she asked.

'Do you still want it?'

'Of course I do. Why wouldn't I?'

'I don't know. It's just that I thought – since you didn't come in yesterday ...'

'You know why, don't you?'

'Yes, I know.'

'I did want to'

'I know.'

'Are you going to give it to me or not then?'

'Actually, I want to write it out again.'

'Oh.' She sounded disappointed.

'Could you pass me the paper and pen, please?'

'Here you are,' she said, passing them to him.

'Thanks,' he said, taking them and pausing, pen in hand. 'You'll have to go, I'm afraid.'

'Will you give it to me later?'

'Yes.'

'Before you leave hospital, I mean?'

'Of course.'

'Promise?'

'Promise.'

'I'll leave you to it then.'

She hurried off, while he started writing. He watched her bustling about the ward as he wrote. The title was 'Resurrection'. It was about how she had rescued him from the 'tomb' of his despair, like the angel who had rolled back the rock from the tomb of Christ. It was about how she had resuscitated him and brought him back to life. It was about how she had given him new hope and belief – belief that he was normal, that life was worth living, that love was worth living for. It was about love and how he loved her and wanted to love her for ever ...

'So, this is it,' Nurse O'Grady chirped.

Fran was sitting in the chair by his hospital bed, dressed in the black clerical suit he had come to hate, his left leg stretched out stiffly, a walking stick to hand. He was waiting for Mike Cummings to pick him up and take him back to the seminary.

This was the day he had dreaded for so long. He felt depressed, especially since Nurse O'Grady sounded so cheerful. Or was she just trying to cheer him up?

While waiting, he had dozed off and dreamt about her. They were walking in a park, holding hands, just like a normal, happy courting couple. Then they stopped, put their arms around each other and kissed, bodies pressed close together. His body seemed to dissolve with pleasure, his soul to fill with ecstasy and fly free. He felt as if he had died and was floating up to Heaven with her in his arms ...

But he was brought back down to earth in the ward by a sudden noise and realised with an inward groan of despair that it was only a dream, hadn't really happened and probably never would.

'Did you read the poem?' he asked her.

'I did – it's lovely, thank you,' she said, blushing. 'No one has ever written anything like that about me before.'

'I mean it.'

'I know you do, but – '

'But what?'

'It's impossible.'

'What's impossible?'

'You know – to see each other.'

'Why?' he asked, dismayed.

'You're going back to the seminary.'

'It won't be impossible when I leave.'

'Yes, but ...'

'But what?'

'I don't know. I don't want you to leave because of me.'

'I'm not leaving just because of you, I told you.'

'You might feel differently when you go back. You might change your mind. You might forget me.'

'I won't forget you. I'll never forget you, whatever happens. And I won't change my mind. I'm going to leave. I have to leave. I can't carry on any longer.'

'I'm sorry,' she said, sadly.

'Why?' There was a lump in his throat.

'It must be so difficult for you, after all those years.'

'It won't be so difficult if I can look forward to seeing you.

171

Can I?'

She didn't say anything.

'Don't you want to see me?' he asked, driven to audacity by a sense of desperation.

'Yes,' she said. 'Yes, I'd like to, very much. But when? When are you going to leave?'

'As soon as my leg's better – in a few weeks. But maybe I could see you before then. I have to come to the hospital twice a week for physio. Maybe I could come and visit you?'

'How? Sister Docherty's already got her knife in me for talking to you.'

'What if you're off duty? Couldn't I come and see you in the Nurses' Home?'

'Visitors are not allowed, officially.'

'Oh.' It seemed as if she didn't really want to see him. He was wasting his time. He was fooling himself.

'It's room number twenty-six.'

'I can come?'

'Yes, but you have to be careful not to let anyone see you.'

'I will be. Thanks.' He saw the porcine figure of Mike Cummings waddle into the ward corridor, in clerical suit and collar. His heart sank. 'Here he is,' he said, gloomily.

'I'd better go. I'll see you. Bye. Good luck.'

'I'll see you. Bye. And thanks for everything.'

She smiled and was gone. A moment later Mike Cummings was standing in her place. 'And who was that, might I be so bold as to ask?' he demanded pompously, not even saying hello.

'Just one of the nurses,' Fran said.

'I see. One of the prettier ones, eh? Ho ho ho!' He gave a false, Father Christmas laugh.

'I suppose so,' he blushed, annoyed with himself and with Mike.

'Well, are you ready? Got everything? Can you walk? Or do I need to carry you? Ho ho ho!' He chuckled at his own joke again.

'I think I can manage,' Fran said, picking up his walking stick and standing up.

'Let's go, then,' Mike said, picking up the small suitcase with his things in it. 'I suppose you'll be glad to get out of this place.'

'Yes,' Fran said, without conviction.

'Not exactly a holiday camp, is it? Ho ho ho!' He chuckled yet again at his own joke.

'No, not exactly,' Fran mumbled, limping after Mike. And neither is the place I'm going back to, he thought, morosely. More like a concentration camp. I have to get out!

He exchanged goodbyes with a few of the patients. At Peter's bed he stopped, took a packet of sweets out of his pocket and gave it to him. He stopped again to say goodbye to the nurses in the office at the end of the ward. Unfortunately, only Sister Docherty was there.

'Goodbye, Mister Walsh,' she said. 'I hope you'll invite me to your ordination.'

'Yes, of course,' he said, cringing inside.

'Goodbye, Father,' she said to Mike Cummings. 'Take care of him, won't you?'

'Oh, yes, we shall, Sister, don't worry,' Mike said, pompous as ever. 'We'll put him straight into intensive care. Ho ho ho!' Sister Docherty rewarded Mike's joke with a sour smile and Fran limped out of the office with him.

'Oh, Father, could I have a word with you in private?' she called Mike back.

Mike went back and closed the door, to Fran's annoyance. He hovered outside, trying to overhear what she was saying to him, but couldn't. Was it about his leg, he wondered, or about Nurse O'Grady? Surely she wouldn't be that officious and interfering?

'Let's go,' Mike said tersely, coming out. His mood seemed to have changed from pompous jollity to self-importantly serious.

He tried to tell from Mike's expression what Sister Docherty had said to him, but couldn't. He was tempted to ask him, but knew it would be pointless. Anyway, he didn't want to give him the satisfaction of not telling him or fobbing him off with some pompous platitude.

He limped along the corridor after him, feeling as if he was being led back to prison, as in a way he was. The only thing that kept him going was the thought of seeing Nurse O'Grady again and the thought that maybe, just maybe, the dream he had had would one day come true ...

CHAPTER SIXTEEN

'Hello,' Angela whispered, letting him into her room and shutting the door quickly. 'Have a seat. Would you like to sit on the bed?'

'This is all right, thanks,' he said, far too shy to sit on the bed and lowering himself into the easy-chair instead, keeping his left leg stretched out stiffly and propping his walking-stick against the arm.

It was a relief to sit down. His leg was aching fiercely after limping from the car park to the nurses' home and upstairs to her room. Mike Cummings had dropped him off at the hospital for his physiotherapy appointment and gone off to do some errands in town. He had to meet him back in the car park in an hour.

'Would you like a cup of tea?' she asked.

'Yes, thanks,' he said.

He felt awkward. He had never been in a girl's room before. While she made the tea he glanced around. It was like his own room in the seminary, but much more homely, with posters and photos on the walls, curtains on the window and a rug on the floor, as well as the electric kettle, which was now boiling. There were books on the bookshelves, but medical, he noticed, not philosophy and theology. On the desk was a cassette-player, a bowl of fruit and a women's magazine. On the shelf above the washbasin, where she was making the tea, was an array of toiletries and cosmetics.

None of those things, he observed wryly, were to be found in his own room. However, he noticed one similarity – on the wall above her bed hung a crucifix. He glanced away from it quickly – he now found crucifixes repellent, symptomatic of the more lurid and sadistic side of Catholicism. How incongruous, he thought with a wince, to have the image of a man being barbarically executed hanging over your bed – especially for a nurse!

'Here you are,' she said, handing him a mug of tea and a plate of biscuits.

'Thanks,' he said, taking them.

'Would you like some music?' she asked.

'All right,' he shrugged.

'What would you like?'

'I don't know – anything.'

'Do you like the Beatles?'

'What a funny name!' he exclaimed. 'What are they?'

'A pop group. Haven't you heard of them?'

'We're not allowed to listen to pop music.'

'I'm sorry – I forgot.'

'It's all right – put them on if you like.'

She put a cassette on and sat on the bed with her back against the wall and her legs tucked under her. She was wearing jeans and a blouse, so that he could see parts of her he had never seen before, such as her throat and the top of her chest, both as white as porcelain. He had never seen her out of her nurse's uniform before. Also, her blonde hair cascaded down over her shoulders, instead of being bunched up beneath her nurse's cap. He dared no more than glance at her, because she looked even prettier and more feminine than ever and it made his heart beat faster.

'Do you like them?' she asked.

'Yes, they sound good, despite the name,' he said.

'I love them.'

He nodded and smiled, not knowing what to say.

'How's the leg?' she asked.

'A bit better, but I get terrible cramps.'

'You poor thing.'

Again, he didn't know what to say, not being used to such expressions of sympathy, especially from a pretty girl.

'Have you been to physiotherapy?' she asked.

'Yes, I went last time.'

'Have they given you exercises to do?'

'Yes.'

'And do you do them?'

'Oh, yes, but they don't stop the cramps.'

'It'll get better in time.'

'I suppose so.' There was another uncomfortable pause.

'How did you get here?' she asked.

'One of the student priests brought me – Mike Cummings. The one who picked me up when I left hospital. Did you see him?'

'Yes. Does he know you're here?'

'I hope not – he thinks I'm at physiotherapy.'

'You haven't told him about visiting me?'

'No, I haven't told anyone, especially him – he'd go straight to the Superior. Not that it'd matter too much.'

'What do you mean?'

'I'm going to leave, anyway. But I don't want them to have an excuse to throw me out.'

'Are you sure you still want to leave?'

'I don't want to, but I have to.'

'You don't want to?'

'Well, I do now,' he said, blushing. Now that I've met you, he wanted to say, but didn't dare.

'I hope you're doing the right thing.'

'Oh, I know it's the right thing – it's just that it's so difficult to actually do it, after nine years.'

'How long have you wanted to be a priest?'

'As long as I can remember. Since I was about four or five years old.'

'I'm sorry.'

Again, he didn't know what to say.

'So how old were you when you left home?'

'Twelve.'

'Sure that's terrible.'

'Why do you say that?' He could guess, but he wanted to hear her say it.

'It's terrible to take a child away from his home and family at such an early age.'

'Yes, I agree.'

'You couldn't have had any idea what you were letting yourself in for.'

'That's right. It shouldn't be allowed. It's criminal.'

'What was it like?'

'The junior seminary?' He wasn't sure if he was able to talk about it, even to her.

'Yes, what was it actually like?'

'It's strange – it didn't seem too bad at the time, but looking back it was pretty grim, I suppose.'

'Tell me. I'm curious. My brother would never talk about it.'

'Well, to start with, you were cut off from your family, as you said. There were no women of course, not even nuns, so it was a totally male environment, which I think now is pretty unhealthy – in fact, you were taught to fear women. You had to pray or study nearly all day. Or do manual labour. You were only allowed out once a week, to go for a walk, all together, in a 'crocodile', as we called it. You had to keep silence nearly all the time. There were rules about almost everything and if you broke one you were liable to get the strap. And the food was awful, except for the priests – they ate like lords. Does that give you an idea?'

'It sounds awful!'

'It was. It's not much better at the senior seminary.'

'Why did you stick it?'

'I thought I wanted to be a priest.' He gave a hollow laugh.

'Surely it doesn't have to be like that though?'

'Of course not. Most of it is unnecessary – stupid. They're still living in the nineteenth century. In the Dark Ages.'

'It's even worse than I imagined.'

'I think the worst thing about it is that there is no love, not in the normal, human sense of the word. They deliberately try to kill that feeling.'

'How do you mean?'

'Well, I mean, you're cut off from your family, as I said. You aren't allowed to have friends, either outside or even among each other. And of course, you aren't allowed to have a girlfriend or anything like that. It's all just – just so *abnormal*. That's what I hate about it now – the *abnormality* of it all.'

He stopped, reminded by the word 'abnormal' of what had happened with the Director – he didn't feel able to tell her about that. He hadn't expected to be able to talk so freely about it at all, but somehow it was easy – maybe because she was a girl and seemed so normal herself, the very essence of normality, sitting there on her bed, shapely legs tucked under her, surrounded by the normality of her room.

Talking to her was therapeutic. He could feel the tension draining out of him like poison out of his veins. He suddenly wished she would hold him in her arms and hug him, as his mother had done when he was a little boy – then he would be healed. But that was too much to hope for. It would probably be too much for him to take. It was enough to be with her, just to be in her presence …

'Do you see what I mean?' he said, glancing at her. His eyes met hers looking at him for one heart-stopping moment, but he looked away. It was too painful – he wanted to throw himself into her arms, but hardly dared even to look at her.

'Yes, I think so,' she said, softly.

'I hope I'm not boring you.'

'No, I want to hear all about it.'

'Why?'

'I want to understand you. And my brother.'

'Didn't he tell you about it?'

'No, he wouldn't speak to anyone about it, especially me – I'm just his kid sister. I think he's still very screwed up about it, even though he's married with kids.'

'It does screw you up, I suppose.' It wasn't an expression he would normally have used, but it somehow sounded apt.

'It certainly screwed him up, I think.'

He wondered if he should tell her about Father Director, but couldn't bring himself to. That part was still too painful and unpleasant, to tell even her. Besides, it might shock her. It might even make her think there was still something abnormal about *him* and put her off him – if she liked him at all. He was by no means sure himself that he wasn't abnormal, though maybe the fact that he liked her as he did was proof enough.

'What about you?' he asked her.

'Oh, I'm not very interesting, I'm afraid,' she said.

'I think you are,' he said, glancing at her again and making her blush. 'Tell me all about yourself.'

'What do you want to know?' she asked.

'Well, what part of Ireland did you say you were from?'

She told him she was from County Galway, where she had

been brought up on a farm, the youngest of six children, and she was now eighteen years old. He told her about his own memories of childhood holidays in Ireland, on the farm where his mother had been brought up, and he suddenly realised how much those memories meant to him.

'When did you go last?' she asked.

'I haven't been since I was sixteen – five years ago,' he said. 'I'd love to go back again, but I suppose I never can now.'

'Sure, why not?'

'Not if I leave the seminary.'

'Ah, you mustn't say that.'

'No, I could never face them again.' The thought sent a pang of regret through him.

'You could always come to Galway,' she grinned.

'I'd love to,' he said, touched. 'I've never been to the West. It's supposed to be very beautiful. Is it?'

'It's the most beautiful place on earth.'

'Do you miss it?'

'I do miss it terrible. But I miss my family more.'

'Tell me about them.'

She told him about her family and he told her about his. They continued chatting for a while, about Ireland, their families, the hospital, her job and the seminary. Then he looked at his watch. 'I'd better go,' he said.

'Would you like another cup of tea?'

'There isn't time,' he said. 'I'd better not be late or he might be suspicious.' He picked up his walking stick and stood up unsteadily.

'Here, let me help you,' she said, jumping up, standing in front of him and offering him her hand.

'It's all right,' he said, too shy to take it, and tried to stand on his own.

However, as soon as he put a bit of weight on his bad leg, the muscles at the back seemed to snap like elastic bands under the strain and roll into tight, knotted balls. His leg buckled and he toppled forward. She caught hold of him and helped him to the bed, where he lay writhing in agony, while she lifted his leg up and tried to rub the muscles back into life.

When the cramp subsided, he sat up and she put an arm

around him. He felt embarrassed but happy, because he had never been so close to a woman since his mother had hugged him as a little boy. He felt like a little boy again, wished he could stay in her arms, here in this room ...

'You poor thing,' she said, rubbing his back.

Was this the moment to tell her he loved her? That she was his Catherine? He opened his mouth. 'I'd better go,' he said, looking at his watch, bending down and picking up his walking stick. Oh, God, what an inadequate fool he was! He stood up unsteadily, eager to leave now, embarrassed at his own gaucheness.

'Are you ok?' she asked, putting her hand on the door handle.

'Yes, thanks,' he said. 'Sorry I've got to go.'

'I'm sorry too,' she said. 'I enjoyed the chat.'

'I feel like a prisoner on parole,' he laughed.

'Ah, you shouldn't say that,' she reprimanded.

'Why not? It's true!'

'You're not a prisoner. If you feel like that you should leave!'

'I have to leave. I have to tell the Superior.'

'When will you tell him?'

'I'll go and see him as soon as my leg's better.'

'Why don't you go and see him now? Don't wait! Oh, God forgive me, I shouldn't be telling you that!'

'I'll go and see him tomorrow.' He smiled weakly, wondering why she had said that. Maybe this was the moment to tell her? But he didn't have the courage. What a coward he was!

'Well, bye and thanks for coming,' she said opening the door and looking out to check. 'All clear,' she said.

'Bye,' he said. 'Thanks.'

'Bye,' she said, giving him a peck on the cheek, and he limped away down the corridor.

He moved as quickly as he could, using his walking stick, because he was in such a state of emotional turmoil. Besides, he was afraid both of being seen and being late. On his way to the car park, he paused only to put back on his clerical collar, which he had removed and hidden in his pocket before visiting her.

'Have you seen him?'

That was the first question Angela asked him every time she saw him and each time he had to shake his head sheepishly and say no. He just couldn't summon up the courage to do it. He made it as far as the Superior's office door once and was about to knock, when his courage failed him and he hobbled on his walking stick as fast as he could back to his room, where he lay on his bed sweating and trembling.

'Anyway, I thought you didn't want me to leave,' he laughed.

'I don't want you to leave,' she said. 'Certainly not because of me.'

'So you don't like me?' he smiled, wounded. He wanted to say 'love' not 'like' but didn't dare.

'I do like you, I suppose,' she said. 'Even though I shouldn't,' she added, laughing.

'Why do you like me?' he asked, ignoring the last bit.

'You're – ' She hesitated. 'Different.'

He winced at the word. 'What do you mean, 'different'?' Of course, he knew he was different – he was a seminarian, a clerical student, a religious ... But it wasn't what he had wanted to hear her say!

'Different from other men,' she shrugged.

'In what way exactly?' he asked, a stab of jealousy going through him at the very thought of other men, irrational as it was.

'Most of them want just one thing,' she said.

'I see,' he said, blushing.

'Especially doctors,' she added,

'Oh,' he said, shocked. 'Well, I suppose I am different, but I'm not sure if I want to be.'

'Don't be ashamed of being different,' she laughed. 'That's why I like you.'

'I see,' he smiled, but felt uncomfortable about it.

'I don't mean I like you just because you're different,' she said quickly, sensing that he was offended. 'I mean, I like you because you're you. And you are different. If you see what I mean.'

'Yes, I suppose so,' he shrugged.

'You're not offended, are you?' she asked.

'No,' he laughed, but inside he suddenly felt depressed. There seemed to be a barrier between them. He was deluding himself. 'I'd better go,' he said, after a while, looking at his watch. 'I'm late already.'

Limping as fast as he could back to the car park after leaving her, he saw Sister Docherty hurrying into the hospital and paused to let her disappear. When he got to the car park, the car was there, but Mike wasn't. He'd probably got fed up waiting and gone to the physiotherapy department to look for him, he thought, annoyed with himself for being late. He'd have to be more careful. Better still, he should go to see the Superior tomorrow and tell him he wanted to leave – then he wouldn't have to worry about Mike Cummings or any of them any more.

'Ah, there you are, Mister Walsh!' Mike exclaimed, turning up a few minutes later. 'I was on my way to the physio department, when I saw you. That's not the way, is it?' he asked, pointing in the direction Fran had come from, the nurses' home.

'No, I – er – finished a bit earlier than usual, so went for a stroll around the grounds,' Fran fibbed, trying not to look guilty.

'The leg must be getting better then, eh?' Mike remarked, with just the faintest hint of irony.

'Yes. Yes, the exercises help,' Fran said, quickly.

'Good. Well, we'd better get back or we'll be late for tea,' Mike said, opening the car and getting in, then opening the passenger door from the inside for him.

'Thanks,' Fran said, easing himself into the seat with difficulty, keeping his bad leg straight.

'All right?' Mike asked, starting up the car.

'Yes, thanks,' Fran said, deciding with relief that Mike didn't suspect anything.

'Let's go, then,' Mike said, putting the car into gear and driving off.

As they drove, he glanced at Mike's bespectacled, plump profile with a mixture of envy and contempt. He was in his clerical suit and collar as always, the collar digging into the fat folds of his neck. He seemed to have no doubts, to be so sure of himself, his faith and vocation, everything ...

That was how he had been himself once, he reflected sadly. He half-wished he could be the same again, but knew he never would. He didn't understand how someone like Mike, who was highly intelligent, could believe so unquestioningly. There was something childish, silly, even stupid, about such irrational faith, he thought now.

The only thing he was sure of now was that he had to leave and leave as soon as possible. He would go to see the Superior tomorrow, he resolved. The thought still daunted him, but the image of Angela in his mind gave him courage: Angela, slim, and fair, and pretty, with her soft, lilting Irish voice, twinkling blue eyes, lily-white skin, slender fingers and lovely, cherry-red lips.

But did she really like him, he wondered? Or was he just fooling himself? The thought was so depressing he shut it out of his mind. She was the one, bright star shining in the infinite emptiness, darkness and desolation of his universe. He had to believe in her!

As soon as he got back, he'd write another poem for her, he decided.

CHAPTER SEVENTEEN

Fran finished writing the letter to his parents, telling them that he was leaving the seminary, put it in an envelope and slipped it into the inside pocket of his cassock. Now all he had to do was go and tell the Superior. This was it. The time had come. He couldn't put it off any longer.

However, he continued sitting at his desk for a while, gazing out of the window at the scene he knew so well: the landscaped gardens, with their lawns, flower beds, gravel paths and trees; the bowling green with its thatched pavilion; the tennis courts; the farm and orchard, where he had spent the afternoon's manual labour picking apples. A few fellow-students were walking around in their habits reading their breviaries. A pang of regret went through him to think he might be looking at the scene for the last time.

He stood up quickly. If he started moping, he told himself, he would never get to the Superior's office. He straightened his habit, brushing the dandruff off his camail, limped to the door, opened it and stepped into the corridor, closing the door behind him. The corridor was dimly-lit and narrow, like a corridor in a ship. To his relief there was no one in it – most of the others would be in their rooms, studying their philosophy or theology books. He felt like a deserter abandoning ship.

As always, he started to tremble at the thought of what he was about to do and felt the familiar, suffocating tightness in his chest. However, he took a deep breath and started to limp along the corridor, holding onto the wall and taking deep breaths as he went, while rehearsing mentally what he was going to say. The nearer he got to the Superior's office, though, the harder it became both to breathe and to move. He felt like a deep-sea diver who had run out of oxygen, but he forged on until he made it to the door.

There he paused, feeling dizzy, and leant back against the wall for a while, afraid he was going to faint. He was tempted to scurry back to his room, as he had done several times before, but before he could, he took another deep breath, raised his fist and knocked tremulously on the door, half-hoping the Superior might not be in or wouldn't hear him.

'Come in,' he heard the Superior's familiar, peremptory voice, making his heart jump.

He reached slowly for the door knob, but hesitated, trembling. It still wasn't too late, he thought, his head pounding with an almost intolerable pressure, as if it was about to burst. He could turn and flee. But then he heard the Superior call 'Come in!' again, even more loudly. It was too late. This was it. There was no turning back now. He took another deep breath, gripped the door knob, turned it and opened the door.

The room seemed to be swaying, like a ship on a stormy sea. The Superior, sitting at his desk, reading his breviary, was rocking from side to side. Fran had to struggle to keep his balance. The Superior glanced up at him over his gold-rimmed glasses.

'C – Could I speak to you, please?' Fran stammered. He should have said 'Father', but the word stuck in his throat.

'What is it?' the Superior demanded tersely.

'It – It might take a few minutes,' Fran said, holding onto the jamb of the door – his bad leg was trembling so violently he was afraid he might get cramp and collapse.

'I see – come in and sit down then,' the Superior said brusquely, indicating the chair in front of his desk.

With relief, Fran limped over and sat on it, keeping his bad leg stretched out and hoping he wouldn't get cramp – it would spoil everything if he collapsed to the floor writhing in agony. While he waited for the Superior to finish reading his breviary, he rehearsed again what he was going to say, taking long, slow, deep breaths to try and calm himself.

He looked at the Superior. His nickname was 'Sharky' and he looked like a shark, with his bald, pointed head, mean little eyes, chin that disappeared into his clerical collar and thin lips. They were lips that had never kissed or been kissed by a woman, Fran suddenly thought, with a mixture of contempt and pity. He was as cold as a fish, too, living a false, illusory, meaningless life. How could he have ever wanted to be like him, he wondered, with a shudder of revulsion?

'Well, Mister Walsh?' the Superior demanded, closing his breviary, clasping his bloodless hands together like a pair of fins and resting them on it.

'I – I've been thinking about this for a long time,' Fran said, struggling to keep his voice steady, 'and I've decided that – that I'm no longer suited to this way of life.' The words almost choked him, but he had said them, they were out. There was no going back now. The room started to swim again and he had to hold onto the chair to stop himself fainting.

'Do you mean that you want to leave the religious life?' the Superior asked bluntly.

'Yes,' Fran gulped.

'I see,' the Superior said, impassively.

'I know it probably comes as a surprise to you,' Fran said and realised it was a mistake even before the Superior spoke again.

'Oh, it's not a surprise, Mister Walsh,' he replied, sarcastically.

'What do you mean?' Fran asked, flushing despite himself.

'It has been noted that you have been participating less than wholeheartedly lately,' the Superior said, with an ironic smile.

Fran was going to ask him what he meant again, but knew it would be pointless, especially since the Superior was right. The Superior was making him feel vulnerable and he had to feel strong. He said nothing.

'Tell me, Mister Walsh,' said the Superior, having enjoyed Fran's evident discomfiture for a while, 'what makes you think you're no longer 'suited to this way of life', as you put it?'

'I – I don't believe in it any more,' Fran said vaguely, not wanting to explain or justify.

'What exactly don't you 'believe in'?' the Superior repeated Fran's phrase mockingly.

'I don't believe in – in the faith,' Fran replied, still somewhat vaguely.

'Aha, I see,' said the Superior, leaning back in his chair with his hands joined at the fingertips, wetting his lips at the prospect of a theological dispute with him.

Fran had often crossed swords with him in class, but it was

the last thing he wanted now. All he wanted was to leave, leave both the room and the place, as soon as possible.

'And could you tell me precisely what aspects of the faith it is you have difficulty with?' the Superior asked, the glint of combat in his eyes.

'I – I don't believe in God,' Fran confessed, deciding not to beat about the bush.

'You don't believe in God,' the Superior repeated, equably.

'No,' Fran said, needled.

'How long have you had this problem?' the Superior enquired, as if he were some sort of doctor. Well, he was a doctor of theology, apparently.

'About a year,' Fran said, resenting the word 'problem', as if he had contracted some nasty disease.

'Have you spoken to your confessor about it?'

'No.'

'Have you spoken to anyone about it?'

'No.' It was a fib – he had spoken to Angela, but he could hardly tell the Superior that.

'Why not, may I ask?'

'I didn't think there was any point.'

'Oh, you didn't think there was any point,' the Superior repeated sarcastically.

'No.'

The Superior leaned forward in his chair. 'Surely the point is, Mister Walsh, that not only your religious vocation, but your immortal soul, is at stake?'

'I don't believe in an immortal soul any more,' Fran stated, starting to feel argumentative.

'Oh, I see,' the Superior said scornfully, leaning back again. 'And what, I wonder, has brought you to that remarkable conclusion?'

'I can't see any evidence for it, just as I can't see any evidence for the existence of God,' Fran replied.

'So, because *you*, Mister Walsh, can't see any evidence, you think there is no evidence?' the Superior sneered .

'I can only go by what I see for myself,' Fran replied, weakly.

'That's exactly where you're mistaken. That's where faith comes in. And humility,' the Superior added, pointedly.

'I can't believe in something I see no evidence for, just for the sake of believing,' Fran insisted.

'What about the five proofs?' The Superior was referring to the five so-called proofs of the existence of God of Saint Thomas Aquinas, which they had studied in class and which he had studied over and over again in private, hoping and praying they would somehow convince him.

'I don't find them convincing,' Fran replied, surprised at his own audacity – he only wished he did.

'You don't find them convincing,' the Superior repeated.

'No. They're arguments, not proofs. Not evidence,' Fran replied, even more audaciously.

'So you need evidence, do you?' the Superior asked.

'Yes,' Fran said.

'Have you looked for evidence?' the Superior demanded.

'Yes, hard,' Fran replied.

'I don't think you've looked hard enough,' the Superior riposted.

'What do you mean?' Fran asked.

'The evidence is all around you, Mister Walsh,' the Superior asserted.

'Where?' Fran asked, half-hoping, absurd as it was, that the Superior was going to show him or tell him of some conclusive, indisputable, irrefutable evidence that he had somehow failed to see, so that all this would become no more than a brief aberration, a bad dream.

'The whole universe is evidence, Mister Walsh!' the Superior declared testily. 'From the stars and planets above to the human eye! Are you trying to tell me that something as complex and intricate as the human eye was formed by chance out of nothing?'

'No, by evolution, out of matter,' Fran replied.

'And where does this primordial matter come from?' the Superior demanded.

'I don't know,' Fran admitted, 'but – '

'There's a lot you don't know, Mister Walsh,' the Superior cut him off. ' "There are more things in Heaven, Horatio, than are dreamt of in your philosophy." Do you know who said that?'

'Yes, Hamlet,' Fran replied, refraining from telling him that he had quoted it incorrectly.

'I don't think you should leave, Mister Walsh,' the Superior said categorically.

'Why not?' Fran asked, annoyed.

'If you left now, in your present state of mind, I think your immortal soul would be in grave danger,' the Superior told him. 'I think you should stay and pray your way through this.'

'That's what I've been doing for the last two years!' Fran expostulated.

'All the same, I think you should wait, at least until Christmas,' the Superior insisted. 'It will take a few weeks to arrange a dispensation from your vows, anyway.'

As if his vows mattered to him now, Fran thought angrily, when he didn't even believe in the God they were supposed to have been made to! However, he decided it would be tactical to please the Superior. 'Could you begin the process, please?' he asked.

'On condition that you agree to wait until Christmas,' the Superior stipulated.

'If you think I should,' Fran agreed reluctantly. Christmas – that was nearly three months away! He couldn't wait that long! He wanted to go tomorrow! Today!

'Meanwhile, I'll pray for you,' the Superior said.

'Thank you,' Fran forced himself to say, starting to get up.

'Before you go, Mister Walsh,' the Superior stopped him with a raised finger. 'Is there anything else that might be having an influence on this decision?'

'What do you mean?' Fran asked, alarmed.

'You see, Mister Walsh,' the Superior said, a triumphant glint in his eyes, 'I have reason to believe that you have struck up a liaison with one of the nurses at the hospital.'

'I was friendly with one of them,' Fran admitted, reddening again despite himself and wondering how the Superior knew, desperately hoping he knew no more.

'I am also led to believe that you sometimes visit her instead of going for physiotherapy,' the Superior went in for the kill.

Fran blushed furiously, realising the Superior knew everything. Mike Cummings must have told him and Sister Docherty must have told Mike Cummings. They had been spying on him! And they had betrayed him!

'Well, is it true, Mister Walsh?' the Superior demanded.

'Yes, it's true,' Fran confessed, deciding to make a clean breast of it, feeling like a criminal despite himself.

'And what, may I ask, passes between you at these rendezvous?' the Superior probed, gloating.

'We just talk to each other, that's all,' Fran protested. It was true, though he wished it weren't, wished there were more. But even if there had been more between him and Angela, he wouldn't have admitted it – as far as he was concerned, the Superior had no right to ask him, had no authority over him any more.

'And what do you talk about?' the Superior pursued.

'About religion mostly,' Fran said, which was half true.

'Is this young lady – if I may call her a young lady – a Catholic?' the Superior enquired.

'Yes, she is,' Fran answered.

'What's her name?' This was starting to feel like the Spanish inquisition!

'I don't think I should tell you that,' Fran said, trembling at his own audacity again.

'I order you to tell me, Mister Walsh, under your vow of obedience,' the Superior insisted, threateningly.

'I'm sorry, but I don't think I should,' Fran stood his ground.

'I see. Well, it doesn't matter. I happen to know who she is,' the Superior replied, cryptically.

Why were you asking me, then, Fran wondered? The Superior was playing a game with him, testing him, trying to catch him out, he thought angrily. Never mind, he tried to calm himself, he couldn't win, he couldn't stop him leaving and he couldn't stop him seeing Angela again. He had the upper hand in the end.

'You've been playing a very dangerous and duplicitous game, Mister Walsh,' the Superior continued, sternly. 'Not only with your own immortal soul, but this young woman's. I hope and pray that your relationship has not strayed beyond the platonic and you have not broken your holy vow of chastity as well.'

'Of course not,' Fran protested, blushing even though it was true, wishing it weren't.

'You are still under a vow of chastity, you know,' the Superior told him.

'I know,' Fran said, to placate him – not that it meant anything to him any more, having been made like his other vows to a God he did not believe in any more. It was not only null and void, but unnatural.

'Apart from anything else,' the Superior continued, menacingly, 'you have both broken the hospital's rules by visiting her in her room. It could be construed as unprofessional conduct on her part.'

What exactly was he implying by that, Fran wondered apprehensively? He was about to ask, but thought better of it. His best policy now was to appease him and play for time, he decided, while he decided what to do.

'I forbid you to see this nurse at the hospital or anywhere else again,' the Superior decreed. 'In fact, I've been in touch with the hospital and they tell me you can do your exercises here, that you don't need to go to physiotherapy again. All you will need is a check-up in a month's time. So, you are not to leave this house for any purpose without my express permission. Do you understand?'

Fran was about to protest, but bit his tongue. 'Yes,' he said, meekly.

Suddenly, the bell for Vespers started ringing. 'You may go,' the Superior said curtly, when it had finished.

'Thank you,' Fran said, standing up.

'Thank you what, Mister Walsh?'

'Father,' Fran said, the word sticking in his throat, and limped out of the office as quickly as he could, feeling sick.

He hurried to the washroom, where he vomited into one of the toilets. Then he went back to his room, unable to face Vespers. He closed the door, collapsed on his bed and lay in the dark, trembling and sweating. Well, he thought, that was it, he had burned his boats now. He had wiped out nine years of his life, his whole past. His leg ached mercilessly, but it was nothing compared to the pain in his soul. A lump came to his throat and tears to his eyes. The only thing that stopped him breaking down and crying was the thought of Angela.

He had to find a way of seeing her or at least getting in touch

191

with her, but it was impossible – he had no access to a phone or letter box and no money. Under their vow of poverty they were not allowed to carry money and normally had no need for it, since everything necessary was provided.

'You are not to leave this house' – the Superior's words echoed grotesquely in his mind. They made him feel like a prisoner under house arrest. He *was* a prisoner! What would Angela think when he didn't turn up on Wednesday afternoon? She would probably think he had changed his mind and decided not to leave the seminary, had decided to leave her instead. The thought of how disappointed she would feel made him writhe. He had to find a way!

On Wednesday afternoon he sat in his room, trying to read a novel, while the others were playing football as usual. However, he couldn't concentrate. He could think only of Angela and what she would think when he didn't turn up. The thought was unbearable. He couldn't wait until Christmas to leave and see her again. Then, suddenly, he had an idea – he would go and see her secretly, by hitching a lift to the hospital and back.

At first the idea scared him, as if he really were a prisoner trying to escape. But it was irrational, he told himself – he wasn't a prisoner, he could walk out if he wanted and nobody could stop him. He was twenty-one years old, an adult, a free agent. He stood up, took off his habit and put on his black anorak. Suddenly, there was a knock on his door.

'Yes?' he called out, panic-stricken, sitting down at his desk, opening a theology book and pretending to read it, hoping desperately that whoever it was wouldn't open the door and see him in his anorak.

'I'm going into town. Do you want anything?' It was Mike Cummings, the person he least wanted to see or be seen by.

'No, thanks, Mike,' he called out, as casually as he could, though his heart was palpitating.

To his relief the door didn't open. He waited a few minutes for Mike to disappear, then opened the door, checked the coast was clear and slipped into the corridor, closing the door behind him.

Quietly, he made his way along the corridor, downstairs and out of the house by a back door. Luckily, as he had expected, there was no one around – the other students were all playing football and the Fathers were all in their rooms. Nervously, he limped along the drive, afraid an alarm would sound and a megaphone call him back any moment. Maybe the voice of God booming from the sky! However, a few moments later he was standing at the side of the road, out of sight of the house and thumbing a lift, feeling like a fugitive.

'She's gone.'

'You mean, she's on duty?' Fran asked.

He was talking to Carmel, the girl who lived next door to Angela, also Irish. There had been no answer when he knocked on Angela's door and he immediately knew something was wrong. He had knocked on Carmel's door, evidently waking her up, since she was in her dressing-gown.

'No, she's gone home.'

'You mean – to Ireland?'

'Yes.'

'For a holiday?' He knew he was clutching at straws.

'No, for good, I'm afraid.'

'For good?' His brain reeled.

'Yes. She left this for you.' She handed him an envelope with his name in Angela's writing on it, marked PRIVATE AND PERSONAL.

'Oh. Thanks,' he said, taking it, in a daze. 'You mean, she isn't coming back?'

'No. I'm sorry. You'd better go. They're watching the building, because there've been intruders.'

'Yes, OK, thanks,' he said, turning and limping away, still in a daze.

He limped down the stairs out of the Nurses' Home to a bench in the hospital grounds and sat down. Opposite him was a sign pointing in one direction to CASUALTY and in the other to MORTUARY. He ripped open the envelope, pulled out a letter and read:

Clayfield Hospital, Saturday

Dear Fran,

This is the hardest thing I've ever had to do, but I think it's for the best. Father Prothero, your Superior, came to see me yesterday. Sister Docherty (the jealous old bitch) told him about us. He accused me of 'seducing' you from your vocation and warned me that I was committing a terrible sin by doing so, which God would not forgive. He threatened to report me to the hospital authorities for 'unprofessional conduct' if I did not promise never to see you again. I refused and they've given me the sack.

I'm going back to Ireland tomorrow, Sunday. Please don't try to follow me or even write to me. I love you, but I think it's for the best. After what has happened, I don't think we could ever be happy together. I would always feel guilty, though I know you were going to leave the seminary anyway. I also know your family, especially your mother, would never accept me, just as mine would never accept you. It would be impossible for us.

Believe me, I do love you with all my heart and you will always be in my heart. I hope and pray that you make the right decision. As for me, don't worry, I'll find another job in Ireland or I might even go to America, as I told you I wanted to before I met you, after I had finished my nurse's training.

Thank you for loving me. I will always remember our love. It was wonderful while it lasted, but it was too good to last. I think it was doomed from the start, just like Romeo and Juliet's. I'm crying now, but I'll be all right. I hope you'll be all right too and will forgive me. Please don't be too angry or sad and say a prayer for me sometimes, though I know you don't believe in it.

I can't write any more, because I'm crying too much. Goodbye and God bless.

With deepest love,

Angela

P.S. I hope your leg gets better soon. X

He had to read it several times for it to sink in that she had gone, she had left him. He was suddenly filled with a rebellious rage. He couldn't accept it. He couldn't let them take her away from him like that. He couldn't let them win. He wouldn't go back to the seminary. He'd go to Ireland and find her!

The more he thought about it though, the more he realised how impossible it was. For one thing, he wasn't fit to travel. For another, he had no money. And anyway, he didn't even have her address. It was hopeless. *They* had won. He crumpled the letter up and tossed it into the litter bin beside him. He couldn't help feeling betrayed by Angela, though he knew she had had little choice. A lump came to his throat and hot, stinging tears to his eyes, but he fought them back, refusing to cry, refusing to break down, refusing to be beaten.

What was he going to do now, that was the question? The familiar black wave of despair swept over him. He felt like committing suicide again. If he had had a bottle of pills, he would have swallowed them. But he had only two choices: he could either hitchhike back to the seminary or try to hitchhike home. Both prospects dismayed him, but he couldn't sit here much longer – it was getting dark as well as cold. He had to make a move. He had to go, one way or the other.

He stood up, pulled the collar of his anorak up and limped out of the hospital gates. On the pavement outside, he hesitated. To go back to the seminary, he had to turn left. To go home, he had to turn right. It would be easier to turn left. He would be back for tea and, he hoped, no one would have noticed him missing.

No, he couldn't go back now, he decided. He waited until the road was clear, limped across and started thumbing in the opposite direction. He felt scared, but also strangely elated – he was free! After half an hour, though, his elation had turned to despair again. A couple of cars stopped, but nobody was going far enough. It was getting dark, he was cold and hungry and his knee was aching madly. It was hopeless, he realised. Crazy! He had to go back.

Despondently, he crossed to the other side of the road and started thumbing again, hoping Mike Cummings wouldn't pass by. He'd go back and if necessary wait until Christmas.

Then he would leave. Then he'd be free. Then he'd go home. But somehow that thought just sent yet another black wave of despair over him …

CHAPTER EIGHTEEN

After leaving the seminary, he was in a state of shock. He moved around the house like an automaton – the house was semi-detached, but he was completely detached. It seemed strangely small to him, almost like a toy house, after nine years of refectories, study halls and dormitories. The furniture and fittings were strange too – he wasn't used to armchairs, carpets, curtains, wallpaper or tablecloths. As for his family, they were strangers to him and he to them – they hardly knew what to say to each other. He even felt strange in normal clothes, after three years in a black frock ...

He killed time by lying in bed for as long as possible, reading in the public library, sitting in the park or just wandering the streets. 'Wandering Jesus', Kevin, his youngest brother, called him, cuttingly. There were times when he felt like killing time for ever, but having tried and failed once, he didn't have the guts to try again. Or maybe he just wasn't quite desperate enough.

Sometimes he went into a pub for a pint, if he could afford it – he had no money except the pocket money his parents gave him, though he was twenty-one years old. Alcohol, he had discovered, assuaged his pain for a while and he graduated from one to two or three or even more pints, whenever he could afford it, saving his money specifically for the purpose of the brief, but blessed, anaesthesia. If there was a jukebox in the pub, so much the better – he found pop music relaxing and enjoyed it all the more because it had been forbidden in the seminary. His parents knew nothing about this – they thought he spent all his time outside in the library.

'You can't carry on like this, Fran,' his mother said to him in the kitchen one evening, when he came home from the pub, 'lying in bed, moping about the house, mooning about the streets, drowning your sorrows in the pub.'

'Ahem. Your mother's right, Fran,' his father chimed in, taking his pipe from his mouth and looking up from his 'Evening News'. 'Sooner or later you've got to face up to reality, go out and get a job, apply for university, do something.'

'Reality' – the word went through him like a rapier. He was tempted to answer back by asking them what they meant by it, but resisted. Of course, he knew – reality for them was the ordinary, normal, everyday, material world, which revolved around earning money and making a living. For nine years though, he had lived in another world, a rarefied world of study, prayer and meditation, a world that revolved around 'God'. Ironically, he didn't believe in God any more, while they did. He left the room without replying, as usual unable to communicate with them.

He sensed that his mother took vindictive pleasure in saying such things to him. She took revenge in other ways, too, in barbed remarks and acts of petty spite. For by leaving the seminary he had shattered her dream of having a son a priest and betrayed the special love she had always had for him. 'I built a monument and it's all fallen down,' she had written to him in reply to his letter telling them he was leaving the seminary. The phrase echoed hauntingly in the shattered temple of his soul, would haunt it, he knew, for ever more, even after he had finished razing the ruins and rebuilding – if he was ever able to.

His leaving the seminary she could have accepted. What she couldn't accept was his leaving the Church. After the first few Sundays at home, he stopped receiving Holy Communion at Mass – it almost choked him to swallow the host, which Catholics believed was the body of Christ: 'Who, the day before He suffered, took bread into His holy and venerable hands, and having raised His eyes to Heaven, unto Thee, O God, His Father almighty, giving thanks to Thee, blessed, broke it and gave it to His disciples, saying: Take, all of you, and eat of this. FOR THIS IS MY BODY.' He now found the idea not only incredible, but revolting, as revolting as cannibalism.

He didn't mind the wine – which Catholics believed to be

the blood of Christ – so much. At least it put a warm glow inside you, like sherry. The trouble was, you only got a sip, whereas he felt like knocking back the whole chalice-full. He remembered how, as sacristans at the junior seminary, they used to drink it straight from the bottle, at risk of six of the best if caught.

Gradually, he stopped going to Mass altogether. He found it absurd, like a séance or voodoo ceremony, full of hocus-pocus and mumbo-jumbo. For a while, he pretended to go at a different time, but there was no fooling his mother.

'Why've you stopped going to Mass?' she demanded out of the blue one day, taking him by surprise.

He was about to deny it, but decided there was no point. 'I just don't feel like going any more,' he said feebly, not wanting to get into a theological debate with her.

'So, you've lost your faith as well,' she said, more in sorrow than anger.

The words 'as well' were like another twist of the knife. She meant that he had lost his faith as well as his vocation, which until recently had been the two most important things in his life. He slunk away without answering her, like a wounded animal.

He understood his mother's reaction. She was a typical Irishwoman of her background and generation, whose faith was part of the very fabric of her being – she would probably have died for it. He had only found out recently, from his elder sister, Molly, that she had been in a convent when she was young, but left, to emigrate to England, become a nurse, get married and have a family – his two brothers, two sisters and himself, her eldest son, whom she had once idolised.

Was that why she had wanted him to be a priest so much, to make up to God for her own 'desertion', he wondered now? By leaving the seminary, then, he had dealt her a double blow – he had not only deprived her of the prestige of having a son a priest, but also prevented her from 'atoning' for her own lost vocation. By losing his faith though, he was dealing her a mortal blow, one that he knew would kill her love for him completely. Yet there was nothing he could do about it. He could pretend, he supposed, but he was sick of pretence.

His father was a Catholic too, but had been born and brought up in Manchester of Irish parents and was proud to call himself Irish. Catholicism was an important part of his identity and he taught in a Catholic primary school, but he had an anti-clerical streak, partly because he was an Irish nationalist and the clergy, or at least the hierarchy, in Ireland had traditionally been anti-nationalist, and partly, he suspected, because of his lack of advancement in the Catholic school system, which was run by the clergy. So his leaving the seminary didn't bother his father so much – in fact, he suspected he was secretly pleased about it. However, losing his faith to his father was like a betrayal not just of his religion, but also of his Irishness. By losing his faith, therefore, he was effectively alienating both his parents.

Unfortunately, he felt that his father had a point. He had always been proud to call himself Irish - at school had always chosen to play for 'Ireland' in football games. He loved Ireland, though it meant little more to him than happy childhood summer holidays on his uncle's farm, where his mother had been born and brought up. But Ireland and Catholicism went together, so by rejecting Catholicism he was rejecting an essential part of his Irish heritage, and that hurt him almost as much as it hurt his father or mother. He certainly felt that, having left the seminary, he would never be able to go back to the part of Ireland where his relations lived. And now, having left the Church as well, he felt that he would never be able to go back to Ireland at all, or at least would never feel so at home there again. But, he told himself sadly, that was part of the price he had to pay for liberation.

Despite his apostasy, his parents continued to keep him, though they nagged him to apply for university and meanwhile find a temporary job. The thought of looking for, never mind doing, some meaningless, menial job depressed him, while the thought of going to university for three more years of study depressed him even more. After nine years of intensive study, since going to the junior seminary at the age of twelve, he was sick of it, much as he loved reading.

Reading was the lifeline that saved him from sinking into suicidal depression or having a nervous breakdown. His favourite writers were Hemingway, Lawrence and, above all, Joyce – Hemingway for his romantic worldliness, Lawrence for his poetic passion and Joyce for his devilish brilliance. He associated them with the World, the Flesh and the Devil respectively, the 'unholy' trinity he was supposed to have renounced, but had now begun to see in a very different light.

Hemingway helped him to see that the world was an exciting place, not to be rejected, but to be explored and enjoyed. Lawrence, more importantly, helped him to realise that there was nothing wrong with women, that they were interesting and attractive, despite all the years of brainwashing against them, despite his failed mini-romance with Angela, despite the fact that it was Father Director and Mark who haunted his dreams still. Lawrence helped him to think that he might be normal, despite them, and that thought gave him a slender thread of hope, saved him from total despair.

Joyce's 'A Portrait of the Artist as a Young Man' was an epiphany to him. Its pages were like a crystal ball in which he saw himself, his very soul, revealed, as if in a past incarnation. It inspired him with the boldness to say with Stephen, 'Non serviam'. It inspired him with the courage to face the future. Above all, it inspired him with the idea of becoming a writer himself, so giving him a new purpose in life.

To become a writer, he realised, he needed some experience of life. After nine years in a monastery, he was hungry for experience, anyway. He couldn't get it at home in Manchester, living with his parents, dependent on them, being monitored by them almost like a child. The best place to get it, he decided, was London, which had always fascinated him. It would kill two birds with one stone – help him to escape from his parents and give him experience. He decided to go, but when he told his parents, they poured cold water on the idea.

'Why do you want to go to London?' his mother demanded indignantly. 'Where would you live? Who do you know there? What will you do? How will you live? You have a home and family here! Go out and get a job! Apply for university! Get some proper qualifications, then go gallivanting round the world, if you must! But come down to earth first!'

'Ahem. Your mother's right, Fran,' his father said, as usual, removing his pipe from his mouth and glancing up from his 'Evening News'. 'You've got no proper qualifications. What would you do in London?'

'I'd like to try my hand at writing,' he said, reluctantly.

'Huh – that's just pie in the sky,' his father said, scornfully. 'Go to university and get yourself a degree – that's the thing to do. That'll provide you with a meal-ticket for life.' He put his pipe back in his mouth and returned to his paper.

He couldn't help feeling a spasm of contempt for them, especially his father – he knew his father wanted him to go to university partly because he hadn't gone himself. Also, his father could have been a professional singer, possibly even a famous singer, but hadn't had the courage to pursue it, had chosen instead the safe, secure, boring, conventional path, was advising him to do the same ...

But he didn't have the courage to argue with them. He didn't have the courage to actually leave and go to London or anywhere else. He hardly had the courage to get out of bed in the morning! As for the idea of being a writer – it did sound airy-fairy, even in his own ears. He was well and truly trapped!

The thought of three more years of study depressed him, as did the thought that he would have to live at home like a schoolboy – he wouldn't be able to go away to university, because he wouldn't get a grant, having already had one at the seminary. However, he resigned himself to it – he owed it to them to get a degree, he supposed, after all they had done for him. He would do it, he told himself, and then he would be free. Reluctantly, he sent away for application forms, filled them in and sent them off. Then he summoned up the courage to go out and look for a job.

He worked for a while as an encyclopaedia salesman, a van driver and a milkman. Then he worked in a mineral bottling factory and finally in Kellogg's Corn Flakes factory, as a 'machine minder', which meant all he had to do was keep an eye on one of the enormous ovens. It was mindless, but it suited him – he spent most of the time reading newspapers, magazines and novels or chatting shyly to the girls on the conveyor belts.

One of them, to his surprise, seemed to take a fancy to him – at least she smiled a lot at him and laughed at his little jokes.

Her name was Sharon, she was seventeen and looked like a doll, with curly black hair beneath her white cap, enormous black eyelashes that she fluttered alluringly at him, porcelain skin, rosy cheeks and cherry-red lips. He eventually plucked up the courage to ask her out – the first time in his life he had ever actually asked a girl out, although, he reflected wryly, he was twenty-one years old.

To his surprise, she said yes. At first, he was over the moon, but afterwards the thought of actually going out with her terrified him. For the next few days he tried to think of an excuse for cancelling it, but couldn't, didn't really want to. By the time Saturday evening came and they were sitting beside each other in a pub in town, he felt so nervous that, after a few banalities, he didn't know what to say to her. She didn't seem to know what to say to him either, so for a couple of hours they sat beside each other in embarrassed near-silence. Then with relief he put her on the bus home, not even daring to give her a peck on the cheek.

He went home cursing himself. He had made a complete mess of it! What was wrong with him, he asked himself angrily? What was wrong with him, he told himself sardonically, was that he had spent nine years locked up in a seminary, so had no idea how to behave with girls. Maybe he was queer after all? No, he refused to believe that! He liked her. He found her physically attractive. He had wanted to kiss her, but was too shy even to touch her or sit close to her, as if she had some terrible, contagious disease. *He* was the one with the disease, a mental disease!

In bed, to convince himself he was normal, as well as to relieve his frustration, he imagined making love to her and masturbated. As always, it left him feeling physically relieved but ashamed, not that he believed it was a sin any longer – he no longer believed in sin at all. No, he was ashamed because it seemed just another symptom of his inadequacy, his maladjustment, his isolation …

In spite of this fiasco, he plucked up the courage to ask her out again and to his surprise she said yes. As before, he arranged to meet her at eight o'clock in front of the town hall in Albert Square, that soot-black, Victorian-gothic civic

cathedral that was a favourite trysting place for Mancunians.
By nine o'clock she still hadn't turned up. He waited for
another half-hour, enviously watching other couples meet with
deepening depression. Then he went and got drunk, so drunk
that he was sick and sank into a stupor on the floor of the bus
station on the way home.

Coming to in the cold early hours of the morning, he
discovered he had either lost his wallet or it had been stolen, so
had to walk home. As he trudged along the deserted, Sunday-
morning suburban streets, the dawn broke with breathtaking
beauty above the city skyline, but he wished he had never woken
up to witness it.

'Hello,' he said to her, the next day at work.

'Hello,' she said sheepishly, as she monitored a conveyor belt
full of corn flakes.

'What happened last night?' he asked.

'I wasn't feeling well,' she said, blushing, which made her
look prettier than ever.

'What was wrong?' he asked, but before she could answer a
supervisor hove into view.

'I'll see you later,' he said, nipping back to his oven.

Later though, he saw her chatting to another bloke and a stab
of jealousy went through him. He noticed them chatting
together several times and each time the dagger twisted in his
guts. She had jilted him! He never spoke to her again, even
though he might be cutting off his nose ...

He looked for another girlfriend, but all the girls he met at
work, pubs and parties seemed to belong to a different species
from the ones he read about in novels or imagined. He found
some of them attractive, but his frail confidence was shattered –
he was too shy to talk to them and if one of them tried to talk to
him, he was seized by the old, familiar paralysis.

It was like being bloody crippled, he thought bitterly, but it
wasn't surprising, after nine years of being isolated from
women and brainwashed against them. Maybe he was
homosexual after all. It would be a miracle if he wasn't, after
nine years living among males only and being messed about

with by the Director. The Director must have been in love with him, he realised now, just as later, in the Sixth Form, he had been himself with Mark Brown, which ironically was why the Director had tried to expel him.

It worried him that he still sometimes remembered Mark with a pang of nostalgic affection. That more than anything made him afraid he might be queer. It was an idea that revolted him, that he couldn't live with, both because it was abnormal and would mean that they – the 'Ghosters' – had won. More than anything else he wanted to be normal, in every way, but especially sexually. What reassured him was that he felt no attraction to men now – indeed found the idea repulsive – and had started to find women attractive, even if he couldn't manage to have a relationship with one.

Why did he find homosexuality so abhorrent, he asked himself? It was probably as much because of as despite his experiences in the seminary – it had been condemned even more fanatically there than by society in general, especially, ironically, by the Director himself. *He* had really been screwed up, he realised now.

That was the trouble with priests, he thought – they renounced and denounced all sex, and not just sex, but all feelings of love, or affection, or even friendship. For some of them though, like the Director, celibacy or at least chastity proved impossible, so they released their sexual frustration in perverted ways, such as by playing around with boys or beating them – or both. What a bunch of screwballs they were, he thought! It disgusted him now to think he had once been one of them. Thank goodness he had escaped, even if he was emotionally crippled.

All the more reason, he resolved, to rehabilitate himself. The best way to do that, he knew, would be by finding a girlfriend – he was fed up with fantasizing and masturbating. But it was 'Catch 22' – as soon as he got near a girl, all the years of conditioning came into play and he froze. Girls seemed to recoil from him too, when he got close, as if he came from another planet – which in a way he did.

He hoped to meet a girl at university, where he went to read English and philosophy. He went only to please his parents and because he seemed to have no other choice. He was depressed by the thought of three more years of study and afraid he might not be able to cope with the pressure. He continued to live at home and travelled by bus every day to the university, or 'College of Knowledge', as one of the conductors amusingly referred to it.

Somehow, with a minimum of effort, he managed to keep up with the course. Lectures were optional and he attended very few, preferring to sit in the library reading novels unconnected with the course, trying to learn about the new world in which he found himself, like a traveller in a foreign country. Tutorials they had to attend, but he did so apathetically, feeling no interest in discussing metaphysical poetry or existential philosophy.

There were some attractive girls on the course, but they were very middle-class and intimidated him even more than the working-class girls he had already met, with their apparent poise and sophistication, so that he didn't dare to speak to them. They never spoke to him either – except for one called Laura, who suddenly started sitting next to him in Anglo-Saxon class, chatting to him and asking him to help her with her translations.

He was only too pleased to do so – she was lovely, like an Anglo-Saxon princess herself, with long, wavy, flaxen tresses, exquisitely chiselled features, a rose-petal complexion and a fetching figure. She usually wore waistcoats, midi-skirts and knee-length boots. He suddenly started to look forward to Anglo-Saxon classes and felt irrationally jealous if she sat next to anyone else. He started to imagine what it would be like to go out with her, kiss her, make love with her ... Eventually, one cold, wet, winter morning, while the lecturer was babbling on about ablauts, he plucked up the courage to ask her out for a drink.

'I'm sorry, I can't,' she said.

'Why not?' he asked, puzzled.

'I've already got a boyfriend.'

'Oh,' he said casually, but inside he was crushed, realising she had only been using him.

At a fellow student's party soon afterwards, he drank enough beer and wine to give him the Dutch courage to dance with a girl in a flowery trouser suit. She was bespectacled and plain, probably the plainest girl at the party, but she had big boobs and he was crazy with frustration.

'What's your name?' she shouted in his ear, above the deafening din of Led Zeppelin, after they had gyrated together for a while.

'Frank,' he shouted back in hers, catching an exciting whiff of perfume. 'What's yours?'

'Barbara,' she shouted back. 'What are you reading?'

'English and philosophy. What about you?'

'Physics.'

He would hardly have known how to continue the conversation even if the deafening music hadn't made it so difficult – the word 'physics' made his brain go straight into neutral. It didn't matter though, because after dancing on for a few minutes, she leant forward again and shouted in his ear: 'Let's go upstairs, shall we?'

He nodded eagerly. This was it – at last he was going to have physical contact with a real, live, flesh and blood girl! She took him by the hand and led him upstairs to one of the bedrooms, where it looked as if there was an orgy going on – there were couples everywhere, on the bed and on the floor, writhing and wriggling like eels. He hesitated, feeling a sudden revulsion, but she tugged him in, found a space on the floor, which was pulsating to the beat of the music, and pulled him down beside her.

She removed her glasses, grabbed him in her arms and wrapped her legs around him like a hungry octopus. Then she clamped her mouth on his and started kissing him greedily. He tried to respond, but felt only disgust, especially when she thrust her tongue into his mouth and started trying to force it down his throat. While she did so, she took his hand and placed it on one of her ample boobs. He squeezed it perfunctorily a few times, but it felt like a soggy sponge. Revolted, he took his hand away, but she grabbed his wrist and forced it down between her thighs, where she was wet. Suddenly feeling sick, he pulled his hand away.

'What's wrong?' she demanded.

'Nothing. I've just got to, er, go to the loo,' he fibbed, jumping up and stumbling over bodies as he rushed from the room.

He ran downstairs, bumping into people sitting on them, and staggered out into the front garden, where he vomited into the hydrangeas. When he had recovered, he slunk off along the tree-lined, suburban streets, dark and deserted except for the ghostly glimmer of street lights. It was a relief to escape from the stuffy, smoky, noisy house and the frosty night air felt both sobering and cleansing.

He felt dirty. He wanted sex, he needed sex, both for the experience and to relieve his frustration, but not like that, like an animal on the floor, with someone he didn't even know. It was disgusting. Or was he just making excuses? None of the others seemed to be bothered about doing it. Maybe he only felt disgusted because he wasn't normal ...

No, he refused to believe it! The problem was, he was not only an ex-Catholic, but an ex-seminarian, so he felt guilty about sex without love. He would probably feel guilty about sex with love, too. God, he had a first-class honours degree in guilt! He wanted love, of course. That was what he wanted above all: to find a girl to fall in love with, to love and be loved by. But it seemed impossible. Maybe he never would. Maybe the idea of falling in love was just a romantic illusion. No, he refused to believe that, too. What else was there to live for?

Until he found a girl to fall in love with, what was he supposed to do – live like a monk? He had had enough of that, thank you! If *they* were against sex, there couldn't be anything wrong with it. Of course there was nothing wrong with it. Catholics were just screwed up about it. It was natural, normal, healthy. He wanted to have sex to prove that to himself as much as for any other reason. Above all, to prove to himself he was *normal*.

But when he found a girl willing to have sex with him, like tonight, he was too inhibited to do it. God, he was well and truly screwed up! Meanwhile, he was lonely and frustrated and the only way to relieve his frustration was through masturbating, which left him feeling physically relieved, but ashamed and even more lonely. What a hopeless case he was!

He stopped to look up at the night sky – it was glittering with stars, like diamonds strewn carelessly across a cloth of purple velvet. It was an awesome sight, suddenly made him feel small and insignificant. There was a time when he would have seen such a sight as a manifestation of God and been inspired to adoration by it. But now that he did not believe in God, it all seemed so mysterious, so meaningless, so utterly incomprehensible.

I don't believe in God. The thought still sent a tremor of terror through him, as though God might strike him down dead for it. That was the power of twenty years' indoctrination and brainwashing! But was it really possible to look up at the stars and not believe there was something or someone behind them? Yes, unfortunately, he thought it was. Maybe it was all just the result of some cosmic explosion. But where did the material of the cosmos come from in the first place? Aha, that was the million-dollar question! If he could answer that, he would be a genius, a prophet, a god himself!

He certainly didn't believe in the God he had been brought up to believe in, the God of Catholicism, of Christianity, of the Bible. He didn't believe in God the Father, Son or Holy Ghost, Heaven or Hell, angels or devils ... If there was a God – and maybe, for all he knew, there was – He or It was unknowable. Why should He make Himself known to mere human beings? Maybe human beings were no more than guinea pigs in some divine cosmic experiment or pawns in some divine game: 'As flies to wanton boys are we to the Gods, They kill us for their sport,' as Shakespeare wrote. Maybe God was evil, rather than good. Maybe He was beyond good and evil ...

Religious people were so naive and so conceited to believe God cared about them, they were important to Him. If there was a God and He did care about human beings, if He did love them, He had a funny way of showing it, what with all the suffering He exposed them to. Keeping Himself so well-hidden, so invisible, so mysterious, so inaccessible, was not the least of the suffering. And then He condemned them all to death in the end, good or bad!

Of course, Catholics and other believers in religion had

answers for all these questions – there were thousands of theology books and he had even read a few of them. But even at the seminary theology had struck him as waffle – he had never been able to take it seriously or read it without impatience. No, the God of Catholicism, the Judaeo-Christian God, struck him now as no more than a fairy tale – a rather grisly, Gothic fairy tale. It seemed more honest to him now to admit you did not know, could not know, the answer to these questions, more honest than inventing them.

It might be more honest, he told himself, but it was also depressing. It meant life was meaningless. It meant human beings were just like insects, scurrying about on this minor planet called Earth, itself a minute speck of dirt in the vastness of the universe. It meant he, Francis Walsh, was of no more importance than a cockroach. Was that really what he believed? Better not to think about it, better just to get on with it, he told himself, lowering his head and walking on through the ghostly suburban streets.

Anyway, life was worth living, whether it was meaningless or not, he reflected. He had to believe that, otherwise he might as well not have bothered leaving the seminary, might as well have killed himself. There were lots of things that made life worth living: love, friendship, literature, music, beer, food ... Life might be meaningless or mysterious, but it was a great *adventure*, an adventure not to be missed. That was the best way to look at it, he decided.

The trouble was, he felt the adventure hadn't started yet, because he was still a student and had to live at home. He was in a kind of limbo. But it would start, he knew. The world was out there and life was all before him. He just had to be patient. Another two years and he would have finished university, fulfilled his obligations to his parents and be free to leave home.

That was what he needed to do, get far away from both home and family – especially his parents – go somewhere no one knew him, somewhere he could start a completely new life, find a new identity, be himself. The best place to do that, he had decided, was London. That was where life was. That was where he would go. That was where he would both lose and find himself!

CHAPTER NINETEEN

'Nice arse on that, eh?'

Fran looked round in surprise. Kevin had come into the bathroom and caught him peeping through the open window at the girl in the garden next door – she was lying on her front on a blanket on the lawn, in her bikini, sunbathing while studying. He shouldn't have left the door open, he thought, annoyed with himself.

'What? Oh, yeah,' he agreed, blushing and turning away to wash his hands for the second time.

'Not a bad pair of tits, too,' Kevin remarked, ogling the girl through the window.

Frank laughed uncomfortably.

'Wouldn't mind giving her one,' Kevin said, unzipping his flies and peeing noisily, which embarrassed him still more. 'What do you say?'

'She's all right, I suppose,' Fran shrugged, drying his hands quickly and hurrying out.

He went back to his deckchair in the garden, from where he could only glimpse the girl through the rose bushes, picked up his book – Bertrand Russell's 'History of Western Philosophy' – and started reading again. But he couldn't concentrate, because he couldn't stop looking at her.

He was annoyed with himself for having been so embarrassed in the bathroom. It was all a hangover from the seminary, he reflected. Girls were the agents of the Devil! You weren't allowed to think about them or talk about them, let alone look at them – not that there was any chance of that. You weren't even allowed to pee in each other's presence, they were so hung up about the body. God, he was near the end of his second year at university, it was three years since he had left the seminary and he still had these hang-ups!

He was annoyed with Kevin too, for talking like that about her. He had noticed her for the first time a few days ago and been secretly watching her since, sunbathing, going shopping with her parents or coming home from school in her green gymslip, cream blouse and panama hat, the uniform of the girls' grammar school she went to and in which she looked so sexy. He had even started fantasising about her, imagining what it would be like to have her as his girlfriend, kiss her, touch her, be touched by her ...

Kevin's remarks made him feel irrationally jealous too, as if she actually was his girlfriend. But the thought of how unlikely that was suddenly depressed him. He had tried to pluck up the courage to say hello to her several times, but always funked it. This was another golden opportunity. Why didn't he grab it, before she went in? If he didn't, it would mean *they* had won again. That thought decided it. He stood up, ambled over to the fence and pretended to examine the roses, with Bertrand Russell under his arm.

'Hello,' she said, looking up from her books with a smile.

'Oh, hello,' he said, surprised, trying not to blush.

He was glad she had spoken first. To his relief she sounded friendly, not snooty like the girls at university. Quick, say something else, he told himself!

'What are you studying?' he asked, still trying not to blush.

'I'm revising for my O-levels,' she said.

'Oh,' he said, surprised again – that meant she was only sixteen.

'Yes, that's right, 'O' levels,' she quipped.

He laughed, pleased she had a sense of humour.

'What about you?' she asked, glancing at his book.

'I'm revising for my second-year university exams – philosophy,' he elucidated, hoping that didn't put her off.

'Oh,' she said in turn, sounding impressed. 'So you're a philosopher, are you?'

'Not much of a one, I'm afraid,' he laughed. 'What are you revising exactly?'

'Latin,' she said.

'Oh, good,' he said, surprised yet again. She pulled a face and moved a strand of blonde hair from over her eye, tucking it behind her ear, a gesture that made his heart skip a beat. 'Don't you like it?' he asked.

'I just can't do it,' she said, with a pout.

'Do you want some help?' he asked, impulsively.

'Have you done Latin?'

'I did it for A-level – it was my best subject, after English,' he told her. Little did he think, back in the Sixth Form at the junior seminary, that it would ever come in so useful! 'I can help you, if you like.'

'If you don't mind,' she said, eagerly.

'Not at all,' he said, suddenly nervous at the thought.

'Why don't you come round?' she suggested.

'Have you got some smelling salts?'

'What for?'

'To help me come round.' To his relief she laughed, feeble as the joke was. 'Shall I come round now?' he asked, stalling.

'If you're sure you don't mind.'

'No, not at all. Shall I come round the front?' he asked stupidly, still stalling.

'Unless you want to jump over the fence,' she said. 'But I wouldn't advise that.'

'Why not?' he grinned.

'You might break something.'

'You mean my leg?'

'No, the fence.'

He laughed. 'I could dig a tunnel,' he suggested. Christ, he was *still* stalling! What was wrong with him? Why didn't he just go?

'Yes, but I think the front way might be quicker,' she said, dryly.

'All right, I'll come round the front,' he agreed, and did so.

When he reached her, he stood awkwardly looking down at her, his senses swimming at the sight of her semi-naked body, which was still lily-white, despite her time in the sun.

'Sit down,' she said, patting the blanket beside her.

'Thanks,' he said, but sat cross-legged on the grass at a safe distance from her and put Bertrand Russell down beside him.

She was still lying on her front, propped up on her elbows. He had to struggle to keep his eyes off her bikini-clad bottom, round as an apple. Every now and then she bent a bare, white, well-turned leg up and let it fall, in a way that almost hypnotized him. His heart was racing and to his embarrassment he had an erection – but at least that meant he was normal, he told himself.

'What's your name?' she asked.

'Frank,' he told her, his voice hoarse. 'What's yours?'

'Sally.' He smiled and there was an awkward silence, which to his relief she broke. 'What university do you go to?' she asked.

'Manchester,' he told her.

'What are you doing?'

'English and philosophy.'

'Wow, you must be good!'

'Why?' he asked, glad she was impressed.

'It's supposed to be hard to get into.'

'Is it?'

'That's what we're told. I'm hoping to though.'

'Yes? To do what?'

'Chemistry.'

'Oh.'

'Don't say it like that!'

'Sorry, I didn't mean it like that.' He cursed himself silently.

'It's all right – I know it's not everyone's favourite subject. It just happens to be mine.'

'Well, I hope you make it. I'm sure you will.'

'Thanks.'

'I can't help you with it though, I'm afraid,' he said, wishing he wasn't such a scientific ignoramus. Absurdly, there had been no science at all at the junior seminary, he recalled. They had been afraid – rightly, no doubt – that science and superstition wouldn't mix.

'I don't need help with my chemistry, but I do with this,' she said, tapping the book with her pen.

'What is it you can't do?' he asked.

'I can't translate this stuff.'

'Let's have a look.'

She handed him the book – it was a passage from Julius Caesar's 'De Bello Gallico'. 'This is a doddle,' he grinned.

214

'Do it for me then.'

'Have you already tried it?'

'Yes, but I didn't get very far.'

'OK, I'll, read out the translation and you write it down. Then we can go through it. All right?'

'Yes, please,' she said, pen poised.

He went through it, cracking a few jokes as he did so and making her laugh. When they had finished, he looked at his watch – he was worried about staying too long with her and about his mother coming home from work and seeing him with her, ridiculous as that was at his age. Besides, it was torture being so close to her and being able to see so much of her, without being able to touch her.

The thought that he probably never would be able to touch her suddenly depressed him again. She only saw him as a friendly neighbour or at best a big brother, he supposed glumly, especially as she had no brothers or sisters. Did she have a boyfriend, he wondered? She must have, he supposed, being so attractive, though he hadn't seen or heard any evidence of one. That was an even more depressing thought.

'I'd better go,' he said.

'Oh, why?' she asked, sounding disappointed.

'I've got to peel the spuds before my mother comes home.' It sounded comical, though it was true.

'Well, thanks for your help,' she said. 'I could never have done it on my own.'

'That's all right,' he said, picking up his 'History of Western Philosophy'.

He couldn't just leave her like this, he thought. He had to ask her out. He had to!

'Are you doing anything on Saturday evening?' he screwed up his courage to ask, trying to sound casual.

'I'm babysitting,' she said.

'Oh,' he said, gutted, but trying not to show it. That was it. She wasn't interested in him. He was stupid ever to think she might have been.

'What are you doing?' she asked.

'Me? Oh, I'm not sure yet,' he shrugged, as if he had so many options he didn't know which one to choose.

'Why don't you come and keep me company?'

For a moment he couldn't quite believe he had heard right. His heart seemed to miss a beat. 'All right,' he shrugged, trying not to sound excited. 'Where?'

'Number ten, just across the road.'

'What time?'

'Nine o'clock?'

'OK. I'll see you then. Bye.'

He stood up and hurried away, hardly able to hide his excitement any longer. He ran up to his bedroom and flung himself on his bed with a whoop of delight. Only then did he notice Kevin lying on the other bed, reading.

'You sound as if you've cracked it, you crafty bugger,' Kevin commented.

'I think I have,' he laughed, embarrassed, but too excited to care.

At nine o'clock on Saturday, having bathed and groomed himself, he knocked nervously on the front door of number ten and waited, half-hoping there would be no answer. However, the door opened almost immediately and there she was, in a green silk blouse and tight white cords, blonde hair tied back with a green ribbon. She looked so pretty that his heart leapt with delight.

'Hello,' he said.

'Hello,' she said, as if surprised to see him.

Oh, God, he thought, she's forgotten or changed her mind! 'You haven't forgotten, have you?' he asked.

'Oh, no,' she said. 'It's just that I never really thought you'd come.'

'I always carry out my threats, I'm afraid,' he joked. She never really thought he'd come? Wild horses couldn't have kept him away!

'Well, come in,' she said.

'Are you sure it's all right?' he asked.

'Yes, come in, please,' she insisted, opening the door wider for him.

'Thanks,' he said, stepping into the plushly-carpeted hall.

She shut the door behind him, put a finger to her lips and with another finger beckoned him to follow her. Nervously, he did so, into a large, elegantly-furnished lounge, where a colour television was on low.

'Would you like a cup of tea?' she asked.

'That'd be nice, thanks,' he said, even more nervous now at the prospect of being alone with her. He noticed that she had put on some mascara and lipstick, which made her look slightly older.

'Have a seat, I'll be back in a jiffy,' she said, going out.

'Thanks,' he said, and glanced around the room, wondering where he should sit. The obvious place was on the settee in front of the telly, but she was evidently sitting there – there was a women's magazine open on it – and he didn't have the nerve to sit so near her. Instead, he pulled an expensive-looking chair out from under the mahogany dining table and sat on it, trying to calm his nerves. After a few minutes, she came back in with a cup of tea on a saucer and a plate of Rich Tea biscuits, which she handed to him.

'Thank you,' he said, taking them, his hands trembling so much that the cup of tea almost spilled. Embarrassed, he put them down on the table quickly, hoping she hadn't noticed. She went over to the settee, kicked off her shoes and curled up in the corner. Her blouse, he noticed, accentuated her small but pert breasts, while her trousers accentuated her shapely hips and legs. God, she was pretty! She didn't really like him, did she?

'How's the revision going?' he asked, to make conversation, while he drank the tea and nibbled a biscuit, though he didn't really feel like either.

'All right, thanks,' she said. 'How about yours?'

'All right,' he said, though he had done so little work he was worried about his exams. 'When's your first exam?'

'Next Thursday,' she said.

'How do you feel?'

'Scared,' she confessed.

'You'll be all right,' he reassured her. 'Eight grade As!'

'You must be joking,' she laughed. 'I hope to get one in chemistry though.'

'Best of luck – I'll keep my fingers crossed for you.'

'Thanks.'

'Toes, too, if you like.'

'I don't think that'll be necessary, thanks,' she laughed. 'Except for Latin,' she added.

'Don't worry,' he reassured her, 'you'll pass.'

'With your help.'

'I haven't helped you much.'

'Can you help me again?'

'Sure. I'd be glad to.' Only too glad to, he thought!

There was an awkward pause.

'That was nice, thanks,' he said, finishing the tea.

'Why don't you come and sit over here?' she suggested, patting the plush dralon upholstery beside her. 'It's more comfortable.'

'I'm OK, here, thanks,' he replied, cursing his cowardice. 'Besides, it's bad for your eyes to be so near the telly,' he added, fatuously.

'I can always switch that off,' she said.

'Switch it off? It's just getting to the exciting part!' he exclaimed, even more fatuously. Oh, God, he thought, what a prat he was! Here he was, for only the second time in his life, on his own in a room with a pretty girl and he was too shy to go near her. He felt like rushing out of the room.

However, he stayed where he was, at a safe distance, as if glued to the chair, and continued to make nervous small talk with her across several yards of Axminster for another hour. By half-past ten he couldn't stand the strain any longer.

'What time are they coming home?' he asked, looking at his watch.

'About eleven,' she said.

'I'd better go,' he said. 'They won't want to see me here.'

'They won't mind,' she said.

'I'd better go, anyway,' he said, standing up, eager now to escape.

'If you want to,' she said, getting up and leading the way to the front door.

'Thanks for coming,' she said, turning to him without opening the door.

'That's all right,' he said.

Did she want him to give her a kiss? He ought to, he supposed, but didn't dare. He wished she would open the door – all he wanted to do was leave as quickly as possible. 'I'd better go,' he said, glancing past her at the door, and to his relief she opened it for him.

'Goodnight, then,' she said. 'And thanks for coming.'

'I'll see you. Goodnight,' he said, stepping out and hurrying away.

It was a warm spring night, so he went for a walk. He needed to be alone for a while. Besides, he didn't want to go home before his parents went to bed, because they would ask him where he had been. He didn't want them to know he had been seeing a girl, especially the girl next door. It was ridiculous at the age of twenty-three, but that was what came of being stuck in a seminary till he was twenty-one, he reflected morosely – he was doing now what he should have been doing seven or eight years ago, when he was fifteen or sixteen. Instead, he had been in love with Mark Brown, he remembered shamefully.

He was furious with himself for the way he had behaved with Sally – just like a bloody, wet-behind-the-ears adolescent! He had to conquer this shyness with girls, he told himself. If he didn't, he would never find a girlfriend and they, the 'Ghosters', would have won. He might as well have stayed in the seminary – except for the small problem that he didn't believe in God. Tonight had been another disaster. She would probably never want to see him again and he wouldn't blame her.

All was not lost though. She had asked him to help her with her Latin again, though they hadn't actually arranged when. He would have to make a point of going to see her, preferably in her garden – he didn't fancy confronting her parents. It would take a bit of nerve, but he'd have to do it. She was so lovely! He really liked her, and not just physically – she was a lovely person, too. And amazingly, she seemed to like him, though he wasn't so sure after tonight.

The velvety night air and the silence of the leafy suburban streets helped to relax him, as did the exercise of walking. The air was perfumed with the scents of flowers wafting from the neat, well-kept gardens, as well as the still blossom-laden cherry trees that lined the streets. He paused to gaze up at the purple sky, where stars twinkled like sapphires. His mood suddenly swung upwards too.

Maybe this was the best anyone could hope for, he reflected, standing to take it all in – a few moments of ephemeral happiness here and there. Maybe there was no such thing as long-term happiness – maybe it was just an illusion. Life was hard. You were lucky if you were healthy, with a roof over your head, a shirt on your back and food in your belly. In the end your luck always ran out too, because you snuffed it. It was all futile, meaningless, a waste of time and effort ...

As always, this thought brought him back down to earth with a bump, so he banished it. Life *was* worth living, no matter how hard or meaningless, he told himself. It was worth living for moments like these. It was worth living for a few moments with someone as lovely as Sally. It was worth living just to have known her, even if he never saw her again. It would be worth living for the memory of what had been and what might have been. Maybe he should write that in a poem for her, it suddenly occurred to him. Yes, he would, he decided, tonight, right now, and turned to walk back home, spirits high again.

He didn't make the same mistake the following Saturday. He politely declined the cup of tea and sat nervously on the settee, but with a 'safe' distance between them. She was wearing a lemon silk blouse and white jeans, with a silver hair band holding back her blonde hair and just a touch of make-up again. She looked so lovely that he hardly dared to look at her or speak to her.

'How are your exams going?' he forced himself to ask.

'OK, so far,' she said.

'Good,' he said. He was so nervous he couldn't think of anything else to say and there was an awkward silence.

'Thank you for coming,' she said, breaking it.

'You don't need to thank me,' he said. 'I wanted to.'

'I'm sure you'd prefer to be going for a drink with your brother or something, wouldn't you?'

'I'd much prefer to be here with you.'

'Would you?'

'Yes.'

'Are you sure?'

'Absolutely.'

'Why?'

This was the moment to tell her, he realised, and took a deep breath.

'I like you,' he said, glancing at her and trying not to blush.

'I like you, too,' she whispered, bashfully.

Her hand was lying on the settee between them. Impulsively, he picked it up and held it. It was only the second time in his life that he had held a girl's hand and he was surprised by how small and soft and delicate it felt. His heart was palpitating with both excitement and apprehension that she would pull it away, but to his relief she didn't. Instead she leant towards him and he towards her. A moment later he was holding her in his arms and they were kissing, his heart pounding.

'I love you, Sally,' he whispered in her ear, taking his lips from hers.

'I love you, Frank,' she sighed, clinging to him even more tightly and they kissed again.

While they kissed, he caressed her, letting his hand brush her breasts. She didn't object, so gradually he became more daring and started to fondle them. To his delight, she still didn't object. They felt small, but he didn't care – it was the first time he had ever touched a girl's breasts and anyway he loved her. His heart was pounding painfully and he had a huge erection. He became even more daring and tried to slip his hand between her thighs.

'Not there, Frank, please,' she said, sharply.

'Sorry,' he said, pulling his hand away quickly and letting go of her, his face burning with shame. He'd gone too far! He'd blown it!

'It's all right,' she said. 'It's just that I've got, you know, my thing.'

It took him a moment to realise what she meant. 'Oh, I'm sorry,' he said again, blushing madly despite himself.

'No, *I'm* sorry,' she said.

'No, *I'm* sorry,' he insisted.

They both laughed, threw their arms round each other and kissed again.

'I love you,' she whispered in his ear.

'I love *you,*' he whispered in hers, caressing the nape of her neck with his fingertips tenderly.

This was it, he thought, triumphantly! At last he had a girlfriend! He was in love! He was normal! He was happy! He was happy just to hold her in his arms like this. He would be happy to hold her in his arms like this for ever. If only it could last for ever! It *would* last for ever! It would transcend time and space. It would be like a star – even after they had gone, its light would shine on. And somehow, maybe they would survive with it, on some other plane, in some other dimension ...

'What are you thinking about?' she whispered.

'About you and me,' he whispered back.

'Tell me,' she insisted.

'Not now.'

'Please.'

'I'll write it for you, in another poem,' he said.

'Oh, Frank, I love you so much,' she sighed, tears in her eyes. 'You do love me, don't you? Tell me!'

'Yes, I love you, don't cry,' he laughed, almost in tears himself, holding her tight and kissing the tears from her eyes, then kissing her on the lips again.

CHAPTER TWENTY

'I'm going out,' he said to his parents, passing through the kitchen one evening.

'With that one over there?' his mother asked, sarcastically.

'Yes, as it happens,' he admitted, flushing – so she knew.

'Sure, she's only half your age,' she sneered.

'Two thirds my age, to be exact,' he replied. Sally was sixteen.

'Ahem. She is a bit young for you, isn't she, Frank?' his father said, lowering his newspaper and removing his pipe.

'I don't think so,' he said, annoyed. If only they knew how little it mattered to him! All that mattered to him was that he had a girlfriend – he was normal!

'Baby snatcher!' his mother jibed.

'Say what you like,' he retorted, going out and closing the door angrily behind him.

He had tried to keep his relationship with Sally secret, especially from his mother, but knew it would be impossible for long. He knew she would take it badly when she found out. Little did he know how badly.

'Why's she like that?' Sally asked, when he told her later in the pub.

'She's jealous,' he said, though it pained him to say it.

'Jealous of me?' Sally asked, ingenuously.

'Not just you – she'd be jealous of any girl I went out with,' he said, realising he was on dangerous ground.

'Why?' Sally asked, frowning.

He hadn't told Sally anything about his past and didn't really want to now. It was too painful – he didn't want to talk about it with anyone, wanted to forget about it. Anyway, he didn't think she would understand, especially as she was neither Irish nor Catholic. When she asked him why he had gone to university so late – always an uncomfortable question – he just said he had worked for a couple of years after leaving school.

'Because I'm her eldest son and she idolises me,' he said, though it was only part of the truth.

'I can understand that,' Sally said, putting her face near to his and gazing into his eyes.

'Can you?' he smiled, flattered. The smell of her perfume excited him, made him want to kiss her, but he was still shy about kissing in public.

'I'd idolise you if you were my son.'

'Would you?' he laughed, glad she didn't seem to want to ask any further questions or to be too upset by what he had told her.

'Do you still love me?' she asked anxiously, still gazing into his eyes.

'Yes, of course,' he said, gazing back into hers.

He suddenly felt sorry for her, being caught up in the crossfire between his mother and himself. He put his arm around her, pulled her close and kissed her. As always when they kissed, his senses swam. However, at the back of his mind lurked the memory of his mother's words, like a maggot he was afraid would destroy this first delicate bloom of love that had budded in the desert of his heart ...

One afternoon a few days later, he wandered into his parents' bedroom and saw his mother taking a slug from a bottle of sherry. She turned and stared at him wide-eyed, like a startled animal, the bottle still to her mouth.

'Sorry,' he mumbled, hurrying out, as embarrassed as if he had found her naked. He was both shocked and guilt-stricken. He had suspected that she drank and now he knew. She was obviously very unhappy. Was it because of him? It made his heart bleed to think so. But what could he do?

He knew what she would like him to do – go back to the seminary and become a priest. That was impossible, of course, even if he wanted to, which he certainly didn't – it would be like going back to a living death. Apart from anything else, it would mean giving up Sally and he wasn't going to do that – he loved her.

She would like him to at least start going to Mass again, he supposed, but he couldn't even bring himself to do that – it would be like going to a voodoo ceremony or séance. He found the very thought abhorrent. There was only one solution really, to leave home, but he couldn't do that until he had finished university, and he still had one more year to do.

He was fed up with university. He wanted to leave and run off to London, but couldn't do that to his parents. He had to stick it out, though he didn't know how he was going to get through his final exams in his present state of mind. Besides, if he did go to London, what would happen to Sally? That was a question he didn't even want to think about yet.

'Get that slut out of my house!'

His mother had come home late from work and walked into the kitchen to see Sally there, sitting in her school uniform at the kitchen table with his father and himself. It was the first time he had dared to bring Sally into the house and his father at least was doing his best to be polite. His mother, obviously, felt differently. Having given her greeting, she turned and left, slamming the door behind her.

Mortified, he jumped up and yanked open the door. His mother was standing unsteadily in the hall, her nurse's bag in one hand, the other one holding onto the banisters. With a shock he realised she was drunk. He felt a stab of pity for her. 'Who are you calling a slut?' he demanded.

'That one in there!' she shouted drunkenly. 'That trollop! That English trollop! Get her out of my house!'

'You're sick!' he shouted back at her – the bigotry of the word 'English' hurt him even more than the other words.

'Frank! Nan!' his father, embarrassed, came into the hall to mediate.

'She's sick!' he shouted at his father and went back into the kitchen. Sally was standing up, looking bewildered.

'Come on, let's go,' he said, taking her by the arm and ushering her towards the door. 'That's it!' he yelled back at his parents, both still in the hall. 'I'm leaving! I'm not living here any more! I'm going for good!' He ushered Sally out, slamming the door.

'I'm sorry,' he said to her later, sitting on a park bench with an arm around her shoulders. 'She didn't really mean it. She was drunk. She didn't know what she was saying.'

'It's all right, Frank,' Sally said, sweetly.

'You're not upset?'

'Yes, but it doesn't matter, not as long as you still love me.'

'I love you more than ever.' He pulled her close and kissed her, a long, slow, lingering kiss …

As he did so though, he couldn't get the echo of his mother's shocking words out of his mind, nor the thought that she was behaving like this because of his own behaviour and how much it must hurt her. It was understandable – she had given him birth, brought him up and loved him, at least for the first twelve years of his life, and now he had rejected her and all she believed in. Of course she couldn't accept Sally – she wouldn't be able to accept any girl he went out with, except possibly the Blessed Virgin Mary! Hell indeed had no fury like a woman scorned. It was a bit like 'Sons and Lovers', which he was reading.

'What are you thinking?' Sally asked.

'I was just thinking it's like 'Sons and Lovers'.'

'What's that?'

'It's a novel by D. H. Lawrence. Have you heard of it?'

'I've heard of D. H. Lawrence, but I haven't read anything by him. Didn't he write 'Lady Chatterley's Lover'?'

'That's right, but I think he'd gone a bit crackers by then. 'Sons and Lovers' is brilliant though. I'll lend it to you.'

'What's it about?'

'It's about a boy growing up and breaking free, especially from his mother.'

'Like you?'

'A bit,' he laughed.

She gave him a peck on the cheek. 'What are you going to do?'

'There's only one thing to do,' he said.

'What's that?'

'Leave home. I've got to. I should've done it ages ago. I can't live with them any longer.'

It would be the second time he had left home, he reflected ironically. Of course, he should never have gone back home when he left the seminary, but he had had nowhere else to go. He couldn't tell Sally that though.

'Where will you live?' she asked.

'I'll have to find a room or something.'

She looked worried.

'What's wrong?' he asked.

'You won't leave me as well, will you?'

'Of course not,' he said, hugging her. 'That's part of the reason for leaving home – if I have a place of my own, we can be together more.' At the back of his mind was the hope that, if he had a place to take her to, she would go to bed with him. Until now she wouldn't go further than petting – she was afraid of getting pregnant, which he understood, but he was finding it more and more frustrating. He wanted to go to bed with her both because he loved her and for the experience. He was twenty-four and still a virgin! 'Don't you want that?' he asked her.

'Yes, you know I do,' she said, offended.

'Will you help me find a place then?'

'Yes, of course.'

'Thank you. I love you.'

'I love you.'

He pulled her closer and they kissed. He slipped his hand under her school blazer, felt for one of her breasts and squeezed it softly. As always, it gave him an erection. He could hardly wait to make love to her properly and at last prove to himself he was a man, a real man, a *normal* man ...

'What do you want to move into some filthy old flat for, when you've got a good home here and someone to look after you?' his mother demanded indignantly, when he told his parents he was leaving home.

'I don't need to be looked after,' he replied, suppressing the impulse to point out that he had had no one to look after him since he was twelve. 'I'm not a child.'

'Ahem. We all know why he wants to move into a flat,' his

227

father took his pipe out of his mouth and remarked cryptically from behind his 'Evening News'.

'I need a place of my own to study. I can't study here. I've got my finals in a few weeks,' he said, stung by his father's remark, but ignoring it.

It was partly true – he was worried he might flunk his finals and he couldn't study properly at home, still couldn't adapt to family life in a suburban semi after nine years in a 'monastery'. He needed privacy. He had opted to do a long essay on Hemingway, instead of one of the examination papers, which he hadn't even started yet and which had to be handed in by Easter. He was also behind with his other essays. He felt like giving up and taking off for London, but couldn't let his parents down now, having come so far. Besides, there was Sally to think of ...

'If you need a room to study in you can have Aunty Aggie's, now that she's gone. God have mercy on her soul,' his mother said.

God have mercy on the whole damn lot of us, if there is one, he thought bitterly. Aunty Aggie had been an old maiden aunt of his father's whom his parents had taken in a few years ago. By 'gone' his mother meant 'died' and, no doubt, gone to Heaven – belief in which now struck him as pathetically childish.

The old lady had died a couple of weeks ago, on a sunny, spring afternoon. Somehow the fact it was spring and the sun was shining when she died made it all the more poignant. The whole family – all seven of them – had gathered in the small back bedroom around her bed to watch her die. As the end approached, they knelt and said the rosary, led by his mother. He joined in reluctantly, mumbling the words he still knew so well, but now found so much mumbo-jumbo. The old woman lay there, her eyes rolling, one hand clutching the bedclothes, the other one clawing the wall, gasping more and more desperately for air, as if she was suffocating – which in a way, he supposed, she was.

It was the first time he had ever seen anyone die and what he felt, more than anything else, was anger, to think that this was how it all ended, not just for her, but for everyone, no matter

who or what they were or how well or badly they had lived –
it all ended in this indignity and defeat. Death *did* have
dominion! His mother kept glancing at him, probably hoping
that the experience of witnessing death might shock him back
into belief, but if anything it only confirmed him in his
disbelief. How could this horror, this obscenity, be reconciled
with the idea of a loving, benevolent, omnipotent God, he kept
asking himself?

When his sister, Molly, a nurse like his mother, who had
taken hold of one the old woman's hands, finally said, 'She's
gone,' it was hard to believe. It was hard to believe that
suddenly, at two minutes past four precisely, after eighty-six
years, the old woman was no more, had ceased to exist, would
never wake up, or blink, or breathe, or speak, or eat, or laugh
again. She was *dead*. She was suddenly no more than a bag of
guts and bones, to be disposed of as soon as possible, like so
much garbage or offal. What a shame, he thought, to die on
such a beautiful day and only hoped that when his turn came
there would be someone as competent and compassionate as his
sister to hold his hand.

Later that evening, he went nervously on his own into the
room where the old woman's body lay. It was a warm evening,
yet the room was icy cold and filled with a repellent, fishy
odour. He felt sick, but forced himself to remain in the room for
a few minutes. The body, which his mother and sister had
washed and dressed, lay in the bed as still as a statue. They had
tied a bandage under the chin and around the top of the white-
haired old head with a bow, like a macabre ribbon – to keep the
mouth closed, he supposed. Around the hands they had
entwined some rosary beads and on her chest placed the crucifix
that normally hung on the wall over the bed. He was shocked by
how small and shrivelled she looked, as if she had shrunk.
Before leaving, he steeled himself to kiss her forehead, which
was as white and cold as marble, and whispered, 'Goodbye',
blinking back tears.

The next day two undertakers in black coats came, carried the
corpse downstairs in a metal box, shoved it in the back of a
black van and drove off. He didn't go to the funeral and his
father, he knew, hadn't forgiven him. He couldn't bring himself

to go, not out of any disregard for the dead woman, but because he couldn't bring himself to take part in what seemed to him a superstitious and hypocritical charade. Most of the relations who would be there had shown little or no interest in the old woman when she was alive. Ironically, *he* used to visit her regularly once or twice a week when he was home on holiday from the seminary and had probably shown her more kindness during her lifetime, when it mattered, than all the rest of them put together, except for his parents themselves. He didn't point this out to his father though.

Childish as it seemed, the idea of moving into the old woman's room, which had remained empty since she died, gave him the creeps. Anyway, he was determined to leave home – he couldn't stand the claustrophobia or his mother's hostility any longer. Even his father had turned against him now, because he hadn't gone to the funeral.

'I need peace and quiet to study, if I'm going to get my degree,' he replied to his mother's suggestion.

'I shouldn't think you'll have much difficulty getting your degree,' his father remarked, acidly.

Little do you know, he thought, biting his tongue. None of them knew the strain he was under, the sheer effort of will it took for him just to get up in the morning and face another meaningless day, never mind the pressure of essay deadlines and exams. He was really afraid he might fail his finals. He hardly knew how he had managed to get through the first two years. One student had already committed suicide under the strain and two others had had nervous breakdowns.

He was tempted to tell them this, but bit his tongue again – it would not only be futile, but counter-productive. Ironically, it was as much for their sake that he wanted to move, so that he wouldn't fail or have a nervous breakdown or worse. Even more ironically, the fact that he had made it this far was in no small part thanks to Sally, whom his mother refused to let into the house.

'I'm sorry, I'm going,' he said adamantly, though there was a lump in his throat, and walked out of the room.

However, tensions from within as well as without were already causing strains in his relationship with Sally. With exams approaching for both of them, they went out only once a week, on Saturday nights. Afterwards, they would go back to his flat and sit on the settee, drinking coffee, chatting and kissing. Then she would sit on his lap and they would continue petting more and more heavily. Eventually, he would carry her, limp in his arms, over to the bed.

There they would carry on kissing, caressing and fondling each other even more intimately. She would let him touch her anywhere, but she wouldn't let him take any of her clothes off, not even her tights. Whenever he tried to, she stopped him, pleading, 'No, Frank, please.' He knew she was right, since neither of them had any form of contraception – she was not on the pill and he was too shy to buy condoms, even from a machine, never mind use one. He was also secretly afraid of actually doing it properly, because he wasn't sure if he would be able to ...

However, she wouldn't relieve him with her hand either and he was too shy to ask her. As a result, he became more and more frustrated, which wasn't helped by frequently hearing the amorous activities of Barry, the young photocopier salesman upstairs, and having to listen to him boasting about them as well. Barry was into reproduction in a big way, though as far as he knew he had no children to show for it. He had offered to sell him some condoms cheap, but he was too priggish to take up the offer and ended up buying a second-hand photocopier from him instead.

The only other occupant of the house was a Persian engineering student with a big black moustache, Ali, or 'Ali Baba' as Barry called him. Ali was obviously lonely and had started inviting him upstairs to his room for tea, which he made in the Persian way, in a glass, without milk and with a lot of sugar. At first he went reluctantly, afraid of wasting valuable study time, but Ali was so friendly and good-natured he became glad of the occasional company. He was lonely himself, having left home and seeing Sally only once a week, though Ali was slightly farther away from home and had no girlfriend.

He found Ali interesting, because he was the first foreigner he had met properly, especially from such an exotic place as Persia. He was also the first Muslim he had ever met and he was fascinated to learn about Islam, as well as Persia, from him. He was not at all fanatical, but devout enough to have a prayer mat in his room, which he showed him and said he used to pray five times a day – or as often as possible – facing Mecca. Funnily enough, exactly opposite and in the same direction as Mecca, there was a Mecca Bingo Hall, which became a joke between them.

He was surprised that Ali – or any intelligent person in the twentieth century – could still believe in God and told him so. Ali, for his part, was shocked that he did not believe in God. So they started discussing religion. Having studied philosophy and theology, he felt he might have an unfair advantage, but Ali was able to defend his corner well. His last line of defence was that the universe must have been created by Someone and could not have come about by chance, as he had suggested.

'It's like to say this watch could be make by the chance,' Ali argued, taking his watch off his hirsute wrist and waving it at him. 'Someone must have make it, no?'

'I'm not saying the universe could have happened by chance just like that, overnight,' he replied, snapping his fingers. 'It's evolved over millions and millions of years. In a sense, the watch is a product of evolution, too. It's taken human beings millions of years to develop the skill and technology to produce it.'

'You still do not explain where basic material of universe is coming from.'

'I admit I don't know. Maybe it was always there. Isn't that a possibility?'

'What do you mean?'

'Maybe the universe had no beginning, so it didn't need a maker.'

'Had no beginning? It must be!'

'Not necessarily. Maybe it's infinite, with no beginning or end.'

'I cannot imagine.'

'Does Allah have a beginning or end?'

'No, He is infinite.'

'There you are, then. Maybe the universe itself is infinite.'

'It cannot be!' Ali shook his head.

'It's all a question of time and the concept of time. Talking about which,' he said, looking at his own watch, 'I think it's time we went for a drink or they'll be closing. We'll leave the concept of time for another day.'

They had started going for a drink towards the end of the evening. Ali, being a Muslim, did not drink anything alcoholic, because it was against his religion, he told him. However, he was interested in girls and hoped to meet one in the pub. Of course, he never did. He must be crazy with frustration, Frank thought, and wondered if he masturbated or if that was also a sin in the Muslim religion.

'If you want to meet girls, you have to go to a disco or club,' he told Ali, giving him the benefit of his extensive worldly experience.

'We go together, yes?' Ali suggested eagerly.

'I've got to study,' he said, glad of the excuse – he didn't fancy going on the pull with Ali. 'Besides, I've got a girlfriend, haven't I?'

'Ah, yes. She is very nice. You are lucky,' Ali said, hangdog.

'I suppose so,' he said, though he was starting to wonder.

His relationship with Sally had become strained close to breaking point. They were seeing less and less of each other, with the excuse that they were both under pressure of exams, and when they did see each other they had started arguing. They had their worst argument ever when he told her he wanted to go to live in London after his exams. Through helping Ali with his English, he had realised what he could do to earn a living there – teach English to foreigners.

'And what about me?' Sally had asked, hurt. They were sitting next to each other in their favourite pub.

'You can come and visit me. I'll come back and visit you.' Even as he said it though, he knew it wouldn't work.

'It won't be the same,' she said.

'Of course it will.'

'Why do you want to go to London, anyway?'

'I've told you – it's where it's all at, as they say. I want to see what it's like.'

'What's wrong with Manchester?'

'It's all right, but it's too – small, provincial, boring. I mean, I know it too well. I want to get away from it, live somewhere new, somewhere different.'

'You want to get away from me, too, don't you?' she said, tears in her eyes.

'Don't be silly, I love you,' he said, choking and giving her a hug, though he knew there was a horrible germ of truth in what she said – he wanted to get away not just from Manchester, but everyone in it, his family and, yes, even her. He wanted to make a completely new start.

'If you loved me, you wouldn't leave me,' she sobbed, dabbing her eyes with a hankie.

'I'm not leaving you,' he said, annoyed.

'Yes you are.'

'You're not being logical, Sally,' he objected, exasperated.

'Love isn't logical.'

That cut through all his pretences and defences like a scalpel. It was the simple truth and the sharpest thing he had ever heard her say. He had no answer to it.

'I want to go home,' she said, picking up her coat.

'Now you're *really* being silly,' he protested, alarmed.

'Take me home, please, Frank,' she insisted, standing up.

'You're being childish. Let's talk about it at least.'

'I'm fed up talking about it. If you want to go to London and leave me, that's all there is to it. I'm going home.'

'If that's the way you feel, go home,' he said, his patience suddenly snapping.

She walked out of the pub on her own. He knew he shouldn't, but he sat there and let her go, feeling ashamed of himself. But he felt angry, too, because she was trying to stop him doing something he really wanted to do, needed to do. 'If you loved me, you wouldn't leave me.' That was emotional blackmail! It made him feel trapped and he never wanted to be trapped again, not after nine years in a seminary.

Maybe she was right though. Maybe he didn't really love her. Maybe he was deluding himself and her, playing a game, playing with her. Maybe he was incapable of love. After all, those nine years were largely devoted to crushing the capacity for love in any normal, human sense. Maybe he would never be able to love properly. Maybe he would be an emotional cripple for life. The thought, as always, depressed him.

He stayed in the pub and drank several more pints of Guinness, then staggered back to his flat. There he put on Simon and Garfunkel, poured himself a large glass of Bushmills and, crying tears of remorse and self-pity, drank himself unconscious ...

'Can you come and see me?' Sally asked on the phone the following evening.

He was in the middle of typing up his long essay on Hemingway, which was already late and had to be on his tutor's desk first thing in the morning.

'Why?' he asked.

'I think we need to talk.'

'About what?'

'About us.'

'Couldn't you come here?' he suggested, though he didn't really have time to see her at all and was in no mood to talk.

'Don't you want to see me?'

'Of course I do, but I've got to finish this tonight, Sally. You know that. Please try to understand.'

She said nothing. There was a knot in his stomach. 'I'll come and see you tomorrow night if you like,' he said, by way of mollification.

She still said nothing. The knot in his stomach became tighter. At last she gave a long sigh and spoke. 'I think it's better if we don't see each other any more, Frank.'

His stomach lurched. 'What do you mean?'

She sighed again. 'We don't seem to be getting anywhere these days, do we?'

He knew it was true, so he couldn't argue. It had been coming for some time, like an unstoppable train, yet he couldn't accept it.

'If that's how you feel,' he said coldly and put down the phone. He really didn't need this, with all the pressure he was under!

He went back to his desk, but couldn't concentrate. There was a lump in his throat and tears sprang to his eyes, so that the page in his typewriter blurred. I bet big, macho Papa Hemingway never cried like this, he thought, ashamed, trying to blink them back. But he couldn't. The tears flowed down his cheeks. He had lost her. It was over, finished, the end, kaput. It was his second failure, his second 'farewell to arms' …

CHAPTER TWENTY-ONE

He got up and sat down to spend the morning writing as usual, both of which seemed harder than ever this morning. He had been in London for a few weeks now, but the initial excitement had worn off and he was starting to feel lonely, living on his own in a bed-sitter, with no friends.

It was a large, bright room with three walls painted white and one orange, a threadbare green carpet and all the necessary, if shoddy, furniture – even an easy-chair. He was sitting in the easy-chair now, in front of his Olivetti typewriter, using the coffee table as a desk. In one corner there was a single bed and in another the 'kitchen'. In between there was a large window, overlooking an unruly garden, through which he could see the candelabra-like crown of a horse-chestnut tree against the background of an azure sky.

Gazing round the room, he felt a sudden attack of claustrophobia. It was a pleasant enough room and he was lucky to have found it, especially as the rent was cheap, but sometimes it felt like a prison cell, to which he had been condemned for an indefinite period of solitary confinement, for some unknown crime, by some invisible judge. At weekends, when he felt like this, he just jumped up and went out, but never in the morning – the morning was for writing and that was sacred. He turned his gaze back to the blank sheet of paper in the typewriter and stared at it, frustrated at not being able to think of what to write or how to write it.

He remembered how excited he had felt on first arriving in London, carrying his most important worldly possession – his typewriter – in one hand and all his others in a holdall in the other: books, records and clothes, in that order. He was amazed by how big and busy it seemed and the first time he went on the underground he felt like a child on a funfair ride, each station a comic-strip of adverts for all the exciting things to do and see – plays, films, concerts, restaurants, exhibitions, museums, art galleries ...

The first time he emerged from the underground at Piccadilly Circus, he felt an almost religious sense of awe, as if he had completed a long-dreamt-of pilgrimage – as in a way he had. To him this was not just the centre of London, but of the world, the world he had almost rejected, but now wanted to experience as fully as possible. It was like a shrine, with the statue of Eros as the god in the middle – the God of love, real, physical, human love, not some religious abstraction. The theatres, cinemas, restaurants, clubs and pubs were tabernacles. The throngs of people out to enjoy themselves were the congregation. For music, there was the cheerful sound of pop blaring from record shops and boutiques. While the star-studded sky above was the dome, infinitely more majestic, mysterious and awe-inspiring than any cathedral.

The first few days were hard, but the excitement of being in London carried him through, like a surfer on the crest of a wave. He lived rough, sleeping in bunks in communal rooms in cheap hostels with lorry-drivers and third-world students and once even in a park, eating only takeaways and treating himself to a pint in the evening – which gave him a glimpse of how it must feel to be really poor, hungry and homeless. During the day he looked for a job and a room, both of which seemed depressingly difficult to find. After a week his meagre savings and his spirits were both running low and he was thinking of giving up, when to his elation he miraculously found both a job and this room on the same day.

By now though, the elation had worn off and he was feeling more and more forlorn, especially at weekends. On Saturday evenings he usually went out for a drink, hoping to meet someone to talk to – preferably female – but always ended up alone and drunk. Sunday afternoons were the worst – he went for a long walk or, if it was raining, to a cinema, art gallery or museum, but always wrapped in an icy shroud of loneliness.

Sometimes he wondered if he had made a terrible mistake, coming here where he knew nobody, leaving home and family and, worst of all, Sally. Sometimes he missed her so much he felt like jumping on a train and dashing back to Manchester to see her, or at least phoning or writing to her. But he didn't, because he knew their relationship had run its course, played itself out, was over. Besides, it would be an admission of defeat. He felt guilty about the way it had ended and had written a letter of apology, but not posted it. It was better to leave it in the past, painful as it was, he told himself, hoping time would heal the wound for both of them.

What he really needed now was another girlfriend. There were lots of girls, from all over the world, in the classes at the private school were he had found a job teaching English as a foreign language. Some of them were attractive, but he was still too shy and insecure to invite any of them out, despite his experience with Sally – it wasn't so easy to overcome nine years of conditioning. But at least he was attracted to women, not men – that was something to be thankful for, he told himself.

There was one girl in particular he liked, who had joined his afternoon class only last week. He had fallen for her as soon as she walked into the classroom the first time. She was from Yugoslavia and her name was Marina. Her name alone was almost enough to make him fall in love with her and he had read Eliot's poem 'Marina' so many times again he now knew the first verse by heart:

'What seas what shores what grey rocks and what islands
What water lapping the bow
And scent of pine and the woodthrush singing through the fog
What images return
O my daughter.'

He felt like writing a poem to her himself, but could hardly hope to improve on that. Maybe one day he would show it to her, he thought wistfully.

She was only eighteen, had just left school and was going to begin studying medicine at Belgrade University in October. He found this out from her not privately, but by asking her about herself in class, like all new students. Since then he had hardly dared to speak to her, even in class, though he could hardly take his eyes off her – which was somewhat distracting while trying to teach.

She was attractive in a natural way that appealed to him. She had a childlike face with the complexion of a baby and blonde hair cut in a pageboy style. She was slightly short and chubby, but that didn't bother him, especially as she had big breasts. She wore no make-up or jewellery, which he liked, and simple clothes – either peasant-style blouses and skirts or sweaters and trousers, with schoolgirl sandals on bare feet.

She was all the more attractive to him because she was also obviously highly intelligent. He had already fallen in love with her. To be loved in return by such a girl would be the most sublime happiness imaginable, he thought. To make love with her would be ecstasy worth dying for! He started to imagine kissing those lovely, pale-pink lips, caressing that silky blonde hair, fondling those beautiful breasts ...

But he stopped himself abruptly. It was stupid, fantasising about her, he told himself – frustrating as well as a waste of time, since it was never likely to come true. She hadn't shown the slightest interest in him or for that matter any of the other students, male or female, though that was probably a good thing – one or two of the boys obviously fancied her, he had noticed jealously. In fact, she seemed rather unsociable, scribbling away studiously during the break and scurrying off after class without talking to anyone.

Maybe she was just shy or suffering from culture shock, he surmised. After all, she was from a communist country, which made her all the more fascinating – he had never met anyone from a communist country before. Amazingly, in view of all the Western and especially Catholic anti-Communist propaganda he had been subjected to, she didn't look like a devil or a freak. If anything, she looked like an angel!

If anyone was a freak, it was he, he reflected wryly, after nine years in a monastery. You couldn't get much more abnormal than that. Here he was, twenty-four, still inexperienced in the ways of the world, still a virgin and still screwed-up. She probably thought he was a typical product of the West – sophisticated, Christian, capitalist. Ironically, he didn't consider himself to be any of those – he could hardly call himself 'sophisticated', he didn't believe in God and, if anything, he was a socialist. Maybe they did have something in common after all.

No, he was making a fool of himself even thinking about her, he told himself. Why should she be interested in him? Who was he? He was a nobody. He had lost both his faith and his vocation. He had left his home and family, for the second time in his life. He had no friends, no money, no proper home or job, nothing except himself and his dream of being a writer one day. But that was all in his mind. Sometimes he felt like the 'Nowhere Man' in the Beatles song, this room felt like a prison cell and London felt like a foreign country where he knew no one and no one knew or cared about him.

He hardly ever even saw the other occupants of the house and didn't want to become too friendly with them anyway, being jealous of his privacy and solitude, despite his loneliness. They were mostly couples or rather threesomes – downstairs two nurses and their cat, next door two homosexual boys and their canary and upstairs a young married couple with a baby daughter. The only other single people in the house also lived upstairs. In the attic lived a chap of about thirty-five who had recently left the RAF and seemed even more lost and lonely than he. In the room immediately above him lived an eccentric opera singer, who flitted in and out of the house in a hooded cloak and started practising her scales at ten sharp every morning.

Suddenly, as if on cue, the silence was broken by an ear-splitting, window-rattling shriek, which meant she had started and it was ten o'clock. The first time he had heard it, he had been about to rush upstairs, thinking she was being attacked. He clamped his hands over his ears, closed his eyes and tried to think of what to write. He had wasted a whole hour and had only two more till twelve, when he would have a quick lunch and rush out to the Shakespeare School of English in Soho.

Outside the tube station, there was an ambulance and a police car, their blue lights flashing. He hoped he wasn't going to be delayed. He bought a ticket and ran down the escalator, but the entrance to the platform was blocked by a crowd of people being held back by a policeman. He joined them and waited impatiently, wondering what had happened.

After a few minutes, the crowd divided and another policeman strode through. He was holding at arm's length a man's tweed sports jacket, similar to the one he was wearing himself, except that it was dripping with blood. The policeman went into one of the station offices, leaving behind him a trail of crimson drops on the stone floor. With a shock he realised what must have happened and suddenly being late for work at the Shakespeare School of English didn't seem to matter so much any more.

'Move back,' the first policeman ordered the crowd, which had started pressing forward again. 'Move back. It's not a pretty sight.'

The crowd moved back reluctantly. This time two ambulance-men came through from the platform, one pulling and the other pushing a trolley. He didn't want to look, afraid of fainting, but forced himself to. On the trolley there was a body, most of it covered by a bright red blanket, except for one leg, which was trailing alongside like a broken doll's. On the foot there was a brown leather brogue shoe – again like the ones he was wearing himself. When they got to the escalator, the ambulance-men lifted the trolley and carried it up, the loose leg dangling grotesquely over the side. One of the ambulance-men kept putting it back on the trolley, but it kept flopping down again.

'Was it an accident?' he asked a middle-aged, head-scarfed woman beside him.

'It weren't no accident, dear,' she said in a Cockney accent. ''E waited till the train were almost aht o' the tunnel an' then 'e jumped. Jumped, 'e did. Driver 'ad no chance. Give me a right turn, it did, I can tell you. Young, good-looking chap 'e were, too, just like you.'

Embarrassed, he was glad he didn't have to answer, because the crowd surged onto the platform, carrying him with them. Nervously, he walked towards the far end, where the train was still standing. A West Indian porter was throwing sand from a red fire bucket onto the track in front of it. He looked down with a shudder of horror – the sand was slowly turning blood-red.

Some 'young, good-looking chap' had just killed himself on

that spot, he thought, appalled. He must have been very unhappy, must have got up this morning knowing he was going to do it. Now he was just a bundle of mangled flesh and bones, soon to be lying on some hospital mortuary slab and cut up like a pig's carcass in a butcher's shop. God, to think he had once been a baby gurgling in his mother's arms, a little boy happily playing with his toys! Why did he do it? How could a loving God allow such a thing to happen? He couldn't! He wouldn't!

'Just like yourself' – the Cockney woman's words reverberated with grim irony in his mind. He knew what it felt like to be so unhappy you wanted to kill yourself. He had tried to do it himself once, but with sleeping pills, not like that. He was glad now he hadn't succeeded, though there were still times when he felt like it, when he thought about what he had lost and the emptiness of life without God ...

It was better not to think about it too much, he admonished himself. It was better just to get on with life and live it to the full, without worrying about what it meant or what came afterwards, if anything. That was what he was determined to do now. He was lucky, he supposed. He had survived the crisis and felt all the stronger for it. He felt strong enough to cope with anything else life might throw at him. He felt invincible. 'Nil carborundum'. He was going to live and he was going to enjoy life!

Suddenly, the station master came striding along the platform, in peaked cap and shirt-sleeves. 'Get this train moving!' he bawled at the porter. 'I don't want any more delays this afternoon!'

Twenty minutes later he dashed up the narrow, bare, wooden stairs of the Shakespeare School of English to the first-floor office to collect his register. To his relief, since he was late, the school principal – a Bunteresque, pompous, ex-public schoolboy called Barry St. John-Ponsonby – wasn't there, but Jill, the school secretary was. He was glad to see her, because she was gorgeous, with long blonde hair, finely-chiselled features and a stunning figure. He wasn't so glad to see the young Arab male student who was trying to chat her up, though she was obviously busy. He said a quick hello to her and she flashed him a friendly smile that made him go weak at the knees. He grabbed his register from the rack and rushed out, as much to escape from the unbearable beauty of Jill as to get to his class.

He dashed upstairs to his classroom, where he was surprised to see Marina, the Yugoslav girl, standing by the open door, instead of sitting inside with the others. She looked as lovely as ever, in one of her peasant blouses and long skirts. He stopped, but his heart, already beating fast from his exertion and the effect of Jill, started to race even faster.

'Hello,' he panted.

'I just wanted give you this,' she said, handing him an envelope and immediately disappearing downstairs without another word.

Taken aback, he stuffed the envelope into his inside jacket pocket and hurried into the classroom. He said hello and apologised for being late, wondering whether to explain why, but deciding suicide might not be the best note to start off on. Then he started the lesson, struggling to keep his eyes off the girls' bodies.

As he proceeded with the lesson, he kept wondering what was in the letter. It was probably just a note to explain why she couldn't come to class today, he supposed. Maybe she wasn't feeling well. But she looked all right. She looked *very* all right! Maybe it was a love letter? He couldn't wait to find out. As soon as he had chance, while the class was working on an exercise on the present perfect, he took out the envelope and opened it.

On a scrappy piece of paper torn out of an exercise book, in childishly large, round handwriting, he read:

'Dear Teacher,
I am sorry I cannot come to class, because I have got new job in afternoon.
Goodbye.
Marina Durajlija'

That 'Goodbye' sounded so final! It was like a dagger in his guts. So much for it being a love letter! Masochistically, he read it again, making the dagger twist. Then he folded the paper up, put it back in the envelope and slipped the envelope back into his inside pocket.

He wished he could slink off to be on his own, but had to carry on with the lesson, trying to appear as cheerful as possible. He would be on his own long enough over the weekend. The thought depressed him. There were several other attractive girls in the class, but somehow he didn't fancy any of them enough to ask out, even if he had the nerve. None of them compared with her.

Then he had an idea: after the class he'd try to catch Jill before she left and pluck up the courage to ask her out – that was if that smarmy Arab student hadn't beaten him to it. He liked her and had a sneaking suspicion she liked him – at least she always smiled at him and laughed at his jokes. On the other hand, he was sure a girl as glamorous as Jill must have a boyfriend already, probably some flashy, affluent type with a sports car. But he had to try – he couldn't bear the thought of yet another weekend on his own.

'Right, let's check through that, shall we?' he said to the class, with as much zest as he could muster.

'Doing anything this weekend?' he asked Jill, casually.

She was on her way out of the building. To his relief there were no other males hovering around her as usual, but there was a girl with her, whom she had introduced as Di, a temp working in the import-export agency on the ground floor. Like Jill, she was wearing hot pants and looked sexy, but she was in the way.

'Yes, we are actually,' Jill chirped.

'Oh, what?' he asked, secretly disappointed. He didn't really want to know now, wanted only to get away.

'At least we might be,' she added and he felt a flicker of renewed hope.

'Oh, let's,' Di said to her.

'Let's what?' he laughed, though he felt like strangling Di.

'Well, this guy's invited us to spend the weekend on his boat,' Jill explained, and, as soon as he heard the word 'boat', he knew he had no chance.

'Sounds great!' he pretended to enthuse, inwardly writhing with jealousy and added jokingly, 'I hope it doesn't sink', though he half-hoped it would. 'So what's the problem? Can't you swim?'

They both giggled. 'The problem is,' Jill said, 'we don't know this guy, do we? We don't know what to expect. I mean, we don't know what he expects.' Jill blushed and they both giggled, to his annoyance, though blushing made Jill look more gorgeous than ever.

'Oh, come on, Jill!' Di said. 'There'll be lots of other people there, not just us two.'

He felt like strangling her again.

'Yes, but we won't know any of them, will we?' Jill said.

'We will by the end of the weekend,' Di retorted.

'What do you think?' Jill asked him.

He was surprised and flattered that she should ask him, yet at the same time annoyed. It meant she only saw him as some kind of big brother or at best platonic friend. He suddenly felt irritated with them, especially Jill, for being so prudish. Wasn't this supposed to be the permissive, promiscuous, swinging seventies? And if she looked and dressed like a dolly-bird, what did she expect?

'What do I think? I think you should go,' he laughed, turning to leave. 'Enjoy yourselves! Don't fall overboard though! See you Monday!' he called back, with feigned good-humour, hurrying out of the building.

He hurried away as fast as he could, glad not to have to put on a cheerful face for them or his students any longer. He felt anything but cheerful. He needed to be on his own for a while before his evening class, when he would have to put on the act again. Being a teacher was a bit like being an entertainer, something of a performance art, he was starting to realise.

He weaved his way through the hordes of office-workers scurrying home and tourists searching for amusement. There was plenty of that available here in Soho: pubs, restaurants, theatres, strip clubs, porn cinemas, sex shops ... He made his way past them all to the public garden in Soho Square, where he sat with relief on a bench. It was a sanctuary of peace and quiet in the hurly-burly of the city: plane trees muffled the din of traffic and screened out the harsh geometry of buildings, while lawns and flower beds soothed both sight and soul. Today there was the added blessing of warm sunshine as well.

He took the Yugoslav girl's letter out of his jacket pocket and read it with a stab of disappointment again. He had really liked her. She was not just attractive, but intelligent too. There were other attractive and intelligent girls around, he supposed, but there was something different about her. Maybe it was just that she came from behind the 'iron curtain', so there was an air of mystery about her. Anyway, he'd never see her again, he thought, making the dagger twist in his guts again. Better to forget her, he told himself. He crumpled the letter up and chucked it in the litter bin beside him.

So, now he was back to square one. That was a joke! It wasn't as if the Yugoslav girl had been his girlfriend or even gone out with him. She probably wouldn't have, even if he had had the guts to ask her. That was an even more depressing thought. He was still so unsure of himself with girls, so screwed up about them. But what could you expect, after nine years in a seminary, cut off from normal human life and relationships, being brainwashed against women? It was hard enough for 'normal' men!

God, what a bizarre experience those nine years had been, when he looked back now! What a barmy way of life! What a massive mistake he had nearly made! Thank goodness he had seen the light and got out before going any further, painful as it had been. It was no use looking back though. He had to forget about it, put it behind him, build a new life, rehabilitate himself.

That was partly why he was here in London. He had had to get away from his family and even from Manchester, from everyone and everything that reminded him of the past, so that he could start a completely new life, find a new self. His parents especially didn't understand that and he couldn't even begin to explain it to them. It would be too painful for both them and him. He hadn't contacted them since he had arrived in London, not even to say he had arrived safely. They had no idea where he was. He had cut himself off. It was cruel and must hurt them, he knew, but it was necessary, necessary for his psychological survival, like life-saving surgery.

On the other hand, maybe they didn't care about him any more. That was a melancholy thought, but he couldn't blame them for it, if it was true – by rejecting Catholicism he had rejected their most deeply-held beliefs, rejected *them*. It was probably the most hurtful thing he could have done to them and it hurt him even to think of it. Yet there was nothing he could do about it. He couldn't change the way he thought and felt, the way he was, because that was a consequence of the past, and he couldn't change the past. He could only hope to escape from it, leave it behind him.

It hadn't been easy for him, either, losing his faith and leaving the seminary. He had tried to commit suicide, unsuccessfully, thank goodness. But it still wasn't easy. Here he was, alone and lonely in this strange city, though it had been his choice to come here and he wanted to stay, had to stay. He could never go back now – that would be an admission of defeat. He had to stay and make a new life for himself and he would, no matter how hard it was. He would never be defeated by life, never succumb to despair again. He had gained a certain strength from his experience, a feeling almost of invincibility. Life couldn't throw anything worse at him. It might prove to be a self-delusion, but that was how he felt.

Meanwhile though, he was lonely and frustrated. He had missed his chance with both the Yugoslav girl and Jill. It was hopeless! He had started to fall in love with the Yugoslav girl. What he felt for her was love, the real thing. He didn't just want to go to bed with her. In fact, he didn't really want to go to bed with her at all. He wanted to be with her, get to know her, look after her, take care of her. She was the kind of girl he could imagine living with for life, even marrying. Now he would never see her again. Another twist of the knife. Forget her!

There were other girls. There was Jill. But he had missed the boat with her, too. 'Boat', ha ha. God, she was gorgeous! The thought of making love with her, kissing those ruby-red lips, stroking that golden hair, caressing those voluptuous curves, fondling those beautiful breasts, made him feel dizzy. Instead of him, though, some loaded, creepy, boat-owning sleazeball would probably have the pleasure. The thought made him writhe with jealousy. *He* would probably end up fantasising and masturbating about her as usual. God, it was pathetic!

Not that he considered masturbation a sin any more. He had educated himself out of that particular piece of Catholic nonsense. It was a normal, healthy, sometimes necessary form of relief. If you didn't do it, it only came out in wet dreams and that just made a mess of the sheets. There was nothing 'sinful' about it, but it was still shameful, if only because it was a substitute for a proper relationship, a symptom of inadequacy, of failure – if he had a girlfriend, he wouldn't need to masturbate.

He wanted more than just sex though. He wanted love. He wanted to fall in love, to love and be loved, as well as to make love. He was twenty-four years old and he had never made love properly – he was still a virgin, still so inexperienced! It was a dismal thought. He could drop dead or be killed any moment and he would die a virgin, without having had that basic human experience. That was an even more depressing thought. It would really mean *they* had won! He had to find a girlfriend soon. He was getting desperate. He almost felt like raping one!

He looked at his watch. Five more minutes and he would have to go back to work – another three hours of teaching! Still, he didn't mind the evening class too much. He usually went for a drink with a few of the students afterwards. And there was an Italian girl in the class he fancied. Her name was Marisa. Maybe he should invite her out – if he could pluck up the courage. That was an idea! She seemed to be a nice girl, shy but sweet. She wasn't exactly pretty, but she was attractive, with a nice figure, long, black, wavy hair and olive skin. She usually wore low-cut tops that showed off her cleavage and mini-skirts that showed off her long, sexy legs. He wouldn't mind going out – or going to bed – with *her,* he thought, shutting his eyes to imagine it …

After class he hurried to put his register back in the office. He was on his way out of the office when in shuffled Mrs. Mullins, the cleaning lady, carrying the tools of her trade, and foolishly he stopped to say, 'Hello. How are you?'

'Mastn't gramble,' she replied as usual and proceeded to do exactly that for the next five minutes or more about some operation her daughter had just had. 'The pills the doctor give 'er don't 'alf look dangerous to me,' she whined on in a Cockney accent, a fag dangling out of the corner of her mouth. 'Still, I s'pose 'e knows what 'e's doin', though yer can't be sure these days, can yer, what wiv thalymide an' all that? They're s'posed to be for – oh, what is it, yer know, when the white corporals takes over from the red 'uns? Thinnin' o' the blood. What's the term? Not leukaemia.'

'Anaemia?' he suggested, impatient to get out and join the students, who would be waiting for him outside.

'That's it,' she said. 'Not as serious as leukaemia. That's serious, ennit? Some sort o' cancer, that, ennit?'

'Cancer of the blood, I think,' he said, trying to edge past her through the door, but knowing that mention of the word 'blood' would get her going.

'Cor, terrible what can 'appen to yer, ennit?' she said on cue.

Like being buttonholed by you when I'm dying for a drink, he thought. 'Yes, I suppose so,' he agreed, 'Well, good – '

'Still, marvellous what they can do these days, too, ennit?' she intercepted him. 'Some o' these operations, 'eart transplantations an' things.'

'Yes, I suppose so. Well, I'd better be off. Leave you to get on with your work.'

'I've 'ad a lung out, you know.'

That was it. There was no way he was going to get out of that office without hearing all the grisly details of her lung operation. 'Oh, really?' he said, resigning himself to it and hoping to get it over with as fast as possible.

'Yeah. It weren't cancer I 'ad, though – it were a cyst. What's this they called it? A congenial cyst, that's it. That means yer was born wiv it.'

'What was the operation like?' he asked, curious despite himself, remembering his own knee operation a few years ago.

'Lavverly!' she declared.

'Lovely?' he laughed sceptically.

'Didn't feel a thing.'

'Weren't you nervous before it?'

'Not once I'd 'ad me pre-med, I wasn't. They give me two, one there an' one there.' She slapped each haunch it turn. 'Dunno why, 'cos I weren't that worried. But I didn't 'alf feel lovely afterwards. I can understand why them drug addicts gets 'ooked. Floatin' on a clahd, I was, when they wheeled me dahn to theatre.'

Suddenly, hearing about this transitory experience of happiness she had had and observing how old and haggard she looked now, he felt a pang of pity for her. 'What was it like afterwards?' he asked.

'Marvellous,' she said, and proceeded to tell him at length how much she had enjoyed being in hospital – unlike himself.

To his dismay, by the time he managed to escape and hurry downstairs into the street, there was no sign of the students. He suddenly felt annoyed, annoyed with Mrs. Mullins for delaying him, annoyed with himself for letting her and annoyed with the students for not waiting for him, though he could hardly have expected them to wait any longer.

He could follow them to the usual pub, he supposed, but why should he, since they hadn't bothered to wait for him? No, that was petty, he told himself. It would be cutting off his nose to spite his face. The prospect of spending the rest of the evening alone – as well as the weekend – depressed him. Besides, he did fancy Marisa, the Italian girl. Pride was no match for loneliness or lust, so off he set.

But when he got to the pub – ironically called 'The Friend at Hand' – they weren't there. Dismayed, he tried a second one, but they weren't there either. Nor were they in the third one. Oh, well, to hell with them, he thought angrily, he wasn't chasing them all over London! He bought himself a pint of Guinness, sat down and started drinking.

His anger was soon dissolved by loneliness. Here he was, he reflected forlornly, in the middle of London, one of the biggest cities in the world, surrounded by millions of people, and he was all alone. He might as well be on the moon! The thought of going home to his room on his own depressed him. The thought of the lonely weekend ahead depressed him even more. There was only one way to make both bearable and that was to get drunk, which he proceeded to do, downing three pints in quick succession, then going to the bar for a fourth ...

What he needed was a girlfriend, he told himself yet again, starting on his fourth. If only the Yugoslav girl hadn't left. 'Marina' – what a beautiful name! 'What seas what shores what grey rocks ... What images return O my daughter.' She seemed like a dream now. Maybe she was a dream. Maybe life was a dream, as Wordsworth suggested in 'Ode to Intimations of Immortality'. Great poem, that. It was funny to think she was a Communist. Communists were supposed to be devils. *She* was beautiful though. It just showed you the power of brainwashing. Bloody religion! Bloody Catholicism! Bloody Christianity! What a disaster it had overtaken the world! What a pity the Romans hadn't exterminated it! It was so bloody repressive, killjoy, life-denying, love-denying. Love – they had certainly tried to kill that in the seminary. Love in all its shapes and forms, not just sexual. They'd even tried to kill the instinct for affection, the simple human pleasure of touch. Stupid bastards, fannying about in their black frocks! Thank God he'd escaped. Escaped? Out of the frying pan into the fire – the fire of Hell, the hell of loneliness. He was a social misfit, a freak, after nine years in a fucking monastery. From the age of twelve. Twelve! Christ! Talk about cradle snatchers! Yes, thank God he'd escaped. What was that book he'd read at the junior seminary about the German prisoner of war who escaped in the Lake District called – 'The One That Got Away'? He still felt like an escaped prisoner of war himself sometimes, lost in enemy territory. He mustn't give up though. That would mean *they* had won, the Ghosters, the Druids, the witch doctors, the wizards, the sorcerers ... There had to be light at the end of the tunnel. Not for that chap who'd thrown himself under a train this morning, poor sod. Why had he done it? Loneliness? He felt bloody lonely himself. He felt suicidal himself! He could never do it like that though. The very thought sent a shudder of horror through him. Electrocuted and mangled at the same time. Mincemeat! Had he bought a ticket, he wondered? 'Single to Eternity, please.' At least all his problems were over. Death was so final, so absolute, so total, so damn *permanent*. It made life meaningless really. Made a mockery of it. Made you wonder if it was worth bothering at all. Maybe it would be better to die and be done with it, get it over with. No. He wouldn't give those bastards the satisfaction. It was better just to get blotto – drown your sorrows, not yourself. That way at least you lived to fight another day. Another day? Another day on his own, another day with no meaning, no purpose. Mustn't get morbid though! You had to look on the bright side, count your blessings. He had counted them and could do with a few more, thank you very much. Come on, you're better off than a lot of people: young, healthy, intelligent, well-educated, not too bad-looking. Not that looks mattered. Oh, yes they did, up to a point. Especially when it came to women. He might as well be King Kong for all the luck he had with them. God, that Yugoslav girl! She was so lovely! And so interesting! To think he'd never see her again. The thought was like a knife in his guts. The pain was almost physical. It was funny he felt like this – he hardly knew her. They'd just been ships in the night really. 'Bridge Over Troubled Water' on the jukebox. Funny coincidence! Great song. It suited his mood exactly. 'Sail on, silver girl.' Without him. Sea of heartbreak. Another good song. Was it Don Gibson? Sea of tears! Christ, he was almost crying! Was that the last bell already? For whom the bell tolls. It tolls for thee, Frankie boy, for thee. He was getting maudlin now. He'd better go while he could still walk in a straight line. He didn't want to fall under a train. He'd go home, put some Dylan on and finish the job off with Jameson's ...

CHAPTER TWENTY-TWO

'Well, did you enjoy your cruise?' he asked Jill on Monday morning, breezing into the school office for his register.

'It was all right in the end,' she said, smiling and stroking her long blonde hair back from her face.

What exactly did that mean, he wondered, with a stab of jealousy? However, he couldn't bring himself to enquire further. There was an awkward pause and he turned to go.

'Did *you* have a good weekend?' she asked.

'Oh, not bad, thanks! See you,' he said, hurrying out before she could ask him what he had done.

He had spent the weekend on his own as usual. On Saturday he had done his shopping, laundry and cleaning. On Saturday evening he had had a few pints here in Soho, gone to a disco in Leicester Square, met nobody, missed the last tube and had to walk most of the way home. On Sunday he had read the papers, gone for a walk by the river, had a couple of pints at the Anchor and Hope overlooking the Marshes, eaten a takeaway on the way home, watched TV, read and gone to bed alone and lonely.

During the class he was tormented by the thought of Jill making love with the creep who owned the boat, while he had spent it on his own. There were several girls sitting in front of him right now whom he wouldn't mind having fun with, which didn't help his state of mind. He had to stop himself ogling their bodies, arrayed tantalisingly in front of him like mouth-wateringly delicious but forbidden fruits, because it was making him have an erection, as well as lose concentration.

He reached the end of the lesson with relief and, deliberately avoiding Jill, escaped to the garden in Soho Square, sitting with relief on one of the benches. As always, he immediately felt himself unwind in this oasis of peace and tranquillity. It was stupid to get so worked up over women, he told himself.

He would find a girlfriend eventually. It was just that meanwhile he was so lonely and frustrated.

What did other men in his situation do about sex, he wondered? They relieved themselves, he supposed. He was fed up with masturbating though, and ashamed of it – not because he considered it a sin any more, but because it was a substitute for real love, a symptom of inadequacy. He wanted a real, live, flesh-and-blood woman to love and be loved by – and to make love with. He wanted love, the love that poets wrote about and singers sang about, romantic love. What if it was only an illusion though? He refused to believe that. He believed in love. He had to, because he didn't have anything else to believe in or live for.

It was an alarming thought, but true. He didn't believe in God or an afterlife any more. This was the only life there was, so what was there to live for? The only thing he really wanted to be was a writer, but that wasn't enough, whether he succeeded or not. No, the only thing worth living for was love. Without it life would be pointless, empty, sterile.

He just had to be patient, he told himself, shutting his eyes. He still had plenty of time. He would find someone sooner or later. Maybe he would pluck up the courage to ask Marisa out tonight ...

He had just started his evening class when the door burst open.

'Can I come in?' she gasped, breathless from running upstairs.

For a moment he just stared at her, too taken aback to answer – it was the Yugoslav girl, Marina. She was wearing a peasant-style blouse and skirt as usal and clutching some books in one hand. She looked flushed and lovelier than ever.

'Yes, of course,' he said at last. 'Do you want to join this class?'

'If is possible,' she panted.

'Of course,' he said, secretly delighted. 'But I thought you had a job and couldn't come to school any more?'

'I can come in evening, if is all right,' she panted.

'Sure. Take a seat,' he said, looking round the small, crowded classroom for one, hardly able to hide his excitement. However, there didn't seem to be one free. He started to panic, afraid she might go away, when Lorenzo, a young, bespectacled, Spanish student, came to the rescue.

'Here ju are,' he said, moving his rucksack and jacket from the seat beside him.

'There you are,' he said quickly, directing her to it, before she could change her mind and go.

To his relief she went to it, deposited her books on the flap and manoeuvred herself into the seat. Carrying on with the lesson, he watched her out of the corner of his eye. She put on a pair of what looked like National Health Service glasses, but their ugliness only accentuated her prettiness in his eyes. Then she took a pen from a pencil case and opened an exercise book and dictionary. With a stab of jealousy he saw Lorenzo offer to share his coursebook with her and heard him explain, in an annoyingly loud voice, what they were doing. For the rest of the lesson he had to struggle to suppress both jealousy and the temptation to keep glancing at her.

During the break he didn't get chance to speak to her, because he was buttonholed by other students asking him questions. He was half glad of the excuse, because he was nervous about speaking to her, anyway. Besides, she herself was buttonholed by Lorenzo. He watched jealously as Lorenzo tried to chat her up and noticed with satisfaction that she hardly answered him, preferring to scribble away beaverishly in her exercise book. She made no effort to talk to any of the other students either. He was disconcerted by this, but supposed it was just shyness, this being her first evening.

During the second half of the lesson he had to struggle even harder not to look at her. She answered a couple of questions that none of the others could answer, confirming his impression that she was bright and making her all the more attractive to him. Towards the end of the lesson he asked her if she would mind the rest of the class 'interviewing' her about herself, as he usually did with new students.

'You already know about me,' she objected.

'*I* know, but they don't,' he replied, afraid she would refuse, which would be both embarrassing and disappointing, because he hoped to find out a little more about her. 'Anyway, it's good practice for your English,' he added, to persuade her.

'All right, if you want,' she agreed, to his relief.

She told them her name was Marina, she came from Yugoslavia, she spoke Serbo-Croat, she had been in London for three weeks, she lived in a student hall of residence in Bloomsbury, she worked as a chambermaid in the hall, she was eighteen years old, she wanted to be a doctor, she was going to begin her medical studies in October at Belgrade University, she had no brothers or sisters, her father was a university professor of history and her mother a doctor.

'Do you like London?' someone asked.

'Yes,' she said.

'Is it different from Belgrade?' someone else asked.

'It's not very different,' she replied. 'Belgrade is big, modern city too.'

'Yugoslavia is a communist country like Russia, isn't it?' someone else asked.

'Yes, it is Communist country, but not like Russia,' she replied, defensively. 'Is independent from Russia.'

'Are you free?' someone else asked.

'Of course we are free. I would not be here if we are not free.' She sounded annoyed. He was starting to feel nervous, because this was dangerous territory.

'Who is the president?' someone else asked.

'President is Marshal Tito. He is great hero,' she declared proudly. 'He beat Germans in Second World War.'

Luckily there were no Germans in the class!

'Do you believe in God,' someone else asked.

'Of course not!' she declared scornfully. 'God is just stupid superstition.'

He winced secretly, though he agreed with her.

'Are you a Marxist?' someone else asked.

'I do not like labels,' she said. 'We learn about Marx in school, but we do not have to believe everything we are told.'

'Do you believe in astrology?'

'That is even more stupid than religion,' she said contemptuously, which he was pleased to hear.

'What do you do in your spare time?'

'I like reading and looking at paintings.'

'So who's your favourite writer?' he couldn't resist asking himself.

'He is German writer called Herman Hesse,' she said.

'Who's your favourite painter?' someone else asked, before he had chance to ask her about Herman Hesse, whom he had never heard of.

'Van Gogh,' she said.

There was a pause. Some of the students were starting to get up. He looked at his watch. 'Well, it's nine o'clock, time to go,' he announced, regretfully. 'Thank you, Marina. Goodnight everyone.'

He started collecting his books and papers, trying to pluck up the courage to invite her to the pub. However, by the time he looked up again, she had disappeared. Maybe one of the other students – Lorenzo, for example – would invite her on the way out. But by the time he got outside, there was no sign of her. He was crestfallen.

'OK, let's go!' he said cheerfully to the ones who were there and led them off, trying to put her out of his mind.

But he couldn't, for neither the rest of the evening nor the week. He found himself looking forward to his evening class more and more. He was afraid she might suddenly stop coming, as she had done before. She was always a few minutes late, so that every evening he was in an agony of suspense until the door opened and she burst in. It was because of her job, she explained – she had to set the tables for breakfast in the refectory before leaving.

Evening classes became a form of exquisite torture for him. She always sat next to Lorenzo, who doggedly chatted her up, while she was slowly becoming more friendly with him, which made him feel absurdly jealous. During the lesson, he had to struggle not to keep looking at her. Then, at the end of each lesson, he resolved to invite her to the pub, but could never pluck up the courage.

He hoped Lorenzo or one of the others might do so, but if they did, she obviously declined, because she always disappeared quickly, to his dismay. He didn't ask them, because he didn't want them – especially Lorenzo – to know he was interested in her. He continued to go to the pub with them, but wasn't really interested in them any more, only her.

Every evening the torture became worse, because he found her more and more attractive, with her blonde, pageboy-style hair, girlish face, baby-like complexion and lovely figure. She seemed to be composed of appealing contrasts – her boyish hairstyle contrasting with her girlish face and her girlish face contrasting in turn with her womanly figure. The National Health Service-style glasses she wore in class only accentuated her prettiness.

He liked the way she dressed, too – simply, in sweaters and trousers, though never jeans, he was glad to see – or peasant-style blouses and skirts. She never wore anything on her feet except schoolgirl's sandals, which he found peculiarly appealing. Also, she never wore any make-up or jewellery, neither of which he liked, except occasionally a necklace of wooden beads. He liked naturalness and she was the most naturally beautiful girl he had ever seen. He even liked that sexy Serbo-Croat accent!

His impression that she was exceptionally bright was confirmed by how quickly she caught up with the class and picked up everything new. She almost always answered questions correctly, even ones none of the others could, though only when he asked her directly – she never answered voluntarily, which struck him as charmingly modest. Anyway, she must be pretty bright to have a place in medical school, he supposed.

He gave the class a composition to do for homework, which he collected on Friday. He could hardly wait to read hers and did so as soon as he got home from the pub, slightly drunk. It was written on scrappy exercise paper, in large, round, childish handwriting, complete with doodles. He was disconcerted, as well as amused by this, but as soon as he began reading he was impressed, becoming more so as he read, brief as it was:

An Adventure that Recently Happened to Me

I think that a human life must be considered as a lot of adventures, which are sometimes dull or naive, but sometimes exciting or dangerous. Usually we get used to our everyday life and new book, face, garden or some other unimportant thing could change our way of living at once.

For me, the most exciting 'adventure' recently was reading 'Demian' by Herman Hesse. I really experienced something what was inside of me, some kind of feeling which I could not animate before. I cannot explain that to anybody, but it was an adventure, because after that book I started to look at the things from another point of view. Some of my truest inside beliefs were knocked out and I cannot find myself now.

Reading it over and over again, he experienced 'something what was inside of' *him*, 'some kind of feeling' which *he* 'could not animate before'. He knew he was only torturing himself, but couldn't help it. It was something he could not 'explain to anybody', except to say that he felt as if he was reading something he might have written himself when he was eighteen. It was as if he had heard an echo or glimpsed a reflection of his most secret, innermost, deepest self. At last, he thought, he had met a girl who thought and felt as he did, with whom he could sense that harmony of thought and feeling, mind and body, which he had been searching for, with whom he felt sure he could strike that rhapsodic, lost chord that he yearned so desperately to hear in the desolate sanctuary of his soul ...

All weekend he struggled to stop himself thinking about her, because he was sure it was impossible, but he couldn't. On Saturday he kept busy doing his usual chores of shopping, laundry and cleaning, but that didn't help. On Saturday evening he went for a drink on his own as usual, but that didn't help either – if anything he found himself thinking about her even more.

On Sunday he tried to distract himself by reading the papers as usual, but couldn't concentrate. In the afternoon he went to the Marshes for a walk, hoping to forget about her, but it was hopeless – he saw her everywhere. Masochistically, he imagined what it would be like to have her with him and felt his spirits soar. Then he thought how unlikely it was and plunged into a trough of depression.

This was ridiculous, he told himself, and tried to think of reasons for disliking her. For one thing, she seemed rather unsociable, still didn't mix with the other students. During the break she stayed in her seat, scribbling away studiously in her exercise book, and at the end of the lesson always rushed off. Lorenzo persisted in trying to chat her up, but she gave him little or no encouragement, he was glad to see. All the same, he was afraid Lorenzo might wear down her defences. After all, he had more in common with her than he did – Lorenzo was the same age, whereas he was six years older and, more worryingly, Lorenzo was also a fervent communist.

She could be a bit dogmatic, too. Last Thursday evening, for example, in a discussion about racism in class, she had refused to listen to anyone who didn't agree with her in condemning it. She called Magnani – a somewhat simple Sicilian who worked as a chef – a 'Fascist'. It caused quite a scene, which he managed to defuse by launching into an explanation of the term 'Fascist'. Afterwards, he was afraid it might have seemed to her as if he was tacitly agreeing with Magnani, which of course he wasn't – he agreed with *her*.

She was a bit curt whenever she did actually speak to any of the other students or even him. There was a certain impatience, even abrasiveness, about her. She rarely said 'please' or 'thank you' and seldom smiled or laughed. He hardly dared think it, but she seemed to have no sense of humour.

However, none of these failings made any difference to how he felt about her. If anything, they only accentuated her attractiveness. The more he thought about her the more he liked her. He could hardly wait for Monday evening, just to see her again. Life without her hardly seemed worth living. He was in love with her, he supposed. Lorenzo and a few of the other males in the class were too, he suspected. It wasn't surprising – she was easily the best-looking and most interesting girl in the class. Any half-intelligent man would fall in love with her!

Suddenly though, he had a devastating thought, which might

explain why she seemed so cool and unsociable – she probably had a boyfriend. She was too attractive not to have one! If she didn't have one here in London, she must have one in Yugoslavia. Why hadn't he thought of that before? What a fool he was! He had no chance! He was a fool even to be thinking about her!

Yet he still couldn't stop. He lay on the grass and imagined her lying beside him, in his arms. The very thought filled him with an almost unbearable bliss. The reality, unlikely as it was, would be too blissful to bear, he thought, like the Beatific Vision or an apparition of the Blessed Virgin, which he used to try to imagine when he was a junior seminarian.

What a bizarre comparison, he reflected wryly – especially since she was an atheist. He was an atheist himself, he supposed, though somehow he didn't like the word, found it ugly and negative – which just showed the power of conditioning. She seemed quite proud to admit it, because she had been brought up that way. He envied and admired her. She would probably be put off if she knew he had once been a seminarian. It made the chances of her liking him even less. Of course, he wouldn't tell her – he never told anyone, didn't like to talk about it, felt embarrassed about it, as if he had done time in prison.

She wasn't just an atheist, but a communist too. According to the Catholic church, that made her the spawn of the devil. How stupid all that anti-Communist propaganda, indoctrination and brainwashing seemed now, like so much else of Catholicism! It made him feel ashamed of ever having believed it, even though he had been young, innocent and naive. She was living proof, if he needed it, of its stupidity. She was so normal, so natural, so brilliant, so beautiful ...

Suddenly, he realised what he had to do. He couldn't wait. He jumped up and walked back home as fast as he could, instead of going to the pub as usual. He locked the door, put on Blood on the Tracks, poured himself a glass of whiskey, sat in the easy-chair and started to write. When he had finished, it was getting dark and he was getting drunk. He read over what he had written by the light of the moon:

MARINA

the starlight in your eyes
i never thought to see
into the starlight i fell
and am falling still
the blood lay congealed and cold
in the tunnels of my soul
beneath the ruins of my life
i lay crushed
my heart was banging
like a door in the night
the engines of the universe stalled
when you handed me the note
saying goodbye
but you came back
settled like a blanket of snow
upon the embers of my heart
the ashes of my soul
you are a sea against
the Sahara of tomorrows
a sun upon
my glacier of sorrows
i am alive again
but will you ever know
or will the truth
be lost in space
my words drift like broken oars
on the sea of silence
between us
the truth I cannot really tell with words
nor metaphor your mystery
except to say that you have been
my salvation and resurrection
a sword of light
to slay my gloom
a silver axe
to split my tomb

He wondered if he should give it to her, but knew he probably wouldn't have the nerve. He was still such a coward when it came to women. It was like saying 'I love you'. Well, it was meant to be a love poem. It sounded good to him now, drunk, but in the clear light of morning it might read like rubbish. He should probably crumple it up and throw it in the bin straightaway!

But he didn't. Whether she ever read it or not, whether it was rubbish or not, it came from him, from his heart. He put on 'Sad-eyed Lady of the Lowlands' and listened to it again, drinking and thinking only one thought, that tomorrow he would see her again ...

But she didn't come to class. He was so disappointed he could hardly concentrate on the lesson. He kept looking at the door, hoping it would burst open, but it didn't. Then he kept looking at the empty seat next to Lorenzo, where she always sat, and each time a stab of disappointment went through him. The thought that she might never come back tormented him, but somehow he managed to get through the lesson without losing track too often.

Afterwards, he went for a drink with the students, though he didn't feel like it. He chatted cheerfully with them, but all the time was tortured by the thought that he might never see her again.

Then, the next evening, to his delight, she turned up, late as usual, and took her seat next to Lorenzo, who kept it for her. Not only did she come back, to his further delight she went to the pub with them afterwards, for the first time ever. To his annoyance though, Lorenzo contrived to sit next to her there as well and proceeded to chew her ear off about politics and Spanish literature.

'What happened to you yesterday?' he asked her, as soon as he could get a word in edgeways.

'One of staff was sick, so I had to do whole job by my own,' she explained.

'I see' he said, silently cursing whoever it was. 'Glad to have you back. I hope you're going to stay.'

'Oh, yes, I hope,' she said.

'So why haven't we had the pleasure of your company in the pub before?'

'Nobody told me you go to pub after class,' she said, accusingly.

'Oh, I'm sorry,' he said, cursing himself for not inviting her. 'Who told you, then?'

'I invite her,' Lorenzo declared proudly.

'Oh, good,' he said with a forced smile to Lorenzo.

He didn't say anything else to her, partly because Lorenzo continued to chew her ear off in his execrable Spanish accent and partly because he was still shy of her. However, he kept an eye on her while he was chatting with the others and noticed that she seemed a little more friendly, though she still sometimes sounded curt. She still didn't smile or laugh easily either. All the same, he was more in love with her than ever and was determined to make her his. He wasn't going to let Lorenzo – amiable lad though he was – or anyone else take her away from him. All was fair in love and war, he told himself, with uncharacteristic ruthlessness.

The following evening, to his delight, she came to the pub after class again, though to his annoyance Lorenzo parked himself beside her and proceeded to chew her ear off again. She was polite enough to make an effort to understand him and respond, but he could tell she wasn't really interested and would rather be talking to him. Or was he deluding himself? There was only one way to find out.

'So who's this Herman Hesse?' he asked her, as soon as he got chance, ashamed of not knowing.

'Who? Who?' Lorenzo pounced, like a dog on a bone.

'Just a writer Marina mentioned,' he said, not looking at him.

'He was German writer,' she said.

'He's dead then, is he?' he asked, deliberately looking at her, not Lorenzo.

'He died in 1962,' she said. 'He won Nobel Prize for literature in 1946.'

'Oh, is good! Is good!' Lorenzo exclaimed, butting in.

'Yes,' he agreed, ignoring him. 'And what exactly is

'Demian' about?' he asked her.

'What? What?' Lorenzo annoyingly stuck his oar in again.

'It's a book Marina's been reading,' he told him, smiling and biting his tongue.

'It is impossible to explain it,' Marina said to him. 'You must read it yourself.'

'Can I borrow it then?' he asked her, seizing his chance.

'Yes, I bring it for you tomorrow,' she said.

'OK. Thanks,' he said, pleased.

'Perhaps when ju hab finished I can hab?' Lorenzo asked him, puppy-like, bespectacled eyes imploring.

'Yes, sure, if Marina doesn't mind,' he said, turning away from him quickly to reply to a question one of the others was asking him.

Of course, he had no intention of letting Lorenzo anywhere near it and would keep it as long as possible. All was fair in love and war!

The next evening she gave the book to him in the pub. It was a slim, black paperback. On the front was a grotesque, enigmatic illustration of a skull-like face with onyx eyes, Medusa-like hair and a bird with outstretched wings on the forehead. The bird reminded him of the Paraclete, but it couldn't be, he supposed. He found the illustration both repellent and intriguing, but didn't look inside the book yet – he thanked her and slipped it into his pocket quickly, before Lorenzo could get his mitts on it.

As soon as he arrived home, he sat down to read it, hoping it would give him an insight into her mind and heart. First he read the blurb and synopsis on the back:

'Few writers have chronicled with such dispassionate lucidity and fearless honesty the progress of the soul through the states of life.' Dr. TIMOTHY LEARY. 'Herman Hesse has become since his death in 1962 one of the most widely read European novelists of this century. His mystical vision has proved prophetic of the questing spirit of the psychedelic generation, to whom he has become a revered figure.

In Demian he chronicles with clearsighted humanity the

growth to maturity of Emil Sinclair, who falls under the influence of Max Demian, a strangely self-possessed figure. As Sinclair progresses through orthodox education and philosophical mysticism towards self-awareness, he always has the image of Demian before him – right up to the climactic moment of confrontation with destiny on a blood-drenched battlefield.'

It sounded intriguing, the kind of book he could relate to, except for the bits about 'psychedelic generation' and 'blood-drenched battlefield'. Eagerly he opened it and read the biography of Hesse on the inside cover:

'Herman Hesse was born at Calw in Germany in 1877. He began his career as a bookseller, and started to write and publish poems when he was 21. He enjoyed his first major success when he was 26 with his novel on youth and its problems, Peter Camenzind. In the next few years a string of novels followed, including Demian. Later, when as a protest against German militarism in the first world war, he settled permanently in Switzerland, his reputation as one of the greatest literary figures of the German-speaking world was already firmly established. Hesse's deep humanity, his searching philosophy, were further developed in such masterly novels as Narziss and Goldmund and the famous Steppenwolf. At the same time he continued to publish poems and a number of critical works which won him a leading place among contemporary thinkers. The Nazis abhorred him and banned his books, but the world honoured him by bestowing the Nobel Prize for Literature on him in 1946. Herman Hesse died shortly after his 82nd birthday in 1962.'

Turning to the title page, he noticed something written on it in blue biro. His heart missed a beat, thinking it might be a message from her to him, but all it said was:

The name of the God is called Abraxas

He was disappointed and puzzled, yet thrilled just to see her handwriting, to think that maybe she had written it for him and maybe it did contain some secret message, which he would only understand after reading the book.

More eagerly than ever, he turned to the first page, on which there was a brief prologue. He would just read that and go to bed, he thought, since he was tired and it was past midnight. However, it was three o'clock when he finally forced himself to put the book down half-way through and did so.

CHAPTER TWENTY-THREE

After leaving the pub the next evening, Friday, they stood chatting on the pavement for a while as usual. Lorenzo had rummaged a book out of his rucksack and was trying to lend it to him. It was called, 'One Hundred Years of Solitude', by a South American writer called Gabriel Garcia Marquez. He declined to take it, because he knew it would oblige him to lend Marina's book to Lorenzo, using the excuse that his Spanish wouldn't be good enough to understand it. Lorenzo continued to prattle on about it anyway and he pretended to listen, but was more interested in watching Marina.

She was being chatted up by a new, good-looking Swedish student called Per. He could tell she wasn't really interested, but was worried Per might make a date with her for the weekend, which is what he would have liked to do himself. He had been trying to pluck up the courage to do so all evening, but hadn't, and the thought of Per or anyone else going out with her made him writhe with jealousy, while the thought of another weekend alone depressed him.

Suddenly, she said goodnight to Per, turned and walked quickly away, clutching her books in front of her as usual. A pang of disappointment went through him. He wanted to call her back or chase after her, but she disappeared round a corner. Oh, well, that's it, he thought dejectedly, while pretending to listen to Lorenzo, who was still jabbering on about Gabriel Garcia Marquez and 'One Hundred Years of Solitude'. He felt like telling him he had enough of solitude, without reading about it!

'We'd better go, too,' he said, interrupting him, and moved off with the rest of them in the opposite direction, towards the underground.

They had only gone a few yards when they heard a voice

behind them calling, 'Wait, please!' They all stopped and turned to see Marina running towards them. 'Can I come with you?' she panted, reaching them.

'We're going home,' he said, puzzled. It suddenly occurred to him that something might have happened. 'Is there anything wrong?' he asked anxiously.

'No, just I was afraid, that's all,' she said, lowering her head. Then she looked up with panic-stricken eyes and pleaded: 'Please let me go with you.'

'But it's late, we're all going home,' he shrugged, looking at his watch – he had never seen her like this before, looking so vulnerable and frightened, felt a sudden surge of protectiveness towards her.

'Yes, I hab to go,' Lorenzo, beside him, said.

'We have to go,' the others said, starting to move.

'I'm sorry, I will go home, too,' she said, turning and walking away again.

'Do you want me to go with you?' he called after her on an impulse.

'Will you?' she asked, stopping and turning round to look at him with imploring eyes.

'Of course, if you want,' he said, but didn't move, suddenly paralysed by the thought of being alone with her.

'Are you sure?' she asked.

'Sure, come on, let's go,' he said, saying goodnight to the others and walking off quickly before either of them could change their minds.

She had to run to catch up with him. He walked briskly, keeping a careful distance between himself and her. He was too nervous to speak to her. It was like a dream – he could hardly believe it was happening. A few minutes ago he was in despair because she had disappeared and now suddenly here he was walking her home!

But what was going to happen when they got there, he wondered? She'd say goodnight and leave him to get home without so much as a thank you, knowing her. And how was he going to get home? It'd be too late for the last tube, he couldn't afford a taxi and he didn't fancy walking five miles. He shouldn't have offered to go with her. She was only using him, because she was afraid to walk home on her own. She wasn't interested in him particularly – if Lorenzo or Per had offered to go with her, she'd have accepted just as quickly. She probably had her boyfriend waiting for her. What a mug he was! He quickened his pace even more, impatient to get there and get away, so that she almost had to run to keep up with him.

Suddenly, though, she stopped. He stopped too and turned to look back. She had dropped her books on the pavement and was standing there, hands clenched by her sides, staring wildly at him. Oh, no, she's having an attack of some sort, he thought in alarm, really regretting now that he had come with her, because he had no idea what to do if she was and there was hardly anyone else around – this was an area of shops and office blocks, all closed at this time of night.

'What's wrong?' he asked, nervously approaching her.

But she didn't answer, just continued to stand there staring wildly at him. Starting to panic, he glanced around for a phone box in case he needed to call an ambulance, but couldn't see one.

Then, suddenly, she threw herself at him. At first he thought she was attacking him and stepped back, but she only flung her arms around him and clung to him, her head pressed against his chest. For a few moments he was too taken aback to do anything. Then, timidly, he put his free arm around her shoulders – with his other arm he was carrying his plastic bag of books.

'Hold me, please,' she begged, clinging to him even more tightly.

He put his bag down and put his other arm around her. The pressure of her body – especially her breasts – against his excited him so much he started to have an erection, but he suppressed it, because he didn't want to feel like that about her, he loved her, all he wanted was to help her, to protect her, to look after her ...

'What's the matter?' he whispered.

She still didn't answer, just clung to him even more tightly, but he didn't mind – he was happy to be here with her, holding her in his arms, glad it was he and no one else, no matter what was wrong with her. After a while though, he started to feel

271

self-conscious, because one or two passers-by glanced curiously at them – they were somewhat conspicuous, he thought, hugging each other in the middle of the pavement, with her books scattered around.

'Are you cold?' he asked, realising she was trembling – there was a cool night breeze blowing along the valley of the street and she was wearing only a blouse.

She nodded, her head still pressed against his chest, and clung to him even more tightly. He was about to offer her his jacket, but didn't, because he was afraid to let go of her – he might never be able to hold her like this again.

'Let's move into the shop doorway,' he suggested instead, and she immediately started to tug him towards it.

'What about your books?' he asked, picking up his bag, but she continued to pull him into the shop doorway, leaving them on the pavement.

There, to his alarm, she removed her arms from around him, but only to slip them under his jacket. He hugged her close to him, excited again by the pressure of her body against his, even closer now than before. His heart was thumping, to his embarrassment, because her head was on his chest and she must be able to feel it. Even more embarrassing, he had an erection again, which she must also be able to feel, because her stomach was pressed tightly against his.

He tried to suppress it, but with her body pressed so tightly against him, it was impossible and, anyway, she seemed either not to notice or not to mind. He was worried about her books still lying on the pavement, too, but she didn't seem to be bothered about them either, so why should he? They couldn't fall any further, he told himself. Here he was, holding the girl of his dreams in his arms, something he never thought would happen – he should be happy. He *was* happy! He was *ecstatic*! He could hardly believe it wasn't a dream. He loved her!

But did she love him? Or was she just holding him like this because she was frightened or lonely or sick? There was only one way to find out, he thought – at least he would have these few minutes of bliss to remember. Hesitantly, he started to stroke her back, moving his hand up and down. To his relief, she didn't pull away, if anything clung to him yet more tightly.

He could feel the ridge of her bra strap through her blouse, but it was too exciting, so he moved his hand up to the nape of her neck and lightly caressed the soft, warm downy hair there with his fingertips. However, this was even more exciting, so he moved his hand up to her head, stroking it lovingly. Her short blonde hair felt silky-soft, while her skull felt as fragile as an egg, filling him with a tender protectiveness. He only wished he could hold her like this for ever ...

Suddenly, to his alarm, she moved her head from his chest, but only to look up at him with big, blue eyes. They were like two lakes in which he seemed to feel himself drowning.

'Francis?' she said.

'Yes?' he asked, thrilled to hear her use his name for the fist time, half-afraid she was going to say something to break the spell, shatter the illusion.

'I am happy you are here with me,' she said.

'I'm happy to be with you,' he said, his voice sticking in his throat.

'Are you?'

'Yes, I am.'

Her upturned face was so lovely, it made his senses swim. He wanted to tell her he loved her, but the words stuck in his throat. He wanted to kiss her, but didn't dare. He felt weak at the knees and his legs were trembling. He was afraid of fainting. If he kissed her, he was sure he would. For the first time ever he understood what they meant in romantic novels when they talked about lovers 'swooning'!

'Will you stay with me?' she asked.

'Yes, of course,' he said thickly, giving her a hug, though he wasn't sure whether she meant till she got home, for the rest of the night or for the rest of her life. Whichever she meant, he would say yes without hesitation, because he loved her. This was the moment, he realised – if he didn't say it now, he would never be able to. He opened his mouth to do so, but again the words stuck in his throat. 'We'd better go,' he said instead, cursing his cowardice.

'You will stay with me?' she asked again, pleading.

'Of course,' he said, though he still wasn't sure exactly what she meant.

'Oh, Francis, I am so happy!' she exclaimed, smiling up at him.

'So am I,' he smiled back at her.

This was the moment to kiss her, he thought, but the very thought made him feel dizzy and he was afraid of fainting again. Besides, his back and legs had started to ache unbearably. That never happened to heroes in romantic novels, he reflected wryly.

'Shall we go?' he said, cursing his cowardice again.

She nodded and, keeping one arm around his waist, tugged him out of the doorway.

'What about your books?' he asked, pulling her back with one arm around her shoulders – they were still lying scattered on the pavement.

'I do not want them,' she said, trying to tug him forward, but he held her back.

'What do you mean?' he laughed.

'I do not want to carry them,' she said, trying to tug him away, but he resisted.

'I'll carry them then,' he said.

She said something in Serbo-Croat under her breath and let go of him. It sounded as if she was swearing and he was afraid he had annoyed her, but he bent down and picked up her books, putting them in his plastic bag with his own.

'You can't just leave them here!' he expostulated with her, standing up. 'Anyway, you need them, don't you?'

'Shall we go now?' she said.

There was a note of mockery in her voice that stung him. Nervously, he put his arm around her shoulders, afraid she might rebuff him, but to his relief she put her arm around his waist again and they walked on. He was puzzled by her behaviour, but put it out of his mind, thrilled to be walking side by side with her again, the contact of their hips as they brushed together sending delicious currents of excitement through him.

Neither of them spoke. He was too nervous and didn't know what to say anyway. After a while though, he started to feel self-conscious about the silence and, simply to break it, asked her: 'Why don't you carry a bag?' He regretted it immediately, realising it sounded trite.

She stopped walking, turned to face him and, like a teacher telling off an importunate child, put a finger to her lips. Then she walked on, pulling him with her. He felt offended, but realised she was right – it was an inane question and it was better to enjoy the magic of the moment in silence.

A little farther along, she pulled him over to a shop window full of pictures and looked in. 'Oh, look, Francis, they are beautiful!' she exclaimed, her arm still around his waist.

'Which ones?' he asked, touched and amused by her enthusiasm, keeping his arm around her shoulders.

'All of them! I love them all!' she enthused.

'I see,' he laughed. 'Which one do you like best?'

'That one,' she pointed.

'Ah, the Van Gogh,' he said.

'Yes!' she declared excitedly. 'Do you know him?'

'Well, I've heard of him,' he said, remembering incongruously how Van Gogh's pictures were among those on the walls of the junior seminary. He wished he knew more about him, since she was obviously so keen on him. All he knew was that he was Dutch, went mad and cut off his own ear. He would have to read up about him, he decided.

The picture in the window was entitled, 'Cornfield with Rooks'. Gazing at it, he suddenly felt moved by the poetry of the picture, but also vaguely disturbed. Was it because it reminded him of the seminary, that other world he had left behind and wanted to forget, to pretend had never even existed, especially with her, he wondered?

'Do you like it?' she asked.

'Yes,' he said, hesitantly. 'It's – it's got atmosphere.'

'I love him!' she declared, tugging him away from the window.

They strolled on, arms still around each other. He was amused by the way she had said, 'I love him'. It sounded funny to say that about someone who was dead and you had never even known. He even felt a jab of jealousy. Would she ever say those words to him? That was too much to hope for. He would definitely have to find out more about Van Gogh, he decided. Maybe he should even learn to paint. He certainly wasn't going to cut off his ear though!

They came to Russell Square. She pulled him across the road and into the garden in the middle. There were floodlights fixed to the trees, so that it was as if they had suddenly entered another world, a magical world of luminous, ethereal green. They were the only people there too, which made it even more enchanting. As they strolled along, arms around each other, he suddenly felt so happy he wanted to stop, sweep her up in his arms and dance for joy. However, before he could, she stopped herself and turned to point at something.

'Oh, Francis, look!' she exclaimed.

'What?' he asked.

'The tree – it is so beautiful!'

'Yes, it is,' he agreed.

It was – a magnificent cedar of Lebanon, bathed in floodlight and standing on its own in the centre of a lawn as smooth as baize. She started to tug him towards it, but he resisted. 'You're not allowed on the grass,' he said, pointing to a sign and immediately realised it was daft, especially as there was no one else around.

Saying something scornful in Serbo-Croat, she let go of him, ran across the grass to the tree, flung her arms around the massive trunk and declared: 'I love you! I love you!'

Nervously – just in case there was a park-keeper lurking in the bushes – he stepped onto the grass and strolled across it towards the tree, where he stood watching her with a mixture of admiration and amusement – admiration for both her and the tree and amusement at her behaviour. He was also amused to realise he felt jealous – he was jealous not only of a dead painter, but also a tree! He shook his head and laughed.

'Why do you laugh?' she asked, her arms still around the massive trunk.

'Nothing,' he said.

'You do not laugh at me, do you?'

'No.'

'Tell me.'

'Some other time.'

'Now.'

'I was laughing because – I'm happy.' Well, it was half true!

'Why are you happy?'

'Because I'm here. With you. And the tree.' He had to struggle to keep a straight face.

'Come and touch it,' she commanded.

Keeping a straight face, he put down his plastic bag with their books in it on the grass, went over to the tree and self-consciously placed his hand on the trunk. The deeply-furrowed bark felt as hard as rock.

'It's hard to believe it's alive,' he remarked, awed.

'Put your arms round it,' she ordered.

Even more self-consciously, he did so – he liked trees, but this was taking it a bit far. However, he was so infatuated with her he would have done almost anything she commanded. Suddenly, his fingertips touched hers and a current of excitement shot through him. They clasped hands, just about able to reach. He could feel his heart pulsating against the tree trunk, mixing with hers in the heart of this mighty, marvellous, mysterious being. If only they could be like this for ever, he thought, or at least for the life of the tree ...

Suddenly, though, she let go, ran off and started gambolling about on the grass. He watched her, again with both admiration and amusement. After a while, she stopped, flung herself down on the grass and lay flat on her back, with her arms and legs outstretched. He went over and looked down at her, smiling. She looked lovely, like some sylvan nymph or dryad, with her limbs spread-eagled and a rapturous expression on her face. He wanted to throw himself down on top of her, but didn't dare. He didn't even dare to lie down beside her.

'Francis, I feel so happy,' she said.

'Good,' he said.

'Why don't you lie down?' she suggested.

'OK,' he agreed, pleased to comply. He lay down on his back on the grass beside her, but at arm's length – despite what had happened before, he was afraid of getting too close or touching her. Above, the sky glittered with stars – he gazed up at them with wonder. There seemed to be millions of them, millions of miles away, millions of years old. If there was a God, he thought, why would He have bothered to make so many? If there wasn't a God, as he now believed, it was even more of a mystery. It meant planet Earth was no more than an insignificant, microscopic speck of dirt in the cosmos. It meant he, lying here on the grass, was no more important than any of the insects with which it was no doubt crawling.

Normally, he would have found the thought depressing, but not tonight, because she was here with him. She had given life a new meaning for him. What did she make of it all, he wondered: the universe, life, death ...? She was a communist and an atheist. How did communists cope with death? He must find out more about communism, he decided – he didn't really know anything about it. Maybe it had some answers.

'What are you thinking?' she asked,

'I was just wondering.' He wasn't sure whether to tell her – she might think he was morbid.

'Tell me,' she ordered, in her peremptory way.

'I was just looking at the stars up there and wondering what it all means.'

'What?'

'The universe, life ...'

'What do you think?'

'Well, if there's no God – '

'Of course not. God is for children. You do not believe in God, do you?'

'Of course not.' He still felt uneasy about admitting it, even after all this time. 'But in that case, what does it all mean? What's it all about?'

'I think it does not mean anything. I think we must find our own meaning.'

She was right, he suddenly realised. She was so smart. In some ways she was smarter than he, even though he was several years older. She had given life a new meaning for him. He turned and propped himself up on his elbow to tell her so, but his nerve failed him. 'Have you found any meaning?' he asked, instead.

'That is why I have come to London,' she said.

'To find the meaning of life?'

'To find meaning of life for *me*.'

'Have you found it yet?'

'No. Sometimes I think I will never find it.'

'I'm sure you will.' He was disappointed – he had hoped she might say he gave meaning to her life, as she did to his. 'What about death?' he couldn't resist asking.

'Sometimes I think it is easier to die,' she said.

'What do you mean?' he asked, surprised.

'Sometimes I think I would prefer to die. How do you say in English: suicide?'

'Commit suicide?' He tried not to sound shocked.

'Yes.'

'I suppose we all feel like that sometimes,' he said lightly, remembering how he had felt like that himself once, not so long ago.

'I tried to do it once.'

'What, to commit suicide?'

'Yes.'

'How?' He remembered how he had tried to do it himself, with pills, but he didn't want to talk about it.

'Look,' she said, showing him one of her wrists. To his horror there was a fine white scar across it.

'You cut your wrist?' He couldn't help sounding shocked now.

'Yes.'

'What with?'

'A razor blade. My father's.'

'When?'

'Last year.'

'Why?'

'I was confused.'

'About what?'

'About life.'

'What do you mean?'

'It is too difficult to explain.'

'Try.'

'I prefer not talk about it tonight. Tonight I am happy. I will tell you other time. Shall we go?'

She jumped up and strolled off. He stood up, picked up his plastic bag and ran after her. When he caught up with her, to his relief she let him put his arm around her shoulders again and put hers around his waist. They walked out of the garden and through empty side-streets, past closed shops and offices, in silence. He wanted to continue the conversation, but thought better of it and kept silent, enjoying again the pleasure of simply being with her, the brush of her hip against his.

Eventually, they came to a tower block, where she suddenly stopped, let go of him and ran up some steps to ring the bell next to the plate-glass entrance doors, while he waited uncomfortably a short distance behind her. From a plaque on the wall, he could see it was a student hall of residence. She stood in front of the doors, with her back to him, tapping one sandalled foot impatiently, each tap a hammer blow to his heart. This was it, he thought – he had served his purpose, the dream was over. *Thank you and goodnight.* She wasn't even going to give him the chance to kiss her goodnight night or make a date with her!

They waited, but nobody came to open the door. Looking at his watch, he saw it was half-past midnight. How on earth was he going to get home, he wondered? Then he had an even more worrying thought: What if she couldn't get in? He would have to take her home with him! For some reason the thought filled him with panic.

'Somebody comes,' she said at last, to his relief, and he saw an Arabic-looking student approach and start unlocking the doors.

It seemed to take him ages though. He didn't want to be seen, just wanted to say goodnight to her and go. He was about to do so, when at last the door opened, to his surprise she stepped in without saying anything, the student closed the door and she started talking to him. He watched the student nodding and smiling as she did so, then to his discomfort glance at him. What was going on, he wondered impatiently? What on earth was she talking about? Why didn't she just say goodnight and let him go?

Then, to his further surprise, the student opened the door again and she beckoned him in. Puzzled, he reluctantly walked up the steps and went inside. To his even greater surprise, the student locked the door behind him, while she went over to the lift and pressed the button. He stood in the middle of the dimly-lit hall, more puzzled than ever.

She beckoned him over, so reluctantly he went and waited silently beside her, wondering what she was up to. She was tapping her foot on the floor impatiently. She just wanted him to stay with her till the lift came, he supposed. But looking back, he noticed the student had locked the front doors and disappeared. He suddenly felt nervous, wanted to go home. He was about to tell her so, when the lift arrived, she stepped in and beckoned him to follow her.

Reluctantly, he did so. She pressed a button and the lift went up. She stood in front of the door, tapping a sandalled foot impatiently on the floor again. What was she doing, he wondered, afraid of being caught as a trespasser? At the fifteenth floor the lift stopped and she hurried out, signalling him to follow. Nervously, he followed her down a long, narrow, dimly-lit corridor. She stopped outside one of the doors, unlocked it and went into the room, leaving the door ajar. He hovered nervously outside.

'Are you coming in?' she asked, opening the door wide.

'I think I'd better go now,' he said. 'It's very late. I – '

'You promised you will stay with me!'

'Yes, I know, but – '

'Please! Stay with me, Francis.'

'Are you sure it's all right?' She didn't say please very often!

'Yes, yes! Come in!'

Nervously, he did so and immediately, excusing herself, she went out. He put his plastic bag down and glanced around, suddenly excited at being allowed into her private space. It was a typical, tiny, student study-bedroom, with a single bed, washbasin, fitted wardrobe, desk, chair, easy-chair and bookshelf. There were posters all over the walls, including one of Che Guevara, and on a ledge around the bed postcard-size reproductions of paintings.

He went over to the window and looked out. The room was so high up, it was like looking down from a plane coming in to land – the lights of the city, of London, spread out below him like a constellation of red, orange, green and white stars. It was all there for him to explore, he thought, with a sudden thrill. And now he had her to do it with – or at least he hoped so. He was on top of the world, both literally and figuratively!

He turned away from the window and looked down at the desk, where, among a lot of other clutter, he saw several books: 'Steppenwolf' by Herman Hesse, 'Animal Farm' by George Orwell, which they were doing in class, a book about Che Guevara, a book about Van Gogh, a Serbo-Croat dictionary and a tome-like textbook of anatomy and physiology. He picked up the book about Van Gogh and flicked through it. It contained a brief critical biography and colour plates with notes. His eye caught the picture they had seen in the shop window, 'Cornfield with Rooks'. He referred to the notes and read:

'1890. Auvers period. Oils. 50.5 by 105 cm. V.W. van Gogh coll., Amsterdam. Formerly J. van Gogh-Bonger coll., Amsterdam. "There – once back here I set to work again – though the brush almost slipped from my fingers, but knowing exactly what I wanted, I have painted three more big canvasses since. They are vast fields of wheat under troubled skies, and I did not need to go out of my way to try to express sadness and extreme loneliness." (letter to Theo and his sister, no. 649, June 1890). This is the last and perhaps the best known of Van Gogh's works, painted almost on the eve of his suicide. In this famous canvas the peculiar format of the picture, the dilated perspective and the crossed directions all unite to create a sense of extraordinary unease, enhanced by the confused – '

Before he could finish reading, the door opened and she rushed back in, went straight to the bed and yanked off the bedspread. 'You can sleep in bed,' she said.

'What about you?' he asked, putting the book down.

'I will sleep here,' she said, pointing to the easy-chair.

'Oh, no!' he objected, sitting in it quickly. 'I'll sleep here.'

'Please, you can use bed,' she insisted.

'Ah, ah, I'm fine here,' he said, pulling the desk chair towards him and propping his legs on it. There was no way he was going to take her bed off her, he told himself.

She said something exasperated in Serbo-Croat and threw the bedspread at him. With a grin, he draped it over his legs. She switched off the light, sat on the edge of the bed and started taking off her sandals. Because it was a clear night and the blind on the window was open, he could still see her quite clearly. Supposing she was going to get undressed, he closed his eyes. After a few minutes, hearing no noise, he opened them again and saw she was lying curled on the bed, with her back to him, still dressed.

He suddenly felt rejected, but told himself that was silly, closed his eyes again and tried to sleep. But he was too excited. There was something surreal about the situation, he thought – here he was, sitting in this space-rocket of a building hundreds of feet above London in the middle of the night with a beautiful girl a few feet away from him, yet she might as well be a million miles away. And yet only an hour ago he had been holding her in his arms!

This was ridiculous, he told himself – he wanted to get into bed with her, and she probably wanted him to, but he didn't dare. What a wimp he was! She must be disillusioned with him. She'd probably never want to see him again. He'd blown it! There must be something wrong with him – it was absurd to be sitting here like this, after what had happened. A normal man would be making love to her now. He was as incapable of getting up and doing so as if he were paralysed. That was his problem – emotional paralysis. He was an emotional cripple. He might as well be a twelve-year-old sitting here. He was a case of arrested development. He really was screwed up!

He mustn't start thinking like that or he'd get depressed, he told himself. He ought to sleep. It was impossible though. Apart from anything else, he was so uncomfortable. He tried changing his position, but it made no difference. It seemed as if she couldn't sleep either, because he could hear her tossing and turning and muttering in Serbo-Croat. God, what a ridiculous situation!

'Francis?'

The sound of her voice saying his name sent a thrill through him. 'Mmm?' he murmured, pretending to be sleepy.

'Do you sleep?'

'Not yet,' he murmured.

There was silence for a few moments. He peeped through his eyelashes at her. To his surprise she was lying with her head propped on her elbow, her eyes wide open, staring at him.

'Why don't you come here?' she said.

'You mean, on the bed?' he asked. What a stupid question!

'Yes.'

'Is there room?' God, another stupid question!

'Yes. Come!' It sounded like an order.

'All right,' he agreed, trying to sound casual, but as he got up and went over to the bed, he was trembling with excitement – she was going to let him share her bed with her!

'Are you sure there's enough room?' he asked, looking down at her.

'Yes, please,' she said, moving nearer to the wall.

Nervously, he lay down on his back beside her, trying not to touch her, but the bed was so small it was impossible – their shoulders and hips made contact, sending a current of excitement through him. Even more excitingly, she didn't seem to mind. He could hardly believe it – he was actually in bed with her!

He lay like this for a while, not daring to move, hardly daring to breathe, his heart fluttering with excitement. This was really absurd, he thought. He ought to take her in his arms and – no, he didn't want to do that, he didn't need to do that, he told himself! It was enough just to lie here beside her like this. No, that was silly. He was just a coward. She obviously wanted him to.

Did she? Or was she asleep? There was only one way to find out. He turned his head slightly to look at her. To his surprise, their eyes met, they threw their arms round each other and kissed, first lips, then tongues ...

As they kissed, he started to explore her body with his hand, caressing all its curves lovingly, eventually even the soft mounds of her breasts. To his delight, she let him fondle them freely through her blouse, moaning with pleasure as he did so. Then he became more daring, moving his hand down over her stomach and between her thighs.

Suddenly though, she let go of him and sat bolt upright on the bed. For a moment he was afraid he had gone too far, but she just said she was hot, unbuttoned her blouse, took it off and flung it on the floor. He gazed with admiration at her back, gleaming like ivory in the moonlight and naked except for her bra strap, which she started trying to unfasten.

'Please,' she said, over her shoulder, unable to undo it.

He tried to do it, but his hands were trembling with excitement – unfastening girls' bras was not something he had had much practice with. After fumbling with it for a while, he gave up, frustrated and embarrassed, afraid it betrayed his inexperience. In the end, muttering something in Serbo-Croat, she undid it herself, pulled it off and flung it on the floor with her blouse. He propped himself up on an elbow and started kissing her back, at the same time cupping one of her now naked breasts in his hand and fondling it until he felt the nipple become stiff and hard like himself.

Meanwhile, she unzipped her skirt, wriggled out of it and flung it on the floor with her other clothes. Then she lay back on the bed, with her arms crossed over her breasts, completely naked now except for a pair of large, white, schoolgirlish knickers. He looked down at her with awe, hardly able to believe she was lying almost naked beside him. Gently, he removed her arms from her breasts, bent down and began kissing them, at the same time caressing the rest of her body with his hand, admiring its lovely, satin-like smoothness, still hardly able to believe she was giving it to him.

'Francis?' she interrupted him after a while.

'Yes?'

'Haven't you forgotten something?'

'What's that?'

'To take off your clothes?'

'Oh, yes,' he said, feeling foolish.

He sat on the edge of the bed and started to undress self-consciously – he had never undressed in front of a girl before. He was too shy to take off his underpants, especially as he had a huge erection, but when he turned around he saw she had taken off her knickers. She wanted him to make love to her properly, he realised in sudden panic, because he had never done it before, though she probably thought he had, probably thought he was very experienced. He didn't really want to do it with her, hadn't really even wanted to go to bed with her, because he loved her, respected her, admired her ...

But this was the moment he had been waiting so long for, he told himself, when he could at last lose his virginity and become a man. It would be the final symbol of victory over the Ghosters, especially Father Director. It would prove he was completely normal. He mustn't blow it. Besides, she *wanted* him to do it. He *had* to do it!

He pulled off his underpants quickly, turned and took her in his arms. The thrill of holding a naked female body – especially hers – against his for the first ever time went through him like an electric shock. They kissed and caressed each other, his hand gliding smoothly over the waves of her body, making her writhe and moan with pleasure. Gradually, he worked his way down between her thighs, slipped a finger between the wet lips into the secret, soft, moist, warm interior and moved it in and out, faster and faster, kissing her all over as he did so, till she was groaning and writhing convulsively. Then suddenly she gave a jerk, cried out in Serbo-Croat, grabbed his arm, pulled it away and threw her arms around him, clinging to him tightly.

When she let go of him, he continued to kiss and caress her, surprised by the salty taste of sweat on her skin. Supposing she had come, but too shy to ask, he eased himself on top of her and tried to go into her. He thought she wanted him to do it and he wanted to do it himself now, to make their union complete, to become a man at last.

'Francis!' she cried, pushing him off.

'What's wrong?' he asked, his heart pounding, his whole body throbbing with desire.

'I am afraid,' she said.

'Of what?' he asked.

'For me it is first time.'

'It's all right, don't worry,' he whispered, kissing her face and trying to enter her again, thinking: If only she knew it was his first time too!

'Francis!' She pushed him off again.

'What's wrong?' he asked again.

'Please do not do that!' She sounded panic-stricken.

'What?'

'That!'

'Why?'

'It is too dangerous!'

She was afraid of getting pregnant, he supposed, but why had she let him go this far, only to stop him now? Wasn't she on the pill or something? He wanted to ask her, but was too inhibited. That was his inexperience again. If she wasn't, why not? Surely she knew about such things, especially as she was going to be a medical student? But maybe not. Maybe contraception wasn't allowed in communist Yugoslavia. He ought to have something himself, of course. That was another symptom of his inexperience – he was too inhibited to buy them, even from a machine. He felt frustrated, but knew she was right, it would be too dangerous. It was his own fault, he told himself.

'All right,' he said.

'I am sorry, Francis,' she said.

'There's nothing to be sorry about. It doesn't matter,' he tried to reassure her, kissing her, fondling her breasts.

'Yes, it does. I know you want to do it. You are man. You can do it if you want, I do not care.'

'No, we'd better not. You're right, it's too dangerous.'

'Oh, Francis, I am sorry!' she said again.

'You don't need to be. It doesn't matter. Honestly.'

He was secretly relieved not to have to do it, because he still wasn't sure exactly how to, but he was desperate to come. After kissing and caressing her again for a while, he eased himself back on top of her and started rubbing himself up and down on her stomach. To his relief she didn't stop him, but encouraged him, gasping, 'Go on, Francis! Go on!' He moved faster and faster, his heart pounding harder and harder, his whole body throbbing, until at last he came in an explosion of ecstasy and collapsed on top of her.

'Francis!' she exclaimed in alarm, pushing him off.

'What?' he gasped, weak with relief.

'I am wet!' She felt her stomach with her hand and lifted it up.

'Are you?' he said, as if surprised.

'They are your children!'

'Yes, I suppose so,' he grinned.

'Oh, Francis, there are millions of them! I want them! I love them!'

She was smearing his semen all over her body with both hands as if it were a lotion. He smiled, though he was shocked. At last he had been to bed with a girl and made love with her, even if not quite properly. He was no longer a complete virgin. He was a man! He was normal! He had done it!

'Thank you!' he said, kissing her on the cheek.

'Oh, Francis, you must not say that!' she remonstrated.

'Why not?' he asked.

'It sounds so polite, so English.'

'Oh, sorry,' he said, trying not to take offence – he didn't want anything to spoil his or her happiness. 'Are you all right?' he asked her, after a pause.

'I am tired,' she said.

'So am I,' he laughed.

'Shall we sleep?'

'OK.'

'Shall we use sheet?'

'Sure.'

She pulled the sheet up over them and to his dismay curled up with her back to him. Oh, God, he thought, he'd upset her. What an anti-climax!

'Francis?' she said to the wall.

'Yes?' he asked.

'Hold me.'

It sounded like an order as usual, but it was one he was only too happy to obey. He snuggled up to her, his belly pressed against her buttocks, his cock between her thighs and his hands cupping her breasts.

'Francis?' she said again.

'Yes?' he asked,

'I love you.'

'I love you,' he whispered into the nape of her neck, kissing it tenderly and squeezing her breasts softly. At last, they had said it!

'Goodnight,' he whispered.

She didn't reply, but he didn't mind – he was happy! He was happier than he had ever been in his life. He would be happy to die, if this could last for ever, he thought, just like Keats in 'Ode to a Nightingale':

'Now more than ever seems it rich to die,
    To cease upon the midnight with no pain ...'

He felt as if he had already died and gone to Heaven! Heaven couldn't be better than this, could it? Except that this couldn't last for ever, he reflected with a pang. But all the more reason to enjoy it fully while it did last, he told himself, hugging her even more tightly as he drifted blissfully off to sleep ...

CHAPTER TWENTY-FOUR

When he woke up the next morning, with her naked body still curled up against his, he could hardly believe it wasn't a dream. For a while he didn't dare open his eyes, in case it was, and he would find himself alone in bed in his own room as usual. He kept his eyes closed and snuggled up closer to her, hugging her tightly, one arm under her head, a hand cradling each of her breasts, their legs entwined, her buttocks pressed into his belly. It was as if their bodies had become one, joined like Siamese twins.

This was heaven, he thought – or at least, it would be if it could last for ever. If he had to die to make it last for ever, he'd be happy to do so. Who needed all that metaphysical or supernatural claptrap? He couldn't imagine any greater happiness than this, didn't need or want it. He could still hardly believe it – he was in bed, naked, with a naked girl, at last! He'd made love with her! He was no longer a virgin! He was a man! He was normal! He'd done it!

Well, nearly done it. She hadn't let him go all the way, actually go inside her, but that didn't matter. They had as good as done it. It was enough. It was more than enough, more than he'd ever hoped for. They'd make love properly in time no doubt. Meanwhile, he was happy. He was in bed with her. He was in love with her. And she was in love with him. Yes, it was heaven, all the heaven he ever wanted, anyway – it certainly beat sitting on a cloud, playing the harp and singing hymns!

When he opened his eyes, he was relieved to find he really was in her room with her. It was dazzlingly bright, with sunlight beaming in through the window, which struck him as symbolic – for him this was now a place of light, a holy place, a sacred place, a shrine. It was where he had lost his virginity, discovered love and become a man. He looked at her head on the pillow beside him adoringly – if the room was a shrine, she was his goddess. She was beautiful and brilliant. He loved her, he worshipped her and, he vowed to himself, he would do so for ever.

The weight of her head on his arm was making it numb, but he didn't move it for fear of waking her. He wondered what time it was and when she had to get up for work, but he had left his watch on the desk and couldn't reach it without disturbing her. Anyway, he wanted these moments of bliss to last as long as possible, to last for ever if possible. He shut his eyes and continued to hold her close without moving, enjoying the contact between their naked bodies, the closeness, the oneness ...

That was what love was all about, he thought – becoming as one, in both body and soul. That was the meaning of love – oneness, unison, harmony. And to think that by becoming a priest he would have missed out on this. Christ, what a mistake! It would have been a living death. Thank goodness he'd seen the light and got out. It was worth all the pain of leaving just for this one night in bed with her!

He wished he could tell her, but it was out of the question. He still found it too painful to talk about to anyone, even to think about for long. It was like a shameful secret that he wanted to keep locked deep inside himself, even to forget if possible. That was partly why he had come to London, to bury the past and start a completely new life, find a new identity. And he had done so, or at least started to. This morning certainly he felt like a new man, thanks to her.

He couldn't bear the pressure of her head on his arm any longer – it felt dead. He removed it as gently as he could, but in doing so woke her up. She turned towards him, opening her eyes and blinking in the brightness. Even first thing in the morning she looked beautiful, with her babyish complexion and sparkling blue eyes.

'Good morning,' he said, giving her a peck on the forehead.

'What is time?' she groaned.

'That's a very big philosophical question so early in the morning,' he quipped. 'You mean, 'What time is it?'.'

'Please, do not speak about philosophy or English now,'

she groaned.

'It's half-past seven,' he said, reaching over to the desk for his watch.

'It is late!' she exclaimed, throwing back the sheet, jumping out of bed and hurriedly getting dressed and washed.

He watched her, excited to think he was now allowed to witness such a private ritual, amused by the way she dashed about looking for things and swearing – or so it sounded – in Serbo-Croat when she couldn't find them.

'Do you have to go to work?' he asked.

'Yes,' she said, brushing her teeth briskly.

'That's a pity,' he said.

'Why?' she asked, splashing her face.

'We could've spent the day together.'

'You want to spend day with me?' she asked, pausing while drying her face, as if surprised by the idea.

'Of course,' he said.

'Why?'

'It'd be fun,' he said, feebly. *Because I love you*, he had wanted to say, but couldn't. Why not, he wondered, annoyed with himself? That was what she wanted him to say, wasn't it? Or was it? She seemed more interested in rushing off to work. She was brushing her hair furiously. Was she going to rush off without arranging to see him this evening? He ought to ask her, but couldn't bring himself to. What was wrong with him? He was too proud, even though the thought of not seeing her filled him with panic. What a prat he was!

She dashed to the door and opened it. He couldn't believe she was going to rush off without saying anything about meeting again.

'Can I get up now?' he asked.

'Yes, but stay here,' she ordered.

'What do you mean?' he asked, puzzled. Did she want him to stay here all day? He didn't like the idea at all. He was afraid of being found. And what would he do in her room all day, privileged as he felt to be allowed in it?

'I come back.'

'When?'

'In few minutes. You will see,' she said, closing the door and locking him in, to his alarm.

What on earth was she playing at, he wondered? Apart from anything else, he needed a pee. He started to feel annoyed with her. But what the hell, he thought – why should he worry? If she wanted him to stay, he would. He would have been overjoyed at the idea twenty-four hours ago. He didn't want to stay in bed though, in case a cleaner or someone came in. Nor did he want her to find him in bed when she came back, though he wasn't sure why.

He got up and dressed. Then he wandered over to the window and gazed out at the view. Like last night, it was spectacular: the sun was already high over the city, spread out below like an elaborate toy-town, glittering and shimmering in the dazzling brightness. It was a doubly awesome sight – the sun an incandescent star, a huge ball of fire, millions of miles away and millions of years old, shining down on this vast, man-made metropolis of concrete, steel, glass and brick. Like last night he was thrilled to think it was all there at his feet, a whole new world waiting for him to explore it. Even more thrilling, he now had her to do it with. He felt as if he was on a voyage of discovery, both interior and exterior, as if life was only just beginning ...

Unable to wait any longer, he peed in the sink and rinsed it out carefully. Then he sat down in the easy-chair to wait for her and gazed around the room. Every feature, every object, no matter how mundane, had a special aura about it, simply because it belonged to her: wardrobe, washbasin, toothbrush, towel ... It was as if the whole world was transformed. The whole world *was* transformed! His *life* was transformed, transformed by love.

What about tonight though? He still hadn't asked her and she didn't seem to be interested in arranging anything. Well, even if she didn't want to see him again, it didn't matter, he told himself. It was enough to have spent one night with her. That was enough for a whole lifetime. That made his life worth having lived. No, he was deluding himself! The thought of not seeing her again sent a wave of despair over him. It would be like going from heaven to hell. He would have to swallow his stupid pride and ask her out when she came back, he decided.

He glanced at his watch – she had been gone for a quarter of an hour. He looked around the room. The walls were covered with pictures, most of which seemed to be by Van Gogh, Picasso and Dali. He remembered how, at the junior seminary, he used to keep a holy picture of Dali's 'Crucifixion' in his missal, but later had torn it up, finding it, like all representations of the crucifixion, repulsive, all the more so for its pseudo-realism. He had never liked Dali's or Picasso's surrealistic paintings much either, but would have to learn to now, since she obviously did. In fact, he decided, he would have to read up about them, because he knew so little about them, or indeed about modern art in general.

The most striking picture in the room was the large poster of Che Guevara. He had seen it before, in poster shops and students' rooms, but not taken much notice of it. He had always found putting pictures of people on the wall juvenile – even one of his tutors at university had had pictures of famous writers and actors on his office wall. He wondered if this was just another prejudice left over from the seminary, where such a practice would have been unthinkable. Anyway, he now looked at the poster of Che Guevara with new interest, because it was hers – he looked dashing, with his long hair, beard and beret, like a film or rock star.

He suddenly realised he knew next to nothing about him, icon though he was. All he knew was that he was a communist revolutionary somewhere in South America. He also suddenly realised why he knew next to nothing about him – it was because of his Catholic background. Goaded by this, he reached over to the desk and picked up the book about Che Guevara that he had noticed there last night. It was called, 'Viva Che' and had a red and black cover with the same pictures of Che's face as on the poster all over it. He opened it and started reading:

'Che Guevara was born on June 14th, 1928, in Rosario, Argentina's most important city after Buenos Aires, the eldest of five children. His father was Ernesto Guevara Lynch, an adventurous, swashbuckling hell-bender of Irish descent who made and squandered fortunes ...'

Che Guevara's father was of Irish descent! So Che had Irish blood in him, just like himself? He read on with increasing interest and admiration, and not only because Che was evidently a hero of hers. He read how Che was afflicted all his life by asthma, bummed around South America during his school holidays as a teenager, qualified as a doctor – was that why she was going to be a doctor, he wondered? – continued to travel around South America afterwards doing odd jobs, observing the poverty, injustice and oppression and meeting with revolutionaries, met with Fidel Castro and the exiled Cuban revolutionary group called the 26th July Movement in Guatemala, joined as 'fighting doctor' the ramshackle expeditionary force of eighty-two men that sailed in an old yacht to Cuba in 1956 to engage in a revolutionary guerrilla war against the Cuban dictator, Batista, fought heroically in the war, helped to win victory in 1959, worked as a minister in the revolutionary government for six years, left Cuba in 1965 and fought as a revolutionary again in various countries ...

By the time he came to the last paragraph, there was a lump in his throat: 'On October 8th, 1967, in the region of Santa Cruz, Bolivia, a group of specially-trained Bolivian rangers were engaged in action against a unit of guerrillas, whom they had encircled. After a fierce battle, the rangers were able to capture the wounded guerrilla leader. He was taken to the nearby village of Higueras, where he was kept in a tiny school. After repeated attempts to interrogate him, he was shot through the heart towards noon of the following day. His corpse was strapped to the runners of a helicopter and taken to the nearby town of Villegrande. There, it was exposed in a shack, where it was viewed by the local population, as well as journalists and photographers. It was announced to the world that this Bolivian guerrilla fighter, known as Ramon, was in fact Major Ernesto 'Che' Guevara. When Che's brother arrived in Bolivia to claim the body, he was told that the corpse had been incinerated and the ashes scattered.'

To his own surprise, he felt choked with a mixture of sadness and anger – anger not just because such a noble spirit had been so callously snuffed out, but also anger with himself, because he hadn't known the story before. It was as if it had been deliberately kept from him, as in a way it had – yet another deficiency of his Catholic education. It was ironic reading about

Che – he felt the same admiration he used to feel reading about the lives of the saints and martyrs, or even Christ himself. But this was a far more edifying and inspiring story than the lives of the saints, most of whom he now realised were crackpots, including Christ himself – if he had ever even really existed.

Looking at the photographs of Che in the book made him feel even sadder. The photo of Che lying dead, shot through the heart, actually brought tears to his eyes, which he had to blink back. It was exactly how he used to feel when he looked at a picture or statue of the dead Christ. Funnily enough, in some of the photos, Che looked Christ-like. The close-up of his dead face, blurred and streaked as it was, reminded him of the supposed face of the dead Christ on the Shroud of Turin, which used to fascinate him, and still did, though he now believed it must be a fake. But there was one photo that intrigued him more than any other and that was one of Che with his second wife standing behind him, both of them in combat uniform with berets on their heads and rifles slung over their shoulders. To his amazement, she looked exactly like Marina!

Gazing at the photo, he thought he would like to become a revolutionary like Che and she could be his comrade. Together they would fight injustice, oppression and poverty. It would give him the purpose his life had been lacking, something to believe in and fight for. The only problem was he abhorred violence, so couldn't imagine himself fighting physically. But there were other ways of fighting, weren't there? He suddenly realised he knew next to nothing about communism – he would have to read up about it. He was ashamed of his ignorance and prejudice. Again, he realised angrily, it was because of his Catholic education. Thank goodness she didn't know about it – she'd probably despise him if she did.

Suddenly, he heard a key in the door. He put the book back on the desk quickly, not wanting her to find him reading it. He thought of hiding, in case it was a cleaner or someone else, but there was nowhere to hide, so he sat still and waited nervously for the door to open. When it did, to his relief it was Marina who walked in, carrying a tray.

'What's this?' he laughed.

'Breakfast!' she announced, depositing the tray on his lap and sitting on the edge of the bed.

There was a glass of orange juice, a bowl of cornflakes, a plate of bacon and egg, a cup of coffee, toast, butter, marmalade ...

'Thank you,' he smiled. 'I didn't expect room service.'

'Eat!' she instructed.

'Have you had yours?' he asked, picking up the orange juice.

'Yes,' she said. 'Is it good?'

'Lovely,' he said, finishing the orange juice and starting on the corn flakes.

As he ate, she sat watching him, which made him uncomfortable.

'It's like an art gallery in here,' he joked, to distract her.

'Do you like them?' she asked, seriously.

'The cornflakes? Yes,' he said, pretending to misunderstand, and was about to tell her he had worked in the factory in Manchester where they were made, but stopped himself – he didn't want to talk about his past ...

'Not cornflakes, pictures,' she said, impatiently.

'Oh, yes, most of them,' he said, deciding not to correct her for omitting her articles as usual.

'Which do you like best?' she asked.

'Er – the one of the cherry tree, I think,' he said.

'This one?' she asked, picking the card off the ledge above the bed.

'Yes.'

'You can have it,' she said, offering it to him.

'Oh, no, I don't want to take it off you,' he objected.

'Please – I can get other one,' she insisted.

'Well, thanks very much,' he said, taking it and studying it for a moment. It had an exquisite delicacy that he liked. 'Who's it by?'

'It is written on back,' she said.

''Egon Schiele',' he read aloud, turning it over. 'Baumchem, 1912. Was he German?'.

'Austrian,' she said, mispronouncing it.

He turned the card over to look at the picture again, moved by its delicate beauty and the thought that the man who had painted it in 1912 had probably been about his own age but was probably dead by now.

'Which is your favourite?' he asked her, starting on his bacon and egg.

'This one,' she said, handing him another card from the ledge.

'Van Gogh,' he said, able to tell without reading it and turned it over to read: 'Starry Night, 1888.'

'It is beautiful, yes?' she said.

'Yes,' he agreed.

'Have you heard song?' She sang a snatch of it, her fingers fluttering over the keys of an invisible piano.

'You've got a good voice,' he said, impressed.

'He was good person,' she said, ignoring the compliment. 'It was so sad, how they killed him.'

'I thought he killed himself,' he said, handing her the card back.

'Society killed him. Stupid people,' she said, scathingly.

He would definitely have to find out more about Van Gogh, as well as Che Guevara, he thought. God, she was so interesting and so intelligent, as well as attractive! He could hardly believe his luck. But then maybe he deserved a bit of luck. He only hoped he could hang on to her. The thought of losing her now went through him like a knife. He put his real knife and fork down, having finished the breakfast.

'You enjoyed?' she asked.

'It was very good, thanks,' he said, wiping his mouth with the tissue.

'I must go back to work now,' she said, standing up and taking the tray from him. 'You must go too.'

'OK,' he said, standing up, suddenly depressed at the thought.

'I will go first,' she said, moving towards the door. 'You follow in minute or two. Please make sure door is locked.'

'Yes, sure,' he said, starting to panic. Was she going to leave just like that, without ..?

'When shall we meet again?' he asked, fear of losing her and of loneliness overcoming his pride.

'Do you want?' she asked, turning back towards him, as if surprised.

'Of course,' he said – it was an odd question, after all that had happened last night. 'Don't you?'

'If you want,' she said, which wasn't quite the answer he had been hoping for, and turned back towards the door.

'What about tonight?' he suggested. 'We could go for a drink.'

'Yes, that would be good,' she said, opening the door and stepping into the corridor.

'Where shall I meet you?' he asked, following her to the door. It was almost as if she wasn't really interested.

'Entrance downstairs is best place,' she said, hurrying away. 'Please go back in room.'

'Eight o'clock?' he called after her, not caring who heard or saw him

'All right,' she said, disappearing down the corridor.

God, that was a close shave, he thought, going back into the room and closing the door. He had nearly blown it! It was funny, the way she had left. No kiss goodbye, no word about meeting again. It was almost as if last night hadn't happened at all. Maybe she was just pretending. Oh, well, there was no point worrying about it, he told himself. After all, last night *had* happened and he *was* going to see her again tonight. He ought to be happy. He *was* happy!

He picked up his bag and was about to leave, when he realised he had forgotten to ask her if he could borrow the Che Guevara book. He decided to take it and leave a note for her, sure she wouldn't mind. He went over to the desk to do so, slipped the book into his bag and went to the door to leave. Before he did so though, he had a last look around the room, wanting to keep a clear picture of it in his mind for the rest of the day, which stretched out ahead of him like a desert without her.

CHAPTER TWENTY-FIVE

'What would you like to drink?'

They were in a pub near the hall of residence, all fake oak beams and brass, but comfortable. She looked so lovely, in a embroidered peasant blouse and skirt, without make-up or jewellery! He felt proud to be with her.

'I drink what you drink,' she answered.

He brought her back a pint of Guinness and placed it in front of her.

'What is it?' she asked, scooping up some of the creamy head on her finger and licking it off, sending through him an erotic thrill.

'Drink it,' he told her, picking up his glass, and she picked up hers. 'Cheers!' He touched her glass with his own and took a first sup.

'Nasdrovie,' she said.

'What's that?' he asked.

'Serbo-Croat for 'cheers',' she told him and sipped some of the Guinness. He waited for her reaction with amusement. 'I love it!' she declared, and took a gulp.

'You're supposed to drink the beer through the head, like this,' he laughed, showing her.

'Mmm, I love it!' she exclaimed, doing so. 'What is it?'

'Guinness. Have you never had it before?'

'No.' She took another, even bigger gulp.

'Not too fast – you'll be drunk,' he laughed, pleased that she liked it.

'I want to be drunk,' she said.

He laughed. She was wonderful! He was already looking forward to going to bed with her again. But he wanted to have a good chat with her first.

'What did you do?' she asked.

'Today?'

'Yes.'

'I went home. Did some shopping. Cleaned my room. Had a bath. Made something to eat. Came out. Not very exciting.'

'Did you read book about Che Guevara?'

'Yes.'

'What do you think?'

'He was an impressive guy. I didn't really know about him before. It's terrible, the way he was killed. Executed.'

'It was crime,' she said.

'I bought some other books on the way home,' he said.

'Which ones?' she asked.

'About communism. I don't know much about it,' he admitted.

'You are typical Western person,' she said.

'I suppose so, in some ways,' he agreed. 'All we get is propaganda against it.'

'Did you read any of books?'

'I read 'The Communist Manifesto'.'

'What do you think?'

'I found it very inspiring. I'm not sure about the theory of dialectical materialism though.'

'What do you mean?'

'I mean, it's very clever, but I'm not sure if it's true.' He was looking for certainty, he supposed, something to replace the certainty of his lost Catholicism. 'Maybe it doesn't have to be true,' he added.

'What do you mean?'

'Maybe it's just a way of looking at history, a useful tool.'

'It could be,' she agreed. 'You don't have to believe everything.'

'I'm not too sure about the 'dictatorship of the proletariat', either.'

'What do you mean?' she asked again.

'Maybe I haven't understood it properly, but I don't like the words 'dictatorship' or 'proletariat'.'

'You have to read more,' she said.

'Probably,' he agreed, and added: 'It sounds like a good idea.'

'What?'

'Communism. I'm not sure if it's possible, though.'

'Why not?'

'I don't know – maybe it's too Utopian, too idealistic.'

'I think is possible.'

'I hope so. Let's drink to it.'

They clinked glasses and did so. He laughed, shaking his head.

'Why do you laugh?' she asked.

'I just never thought I'd find myself sitting in a pub and drinking to communism with a beautiful girl like you,' he said. The alcohol was loosening him up already, he realised.

'Why not?' she asked, ignoring the compliment.

'Well, I was brought up as a Catholic,' he confessed. 'We were taught that communism was evil, the work of the Devil.' The alcohol was definitely having an effect – he had better be careful, he told himself.

'Are you still Catholic?' she asked.

'No, I don't believe in it any more,' he replied, even now unable to avoid feeling a twitch of guilt at saying it.

'Why not?' she asked, to his surprise.

'I think it's superstitious nonsense, like all religion. Have you any idea what Catholics believe?'

'I know nothing about it.' What charming ignorance, he thought: a mind unsullied by all that superstitious claptrap. 'Tell me,' she ordered.

'Well, they believe in God, of course,' he obliged. 'They believe in life after death – if you're good, you go to Heaven, if you're bad, you go to Hell, for ever and ever. They believe that God created the world. In six days! In about 4000 BC! They believe that Jesus Christ was God, that he came down to Earth to save man. I *think* that includes women too, by the way. They believe that he was conceived miraculously in his mother's womb, without sexual intercourse. They believe that He rose from the dead after he was crucified.'

'What is that?' she interrupted.

'Executed, on the cross, by the Romans. They believe that he could do miracles, like changing water into wine or making the blind see. They believe that the priest can change bread and wine into his body and blood. They believe that God is actually present in the church. And lots more. All fairytales, of course.'

'I do not understand how people can believe such things.'

'Neither do I now, not intelligent people, anyway,' he agreed, ashamed to think he had believed it all himself once, yet still guilty at denying it. 'Of course, if you are taught to believe something from birth, it's easy to believe it. And difficult to stop believing it.' God, he knew only too well how difficult!

'When did you stop believing it?' she asked.

'Oh, when I was about your age and started to think for myself,' he said.

She was eighteen. When he was eighteen, he reflected, he was stuck in a bloody monastery! That was the last thing he wanted to tell her about now though, he thought, shutting it out of his mind – it seemed unreal, like a previous existence, another incarnation ...

'It took you long time,' she said.

'Yes, I suppose so, but that's the power of indoctrination. Would you like another Guinness?' he asked, to change the subject.

'Yes,' she nodded eagerly. 'But I buy it.'

'It's all right,' he objected.

'No, I buy it,' she insisted, fishing a crumpled pound note from her skirt and throwing it on the table.

'Well, in that case, you have to go to the bar,' he said.

'I do not know what to say.'

'Two pints of Guinness, please.'

'I prefer you go.'

'No, if you pay, you go. It's good practice for your English, anyway.'

For a moment he was afraid she was going to refuse, but to his relief she grabbed the crumpled note from the table, stood up and went to the bar, repeating the sentence to herself. He watched her with admiration. This was living at last, he thought, happily: having a drink and an intelligent conversation with a beautiful girl in a pub, with the prospect of going to bed with her afterwards. He wanted nothing more – he was perfectly happy. His only worry was that maybe it was too good to last. It would last though, he told himself. He would make it last. He loved her and would love her always, for ever and ever ...

'Thanks. Cheers,' he said, when she brought the drinks, holding his up.

'Cheers,' she imitated him, and they touched glasses. 'Nasdrovie, too,' he added, touching her glass again

'Nasdrovie,' she said.

He took a sup of Guinness, but she scooped up the cream with her finger and licked it off first, amusing and arousing him as before.

'Why do you want to be a doctor?' he asked, deciding to keep the conversation on her, rather than himself.

'I don't want be doctor,' she said.

'What do you mean?' he asked, puzzled. 'I thought you were going to study medicine?'

'I am going to study medicine, but not to be doctor, not in usual way. I want to do how do you call it – research.'

'Oh,' he said, slightly disappointed. He had hoped she might say she wanted to be a doctor so she could help people and he could imagine them working as a team, she as a doctor, he as a teacher.

'I want to study about disease, try to find cure,' she explained.

'I see,' he said, appeased. 'Like Che Guevara.'

'Yes, but I do not compare myself with him.'

'So when exactly does your course begin?' he asked, though he didn't really want to know, because that was when she would have to leave London and him.

'October,' she said.

He winced – that gave them only about two months together. Maybe he could persuade her to postpone her course for a year, he thought? That wouldn't be fair though. The only other possibility was for him to go back to Yugoslavia with her. He wasn't too keen on the idea, because he had only been in London a few weeks, but he would rather do that than lose her. That was, if she wanted him to ...

'Where are you going to study?' he asked.

'University of Belgrade.'

'Belgrade is where you live, isn't it?'

'Yes.'

'Will you carry on living with your parents, then?'

'I have to.'

What a drag, he thought. He had hoped that if he went to Yugoslavia, he would be able to live with her. 'Couldn't you go away from home to study?' he asked.

'I do not have money to live on my own,' she said.

'Don't you get a grant?'

'Grant?'

'Money from the government.'

'Only for fees and books, not for living.'

'Oh – in Britain most people get a grant and leave home to study.'

'In my country is different.'

She sounded defensive. Yugoslavia was supposed to be a socialist country, but he couldn't help feeling pleased that in this respect at least Britain seemed more advanced.

'Yugoslavia is still quite poor country, you know.'

'Is it?' He realised he knew next to nothing about Yugoslavia. He had some more homework to do!

'I want to help it to develop.'

'That's good,' he said, touched by her idealism. There was a pause. 'Don't you get on with your parents, then?' he asked, emboldened by the alcohol.

'No,' she said, emphatically.

'Why not?'

'They do not understand me.'

'How do you mean?'

'They think I am crazy.'

He shook his head. How stupid parents could be! How could such a brilliant and beautiful girl be crazy? If she was his daughter, he would be proud of her. He was proud to be with her now.

'What do your parents do?' he asked.

'My father is professor of history and politics in university.'

'That sounds interesting.'

'He is very boring.'

'Oh, well,' he laughed. 'What about your mother?'

'She is psychiatrist.'

'And she thinks you're crazy?' he laughed again, nervously.

'Yes.'

'You must be crazy, then,' he quipped.

'Please do not say that, Francis,' she said, seriously.

'Sorry – I was only joking,' he said, taken aback.

'You do not think I am crazy, do you?' she asked.

'Of course not – I think you are brilliant and beautiful,' he declared.

'Please do not make fun of me, Francis.'

'I'm not making fun of you – I'm serious,' he said, stung. 'Why do your parents think you're crazy?'

'Because of what I think, what I say, what I do. They think I was crazy for coming to England.'

'I'm glad you did,' he said, hoping to mollify her, but she didn't respond. 'You're not crazy,' he added.

'*They* are crazy,' she said.

He gave a wry smile and said: 'My parents don't understand me, either.'

'Why not?' she asked.

He half-regretted saying it, realising it was the alcohol loosening his tongue, but decided that was probably a good thing. Anyway, he had to tell her now, he supposed. 'Well, for example,' he said, 'they are very religious and I'm not.' He was going to add 'any more' but stopped himself.

'They are Catholic?'

'Yes.'

'There are Catholics in England?'

'Yes, a few, mostly Irish, I think, like my parents.'

'So you are Irish?'

'Yes. Well, Irish descent.'

'What does it mean?'

'It means my parents were born in Ireland, but I was born and brought up here. I consider myself Irish though.'

'I have Irish friend at hall.'

'Oh, who?' he asked, hoping it wasn't a man.

'She is cleaner. Her name is Norah.'

'Yes, that's an Irish name, all right,' he said, relieved.

'She is old woman, but I like her. I like Irish people.'

'Good. I'm definitely Irish, then!'

'She told me about trouble in Ireland. She said it was because of British. What do you think?'

'She's right. I think they should get out of Ireland.'

'It makes me afraid.'

'Why?'

'I am afraid it will happen in my country.'

'What?'

'Fighting.'

'Why?'

'When Tito dies. He is old man.'

'How old is he?'

'Seventy-nine.'

'Wow – that's pretty old. What will happen when he dies?'

'I am afraid people will start fighting and killing each other. Already Croatians have started to fight.'

'Why?' he asked, sorry again that he knew so little about Yugoslavia.

'They want to be separate from Yugoslavia. You know Yugoslavia is many different people? They are only together because of Tito.'

'Oh, I see,' he said, though he didn't really – he would definitely have to find out more about it, he resolved.

'Do you want another drink?' he asked, looking at his watch to see if they had time.

'Why do you always look at your watch?' she asked.

'The pubs close at eleven,' he explained defensively. 'It's the law.'

'Bloody stupid law!' she declared. She sounded slightly drunk. He was shocked to hear her use the word 'bloody' and wondered where she had picked it up.

'Anyway, apparently Che Guevara was always doing it,' he said.

'What?' she asked.

'Looking at his watch.'

'You should throw it away.'

'Why?'

'Time is not so important.'

'I suppose not,' he agreed – she never wore a watch, he noticed. 'Do you want another drink?'

'I would like to go now.'

'You mean, to another pub?' he asked, alarmed.

'No.'

'Do you want to go home?'

'I want go somewhere else, if you will take me.'

'Of course. Where?'

'I want see where you live.'

'What, now?'

'Yes.'

'Sure,' he shrugged, looking at his watch to see if there would still be transport, excited but nervous at the prospect. 'You don't want another drink first?' It was stupid of him to ask, he thought – if they didn't go now they would miss the last tube and he didn't want her to get drunk.

'It is enough,' she said.

'Let's go, then,' he said, standing up. *You and I.*

'Oh, Francis, I am so happy!' she exclaimed outside and went dancing off along the pavement, pirouetting like a ballerina.

He followed her. She had drunk two pints of Guinness and was obviously a bit drunk. Passers-by turned and looked, but he didn't care – he felt a bit drunk himself, felt as if he was walking on air. But it wasn't just the Guinness, he knew – it was because he was with her, he was in love with her, he had started living at last!

'What nice room!' she declared, when they arrived.

'It's OK,' he said, pleased. 'Would you like some coffee?'

'Whisky!' she demanded, to his alarm.

While he poured out two glasses of Jameson's, she went round inspecting, to his amusement. He gave her a glass and she took a large swig.

'Bookcase is beautiful!' she declared, going over to it.

'It's not bad,' he said and added, with uncharacteristic boastfulness, 'I made it myself.' It was a simple enough affair of bricks and wood, but effective.

'Have you read all books?' she asked.

'Most of them,' he laughed. 'I do like reading.'

'Who is favourite writer?'

He thought for a moment. It was between Joyce, Lawrence and Hemingway, but he thought Lawrence would be the most interesting to her. 'D. H. Lawrence, I suppose,' he said.

'Show me,' she ordered.

He pulled out one of several Lawrence paperbacks at random. It was 'Fantasia of the Unconscious and Psychoanalysis and the Unconscious'.

'I will read it,' she said, holding her hand out for it.

'It's not the best one to read first,' he said, thinking 'Sons and Lovers' or 'Women in Love' would be better, but she insisted on taking it.

Then she turned to his record collection. 'Put some music on,' she ordered.

'Which one?' he asked.

'Who is your favourite?' she asked.

'Bob Dylan,' he said, picking out an album and showing it to her. 'Have you heard of him?'

'Play for me,' she said, shaking her head.

He happily did as he was told.

'I love him!' she declared immediately, taking another swig of the whiskey.

Then she plonked herself down in the easy-chair, picked up from his 'desk' the notebook in which he wrote his poetry, and opened it, to his annoyance.

'Francis, are you poet?' she asked, starting to read it.

'I write a bit,' he shrugged.

'Francis, they are beautiful! I knew you must be poet!' she declared, turning the pages excitedly.

He smiled, no longer annoyed, but amused and flattered. Then she suddenly dropped the notebook, jumped up and flung her arms around his neck. 'Francis, I love you!' she exclaimed, swaying to the music.

'I love you, Marina,' he said, putting his arms around her waist and swaying with her. They were both a bit drunk on Guinness and Jameson's now. Dancing to Bob Dylan with a beautiful girl in his arms and drinking whiskey – this was paradise! Wine – or at least whiskey – women and song at last!

'Oh, Francis, I love this one!' she exclaimed. It was 'I'll Be Your Baby Tonight'. 'Take my clothes off.'

He gladly obeyed, kissing each part of her body as it became naked, kneeling down in front of her to remove her skirt and knickers. Then she took off his clothes, dropping them on the floor and kissing him as she did so, even his by now erect cock. They danced naked together in the moonlight, listening to 'I'll Be Your Baby Tonight', which she made him play over and over again.

'Let's go to bed,' she said eventually.

He didn't need a second invitation.

'I love you, Francis!' she gasped, over and over again, hugging and kissing him wildly as he kissed and caressed her naked body.

'I love *you!*' he whispered, easing himself on top of her and trying to go inside her.

'Francis!' she exclaimed, in alarm.

'Yes?'

'Do not do that, will you?'

'It's all right, I won't,' he assured her, rubbing himself against her stomach.

'Francis!' she exclaimed, pushing him up and taking hold of his cock, sending a shock of pleasure through him. 'You are wet!'

'I know – don't worry, I won't go inside, I promise,' he reassured her again, eager to come.

She let go of him and he carried on rubbing himself against her, faster and faster, until at last he came in an explosion of ecstasy and rolled off her, exhausted.

'Francis!' she exclaimed in alarm again. 'I am wet!'

'Do you want a tissue?' he asked, reaching over to the box on the bedside locker.

'No, they are your children, I want them!' she declared, smearing his semen all over herself, as she had done last night.

'I wonder how many there are,' he said.

'Millions!' she declared.

'Would you really like to have a child with me?' he asked.

'Francis! No, I cannot!'

'I don't mean now. I mean in the future,' he laughed, though he couldn't help feeling slightly disappointed.

'Yes, yes, I do,' she said. 'But I want to make love now.'

'You can make love without getting pregnant,' he told her.

'I am afraid, Francis. It is too dangerous.'

'Not if you use something.'

'What do you mean?'

'I mean – if I wear something.' He felt embarrassed speaking about it to her, never having actually used one or even seen one.

'Francis, I do not like that!' she objected.

'It doesn't matter,' he said, not too disappointed, since he still wasn't sure if he would be able to do it properly, much as he wanted to.

'I know you want to – you are normal man,' she said.

'Yes, but it doesn't matter, I can wait,' he said, delighted to be called 'normal'. 'The important thing is that we are together and we love each other.'

'Oh, Francis!' she declared. 'You are so good! I love you!'

'And I love you,' he said, kissing her. 'Shall we sleep now?'

'Yes, but first touch me again,' she said, taking his hand and putting it between her thighs.

He made her come again with his finger and she made him come again with her hand. Then they curled up spoon-fashion to sleep and he drifted off in a state of perfect bliss – except for the insidious thought, somewhere at the back of his mind, that this was just too good to be true, too good to last ...

CHAPTER TWENTY-SIX

'Francis, no!'

'What's wrong?'

'Is too dangerous!'

It was always the same when he tried to make love properly with her. She was terrified of getting pregnant, he knew, but he was finding it more and more frustrating. 'Why don't we use something?' he suggested.

'What do you mean?'

'One of these.'

He reached over to his jacket hanging on the chair and fished out the condom he had bought earlier from a machine in a gents' toilet. It had taken him a long time to screw up the courage to do so and even then he had had to wait till the toilet was empty.

'What is it?' she asked.

'It's a condom,' he said, trying to sound blasé.

'What is that?' she asked.

Did she really not know, he wondered, even though she was going to be a medical student? Maybe they didn't have them in Yugoslavia. Maybe she was even more innocent than he was. They'd both had somewhat sheltered lives ... 'It's to stop you getting pregnant,' he explained, embarrassed despite himself.

'I do not like,' she declared.

'Why not?' he asked, annoyed.

'You want?'

'We could try it,' he shrugged.

'OK, we try it,' she agreed.

'Are you sure?'

'Yes, I want,' she said, suddenly sounding eager.

He opened the packet carefully and took out the rubber. He had already experimented with one, so he had a rough idea what to do. Self-consciously, he tried to put it on, but started to lose his erection.

'I do it,' she said.

He lay back and played with her one of her breasts while she tried to put it on. It was exciting to feel her fingers on him, but he still couldn't get a full erection back, so she couldn't get it on properly. They tried to make love anyway, but the condom kept slipping off.

'It's no good,' he said, giving up and lying back, more frustrated than ever and furious with himself. He'd failed!

'I knew we wouldn't be able do it,' she muttered, turning away.

What did she mean by that, he wondered? He turned to her, put his arm round her and started kissing her, but she seemed to have lost interest.

'What's wrong?' he asked.

'Is no good,' she said.

'What's no good?' he asked.

'We cannot do it,' she said.

'It doesn't matter,' he said. 'We still love each other, don't we?'

'Oh, Francis, I love you!' she exclaimed, turning and throwing her arms round his neck.

'I love you, too,' he said, relieved, and they made love in their usual way – he made her come with his fingers and she made him come with her hand, rubbing his semen over herself and exclaiming rapturously: 'Your babies, Francis! I love them!' Then they fell asleep in each other's arms, but he had bad dreams ...

They went to parks, pubs, theatres, art galleries and museums together. As well as Herman Hesse and Van Gogh, she introduced him to Rabindranath Tagore, Picasso, Salvador Dali and Munch, her favourite painters, to Che Guevara and Communism, and to slivovitz. He introduced her to D.H. Lawrence, Joyce, Hemingway and Whitman, to Irish music, Bob Dylan, Van Morrison and Ravi Shankar, and to Guinness, which she took to like a duck to water.

He was impressed by how quickly she read and understood anything he gave her to read, even if she didn't like it. She gave him back the D.H. Lawrence book with the comment, 'He is fascistic'. He couldn't help feeling offended, but had to admit she was right – after all, Bertrand Russell had accused Lawrence of the same – and perceptive to have recognised it. He gave her 'Women in Love' instead, which she rhapsodised about. She didn't like 'Animal Farm', the book they were doing in class, dismissing it as 'childish, anti-Communist propaganda'. It was a somewhat simplistic view, perhaps, but he could see her point. He tried to explain that it was anti-Soviet, not anti-Communist, but she wasn't convinced.

Inspired by her, he read about Marxism, communism and socialism for the first time, and the more he read, the more impressed he was. It was like a revelation, as if a blindfold had been taken off his eyes. The Communist Manifesto struck him as eminently sensible and noble in its aims and ideals: freedom from exploitation, oppression, persecution and class distinction; unity, internationalism, comradeship and solidarity; and the abolition of social privilege, tyranny, private property and slavery. As for the abolition of religion, marriage and the family, it seemed to him the world would probably be better off without them as well. Apart from the latter, it was like Christianity, but without the supernatural and superstitious elements. The combination of idealism and materialism appealed to him perfectly. For the first time since losing his faith, he felt that here was something worth believing in, even devoting his life to – especially with her.

He didn't tell her this openly - in fact he argued with her about it, playing devil's advocate. However, she was nearly always able to give him a good answer, despite her linguistic limitations. When he used the argument that communism could never succeed because of 'human nature', she replied that 'human nature' was just an abstraction, that it didn't really exist. What existed, she said, was 'human behaviour', which could be changed – it was just a matter of education.

'OK, so there's no such thing as human nature,' he agreed, unable to think of an effective counter-argument. 'I've got another problem.'

'Tell,' she commanded.

'Violence,' he said, taking another sup of Guinness – they were in their usual watering hole, the Friend at Hand.

'What is problem?' she asked.

'I don't like violence.'

'Why?'

'Because violence means killing people. I could never kill anyone. Could you?'

'Of course,' she declared.

'In what circumstances?' he asked, shocked.

'You cannot imagine circumstances?' she asked, scornfully.

'No, not really.'

'If somebody is going to kill you, for example.'

'Yes, but – '

'You would not kill someone to defend yourself, if they are going to kill you?'

'Well, maybe, if it was necessary.'

'Sometimes it may be necessary.'

'Yes, but self-defence is different from revolution. Surely it's possible to have revolution without violence, without killing people?'

'Sometimes it may be. But usually it is not. Usually violence is necessary.'

'Why?'

'Because usually people in power have got their power and keep it through violence and only way to stop them is through fighting. That is what history teaches us. Most countries and most people have got their freedom only through fighting for it. Your own country, Ireland, for example.'

'Yes, but that doesn't prove that violence is the only way, does it?'

'Finally, violence is usually necessary. It is lesson of history. You must look at history, Francis. Name one country that has become free without violence.'

'India?'

'Even India did not become free completely without violence. But India is exception. Can you name other country?'

He couldn't offhand, though he was sure there must be a few.

He had to admit to himself that she seemed right. 'I still couldn't shoot someone,' he said. 'Could you?'

'If necessary. If he is attacking me or my country.'

'You could point a gun at another human being, pull the trigger and shoot them?' he asked, shocked again.

'Yes, of course,' she reiterated.

'I don't think I ever could,' he said, shaking his head.

'You have not done military training?'

'No. There isn't any in Britain any longer, thank goodness. Is there in Yugoslavia?'

'Yes, everyone must do it.'

'Even women?'

'Yes.'

'Have you done it?'

'Not properly, but we have to do some at school.'

'Well, I hope you never have to do it.'

'What?'

'Shoot someone. Kill someone.'

'Yes, I hope so, too. Probably I never will, because I am going to be doctor. But I am afraid.'

'Afraid? Why?'

'Afraid for my country. What will happen.'

'You mean when Tito dies?'

'Yes. I think people will start fighting each other.' She seemed genuinely worried about it.

'Well, let's hope it doesn't happen. I think if I was in a war, I'd be an ambulance driver or something,' he said, finishing his pint.

'Somebody has to fight.'

'Maybe,' he shrugged. 'Would you like another drink?' he asked, to change the subject.

'I will buy,' she said, jumping up to do so.

Afterwards, he started to think that maybe she was right about the necessity of violence, much as he abhorred it. Maybe freedom and justice were things that had to be fought for and defended with blood. Maybe they were more sacred than life itself. Most countries had only achieved independence through fighting – the United States and Ireland, for example. France had only achieved democracy through violence. Would he have let the Nazis roll into Britain in 1940 without a fight? Would he let the Russians now? No. But he still couldn't imagine himself actually shooting anyone, much less sticking a bayonet in them. Yes, if there was a war, he thought, he'd have to be an ambulance driver like Lieutenant Henry in 'A Farewell to Arms'.

But the more he thought about it, the more he felt his pacifist principles wavering. He started to suspect that maybe they were only another by-product of his Christian indoctrination. 'Turn the other cheek', for example. That was an absurd exhortation, when you thought about it. It was based on the equally absurd idea that pain and suffering in this life didn't matter, in fact were desirable, because there was another, better life in the hereafter. 'The meek shall inherit the earth' – that was another one. Well, it was unlikely, but if they did they certainly wouldn't keep it for long, as the old joke said. There was something sloppy and sentimental about this aspect of Christianity, he decided. Communism, on the other hand, had a rationality, realism and ruggedness about it, combined with idealism, that appealed to him.

He started to see what Marx meant when he said religion was the opium of the masses. If people believed there was an afterlife, for which suffering in this life helped to qualify them, it made the job of keeping them under control considerably easier. He began to understand how religion had been used as an instrument of political and social control throughout history.

He read about Che Guevara with an admiration he used to feel for saints. He would dedicate himself to fighting injustice and oppression, he resolved. He still couldn't imagine himself carrying and using a rifle like Che, but he would fight in whatever other way he could – especially if it brought him closer to *her*.

He had been shocked when she told him she would kill somebody if necessary, but even more shocked when she told him that sometimes she still felt like killing herself. He remembered her telling him about her suicide attempt on that first evening in Russell Square, but he had deliberately avoided the subject since.

'We all feel like that sometimes,' he said, not wanting to take her seriously. They were in the Friend at Hand as usual.

'You know I already tried to do it once,' she said.

'I know. You told me. So did I,' he admitted, as if to make it seem less dramatic.

'You did?' she asked. It was her turn to be surprised. 'How?'

'With tablets.'

'When?'

'About four years ago.'

'Why?'

'I was depressed, I suppose,' he said vaguely, sorry he had mentioned it.

'Why you were depressed?' she pursued.

'Oh, because I'd lost my faith and didn't know what to do with my life,' he said, evasively.

'They did not work?'

'As you can see, I'm still here,' he laughed.

'And now?'

'Now I'm all right. I've sorted myself out. I think.'

'Look,' she said, showing him her wrists. There was a fine, white scar across each one. She seemed almost proud of her handiwork.

'I know.' He didn't want to look, but was horribly fascinated. He remembered she had told him she had used one of her father's razor blades. He looked away, revolted.

'Who found you?'

'My mother.'

'And took you to hospital?'

'Yes.'

'Why did you do it?'

'I wanted to come to London and my parents would not let me.'

'You tried to commit suicide because your parents wouldn't let you come to London?'

'Not just that. That was just – how do you say, 'last straw'? I felt so frustrated at home.'

'How do you mean?'

'They would not let me do anything I wanted. I was not free.'

'What do they think of you?'

'They think I am crazy. What do you think?'

'I think you're beautiful,' he said, putting his arm round her, pulling her close to him and gazing into her eyes.

'I'm afraid, Francis,' she said.

'What are you afraid of?'

'I am afraid maybe I am a little bit crazy.'

'Of course you're not,' he said. 'Why do you say that?'

'I do crazy things sometimes.'

'We all do! Anyway, it doesn't matter. I'll take care of you.'

'I love you,' she said.

'I love *you*.'

'Kiss me,' she said.

He pulled her close and did so. How stupid they were, he thought! To him she was anything but crazy – she was beautiful and brilliant. The fact that she had tried to commit suicide only made him love her all the more. She felt so soft and vulnerable in his arms. The pressure of her breasts against his chest made his heart pound. He'd be happy to love her and look after her like this for ever!

As the weeks went by though, he started to wonder if she wasn't a bit crazy himself. She said and did outlandish things. She would suddenly start prancing about in public places, to his amused embarrassment. She would try to make love in public and accused him of being 'conventional' when he resisted. She sometimes got drunk and would say outrageous things, such as that she would like to be a prostitute. He laughed at her, but noticed she didn't like it when he did so.

She also wrote strange things in the compositions he gave the class, which he read with a mixture of fascination and unease:

FREEDOM

I become aware that freedom is death, because I can't follow my feelings and thoughts freely. I want to go back to earth and water, but there are not enough clean and good ways to do that. Help me, Francis. I know that you can see the meaning of my terrible, meaningless life in just rare experiences, acts, thoughts and words that shine out above the chaos of such a life. Always I was alone and you are the first person who ever came near to me. I feel now that for a peaceful life we need fewness of people if possible and no words at all. Last Sunday at seaside I was madly happy with you. I was in the air more than my body. I usually hate Sundays, they have never brought me any good. The very thought that our time is splited (I am not sure about past participle) into days with one day intended for doing nothing makes me feel trapped. By the way, you must read 'The Person Who Works in the Kitchen Garden' (I do not know exact translation but ...) by Rabindranath Tagore (1861 - 1941), India, 1913 Nobel prize for literature. Please read it. Poem 42 is great.

TRAVEL

I am confused. How can I explain to you the delicate travels of my body? I am still travelling, never reaching my dreams, but it is horrible to find out that all the stations are very similar. I am always in confusion because of my hyper-imagination, which makes chaotic images of present events. But reality is very far from me, you know that better. I would like to be drunk all my lifetime. (Or making love.) Inside of myself I experience strange and beautiful things, which there are no words to describe. Sometimes my whole being travels onto new plane. Most of time I am not in this world with other people, with material things, which I hate. I hate the reality of each day which never changes. I hate it, this reality of each day measured by hands of clock, having to do silly and trivial things all the time. I cannot describe my feelings, which are so fine and fragile beyond words.

FEAR

I have got some sexual frustrations, Francis, I am desperately helpless. I am afraid of having a baby. The men, they are full of them and I am so fertile, like Earth's soil. Sometimes I fear to go out, because I get excited by accidental look at some unknown man and that makes me mad. With you also I am afraid. My instinct is beastly strong and I do not kiss you but the whole Universe. That is why I am never relaxed but 'restless as the sea'. That is why sometimes I start a silly monologue, I talk and talk just to prevent myself of getting devilishly excited and lost. That is why I am writing you these bloody lines which could show you how disintegrated I am. Always I am against the self-blood. Otherwise I would give you just empty sheet of paper.

P.S. Thank you for 'The Graphic Work' of E. Munch, especially 'The Shriek'. I cannot forget the shrieky silence which has lain over my spirit until I met you. Now I feel something very strong and new. I want to say I love you, but these stupid words spoil everything. Forgive me to be such complicated person for you. You are so calm. Just Devil and God know what is happening inside of my cells.

He didn't discuss these compositions with her or even return them to her, but kept them, as she insisted, and read them over and over. He didn't quite know what to make of them. Sometimes he thought they were just the expression of a highly intelligent, highly-strung eighteen-year-old, the kind of thing he might almost have written himself when he was her age. At other times though, he couldn't help thinking maybe there was something a bit 'crazy' or at least neurotic about them. However, he didn't want to believe that, so shut his mind to the idea. Anyway, he told himself, crazy or not, he loved her.

'Oh - hello,' he said, shocked.

There was a man sitting cross-legged on her bed. He looked like a hippy, with long, dishevelled, blond hair, beads, jeans and sandals. He was quite good-looking, in a bony, Slavonic sort of way. A stab of jealousy went through him.

'This is Pavlo,' she said, as if there was nothing odd about a strange man sitting on her bed.

'Hello,' he said again, deliberately sitting down in the easy-chair without shaking hands with 'Pavlo'.

'Hi,' Pavlo said, holding his hand up Red Indian style. He had half-expected him to say, 'Peace'! He noticed he was wearing a bracelet.

'Where do you come from?' he asked, trying to be friendly.

'I come from Yugoslavia,' Pavlo told him, in the familiar, harsh accent he found so charming because of her.

'Oh, really?' he said, dismayed. 'What part?' *Not Belgrade, I hope.*

'Capital. Belgrade.'

'Oh, the same as Marina.' Was it a coincidence or – ? He didn't want to know, not yet, anyway.

'Yes.'

'What are you doing here?'

'In London?'

'Yes.' *And on her bed!*

'I travel around Europe.' *Wrong tense.*

'I see. So, er, where are you staying?' *Not here in the hostel, I hope.*

'I stay here.'

'In the hostel?'

'Yes.' *Not in her room, I hope.* 'Do you like it?'

'It's good.' *No, it's not! It's not good at all! Interloper!* 'How long have you been here?'

'I arrive yesterday.'

Wrong tense again. Here one day and already on her bed! 'Oh. How long are you going to stay?' *Don't stay too long, will you?*

'In London? I don't know. Maybe for good, since situation in Yugoslavia is so bad.' *Oh no!* 'It depends if I can make some money,' he added.

'I see. Are you going to look for a job?'

'He is artist,' Marina, who was getting ready to go out, suddenly chipped in.

'Oh,' he said, wincing secretly.

'Look, he drew picture of me,' she said, passing it to him.

He looked at it reluctantly. 'Quite good,' he said, passing it back to her.

'You can keep,' she said.

'Oh, no, thanks,' he refused. 'It's yours.' It was the last thing he wanted.

'Please keep it,' she insisted.

'If you like,' he shrugged, folding it and slipping it into the inside pocket of his jacket.

To his annoyance, Pavlo hung around until they were ready to go out. He even followed them down to the street, where he and Marina stopped and spoke to each other in Serbo-Croat. He hoped he wasn't going to go to the pub with them. He was quite small and skinny – a bit of a weed really. *Surely she can't prefer him to me, can she?* Eventually, to his relief, he said goodbye and cleared off.

'Did you know him before?' he asked her in the pub.

'No. It's first time,' she said.

'Are you sure?'

'You are jealous!' she teased.

'No, I'm not,' he lied.

'So you don't mind if I see him?'

'You're free,' he shrugged, but inside he was seething.

'Yes, I know,' she said, and he regretted having said it.

To his annoyance, Pavlo was in her room almost every time he went after that, but he tried not to let it show, chatting to him affably. In fact, he was quite an amiable fellow and he would have liked him if he hadn't seemed a rival. He was fairly sure Marina didn't really like him as a man, but she started pretending to, just to tease him. She seemed to enjoy this, though it annoyed him, but he put up with it, because he was infatuated with her.

She made fun of him in other ways, too – for being too conventional, too tidy, always wearing a watch, which she never did, and always looking at it.

'Apparently Che Guevara was the same,' he riposted.

'You do not compare yourself with Che, do you?' she asked, laughing at him.

'No, of course not, but – ' he started, stung.

'Please, Francis, take off watch,' she said. 'You will feel better.'

'OK, whatever you say, doctor,' he laughed, taking it off and putting it in his pocket. He felt guilty. It was the watch his mother had given him for his twenty-first birthday. Did that mean something?

'Time, ladies and gentlemen, please!' the barman suddenly shouted

'You see!' she mocked. 'Bloody stupid people!'

He never wore it again with her. It was inconvenient but liberating. She was right. He loved her.

The following Friday she handed him a note during the break in class:

Tomorrow is your birthday. Let's get drunk together. We can get beautifully drunk with Guinness and slivovitz. I want to give you something special for your birthday. P.S. I am so happy you exist.

They started off in the pub with Guinness and then went back to her room, where she had a bottle of slivovitz. She poured two mugs and gave him one.

'What exactly is it?' he asked her, sniffing it.

'It's brandy made from plums,' she explained.

'How did you get it?' he asked, taking a sip. He suspected Pavlo had given it to her. He wasn't around, thank goodness.

'It does not matter,' she said. 'Do you like it?'

'Mm, yes!' he exclaimed, taking a slug. 'It's wonderful!' It *was* wonderful. *She* was wonderful. *Life* was wonderful. He was twenty-five today and life was wonderful!

As a birthday card she gave him a postcard of a picture by Edvard Munch called, 'The Kiss'. On the back of it she had written:

Let your smile be just a joy,
Like a glaring light upon the waves;
Play on the harp the rhythm
That the moment presents you with.
R.T.

'Thanks,' he said, giving her a kiss. 'A kiss for a kiss.'

He took another slug of slivovitz and lay back on the bed. She put on the Bob Dylan record they had listened to that first night and stood in the middle of the room, swaying to the music and sipping slivovitz. He watched her admiringly, drinking, until the room started to sway as well.

'What's this something special you wanted to give me?' he asked, starting to get high.

She swung round to the bed and said: 'I want to make love properly with you.'

He reached out, took her hand and gently pulled her down onto the bed beside him. He took her in his arms and they kissed long and deep while Dylan sang, 'I'll Be Your Baby Tonight.'

'Let's shut light,' she said, as Dylan sang in his country and western twang the line, 'Shut the light ...', jumping up and doing so.

Then she pulled off her clothes, so he did the same. When they were both undressed, she got back on the bed with him. He took her in his arms, pulled her tightly to him and they kissed, their tongues exploring each other's mouths greedily. While they kissed, he caressed her naked body with his hand, sailing ecstatically over all its most secret, sexy curves.

This was the high point of his life, he thought: he was drunk, the music was good and in his arms he held a beautiful, naked girl, whom he loved and desired with all his heart and soul, and who seemed to love him in the same way, who wanted to give herself to him completely, just as he wanted to give himself to her, in love's most sacred ceremony, its ultimate act of holy communion ...

Francis, always I am confused. My whole being is full of love for you. (Zen.) I feel it in my solar plexus. (You see, I have been reading D. H. Lawrence, even though I think he is fascistic.) I remember beautiful feelings of your touch, your look at my body, which travels through me. I wanted make love with you properly other night, but am still afraid. I cannot satisfy you and that makes me feel guilty and frustrated. Soon I must go back to my country. Yet that fills me with anxiety and sadness. Everyone feel that something is happening there. My country is in danger. I do not want to know, but my presentiment is enough alarming and in case of my country me and society are one. But I cannot open my arms to welcome the bonds of that society. Help me.

This 'composition' disturbed him more than any other she had given him. First, it reminded him that their attempt to make love properly the other night had failed again. It was ironic that she seemed to think it was her fault. In fact, it was as much, if not more, his – he had been too drunk. Or was that just an excuse? Maybe there was something wrong with him after all. Maybe he was impotent. It was too depressing to think about, never mind to speak about. Not that he really cared – he was happy to be with her.

He was more worried by the second part of her 'composition', the bit about going back to her country. She was supposed to go back in a couple of weeks to begin her medical course. He knew, deep down, that if she did go back, he would lose her. He couldn't bear the thought of being apart from her, even for a short time. He should have spoken to her about it before, but couldn't bring himself to. He wanted to pretend she was never going back, that she was here for ever. Now though, he knew he had to, painful as it was. He had been thinking about it and he had an idea.

In the end it was she who brought it up, the very next day.

The day before, according to the newspapers, Croatian separatists had exploded another bomb in Belgrade, as the IRA had been doing in London. They discussed this and the ethics of terrorism in the pub. Even more emphatically than before, he condemned the killing of innocent people – especially children – for any cause. Before, she had seemed to support terrorism. Now she seemed more ambivalent. She said she was confused, didn't know what to do. On the one hand, she wanted to go back home, on the other hand, she said, she didn't.

'Why not?' he asked, trying to sound neutral – secretly he hoped she wouldn't go back, but didn't want to put any pressure on her, didn't want to be the cause of her not taking up her medical course.

'I am afraid, Francis,' she said.

'Of what?'

'Of political situation in Yugoslavia.'

He couldn't help feeling slightly disappointed – he had half-hoped she would say she didn't want to go back because of him, but realised how egotistic that was in the situation.

'What exactly are you afraid of?' he asked.

'Bombs,' she said.

'Bombs? It's probably more dangerous here in London,' he said, playing devil's advocate for a moment. 'Anyway,' he couldn't resist adding, at the risk of offending her, 'I thought you had done military service and were prepared to defend your country.'

'Yes, but maybe I could be more useful in London.'

He was going to ask her how, but stopped himself – why should he stop her staying, if she wanted to? That was what he wanted, wasn't it? This was the moment to ask her, if he was ever going to. He took a swig of Guinness to nerve himself. 'Why don't you stay here, then?' he suggested casually.

'Where?' she asked.

He paused and took another swig of Guinness – this was the crunch. 'You could stay with me,' he suggested, as casually as he could, though inside he was trembling with excitement.

'I could stay with you?' she asked, incredulously.

'Yes, why not?' he shrugged, still trying to sound casual.

'Your are sure?'

'Of course,' he said, taking another swig of the black stuff to fortify himself, hardly able to contain his excitement at the prospect. 'You could improve your English even more, go for the Cambridge Proficiency exam, and begin your medical course next year, if the political situation is better.' He didn't dare suggest he would go with her, but he would. 'Maybe you could even do your medical studies here,' he added.

'What about visa?' she asked. 'I need visa to stay.'

This was it, he thought, taking another swig of liquid courage. 'There is a way to get one,' he said.

'How?'

'We could get married.' He tried to make it sound throwaway, in case she poured scorn on the idea, because he knew she considered marriage a corrupt, bourgeois institution, as he did himself, didn't he? No, not with her he didn't!

'What do you think?' he asked, nervously, since she didn't reply.

'Thank you, Francis,' she said, taking his hand.

'You mean yes?' He could hardly believe it or disguise his excitement any longer.

'If you are sure – '

'Of course I'm sure!' he exclaimed, overjoyed. 'You can move in at the weekend. You have to leave your room in the hostel, anyway, don't you?'

'Yes,' she nodded.

'And we'll get married?'

'Yes,' she agreed.

'Let's drink to it,' he said, and they clinked glasses. 'Cheers! I love you!'

'Nasdrovie,' she replied. 'I love you.'

And then, even though he was still shy about doing so in public, he took her in his arms and kissed her.

CHAPTER TWENTY-SEVEN

She moved in that weekend – with Pavlo's help – and they arranged to get married in a register office the following month. They explored more of London's parks and pubs, museums and art galleries together. They made love, too, but she still wouldn't let him go all the way. Nor would she try using a condom again or any other form of contraceptive. Sometimes he tried to go inside her, but she always stopped him, crying in alarm: 'Francis, no!'

It was frustrating, but he didn't mind too much. She always made him come and anyway he knew it was dangerous without any form of contraception. Besides, after the fiasco of the last attempt, he was afraid of trying again. On the other hand, he wanted to prove to himself that he could do it, that he was completely normal. And he wanted to be able to say to himself that he had made love properly to a woman, that he was no longer in even the slightest sense a 'virgin'. How he hated that word!

Maybe it would be easier after they were married, he told himself, though they would still have to be careful that she didn't get pregnant – he wasn't ready for fatherhood yet.

Then, one night, instead of crying 'Francis, no!' while he was on top of her, she cried out: 'Francis, do it! Do it!'

'Are you sure?' he asked, pausing.

'Yes! Do it, please!'

'Is it safe?' he asked, worried.

'It doesn't matter!' she cried. 'I want it! Do it! Do it!'

Suddenly, he wanted to do it himself, with an overwhelming urgency. He didn't care if she got pregnant – the risk was slight, anyway. He wanted to be inside her, to come inside her, to be one with her, to be lost in ecstasy with her ...

He tried to go in, but couldn't, and lost his erection. He tried to get it back by rubbing himself on her, but couldn't, no matter how hard he tried. It was a fiasco, like the last time. Eventually, he gave up, frustrated and ashamed.

'I knew we wouldn't be able to do it,' she said, flatly.

'Let's try again,' he said, desperately.

'It's no good,' she said.

'Another time, then,' he said, choking.

'It's better not to,' she said, turning her back to him and curling up as if to sleep.

What did she mean by that, he wanted to ask her, but didn't dare? He wanted to put his arm around her, but didn't even dare to do that. Crushed, he lay back. What was wrong with him, he wondered abjectly, staring up into the darkness? Why couldn't he do it? He loved her and she loved him, so why couldn't he make love to her properly? Maybe there was something wrong with her? No, it was *him*. He was impotent. Those bastards had screwed him up after all!

What exactly did she mean by saying it was better not to try again, he wondered? Did she mean she wanted to end their relationship, not get married, go back to Yugoslavia? The thought filled him with panic. He turned to put his arm around her, but still couldn't. It was as if she was a total stranger in the bed beside him.

The next morning they made love in their usual way. He told himself it didn't really matter if they weren't able to make love properly – what mattered was that they loved each other and were together. However, he didn't talk about it with her – he was afraid of what she might say.

She continued to live with him, but her attitude became more and more critical. She criticised him for being too tidy, too organised, too punctual. When she had moved in, she had quite rightly made fun of the cheap plastic lampshade and replaced it with a more artistic, paper one herself. Now she started to make fun of the white walls, threatening to paint them black. One day he came home to find her doing just that, with the Rolling Stones' 'Paint It Black' playing at full blast on the record player.

'What are you doing?' he asked, as calmly as he could, turning the record player off.

'You do not like it?' she said, paintbrush in hand.

He looked around with a sinking stomach. She had slapped black paint haphazardly over most of one wall, like some crazed, surreal artist or delinquent child. 'I think it was better the way it was,' he said, struggling to keep calm.

'Francis, you have no imagination!' she mocked. 'White is so boring! You are so boring!'

He bit his tongue. He still loved her and wanted her, despite everything. He noticed she had been drinking whiskey. That explained it, he told himself. He shut his eyes, hoping it was a bad dream, but when he opened them she was still there, in demonic mode.

'Look at what you write,' she said, scornfully, putting the paintbrush down and picking up the folder in which he kept the manuscript of the novel he was trying to write, much of it about her.

Now he felt anger boiling up inside him like a volcano, but he didn't erupt. He waited and watched in horrified disbelief as she opened the folder and took out the manuscript.

'Is it supposed to be about me?' she demanded. 'It is not true. I am not like this! This girl is crazy!' Then, to his utter disbelief, she started reading in a sarcastic voice what he had written:

'Suddenly she flung herself at him in panic and clung to him like a maniac. Her brain seemed to have swollen and burst like a boil, discharging its venom to the very extremes of her body ... '

'Give it to me!' he demanded, through clenched teeth, stretching out his hand.

' *... making her whole body tremble convulsively as if she were having an epileptic fit,'* she carried on reading sarcastically.

Furious, he lunged forward and made a grab for the folder, but she stepped back nimbly.

'Marina, give it to me!' he demanded again.

However, instead of doing so, to his horror she started flinging the pages of the typescript one by one into the air, exclaiming, 'This is rubbish! So is this! And so is this!'

For a moment he stood and stared, transfixed with horror and disbelief. This was an act of sacrilege, of desecration! It was like disembowelling his own child in front of him. Why was she doing this? What was wrong with her? She seemed to have turned into a monster before his very eyes!

Enraged, he lunged forward again, grabbed her by the arm and yanked her towards him. However, she flung the folder to the floor, jerked away and went crashing into the wardrobe. For a moment he was afraid she had injured herself, but she suddenly started laughing inanely, leaning against the wardrobe door.

'Your parents were right,' he said viciously. 'You *are* crazy!'

She stopped laughing as suddenly as she had started. 'Francis, please, do not say that to me!' she implored, a look of terror on her face.

'You're crazy! You're bloody crazy!' he repeated, even more viciously.

'Maybe I should go and kill myself then,' she said.

'You can do what you like,' he replied coldly, kneeling down to pick up the pages of his typescript. 'I don't care. Go back to Yugoslavia. Go to hell.'

The next thing he heard was the door opening. He twisted round just in time to see her disappear through it and in doing so felt the familiar electric shock of pain as his knee gave way and he collapsed to the floor, almost blacking out. He picked himself up and hobbled out onto the landing just in time to hear the front door slam. Oh, God, he thought, maybe she was going to do something crazy like throw herself under a train. Despite the searing pain in his knee, he pulled the door of his room shut, hobbled downstairs, out of the house, down the front steps and along the street to the underground, just in time to see her running in.

His knee felt as if a bullet had smashed through it and he had to hold onto a railing to stop himself fainting. After a few moments he followed her into the underground and onto the escalator. As it carried him down, he heard the sound of a train thundering through the tunnel into the station. In panic he hobbled down the rest of the escalator and onto the platform, just in time to see the train pulling out. There was no sign of her on the platform, so he scanned each carriage as the train gathered speed past him, but couldn't see her. Then he glimpsed her in the very last carriage, sitting and staring straight ahead, as if into space. Then she was swallowed by the tunnel.

He staggered to a bench and collapsed onto it, his heart palpitating, his knee throbbing mercilessly. He couldn't let her go like this, he thought. When the next train came, he'd get on and follow her. She'd probably gone back to the hostel, to see Pavlo. He'd go and look for her there. He'd tell her he was sorry, he hadn't meant what he said, his room didn't matter, not even his novel, not compared with what he felt for her.

But when the next train came in, he didn't move. His leg was on fire, but he knew that wasn't why. It was because she had wounded him in a way that hurt far more than a twisted knee or broken heart. She had attacked the thing that was more important to him than anything else in the world. Why should he go and apologise to her? Let her go!

He waited for another train, trying to persuade himself that he ought to get on it and look for her, but when it stopped and the doors opened he didn't move. It was as if he was paralysed. He watched the guard look up and down the platform and press the button. The doors slid shut with a hydraulic hiss as the brakes were released and the train pulled away, clattering off into the tunnel, the red light disappearing into the blackness.

He sat on the platform for another few minutes, wondering what do to. He ought to go back and tidy up the mess in his room, he supposed, but the thought made his heart sink. Besides, with his knee as it was, he wouldn't be able to. Maybe he should go for a drink, he thought, looking at his watch and realising that, because of her, he wasn't wearing it. He looked up at the station clock instead – it was quarter to six, so the pubs would be open. It was a bit early to start drinking, but what else was there to do?

Maybe he should throw himself under the next train, he thought, gazing at the electrified rails. No, he'd go for a drink. That would anaesthetize the pain in both his knee and his heart, at least for a while. Grimacing with pain, he stood up and limped off the platform.

When he got back to his room a couple of hours later, he was already drunk. He poured himself a Jameson's and sat on the floor, with his legs outstretched – his knee was still burning, but the alcohol kept the fire down. He picked up the pages of his manuscript to collate them, reading them as he did so. They were full of memories, based on things she had said to him and things they had done together, memories that brought with them a mixture of pain and pleasure, but the alcohol intensified the pleasure and anaesthetised the pain:

She awoke in the middle of the night. The darkness was like a vast sea rolling up against the window, trying to enter the room and engulf her. She opened the window and sat on the side of the bed, letting the spirit of the night enfold her, the universe gather her into the mystery of its infinity. Lost in the mystery, she suddenly felt free. She realised that all her life she had been playing a part. Now she was free. The light of freedom flowed through the prism of her heart and flooded her soul with joy, dispelling the darkness ...

When they reached the top of the dunes, the sea appeared before them suddenly, stretching away as far as they could see. He gasped with awe. The sound was awesome too, like stereophonic thunder. The vast plain of liquid rolled towards them in waves, unfurling onto the satin-smooth beach, spilling forward and sliding back, leaving the sand glistening sleekly. The sky was canvas-grey. Gulls wheeled above in an aerial choreography of breathtaking aerodynamic virtuosity. The wind almost blew them back. He breathed in the ozone like a drug.

'Francis, it is fantastic!' she exclaimed, running down the dune with her arms outstretched towards the sea.

The sea's power and magnitude were awesome. It was like some huge, mindless, primeval organism, beautiful yet terrifying.

'I want to go in!' she declared, taking off her sandals, lifting up her skirt and wading into the waves.

The sight of her bare legs pierced him with desire. They walked along the beach, arms around each other, buffeted by the wind, deafened by the sea's boom. The sea was like a giant womb, he thought, from whose fertile, mysterious depths all life had sprung. The smooth wet sand was speckled with tiny multicoloured bits of shell, like pieces spilt from some giant kaleidoscope. Further back there were heaps of shells and pebbles. He picked up a pebble and gave it to her. It was oval, marbled with black and white stripes, smoothed and shaped to an exquisite symmetry by the sea. She was in raptures. 'It is so beautiful!' she exclaimed.

'I wonder how long it took to get like that,' he said.

'Millions of years.'

'It puts us in perspective.'

'Put it in your pocket.'

They collected several pebbles and shells.

'What are you going to do with them, sell them?' he asked, joking.

'Francis, you are joking!'

'She sells seashells by the seashore.'

'What is that?'

'It's a tongue-twister. Try it.'

He repeated it and so did she, almost perfectly.

Later they lay in the dunes beneath the mother-of-pearl sky and made love to the sound of the sea. It was like the sound of a thousand drum-rolls, followed by a thousand cymbals, reverberating through the tympanum of the earth beneath them. Their bodies moved to its rhythm, faster and faster, until they came together in a crescendo of ecstasy ...

In her dream she was walking through a forest. Through canopies of green foliage sunlight shone as if through a filter, filling the forest with aquamarine light. Between the leaves she could see pieces of blue sky like a jigsaw. The mossy path on which she was walking was strewn with petals of blossom. The silence was like that of a deep well, full of inaudible echoes of a mysterious, mystical music, music that was no more than a pressure on the heart. She stopped, spellbound, enchanted, and tears of an ineffable joy sprang to her eyes. Her heart beat like the heart of a newborn bird, felt as if it would break with joy. She wanted to stay here for ever, become part of this magical place. She lay down on the soft bed of the forest floor, as if on the earth's bosom, and her heartbeat became one with the earth's. She was a seed in the green womb of the forest. Above her the great green boughs swayed hypnotically, cradling her in their arms, rocking her gently to slumber with their arboreal lullaby ...

'Money! Why do you worry about money so much? It's only pieces of paper!' she declared scornfully, grabbing the pound notes and to his horror flinging them out of the window to flutter down to the street below.

He wanted to rush out and retrieve them, but stopped himself. She was right, he realised ...

'Your grandfather is crazy?' he asked, laughing. 'Why?'

'He says crazy things and he does crazy things, just like me.'

'What do you mean?'

'Lots of things. He gets up very early in morning, opens all windows and doors, and goes out!' He chuckled. 'Also he stops in street and talks to everybody. It does not matter if he does not know them. He says marvellous things like, 'The sky is very blue today, isn't it?' or 'Have you heard birds singing?' Of course, they do not know what he is talking about. Other thing he does, he lights fires just for fun, in street, anywhere.'

'He sounds dangerous,' he laughed.

'He is really nice old man. I like him.'

'Why?'

'I understand him and he understands me. No one else does.'

Light was the medium into which she would have liked to pass. However, she was obstructed by the presence of so many inanimate objects. Walls, furniture, buildings, things surrounded her, besieged her. Their lifelessness oppressed her unutterably, filled her with phobia. The city was like a vast concentration camp. She was trapped like a fly in its concrete web, its relentless geometry of angles, surfaces and shapes, which had no life, no meaning for her. She wanted to be fluid. The elements she most admired, which best metaphored her yearning, were light and water, especially light. Light was everywhere, yet it was invisible. It was the nearest thing to pure spirit. She imagined herself transmuted into light, but in fact she was trapped in this maze of materials, obstructing her every movement, even her very thoughts. She was a prisoner within her clothes, even her very body. She wanted to escape it, to fly, to evaporate, to dissolve, to dilute into light ...

Her body burned with the unspent fuel of a thousand desires and dreams. It needed only the ignition of a man's touch, any man. If only they knew the explosive power within her, how helpless she was, how vulnerable! She wanted to throw herself at one of them there and then ...

'I love him! I love him!'

'Who?' he laughed.

'Walt Whitman! Listen to this:

"I will go to the bank by the wood and become undisguised and naked,

I am mad for it to be in contact with me."

I understand him! I understand him perfectly!'

Her naked body in his arms was the fulfilment of a fantasy he had hardly dared to dream – it was like a sacred vessel, too sacred, too precious, too beautiful, to touch, even to look at. He could hardly believe he was actually holding it, hardly dared touch her. His hand sailed like a boat over the smooth sea of her body, leaving in its wake ripples and waves of pleasure. His kisses exploded like depth-charges in the depths of her being, sending through her shockwaves of pleasure. Like a deep-sea diver he explored the secrets of her body. Like a pearl diver his finger gently prised open the soft lips between her shell-white thighs and entered -

He slipped the pages of typescript back into their folder and tossed it onto the coffee table he used as a desk. Then he poured himself another whiskey and took a slug. 'Rubbish' she'd called it. It was as if she'd stabbed him through the heart, mortally wounding him. He could feel the lifeblood of his love running away, feel his love for her draining from him like the blood from a dying man ...

He took another slug of whiskey and tried to staunch it by thinking that maybe she hadn't meant it, but it didn't matter – she'd said it. Why? What had he done to her? Maybe she was right – maybe it was rubbish. No, he couldn't accept that. It was a bit overwritten, might need rewriting, but it wasn't rubbish. She shouldn't've said that. It was the worst thing she could've said to him. He could never forgive her. He never wanted to see her again. He didn't love her any more. Their love was over. It was dead. She had killed it!

Tears sprang to his eyes. He took another slug of whiskey, but it only made him weep more. He'd lost her. It was his fault. If he'd been able to make love to her properly, it wouldn't've happened. There was something wrong with him. The bastards had won after all. He was impotent. He was screwed up. He was inadequate. He felt like ending it all. But he wouldn't do that. That'd really mean *they* had won. He'd just drink himself into oblivion, forget everything. Yes, that was what he'd do. Blessed oblivion. He took yet another big slug of whiskey. He was a loser. He'd lost her. He'd lost Sally. He'd lost his faith. He'd lost his vocation. He'd lost his family. So now he was alone again. He had nobody. He *was* nobody. But he didn't care. It didn't matter. He took another slug of whiskey.

His senses were swirling. The room was revolving. Suddenly, he was floating, up, up, up, to the ceiling. He looked down and saw himself, crying. It was ridiculous, a grown man crying like a little boy. There was nothing to cry about. So she'd left him. It didn't matter. So he was alone. It didn't matter. So he was lost. It didn't matter. Nothing mattered. It was a joke. Life was a joke. It was all a big joke, a sick, stupid joke. It didn't matter. Ha ha ha! Ha ha ha! Ha ha ...

Early in the morning, he came to on the floor and realised with disgust he had been sick all over himself. He undressed, washed himself at the sink in the corner of the room and collapsed into bed. Late in the morning, he woke up with a throbbing headache. For a moment or two, it was as if it had all been a bad dream. When he realised it hadn't, she really had gone and left him, a wave of despair swept over him and he wished he had never woken up.

With a huge effort of will, he got up and made a mug of tea to quench his thirst. He sat in the easy-chair and drank it, staring out of the window into the emptiness of a pale china-blue sky. It seemed to reflect how he felt, the void within him. He sat staring into space like this for a while, too dazed to think or move. It was as if he was in a state of shock.

After a while, though, he started to think. What was he going to do? Should he go out and try to find her? Did he want to find her? Did he want her back? Would she come back? If she came back, would it work? He didn't know the answer to any of these questions. If the answer was no, it meant he would never see her again. Never to see her again! The thought suddenly went through him like a spear and he realised that in spite of everything he still loved her. He had to go and look for her!

But where should he look? The first place was the hostel – she might have stayed with Pavlo. She wouldn't have slept with him, would she? The thought went through his guts like a rapier. The other possibility was Norah, the Irish cleaner she was friendly with. She could have stayed with her, he supposed. She had no other friends as far as he knew. On the other hand she might have slept on the street, might be wandering around the streets on her own now. He suddenly felt worried about her – she was a girl, she was a foreigner and she was in a highly emotional state. He felt responsible for her. He had to try to find her. He had to go and look for her.

'Have you seen Marina?' he asked Norah – thank goodness she was still there, still cleaning bedrooms, a grey-haired old woman in an overall. He felt sorry for her, having to do such menial work at her age, no doubt for a paltry wage.

'I saw her yesterday,' Norah said.

'Did you speak to her?'

'I did.'

'How was she?'

'Well, dear, she seemed very upset. Have yous two fallen out?'

'We had a bit of a row.'

'I'm sorry to hear that, dear. She's such a lovely girl.'

'Yes. You don't know where she stayed last night, do you?'

'I mebbe shouldn't tell you this, but I think she stayed with that young fellow from Yugoslavia – what's this his name is?'

'Pavlo?'

'That's it. They were together anyhow.'

'I'll try his room. Thanks, Norah.'

Nervously, he knocked on Pavlo's door. For a while there was no answer. Then Pavlo opened it, looking scruffily Bohemian as usual in T-shirt and jeans, long hair dishevelled, chin stubbly.

'Hello,' Pavlo said,

'Hello. Have you seen Marina?' He tried to peep into the room.

'She's left,' Pavlo told him.

'You mean, she was here?'

'She was here, but now she's gone. Please, come in.'

'Do you know where she's gone?' he asked, accepting the invitation and glancing around the room – there was no sign of her.

'Sorry, I don't know,' Pavlo said, sitting cross-legged on his bed and rolling a fag. 'Please sit.'

Reluctantly, he sat in the easy-chair in the hope of getting some information out of Pavlo. He seemed friendly enough. Had she slept here, he wondered, but didn't dare ask.

'Would you like cigarette?' Pavlo offered.

'No, thanks, I don't smoke. Did she say anything?'

'She said she had to go and think.'

'Think?'

'Think about what she should do.'

'What do you mean?' *I thought she'd already decided what she should do.*

'She's worried, you know.'

'About what?'

'About our country. Situation is very bad.'

'Yes, I know. What do you think?'

'I think it will be war in our country.'

'Is that why you left?'

'Yes. I don't want fight war. I hate that.'

'You're going to stay here?'

'Stay here if I allowed. Or other place. Maybe Paris.'

'So you think it'd be dangerous for her to go back?'

'I think so, it could be dangerous, yes.'

'Did she ask you?'

'Yes. I tell her stay here.'

'What did she say?'

'She said she wants stay here because she loves you.'

'Oh. Yes. I – I love her, too, I suppose.'

'But also she loves Yugoslavia, so she feels guilty if she stay here.'

'I see. Thanks. I'd better go and look for her.'

He had a look around a few of the places he thought she might be, such as Russell Square and Soho, but there was no sign of her, so he gave up and went home.

Turning into the front gate of his house, he saw her. She was sitting on the steps, in the same blouse and long skirt she had had on last night, with her arms and head on her knees. A wave of relief swept over him. He stopped at the foot of the steps and looked at her. He wanted to rush up the steps and gather her into his arms, but didn't. He loved her, but he was angry with her, the way a father might feel towards an errant daughter.

'What are you doing here?' he asked, coldly.

'Oh, hello,' she said, raising her head and smiling at him as if nothing had happened. 'I came back.'

'I can see that,' he replied, even more coldly. 'Why?'

'Why do you think?'

'To collect your things?' he suggested sarcastically, despite himself.

'You want me to go?'

'I didn't say that.'

'If you want me to go, I will go.'

She jumped up and ran down the steps past him. As she did so, he reached out, grabbed her by the arm and pulled her towards him.

'I don't want you to go,' he said, grasping her arm.

'You are hurting me, Francis,' she said.

There were tears in her eyes. Shocked, he let go of her arm instantly. He had never seen her cry before. It brought a lump to his throat. He wanted to throw his arms round her and hug her, but didn't dare. 'I want you to stay,' he said, choking and blinking back tears from his own eyes.

'Are you sure, Francis?' she asked.

'Yes, I'm sure,' he said, choking.

'Why do you want me to stay?' she asked.

'I love you,' he said, the words almost sticking in his throat.

She looked at him for a few moments through tearful eyes. Then she suddenly threw herself at him, just as she had done on that first night, flung her arms around his waist and clung tightly to him, her head on his chest. He put his arms round her and hugged her to him joyfully.

'Francis, I am sorry,' she whispered after a while. 'I did not mean it. I did not mean to hurt you.'

'I know,' he said, still choking. 'It's OK. It doesn't matter.'

'I am crazy girl, I know,' she said, looking up at him, tears in her eyes.

'No you're not,' he said, guiltily.

'Yes I am,' she insisted.

'It doesn't matter,' he said. 'I still love you.'

'I love *you*,' she said, and they kissed.

'Shall we go inside?' he suggested after a while, afraid of being seen by the other occupants of the house.

'Let' go for walk,' she suggested instead.

'OK,' he agreed, though he was tired. 'Where?'

'Let's go to Marshes!' she suggested excitedly. 'We can make love in grass, have pint of Guinness in pub and watch sun go down!'

'It sounds like an offer I can't refuse,' he laughed. 'Let's go.'

They set off with their arms round each other. It was a mellow September evening, the streets bathed in autumn sunshine, the brown-bricked houses radiating back the day's accumulated heat in warm waves. He could feel her hip brushing against his as they walked, as if their bodies were one. They *were* one, he told himself. They would soon be married and he would never lose her again. He loved her. That was all that mattered. Love conquered everything. Amor vincit omnia, as Chaucer said ...

CHAPTER TWENTY-EIGHT

'Excuse me. Sorry to interrupt. It is Frank Walsh, isn't it?' a slurred, effeminate voice said.

'Yes?' Frank said, turning from talking to Marina and looking up to see a young man standing at their table. He was holding a glass of something like vodka and lemon in one hand and a cigarette in the other and was swaying slightly.

'Don't tell me you don't recognise me!' the young man said.

Frank looked him over. He was wearing a brown leather jacket over a striped shirt and fawn chino trousers. He had the same blond hair, but longer and thicker, the same smooth, soft face but thinner, the same slim, girlish figure, but a bit – only a bit – taller. It couldn't be, could it? 'Mark? Mark Brown?' he asked, incredulously.

'Hello,' Mark transferred his cigarette from his right to his left hand and held his right hand out. A gold bracelet hung loosely from the wrist. Frank stood up and shook it limply.

'Isn't this fantastic?' Mark said, slurred.

'Yes,' Frank said, not so sure.

'You sound somewhat underwhelmed.'

'No,' Frank said, shaking his head. 'It's just that – I can't quite believe it. It's incredible! How long has it been? Seven? Eight years?' He tried to sound excited. He *was* excited, but he was even more apprehensive.

'Too long, I should say,' Mark said. 'I knew we'd meet again though. Didn't you? Destiny and all that.'

Frank didn't know what to say. It was the last thing on earth he had expected or wanted. 'So – er – what are you doing these days?' he asked.

'I'm teaching EFL – English as a Foreign Language.'

Frank laughed in disbelief. 'Me too! Where?'

'Tin-pot school round the corner. Central School it's called.

What about you?'

'Shakespeare School. Not far from here too.'

'Is it destiny?'

'I don't know. It's incredible.'

'Well, anyway, aren't you going to introduce me?' Mark nodded towards Marina.

'Oh, sorry, yes. This is Marina.' He was going to say 'my girlfriend', but stopped himself – he knew Marina didn't like to be labelled. Or was it because of Mark, he wondered? 'This is Mark – an old, er, school friend,' he said to her.

'Pleased to meet you,' Mark said, but didn't offer her his hand.

'Hello,' Marina said, barely glancing at him and continuing to read Time Out magazine.

'Frank, would you mind if I sat down for a minute?' Mark asked, with a hiccup.

'Actually, we've got to go,' Frank said, alarmed – he didn't want Mark to say too much in front of Marina, especially drunk as he was. He signalled to Marina with his eyes and she stood up.

'Oh, what a drag!' Mark exclaimed. 'I mean, we've got so much to talk about, haven't we, Frankie?'

'Yes, I suppose so,' Frank agreed half-heartedly – he didn't like being called 'Frankie' and he wasn't at all sure he wanted to talk about it. Also, there was something about Mark's voice that irritated him. Was it the effete, poncy, southern, RP accent? He should be used to them by now!

'Where are you going?'

'The theatre, actually.'

'Fabulous! Anything interesting?'

'The Caucasian Chalk Circle.'

'Who's that by?'

'Bertold Brecht.'

'Never heard of him.'

'Left-wing German, nineteen-thirties? Well, we'd better go – curtain goes up in a few minutes.'

'Look, we must meet up for a drink and a chat, mustn't we?' Mark said, putting a hand on his Frank's shoulder, making him flinch.

'Yes, sure,' Frank agreed, pulling away and trying to sound enthusiastic – the idea worried him.

'Have you got a phone number or something?'

He was going to say no, but couldn't, especially in front of Marina, so gave Mark his number. Mark wrote it shakily on a beer mat and gave him his. As he did so, Marina rudely walked away to the door, without saying anything to Mark.

'Where is that?' he asked Mark.

'Croydon.'

'Where's that?'

'South of the river?'

'I see.' Good, Frank thought – it was on the other side of London. 'Do you live with your parents?'

'Gosh, no! They threw me out long ago!' Mark laughed ironically. 'No, I live with a friend. He's over there. He's called Costas.'

Frank looked over to see a large-nosed, Mediterranean-looking young man with shoulder-length, black, curly hair and wearing a maroon velvet suit sitting at a table. He gave Frank a forced smile. It must be his boyfriend, Frank supposed, and to his amazement felt a pinprick of jealousy.

'We'd better go,' he said.

'Great to meet you again, Frankie,' Mark said, shaking hands again. 'I'll give you a tinkle. We must get together. We've got so much to talk about, haven't we?'

'Sure, bye,' Frank said, following Marina out with relief. 'What an incredible coincidence,' he told her as they hurried to the theatre.

'Who is he?' she asked, coldly.

'Oh, just an old school friend,' he said casually. 'Not even a friend really.'

'He seems to like you.'

'Does he?'

'Will you phone him?'

'I don't know. I don't really want to. Do you think I should?'

'You are free.'

He could tell she didn't like the idea though. Was she jealous? Why? She didn't know anything about Mark, did she? Or was there some feminine intuition going on?

Eugene Vesey

'He'll probably phone me, anyway,' he said, unsure if he wanted to meet this ghost from his past again, but somehow knowing he wouldn't be able to avoid it.

Gone to Paris with Pavlo. Back Sunday, 4 p.m. Victoria Coach Station.

The note was in her familiar, childish scrawl. She had failed to turn up at class and he had gone to the hall of residence to look for her. Masoud, the Iranian student who had opened the door for them on that first evening and with whom he had become friendly, had given him the note, which he read with disbelief.

'Thanks, Masoud,' he said, trying not appear as devastated as he felt, and hurried out.

In the pub he had to read it several more times before he could fully believe it. So she'd run off to Paris with Pavlo for the weekend, had she, he thought angrily? And she expected him to meet her when she arrived back on Sunday, did she? Well, she had another think coming! This was it. This was the last straw. He wouldn't! He'd show her! It was over! The end!

After a couple of pints though, anger gave way to depression. He had lost her. He was a loser. He was a failure. He was a fucking freak! And he was on his own again. It was weekend and he was on his own again!

No, he wasn't, he suddenly realised. He wasn't on his own. There was Mark. He'd phone Mark and go for a drink with him tomorrow. That'd teach her! That would be sweet revenge!

'Cheers,' said Frank, clinking his pint of Guinness against Mark's vodka and lime.

'Cheers,' said Mark.

Frank took his first sup of Guinness, Mark sipped his vodka. They were in a pub in Soho suggested by Mark, who was wearing the same brown leather jacket and jeans. He offered Frank a cigarette, which he declined, and lit up.

'So, what a coincidence!' Frank declared. 'I still can't quite

346

believe it.'

'Yes,' said Mark. 'When I woke up the next day, I thought I'd been dreaming. Sorry if I was a bit tiddly the other night.'

In fact, he still seemed slightly tiddly. Had he already been drinking? Or was it just his lispy southern voice and languid manner? He didn't remember him being like that.

'That's all right,' said Frank. 'It all seems a bit like a dream, now, doesn't it?'

'What?' Mark asked.

'The Ghosters.' *Might as well get onto the subject straightaway.*

'Oh – yes.'

'A bad dream,' Frank laughed.

'Yes. It wasn't all bad though, was it, Frank?'

'How do you mean?'

'Well, we met each other, didn't we?'

'Yes, I suppose so,' Frank said, taking another sup of Guinness to hide his discomfiture.

'I've never forgotten you, you know.'

'It was pretty grim though, wasn't it?' Frank said, ignoring the remark and trying to divert the conversation.

'That's why I got out quick, Frank.'

'You were right. I left it late.'

'When did you actually leave?'

'Third year of scholasticate – senior seminary.'

'How old were you?'

'Twenty-one.'

'You did leave it late!'

Frank winced. 'Yes. Not too late though. Better than some.'

'What do you mean?'

'Some left much later than me. Some even after they were ordained. They're the ones I really feel sorry for. Just think of the problems of adjustment they must have. I think I was quite lucky really.'

'Why did you hang on so long, though, Frank?'

'I don't know. I just found it so difficult to give up the idea of being a priest. It was all I'd ever wanted to be. Basically, I think I'd been brainwashed into it.'

'Brainwashed? By who?'

'My mother.'

'What do you mean, 'brainwashed'?'

'I mean, I think she put the idea in my mind when I was a kid and cultivated it. There was an element of emotional blackmail involved, too.'

'In what way?'

'Well, Irish-Catholic. I'm her eldest son. She idolised me. She made it clear to me it'd make her happy if I became a priest. I idolised her, so I wanted to please her. I couldn't face the thought of disappointing her.' He felt uncomfortable being questioned about it like this, but realised it was therapeutic too.

'So why did you leave?' Mark asked.

This was like open-heart surgery, he thought, taking another sup of Guinness to anaesthetize himself. 'I stopped believing in it,' he said, evasively.

'What do you mean exactly, Frank?'

'I stopped believing in it all – the whole package, Heaven, Hell, transubstantiation, God ...'

'You mean you've lost your faith, Frank?' His use of the present-perfect made the question all the sharper.

'I suppose you could put it like that. What about you?'

'I'm still a Catholic.'

'You still go to Mass, then?'

'Yes, occasionally. I even sing in the choir. You don't?'

'Last time I went to Mass was about five years ago. It all seems like mumbo-jumbo to me now to be honest.'

'I'm sorry to hear that, Frank. My faith is important to me.'

'I don't believe in faith.'

'What do you believe in?'

'Life,' Frank shrugged. 'Living life to the full.'

'What about afterwards?'

'There is no afterwards, Mark. This is it.'

'What about the soul?'

'I don't believe in the soul. Not in the immortal sense.'

'You don't?'

'No. There's no evidence for it, is there?'

'Do you need evidence?'

'Sure. Don't you?'

'No. That's what faith is, I suppose.'

'It's all superstition to me now.'

'You've changed a bit, Frank.'

'Yes, I suppose so. That's life, isn't it? Another drink?' He brought back another pint of Guinness for himself and vodka and lemon for Mark.

'So what did you do after you left?' Mark asked.

'Worked for a few months. Odd jobs. Then went to uni.'

'Where?'

'Manchester. Just finished actually, a couple of months ago.'

'Me too.'

'Really?'

'Yes. What did you study?'

'English Language and Literature. And philosophy. What about you. What did you do?'

'Modern Languages. French and Italian.'

'Where?'

'London.' There was a pause.

'You left the following year, didn't you?' Frank asked.

'Yes. How did you know?'

'We got a letter. I was in the novitiate.' He remembered how depressed he had felt. Was this the same person sitting in front of him in a pub in Soho? It seemed unreal.

'You never answered my letters, Frank.' There was a note of reproof in Mark's voice.

'You mean you wrote to me?'

'Lots of letters.'

'The bastards must've intercepted them.' A surge of anger went through him at the realisation.

'What was it like, the novitiate?'

'Awful. A complete waste of a year of my life. It depresses me to think about it.'

'Why?'

'Well, it was in the middle of nowhere and like being on retreat for a year – meaningless religious exercises and manual labour all day. Silence nearly all the time. Hardly any recreation. We weren't allowed to read anything, except arid religious crap. We were allowed out once a week for a walk on a Sunday afternoon. And the Novice Master was a brainless, humourless pedant.' He didn't add that he had missed Mark, too.

'I'm glad I didn't make it! What about the senior sem?'

'That was in the middle of nowhere too, but it was better, because there was loads of free time. I did a lot of reading. I mean modern literature, not theology. That was all moonshine to me. Philosophy was quite interesting, though it was mainly scholasticism, you know, Thomas Aquinas and all that.'

'So what do you think of the Ghosters now?' Mark asked.

'They were a bunch of screwballs, weren't they?' Mark laughed. 'Remember the Dean of Studies for example?'

'You bet. He gave me the strap a few times, sadistic swine.'

'And me. Remember that thing? Leather reinforced with whalebone or something? It was a bloody offensive weapon. He was a fucking psycho. Should've been locked up.'

'I wonder what became of him?'

'I think he went back to the order's school in Dublin and became Superior. I suppose he's still terrorising the kids there.'

'Poor buggers!' Mark shook his head. There was a pause.

'Of course, he wasn't the worst of them, was he?'

'Who was?' An anxious look appeared in Mark's eyes.

'Father Director. He was even more of a sadistic bastard, beneath the handsome exterior.'

Mark nodded sadly.

'He was a paedophile, too, of course,' Frank added, deciding they had to talk about it sooner or later.

'I was hoping you wouldn't say that, Frank.' Mark's features twisted as if in physical pain.

'It's the truth, isn't it? He mucked about with me. And he mucked about with you, didn't he? And lots of others I suppose.'

'He screwed me up, Frank.' Mark's lip curled with contempt.

'I suppose we're all a bit screwed up, Mark.'

'He screwed me up good and proper though.'

'How do you mean?'

'That's why I am as I am, isn't it?'

'You mean – ?'

'Yes, fucking queer. Like most of the others here.'

Frank looked around and suddenly realised uncomfortably there were no women. It must be a gay pub! 'Does it matter?'

he asked Mark.

'Does what matter?'

'Being – gay?'

'Of course it fucking matters. I don't want to be queer. I didn't choose to be queer. It was that fucking pervert. That whole fucking place. I was normal till I went there.'

'I'm sorry, Mark.' That probably wasn't the right thing to say.

'I still have feelings for you, you know, Frank. I've never forgotten you.'

Frank shook his head, too embarrassed to say anything.

'What about you, Frank?'

'I'm into women now, I'm afraid, Mark.' Mark's face clouded.

'That girl you were with last night. Is she your girlfriend then?'

'Yes.' Though he wasn't so sure any more.

'Where's she from?'

'Yugoslavia.'

'So she's a communist then.'

'I suppose so. There's nothing wrong with that, is there?'

'Isn't there?'

'Come on, Mark. You don't believe all that anti-Communist propaganda still, do you?' If he was still a Catholic, he probably did.

'Is it propaganda?'

'Of course. Have you actually read any of the literature?'

'Have you?'

'I've started reading it. The Communist Manifesto, for example. It makes a lot of sense to me.'

'This is her influence, isn't it?'

'Partly.'

'So it's serious, then, is it, Frank?'

'Yes. In fact – we're getting married next week.' He wasn't at all sure any more though.

'Oh, fuck! Sorry.' Mark looked shattered.

'It's OK.'

'What about us, Frank?'

'I think what happened between us was an aberration, Mark.'

'Don't disillusion me completely, Frank.'

351

'Sorry – I didn't quite mean it like that.'

'What *do* you mean, Frank?'

'I mean, well, it was another time, another place. There's been a lot of water under the bridge since then. I've changed. I'm different. I suppose I'm – ' He was going to say 'normal', but stopped himself.

'I get the message, Frank.' Mark looked lachrymose. 'Anyway, what about Costas? Isn't he your boyfriend?'

'He doesn't hold a candle to you, Frank. I think it's over between us.'

'Not because of me, I hope.'

'It was over, anyway. But meeting you again doesn't help. Let's give it a try, Frank.' Mark held out a hand to touch him.

'That's not a good idea, Mark,' Frank said, recoiling.

'I still love you, Frank. I never stopped.'

'Please, Mark, don't. I've told you. That was a long time ago. It's over. I'm different now. I'm with Marina.' Was he?

'You're breaking my heart, Frank.'

'Mark, please don't be ridiculous. It's impossible, out of the question.'

'Please don't say that, Frank. Give me a glimmer of hope.'

'It's impossible, Mark. I'm getting married next week!'

'Please, Frank.' There were tears in his eyes now.

'I think we'd better go. You're drunk.'

He felt a bit drunk himself. Loneliness and betrayal were combining with the alcohol to undermine his defences. He'd better go before he said or did something he'd regret, he decided, standing up.

'Help me, Frankie,' Mark slurred, standing up and nearly falling over.

Reluctantly, he took Mark's arm and helped him out of the pub. As he did so he noticed a familiar figure slipping out of another door. It looked like Costas, Mark's boyfriend. Had he been spying on them? Oh, Christ, what a mess! He felt sick.

Outside, he tried to leave, but Mark insisted on being helped to the tube and even down the escalator onto the platform. He had to put his arm around him to do so and to his dismay felt a tiny frisson of excitement.

'Why don't you come home with me, Frank?' Mark slurred,

staggering dangerously near the edge of the platform, so that Frank had to pull him back and hold onto his arm.

'I've told you, Mark,' Frank said, wishing the train would come, regretting meeting him.

'At least give me a kiss goodnight, Frank,' Mark slurred, trying to kiss him on the cheek.

'Please, Mark,' Frank said, pushing him away, embarrassed because some of the other passengers were watching, afraid that Costas might be too, though he couldn't see him. To his relief, he heard the train thundering through the tunnel towards them.

'I might as well end it all here and now then,' Mark said, staggering towards the edge of the platform again.

'Don't be silly, Mark,' Frank said, pulling him back by the arm just in time.

The train rattled to a halt, the doors slid open and Frank pushed him in.

'You won't forget me, will you, Frank?' Mark slurred, swaying in the doorway.

'No, I won't,' Frank said. It was true, whether he wanted to or not.

'Give me a tinkle, won't you?' Mark slurred, almost falling out of the carriage again. 'Invite me to the wedding! I'll be your best man if you like!'

'Sure,' Frank lied, pushing him back in, wishing the doors would shut so he could escape, and at last they started to.

'I still love you, Frank!' Mark shouted, blowing a kiss as the doors slid shut and the train pulled out.

The draught from the train as it disappeared into the darkness of the tunnel was like a wave of relief sweeping over him. He turned and ran through the underground to his own platform. All he wanted to do was get home as quickly as possible to his bottle of Bushmills ...

'Hello,' he said coolly, without touching her, as she stepped off the coach at Victoria.

'Hello,' she said, sheepishly.

She looked lovely, in a white beret and flowery summer frock, with her blond hair, blue eyes and baby-like skin. His heart swelled painfully with love and desire. He was glad he had decided to meet her after all. He wanted to sweep her into his arms and hold her for ever, never let her go again, but waited.

'Where's Pavlo?' he asked.

'He stays in Paris.'

Thank goodness for that, he thought, but still didn't move. She was the one who had deserted him, so it was up to her to make the first move. And suddenly she did.

'Francis, I am sorry,' she said, flinging her arms around him and clinging tightly to him, just as she had done that first night.

'It's OK,' he said with relief, putting his arms around her and hugging her. 'I love you.'

'Kiss me,' she ordered, raising her face to his and he did so, for once not caring about being in public.

A coach horn honked loudly and he looked up to see the coach almost on top of them, with the driver gesticulating to get out of the way.

'We'd better move,' he said, taking her bag off her shoulder and keeping an arm around her as he led her through the mêlée of coaches and people out of the coach station.

'What do you want to do?' he asked her outside.

'Let's go home and make love,' she said, in her usual direct way.

'Can we go for a drink first?' he laughed.

'Yes, I need pint of Guinness,' she agreed, pulling him across the road to the pub opposite the coach station.

'Nasdrovie,' he said, touching her glass with his, when he had brought the drinks.

'Nasdrovie,' she said, and took a mouthful, licking the cream from her lips in a way that always excited him. 'Mmm, I love it!'

'Yes, it's good stuff,' he agreed, taking a mouthful himself. 'You didn't drink this in Paris, did you?'

'I missed it!'

Did she miss him, he wondered, but didn't ask. 'Did you enjoy it?' he asked instead.

'Louvre was wonderful.' He might have known!

'Did you go with Pavlo?' he couldn't resist asking.

'Yes. He is artist. He knows lot about paintings.'

What else had she done with Pavlo, he wondered, but didn't want to know. Whatever had happened between them, she had come back to him. That was all that mattered.

'What did you do?' she asked, innocently.

'I went for a drink with that chap we met the other day,' he said, half-regretting it immediately.

'Which chap?' she enquired.

'You know – the chap from my school.'

'Your boyfriend?'

'Please, Marina.'

'Only joke.'

'I thought I might invite him to the wedding.'

'I hope that is joke!'

'Why not?'

'Why do you want him at wedding?'

'He asked me. Anyway, we do need a witness.'

'Norah is witness.'

'We need two witnesses.'

'We might not need any.'

'What do you mean?' he asked in alarm.

'Nothing.'

'You do still want to get married, don't you?'

'I must get married if I want stay in this country.'

'Don't you want to stay?'

'I want stay, but – '

'But what?'

'I'm afraid, Francis.'

'What are you afraid of?'

'I'm afraid for my country.'

'Why?'

'Situation is bad.' There had been more bombs by Croatian separatists in the news. 'I feel my country needs me. I love my country.'

'I know, but what about me? *I* need you! Don't you love me?'

'Francis, I am tired. I don't want talk about it. Can we go home?'

'All right. Just tell me you love me.'

'I love you.'

'You'll stay?'

'Yes.'

'And we'll get married?'

'Yes.'

'Kiss me.' She did.

'I do love you, Francis,' she said. 'I'm sorry for being such mixed-up crazy girl.'

'It doesn't matter. I love you, too. Let's go home and make love, shall we?' He suddenly wanted to cement their reunion.

'You want make love?'

'Yes, of course. Don't you?'

'Yes! Let's try to make love properly!'

'Is it safe?'

'Francis, I don't care, I want your baby!'

What a bizarre but beautiful thing to say, he thought, looking into her shining big blue eyes with admiration. It was quite impractical, of course – even if he could. He was about to say so, but an inspired thought suddenly crossed his mind. 'Let's go, then,' he said, quaffing the last of his Guinness.

CHAPTER TWENTY-NINE

'Hello. Can I speak to Mark Ward, please?'

'Who it is?' a foreign voice asked.

'It's a friend. Frank Walsh. Who's that?'

'Is Costas.'

'Oh. Hello. Can I speak to Mark, please?'

Silence.

'Sorry. Is not possible.'

'Oh? Why not?' There was another silence. He felt annoyed. Who was this fellow? What right did he have to prevent him talking to Mark? How long had he known Mark? A few weeks? He had known him for nearly ten years! Well, ten years ago … 'Is there a problem?' he asked, biting his tongue.

'Yes. Is proplem,' Costas replied. He sounded hostile.

'So what's the problem?' he asked, sounding annoyed despite himself.

There was yet another silence. He started to feel angry.

'Mark is died.'

'Sorry – what did you say?' He couldn't have heard right.

'Mark is died.'

'Died? You mean – 'dead'?'

'Yes.'

'Mark is dead?'

'Yes. Is dead.'

'What do you mean, 'dead'?' he demanded, unable to believe it.

'Mark is died few days ago.'

'How did he die?' he demanded – this couldn't be true, it was a misunderstanding, a joke, a sick joke.

'I prefer not speak about.' Costas sounded distraught.

'No, please,' he pleaded. 'Please tell me. How did he die? What happened?' Even as he asked, he had a ghastly foreboding of the answer.

'He suicide himself.'

'Oh, God,' he groaned, as if he'd been punched in the stomach. 'I'm sorry. How? How did he – ?' He couldn't bring himself to finish the sentence. Again, he had a horrible foreboding of the answer.

'He jumped in front of train.' Costas was crying now.

'Oh, God,' he groaned again, closing his eyes. 'I'm sorry. Why?' He knew why. He didn't need to ask.

'I prefer not ...' Costas was sobbing.

'I'm sorry. It's all right.'

'I go. Goodbye,' Costas sobbed.

'No, please,' he begged. 'When – when is the funeral?' He hoped it wasn't over.

'Funeral ... is ... tomorrow. Goodbye.' Oh, God – he was getting married to Marina tomorrow!

'No, please! Where?'

'I go now.'

'No, please, don't go! Tell me, please! Where?'

'His parents do it.'

'Have you got their number?'

'Yes, but – '

'Can I have it? Please!'

'I don't think – '

'Please!'

Reluctantly, Costas gave him the number, still sobbing.

'Thank you. I'm sorry. Goodbye,' he said, putting the phone down.

He stood in a daze on the landing for a while, his brain whirling with memories he thought he had forgotten: Mark as a young, blond-haired, blue-eyed, smooth-faced boy, Father Director in his black habit, Father Director's bedroom, the dormitory, the study hall, priests in their black frocks ... They rose up out of the dark subterranean depths of his psyche like grotesque, half-decomposed ghosts out of their graves, dancing like dervishes around him in a macabre, ghoulish, mocking masque, filling him with feelings of horror, guilt, disgust, despair ...

Afraid of fainting, he pulled himself together and tried to

think. Should he go to the funeral? He'd have to. He couldn't not go. That meant he'd have to phone Mark's parents. The thought terrified him. He was tempted to stall it, but knew that if he was going to do it, he'd have to do it now. He took a deep breath, picked up the receiver again and dialled the number.

'Veronica Brown speaking.' She sounded posh. But then so had Mark, because of his southern accent.

'Oh. Hello. I'm sorry to disturb you. Is that Mark's mother?'

'Yes, speaking.'

'My name's Frank Walsh. I – er – knew Mark at school. At the seminary, I mean. I just wanted to say how – er – sorry I was to hear about –'

'Thank you. That's very kind of you. What name did you say?'

'Frank. Frank Walsh.'

'Oh, yes. He used to speak about you a lot. He seemed to think very highly of you.'

'Did he? That's good. I – er – I was just wondering about the – er – funeral ...'

'Yes. It's at ten o'clock tomorrow. Saint Joseph's Catholic Church, Cranbrook Road, Mitcham, Surrey.'

'Thank you ... Would it be all right if I went?'

'Yes, of course, dear. That would be very nice. We'd like to meet you. Mark spoke such a lot about you.' She sounded so dignified!

'Thank you. I'll – er – see you tomorrow then.'

'Thank you for calling. Goodbye.'

Frank put the phone down quickly, paused to compose himself and went back into the room, where Marina was studying at the table, her back to him. He stood looking at her for a moment, still in a daze. It was all unreal, like a dream, a bad dream: the junior seminary, Father Director, meeting Mark again, now Mark dead ...

But was this real, he wondered too? Was she real? Or was it all a dream, as Bishop Berkeley said? No, she was real, he told himself. This was reality. This was *normality*. It was the past that was unreal and abnormal. Suddenly he felt glad she was there. He wanted to go and put his arms around her, just to reassure himself, but didn't dare. He knew she was in a funny mood.

Instead, he collapsed into the easy-chair and tried to think. He still couldn't believe Mark was dead. Why had he done it? Was it because of him? Oh, God, he hoped not! No. It was because of what had happened all those years ago at the junior seminary. It didn't matter now. He was dead. A lump came to his throat and tears to his eyes. He had to blink them back. He didn't want Marina to see him cry and know how upset he was.

'Mark's dead,' he blurted out.

'Who is dead?' she asked, without turning around.

'Mark,' he said, irritated. 'You know, the chap we met the other day. I went for a drink with him.'

'He is dead? How?' She sounded matter-of-fact about it, still didn't turn around.

'Apparently he committed suicide.' He tried to sound matter-of-fact himself, didn't want her to know how affected he was.

'Why did he do that?' Now she turned to face him, interested.

'It's a long story.'

'Tell me.'

She was wearing a white sweatshirt, long flowery skirt and her 'National Health' specs, which she now took off. She looked so pretty and so innocent. He didn't want to tell her. He didn't want her to enter his past, to be tainted by it, to be contaminated by it. He wanted to keep her separate, a symbol of his new life. He didn't want to return to the past himself. 'I don't really know,' he said evasively. 'Maybe because he was gay.'

'That is not reason to commit suicide.' She could sound so sensible at times.

'For some people it is. I think for him it was.'

'It is stupid.'

'What do you mean?' he asked, annoyed.

'This society is stupid.'

'Oh. Yes. Society can be very stupid.' He didn't want to discuss it with her. 'Anyway, the funeral's tomorrow.' She said nothing. 'Do you think I should go?'

'Do you want to go?'

'No, but I think I should.'

'Why you should go?'

'He was somebody I knew. He was a – friend.'

'Just friend?'

'Just a friend, yes,' he said, defensively.

'I think he was more than friend.'

'What do you mean?' he asked.

'I think he was in love with you.'

There was no use trying to deny it, he decided – she was too perceptive.

'He was, once. At school.'

'Were you in love with him?'

'I suppose I was once.' That was the first time he had ever admitted it to anyone. He had hardly even admitted it to himself. It was almost like a confession.

'And now? Are you in love with him now?'

'Don't be ridiculous!'

He should have said: 'I'm in love with *you*.' But for some reason he couldn't. It was as if it would be disloyal to Mark, absurd as the idea was. 'Anyway, he's dead.'

'I think you still love him.'

'Should I go to the funeral?' he demanded, ignoring her remark.

'What about wedding?'

'The funeral's at ten. The register office is at three. I could be back.' It would be tight though.

She said nothing.

'So. What do you think?' he asked. He wanted empathy from her, but knew he could hardly expect her to encourage him to go to his 'boyfriend's' funeral on their wedding day.

'Why do you ask me?' she said.

'I want to know what you think.'

'I think you do not want to get married tomorrow,' she said, turning away from him.

'Of course I do!' he declared, exasperated.

'If you want to go to funeral, you go.' She jumped up, rushed over to the door, grabbed her mac and put it on.

'I don't want to! It's just turned out like that! I didn't arrange it! It's fate! Where are you going?'

He stood up and followed her to the door.

'I am going for walk. To think. Please, do not follow me.'

She opened the door, rushed out and hurried downstairs.

'Marina!' he called after her, going out onto the landing, but all he heard was the slam of the front door – a fateful sound that would reverberate in his mind for a long, long time ...

He arrived deliberately late for the funeral, not wanting to meet anyone beforehand. The first thing he saw, outside the church, was a shiny, black, empty hearse with a funeral limousine behind it, the undertakers lounging around, one of them smoking. It gave him a shock, because it was the first evidence he had seen that this was real, it wasn't just a bad dream – Mark really was dead, though he still couldn't quite believe it.

He sneaked into the church and stood at the back. It was the first time he had been in a Catholic church for several years. Glancing around, he felt as if he had wandered into some exotic temple, with its strange furniture, statues and icons. Or had he mistakenly wandered into a theatre? One way or another, it felt unreal.

At the front of the church a coffin lay on some trestles. The sight of it gave him an even worse shock than the hearse. He couldn't believe Mark lay inside it. Not the Mark he had known as a blond-haired, blue-eyed, smooth-faced boy of thirteen at the junior seminary. Or had that all been a dream? What about the Mark he had met again the other day? Was that the same person? Or had that been a dream, too? Had Mark ever really existed? Was this all just a bad dream after all?

There was something spooky about it all. Did people really believe that God – the creator of the universe – was present in that golden-doored box on the altar? Did they really believe that they could talk to Him, that He could hear them, that He might listen to them? Did they really believe that the priest in his strange, druid-like vestments had supernatural powers, could change bread into the body of Christ, wine into blood? Did they really believe that death was not the end, that Mark was now in some la-la land called 'Heaven'?

Or did some of them believe Mark was in Hell? After all, he had committed two of the gravest sins in the Catholic canon, mortal sins – he was a homosexual and he had committed suicide. Maybe they weren't sins any more though. Once upon a time he wouldn't have been allowed to have a requiem mass like this. What did Catholics believe these days? He didn't know. Did they know themselves?

He glanced at the coffin again. It looked like a beautiful piece of furniture – a sideboard maybe – made of highly-polished dark wood with shiny gold handles. It was a macabre sideboard though, because Mark's dead body lay inside. Did it? What did he look like now? The train must have made a terrible mess of him. He remembered the suicide he had witnessed in the underground just after he came to London. The thought sent a spasm of horror through him. They must have prettied him up, he supposed. It didn't bear thinking about. He averted his gaze, looked around at the congregation.

That must be Mark's parents at the front. The mother was a tall, thin woman, dressed in black with a black hat and veil. The father was a tall, military-looking man with a toothbrush moustache and glasses, thinning fair hair on top. What must they be feeling? Their only son, their only child, dead. He felt a stab of pity for them. How could a loving God have done this to them? It was too cruel for words.

Did they know how Mark had died? They must do, he supposed. But did they know it was suicide or did they think it was an accident? They must have been told it was suicide, surely. Did they know why? They knew Mark was homosexual, according to what Mark had told him the other day. What a shock that must have been to them! But did they know why he was homosexual?

He'd have to talk to them afterwards, he supposed, though the thought dismayed him. Maybe he could just slip off without doing so? No, he couldn't do that. He'd have to talk to them. God, what did you say to someone whose twenty-two--year-old son had just committed suicide? And what if they asked him questions?

That was Costas, near the back like him, but on the other side. He was wearing the same maroon velvet jacket he had had on in the pub. He kept his head bowed, long black curly hair curtaining his face, as if he didn't want to see or be seen. Frank glanced at him with a mixture of pity and disgust. Did

Mark's parents know he was there and who he was, he wondered? Anyway, he was glad he was staying in the background. He certainly didn't want to meet him again.

At last the requiem mass finished and the priest walked around the coffin, incensing it with a thurible while intoning prayers. Somehow it all seemed pathetically inadequate to the horror of death, a pointless pantomime. What else could you do though? You couldn't just bury or burn the dead without any ceremony at all. Was the incense supposed to mask the stench of death, like perfume? The sickly-sweet smell brought back ghostly memories, made him feel slightly sick. He wished it was over. He wanted to escape. He wanted to go back to Marina and his life. He wanted to pretend this hadn't happened, the past hadn't happened ...

He couldn't shake off a feeling of guilt, as if he was responsible for Mark's death. He wasn't, was he? Mark wanted him back, but it was impossible. He was different now. Wasn't he? Oh, Mark! I'm sorry! I wish I could've helped you somehow. I wish I could have saved you. But I've only just managed to save myself. Oh, God, he was starting to cry! He mustn't do that. That'd be so embarrassing! Anyway, it was too late for tears.

At last the service came to an end. The undertakers came down the aisles in their black suits, lifted the coffin and carried it out of the church on their shoulders, preceded by the priest and followed by the mourners. The priest walked in front, intoning a prayer that included the words, 'May the angels lead him to Paradise'. What a beautiful prayer, Frank thought, even if there was no such place as Paradise. He followed at the end of the procession.

Outside, the coffin was slid into the hearse, with a few wreaths, and the mourners got into their cars. He was tempted to slip away, rather than face the burial and Mark's parents afterwards. However, someone offered him a lift and he felt obliged to accept. He got in the car, the hearse drove off, with the official cars behind, and they all followed at funereal pace.

'Are you family or friend?' the driver, a bespectacled, middle-aged man, asked him.

'Just a friend,' Frank said, not wanting to talk. 'What

about you?'

'Sang in the choir with him. Didn't know him very well, really, to be honest. He had a nice voice. Sad, isn't it?'

'Yes,' Frank said, a lump in his throat.

To his relief, the man didn't say anything else, nor did the other occupants of the car. Frank felt like an intruder. Yet he had probably known Mark better than any of them. Or at least he had know one version of Mark, one that had maybe died a long time ago.

At last they arrived at the cemetery. Frank thanked the driver for the lift – it seemed strangely mundane in the circumstances – and walked slowly to the graveside, remaining in the background of mourners around it and well away from Costas. The priest stood at the head of the grave, in white surplice and purple stole, missal in hand. On one side of the grave was a mound of freshly dug brown earth. On the other side lay the box with Mark in it. Or was he? Yes, he was. This was it. Mark was going into that neat, rectangular, deep hole in the ground and disappearing for ever ...

The priest intoned a few more prayers, sprinkled some holy water on the coffin and it was lowered into the hole with ropes. It was impossible to believe that Mark was inside it! A few mourners stepped forward, picked up a bit of earth and tossed it into the grave. It made a dull thudding sound on the coffin lid. He couldn't bring himself to do it.

Then the mourners started to move away. That was it. That was the end. The end of Mark Brown. He was no more. Dead and buried. In a box in the dirt. Already starting to decompose. Dust to dust, ashes to ashes. Death was disgusting, dirty, depressing. Not to most of the other mourners maybe. Being mostly Catholics, he supposed, no doubt they believed in an afterlife, Heaven and Hell, all that. But he couldn't. For him death was the end. There was nothing afterwards. We came from nothing and went back to nothing, came from nowhere and went back to nowhere ...

'Hello. Veronica Brown. Are you Francis Walsh?'

It was Mark's mother, with his father beside her, holding out a thin hand from which she had removed the black lace glove.

'Yes,' he said, shaking her hand and then her husband's. 'I'm very sorry about –' It sounded feeble and he didn't know how to finish the sentence.

'That's all right, dear. Thank you for coming. It's very good of you.'

'No, I'm only too glad,' he mumbled, realising that didn't sound right either. Oh, God!

'Would you like to come back to the house? We'd like to speak to you properly.'

'Er, thank you, but I have to get back to – er – work,' he fibbed. He couldn't very well tell them he was actually getting married that afternoon, could he?

'Oh, what a shame. We were hoping to speak to you about Mark. He often spoke about you. When he was at the seminary, I mean. And for quite a while afterwards. Didn't he, David?'

'That's right,' her husband spoke for the first time.

'I didn't really know him all that well, to be honest,' Frank said. Was that a fib, too, he wondered? 'Only for a year, actually.'

'You know, Mark was never quite the same after he left the seminary,' she said. 'Was he, David?'

'That's right,' Mark's father said again. He seemed stiff, ill at ease, unwilling to talk – understandably.

'We were just wondering if, you know, anything happened?' Mark's mother continued, an anguished, haunted look in her eyes.

His heart went out to them in their grief, which they seemed to be bearing with such dignity. He ought to tell them, he thought. They had a right to know. He ought to tell them the whole sordid story, that the Director had been a paedophile, that he had interfered with Mark, and lots of other boys, including himself. They had a right to know!

'Not as far as I know,' he lied, looking away.

He couldn't tell them, not here and now, next to Mark's freshly dug grave. It was too sordid, too shameful, too painful. He just didn't have the guts. Maybe he would write to them.

'Well, that's some consolation,' Mark's mother said with a sigh. 'Isn't it, David?'

'Yes, yes it is,' he agreed, uncomfortably.

'I'm sorry,' Frank said, guilty about deceiving them in their moment of grief.

'Don't worry, dear,' Mark's mother said. 'It's not your fault. Are you sure you haven't got time to come back?'

'Thank you, but I must get back to work,' Frank said, eager now to escape and worried about being late for the register office.

'Thank you for coming, we appreciate it,' Mark's father said, holding out his hand again and Frank shook it.

'Yes, thank you, dear,' Mark's mother said and then, to Frank's surprise, kissed him on the cheek.

'Sorry, I'd better go,' Frank said, embarrassed.

'Would you like a lift anywhere?' Mark's father asked.

'No, thanks. The station's just round the corner. I'll be all right. Thanks, anyway.'

'Goodbye, dear. Do keep in touch.'

'Yes. I will. Thanks. Bye.'

He turned and walked briskly away, ashamed of his cowardice. As soon as he was out of the cemetery gates, he ran to the underground and jumped on a train, relieved to have escaped, but still worried about being late for the register office. He'd just about make it, he thought, looking at his watch, which he had secretly put on so that Marina wouldn't see it.

A funeral and a wedding all in one day – it was weird, he thought, sitting on the train as it rattled along. He suddenly felt depressed. Why, he wondered? Mark was dead, yes, but Mark didn't really mean anything to him any more, did he? He had been in love with him once, eight years ago, but not now, surely? Or was he subconsciously still in love with him? Of course not! He was in love with Marina, wasn't he? He was going to marry her, wasn't he? This afternoon!

Suddenly he wasn't sure if he wanted to go through with it. It seemed a crazy thing to do, get married at his age – twenty-five – to a girl from another country, another culture. But he loved her, didn't he? He wasn't sure any more. Somehow it didn't compare with what he had once felt for Mark. It would be like a betrayal. Oh, God! He half hoped he would be late.

No, he mustn't think like that, he told himself. He only felt like that because of meeting Mark again, the funeral, meeting Mark's parents, bad memories resurfacing. It was just years of suppressed guilt and shame and loss coming to the surface. Of course he loved Marina. Of course he was going to marry her this afternoon. If he didn't, it would really mean that they, the 'Ghosters', had won! He had to go through with it! He had to, for Mark's sake as much as his own!

He looked at his watch again. He'd just about make it, he thought, as long as there were no delays.

'Where is she?'

Only Masoud and Norah, who were supposed to be witnesses, were there when he arrived at the register office a few minutes late. He knew something was wrong by the look on their faces.

'She left this,' Masoud said, handing him an envelope. He took it, tore it open, pulled out a sheet of exercise paper and read in her familiar childish, loopy handwriting:

Dear Francis,

It was good while it lasted, but it was only dream. Now I must face the reality and go back to my country. My country needs me. I must study medicine, so I can become doctor and help people there. Please try to understand. I am sorry for not being girl you want. I will always remember good times we had together in London. Thank you for all what you gave me. You are only man who could come close to such 'crazy' girl like me. But I know we could never be together. Now each we must go our different paths of life. I hope that you will find right person to love and be happy. I am sorry about death of your friend. Please do not try to follow me or write to me. I think it is better if we keep memory of each other only. I will throw coin in fountain for you. Remember, name of God is called Abraxas.

Love,
Your crazy Yugoslav girl,
Marina

'What does it say?' Norah asked.

'She's not coming,' he said, shaking his head with disbelief. 'She's gone.'

'Gone where?' Norah asked.

'Gone back home. To Yugoslavia.' He still couldn't quite believe it himself.

'Ah, God, I'm sorry, darlin',' Norah said, putting a sympathetic hand on his arm.

'Thanks,' he murmured, trying to think.

She'd gone and left him! Jilted him! At the altar! Well, figuratively speaking. He couldn't accept it. It was all a mistake, a misunderstanding. He had to follow her, find her, apologise, explain ... But how? She would be on her way to the airport now. She might already be there. She couldn't have taken off yet, though, could she? Suddenly he had an idea.

'Masoud, have you got your bike with you?'

Masoud pointed to the helmet under his arm.

'Could you give me a lift to Heathrow?'

'Let's go,' Masoud said, putting the helmet on and heading for the door.

'Bye, Norah, thanks,' he said, running out of the building and around to the car park at the back, where Masoud's gleaming Harley-Davidson waited.

Masoud got on and kick-started it with a deafening vroom. Nervously, he climbed on the pillion and grabbed hold of Masoud's waist. Masoud opened the throttle to a roar, clicked it into gear and they shot out into the busy central London traffic, Frank clinging on for grim life. Masoud rode like some crazed speedway rider, weaving in and out of traffic and banking almost to the tarmac around corners. Frank clung on, eyes closed in terror, half-expecting to be catapulted into eternity any moment.

When they reached the motorway they raced past everything else on the road. By now though, Frank didn't care. A wild elation had taken hold of him, so that he silently urged Masoud to go even faster. All he wanted was to get to the airport before she disappeared out of his life for ever. If she did, life wouldn't be worth living. He might as well be killed, hurtled into eternity now. It would be a release!

Suddenly, though, disaster struck – a police motorbike streaked past them, blue light flashing, and with a gauntleted arm the cop signalled them to pull over. He silently willed Masoud to carry on, but he slowed down and pulled over onto the hard shoulder. That's it, he thought, his heart sinking. He'd never make it now. He'd lost her. A wave of despair swept over him.

The cop stopped several yards in front of them and Frank watched in despair as, indolently, he switched off his bike, said something into his radio, dismounted, took off his gauntlets and laid them fastidiously on the seat, while the radio continued to babble away. Masoud revved his bike a few times as if to hurry him. Frank clung to him, sinking deeper and deeper into despair.

Eventually the cop, who was surprisingly short and fat with gold-rimmed glasses and a ginger goatee beard, ambled towards them, fishing a notebook out of his jacket pocket as he did so. He looked like one of Hitler's storm-troopers in his helmet, uniform and jackboots, Frank thought, flooded with an almost violent hatred towards him. He was obviously going to book them and enjoying every minute of it.

However, just before the cop reached them, Masoud shouted 'Hold tight!', opened the throttle of the chopper and shot off along the hard shoulder, almost catapulting Frank off. He glanced behind as they roared away and saw the cop running back to his bike. *Go on!* he silently urged Masoud, clutching his waist with a mixture of terror and triumph as the bike banked across the motorway back into the fast lane.

He glanced back again and saw the cop following them, gaining rapidly on them. Faster, faster, he silently urged Masoud, regardless of the danger. They reached a roundabout with the cop close behind. Masoud went around it twice at a breakneck speed and angle and the cop followed. Suddenly there was a blare of horns and an almighty clatter. Masoud went around again and they saw the cop's bike lying on the road, blue light still flashing and radio babbling, with the cop himself sitting on the road beside it, looking dazed.

Masoud banked off the roundabout and zoomed away.

Frank felt another surge of triumph. A few moments later they screeched to a halt outside the front of the terminal. Frank jumped off, gave Masoud a clap on the back to thank him and dashed into the terminal.

His heart immediately sank – it was so crowded he'd never find her. He couldn't give up now though. He made his way to a monitor and scanned it, his heart pounding. There it was: BELGRADE. Dep 17.10. It was now quarter to five. Oh, God! It was no good. She would be on it. Or at least in the departure lounge. Unless it had been delayed ...

He sprinted up the nearest escalator to departures and his heart sank again – it was even more crowded. He had to find the Yugoslav Airways check-in desk and ask if she was on the flight. There seemed to be hundreds of desks though. He ran up and down desperately, bumping into people and almost tripping over luggage, but couldn't find it.

In desperation, he asked an official, who pointed it out. There was a girl checking in. From the back it looked like Marina. She had short fair hair and was wearing a brown suede jacket like Marina's. He rushed over, but it was a middle-aged woman. He waited, seething with impatience, for her to finish checking in.

'Excuse me,' he gasped to the girl on the desk.

She looked at him in alarm, as if he might be going to attack her. She was young and looked smart, even sexy, in her uniform.

'Sorry,' he panted. 'Could you tell me if there's a passenger called Marina Durajlija on this flight?'

'I'm sorry, sir, we're not allowed to give out that information,' the girl said, still looking alarmed.

'Oh,' he said, deflated. 'You're not?'

'Why do you need to know?' the girl asked.

'She's – she's my girlfriend,' he stammered, hoping to appeal to the girl's romantic instincts. 'I don't know where she is. I've lost her. I mean, I think she's run away.'

'We're not supposed to – ' the girl said, softening.

'Please,' he begged.

'Well, I'll have a look at the passenger list for you, sir.'

'Thank you,' he gasped.

She pressed her keyboard and scanned the computer screen.

He waited tensely, studying her face for some sign. 'What was the surname, sir?'

'Durajlija.'

'Could you spell that, please?'

He did so.

'Marina?'

'That's right. Is she on the list?'

'Yes, sir – there is a passenger with that name.'

She might as well have put a knife through his heart! 'Could I speak to her?' he asked, desperately.

'I'm sorry, sir. They've boarded. The flight's about to take off.'

'It's absolutely impossible?'

'I'm afraid so, sir. Unless it's an emergency.'

It is an emergency, he thought in despair. *She's left me. She's broken my heart. That's an emergency, isn't it?*

'Is it an emergency, sir?' the girl enquired anxiously.

He thought of telling her that she was ill, had left some vital pills, or even that there was a bomb on board, but didn't dare. It was hopeless. She was going. He had lost her. He might as well accept it, crawl away, find a corner, curl up and die ...

'No, not exactly,' he admitted in defeat.

'I'm sorry, sir. Are you all right?'

'Yes. Yes, thanks,' he said, in a daze, then had an idea. 'Is there a viewing area?' he asked. He might as well see her go, he thought masochistically.

'There's no official viewing area,' the girl told him, 'but if you go to the top floor of the car park – '

'Which way is that?' he interrupted her.

She told him, he thanked her and rushed off to the car park. He ran up the steps to the top floor and joined a group of others gazing out at the tarmac, where several planes stood. Some of the others were obviously plane-spotters, with binoculars and radios tuned in to air-traffic control. How he envied them their simple, innocent pastime!

He scanned around for her plane and eventually saw one with YUGOSLAV AIRWAYS emblazoned on the side. That must be it, he realised with a shock. He could hardly believe she was on it though, so near yet so far. He peered at the windows in the forlorn hope of seeing her, but they were too small and too far away to see anyone. It was hopeless. He'd never see her again.

Suddenly, the plane started to move. It reversed out onto the apron and stopped. It looked like a giant, ungainly, prehistoric bird, with its sharp beak and huge wings. It was hard to believe it could take off into the sky and fly. It was even harder to believe she was inside it. It was unreal, like a dream, a bad dream!

Suddenly it moved forward and trundled, wings trembling, to the far end of the runway, where it stopped and waited for a few minutes. He stared at it in disbelief. Surely that huge, heavy, gawky contraption couldn't leave the ground and fly, could it? Surely she wasn't inside it, was she? Surely it was all a bad dream and he would wake up any moment?

Suddenly, though, the bird darted forward, raced down the runway, lifted its beak and soared steeply into the sky. Then, still climbing, it slowly diminished, became a dot and disappeared. He stood staring into space for a while, still unable to believe it, waiting to wake up ...

But he didn't. He was already awake. It wasn't a dream. It was real. She'd gone. He'd never see her again, just as he'd never see Mark again. He loved her, but she'd gone. In one day he had lost the only two people he had ever really, truly loved. He was alone again.

What was he going to do? There was only one thing to do – end it all. Put himself out of his misery. Go and throw himself under a train. No – he might as well do it here and now – throw himself off the roof of the car park ...

He moved closer to the parapet and looked over. It was a long way down. He would die instantaneously, he supposed. It would all be over in a second or two. No more loneliness, no more sorrow, no more guilt, no more sadness, no more emptiness, no more pain of any kind. Blissful, eternal oblivion!

But something stopped him. No, he thought. That would mean they – 'the Ghosters' – had won. It would mean the forces of evil, of ignorance and superstition, had won. No! He owed it to both Mark and himself to survive, to tell the truth one day. He thought he had exorcised the ghosts of the past. Now he realised it would take him much longer, maybe a whole lifetime. He would never give up though.

He had lost Marina. That was depressing. But he refused to be sucked down into depression. He was still alive. He had survived before and he would survive this. It would make him all the stronger. He would find another girlfriend. One day he would get married and have children. He would live a normal life, be *normal*. He would beat them! He would win!

A feeling of power suddenly flooded through him and with it a strange sense of jubilation. He felt like jumping for joy, like rushing over and telling the plane-spotters: 'Guess what? My boyfriend's dead and my girlfriend's left me, but I don't care! I'm still here! I'm still alive! I'm not going to kill myself! They can't beat me!' They'd think he was mad. Maybe he was a bit mad. He didn't care. He was happy! He was triumphant! He was invincible!

He felt like celebrating. It sounded crazy – he had just lost the only two people he had ever loved, but he felt like celebrating! He was on a high, like the plane now high in the sky somewhere over Europe. He knew that like the plane he would have to come down, but he'd never crash again.

He had to preserve this feeling for as long as possible. There was only one way to do that – go and get drunk. That was what he'd do, he decided – go and get drunk. He turned and walked away, back towards the underground, towards London, towards life ...

About the author

Eugene Vesey was born and brought up in Manchester, where he attended Xaverian College until the age of eleven. He continued his education at Roman Catholic seminaries in the English Lake District and the English Midlands. He obtained an honours degree in English language and literature at the University of Manchester and a teacher training certificate at the University of Liverpool. He now lives in London, where he has taught English as a Foreign Language in private schools and colleges of further education for forty years. Though now retired he continues to do some private teaching. However, he spends most of his time writing, reading, listening to Irish music, studying other languages, gardening, walking, drinking and, for his sins, watching Manchester United. As well as **GHOSTERS** he has published two sequels, **OPPOSITE WORLDS** and **ITALIAN GIRLS**. He has also published two volumes of poetry, **VENICE AND OTHER POEMS** and **THIRTY-NINE POEMS**. All Eugene's books are available from Amazon.

You may contact Eugene at:

veseyeugene@hotmail.com

Eugene is also on Facebook

Some reviews of **GHOSTERS**:

'I liked it ... imaginatively strong ... I was riveted ... sensitively worked out ... intelligently written ... powerfully presented ... this heart-felt painful re-creation of a central hidden part of our culture.'
Kate Cruise O'Brien, Poolbeg Press Ltd.

'...extremely well written and moves at a pace that keeps you captivated. Crucially, it deals with the disturbing subject of child abuse in the Catholic church in a revealing, but sensitive, way, without pulling any punches, drawing on the author's own firsthand experiences ... provides a graphic and disturbing insight into the emotional traumas suffered by both the victims and ironically the perpetrators ... an informative and thought provoking book that could and should be adapted into a television drama.'
John Vesey, Amazon

'This novel deals with some very sensitive and difficult issues in a very interesting, serious, intelligent way. It's very well written. It's obviously autobiographical but that in no way invalidates it in my opinion. The story really carried me along and I couldn't wait to find out whether Frank would be able to turn his life around or not. I won't give the game away by saying whether he does or not! The writing style is unshowy, verging perhaps on plain, but that for me gives the story an extra patina of truth. The story is so engaging that it doesn't need any embellishments of any kind in my view. I'd recommend this book to anyone who is interested in a very good human story, well told, and who is interested in such issues as child abuse, religious indoctrination, love and self-fulfilment. It is a bit slow at the start, but I found it difficult to put down once I got into it.'
Orinoco, Amazon

'Wow! Brilliant! Especially if you're Polish and Catholic like me. Well, I should say 'lapsed Catholic'. This story reminded me why I no longer believe. Every Catholic bishop and priest should read it. So should every parent who tries to indoctrinate their children with any strange, supernatural beliefs – in the end it's likely to be counter-productive. I could identify so closely with Frank even though I'm not a man. My own story is almost parallel. When I was reading this book I felt as if I was looking in a mirror! I actually understand myself better now! That's what good literature should do, isn't it?'

''Ghosters' has a really powerful emotive effect as it charts Frank's life throughout his childhood and as a young adult in a very truthful and honest way ... It deals with faith, religion and love and most of all identity. It is an empowering story that allows the reader to connect to Frank, the main character. This is a thoroughly enjoyable read that grips the reader throughout.'
Miss A. M. Kearney, Amazon

'Christian romance is a bit misleading perhaps, but this book does deal with the question of religious faith – specifically the Catholic faith and theology – in a very intelligent, dramatic and moving way. More accurately, it deals with the loss of faith. The main drama is about how Franks Walsh manages to recover from his drastic loss of faith, reinvent himself and forge a new life, in effect a new identity. But the story also encompasses other themes, such as child abuse [very topical] and romantic love both homosexual and heterosexual. I found the story of Frank's progression from despair at losing his faith [and therefore his vocation to the priesthood] to relative happiness as a young, carefree teacher in London to be completely engrossing. The author deals with all these themes very honestly – sometimes painfully honestly – so for me this was a riveting read.'
Nena, Amazon

'I especially liked the first two chapters. The thoughts Fran had in the train to St. Mary's, about venial and mortal sins – I understand that culture since we, in Spain, are Catholic by tradition. It seemed to me like I had been watching a film of those young lads passing through the gates of St Mary's college. At the end of chapter three it seemed to me the school/castle had more that a couple of ghosts! After reading chapter six, I think how easy it is to manipulate young minds. I like the way the author has introduced the story between Fran and Father Director. It has made me see very clearly how things like that can happen. I am really enjoying it.'
Maria-Angeles Sanchez, Madrid

Amazon Average Customer Review *****

OPPOSITE WORLDS

OPPOSITE WORLDS is the follow-up to **GHOSTERS**. It finds Frank alone and lonely in London, having been jilted by his Yugoslav girlfriend, Marina, on their wedding day. On the rebound from this, he has a passionate affair with Kalli, a gorgeous Greek singer and belly-dancer, who is a student in his class at the school in Soho where he teaches English to foreign students. When Kalli leaves him, Frank finds himself alone again. Then one evening, in a folk club in an Irish pub, he hears a young, attractive girl singing and falls instantly in love with her. Her name is Mary, he contrives to meet her and Mary falls in love with him. Love leads to marriage – reluctantly at first on Frank's part – but their marriage proves to be a collision of two very different, indeed opposite, worlds ...

'Opposite Worlds is an extremely well-written book – thoughtful, descriptive and emotive. The journey of exploration and discovery for Frank Walsh enables the reader to identify with him on a deep emotional level. As you read, you feel how Frank is feeling and thinking as if you're in that moment with him. Overall, it's a great read as it explores identity, relationships and belonging. A definite recommendation! It gives a clear insight into the life of Frank Walsh and touches the reader on a deeper level.'
Miss A. M. Kearney, Amazon

'I read it with great enjoyment. Couldn't put it down.'
John Barber

ITALIAN GIRLS

At the end of **OPPOSITE WORLDS**, the prequel to **ITALIAN GIRLS**, Mary, Frank Walsh's wife, has left him, frustrated by his philandering ways and apparent infertility. Unlike Mary, Frank doesn't believe in marriage, nor does he believe in God any more, though like her he was brought up as a Catholic. He even spent nine years training to be a priest, an experience described in GHOSTERS, the first book in Frank's saga, and an experience that still haunts him. The beginning of ITALIAN GIRLS finds Frank feeling liberated but lonely, as well as guilty about the break-up of his marriage. He tries to find solace in love affairs with his international students at the colleges in London and Dublin where he teaches English. Ironically, though, these affairs make him realise what he really wants is a wife and children after all. He has always had a thing for Italian girls, ever since a boyhood crush on Gina Lollobrigida, so when he falls in love with Cinzia, an Italian student, he thinks he has found the love of his life and the wife of his dreams. But has he? Or will his quest lead him to a different continent entirely?

'Italian Girls is a very well-written, intelligent and technically adept, well-structured novel, just like Ghosters and Opposite Worlds. Eugene Vesey is obviously an excellent writer. He especially expresses the characters' emotions very well. The story takes you on a journey, the journey of Frank Walsh's search for lasting love. It explores themes of love, loss, sex and self-discovery, as well as giving an insight into the world of a college of further education. I found it very moving- in fact, it brought tears to my eyes! I was gripped from the first to the last page. It's a very good read and I really enjoyed it even though it made me cry. What a great writer! He deserves to be much better known. I can't wait for his next novel, which I hope will continue Frank's story.'
Miss A. M. Kearney, Amazon

VENICE AND OTHER POEMS

VENICE AND OTHER POEMS is Eugene's first book of poetry. It includes poems written when he was a teenager to poems written recently. In other words, it covers a span of nearly fifty years, from his schooldays in the sixties to 2014. However, the poems are in alphabetical not chronological order. Each poem expresses a state of mind or emotion at the time, an observation of a scene or a reflection upon some experience. So in a sense the poems are autobiographical, though not necessarily an exact mirror of the author's life – there may be some 'poetic licence' here and there. Perhaps it would be better to describe each poem as a prism. As well as reflecting his own life-experience though, the author hopes that in at least some of these poems readers may catch a glimpse of their own lives, past, present or even future.

'This is a very appealing collection of poems. They are well constructed with lots of descriptive, emotive language. The writer explores deep subjects such as Love, Identity and Loss. I would recommend this collection as it has a lovely selection of poems that touch you with many emotions.'
Miss A. M. Kearney, Amazon

THIRTY-NINE POEMS

THIRTY-NINE POEMS is Eugene's second book of poetry after **VENICE AND OTHER POEMS**, which he published in 2011. Unlike the poems in that collection though, it contains mostly poems written in more recent years. As in that collection, the poems are in simple alphabetical order rather than chronological order. Like the poems in that collection, each poem expresses a state of mind or emotion, an observation of a scene or a reflection on some experience. So these poems too are autobiographical, without necessarily being an exact mirror of the author's own life. And he still hopes that, as with the poems in his first collection, in some of them at least readers may catch glimpses of their own lives, past or present.

You can contact Eugene at:

veseyeugene@hotmail.com

Eugene is also on Facebook

All Eugene's books are
available from Amazon